DELUSION

DELUSION

Dwayne Morrow Mystery #8

DARIN MILLER

ISBN: 978-1-963325-11-9 (Paperback)

Library of Congress Control Number: 2025914630

Any references to historical events, real people, or real places are used fictitiously. Names, characters, and places are products of the author's imagination. No portion of this book was created through use of artificial intelligence (AI), nor may any portion be used to train AI.

Cover image licensed for commercial use from Adobe Stock Images (stock.image.com)

Printed by Kindle Direct Publishing, in Columbus, OH, USA.

First printing edition 2025.

www.darin-miller.com

DARIN MILLER
Dwayne Morrow Mysteries

For Dad and Gina
with all my heart

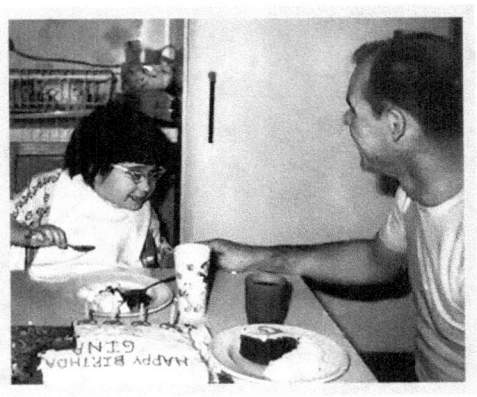

TABLE OF CONTENTS

CHAPTER ONE

"I am *out!*"

Jasmine stormed past me toward the house, her curly red hair reflecting each exaggerated step. I shot a startled look at Melanie, who was equally perplexed. She shrugged her shoulders as best she could while holding a massive bowl of potato salad in her arms. "Who knows? I'll check on her in a minute."

It was an unseasonably warm Easter Sunday in early April, and we were hosting our first shindig as a family unit. Invitations had been extended to family, friends, and our co-workers at Boggs Investigations, where I was nearly halfway through a two-year apprenticeship and Melanie was Boggs' newest hire.

I squinted against the bright sunlight into the side yard where most of our company had collected around my recent acquisition, a 10-foot Amish-made picnic table that could comfortably accommodate twelve. A junior version sat behind it, coming in at 5-foot, although one end had been modified to accommodate Billy Garrett's wheelchair. Billy was currently motoring his all-terrain ride through the open field with his buddy, Scott Nichols, jogging along beside him. They were attempting to collect some of the brightly colored eggs we had hidden around the yard before little Brianna Graves could hoard them all, gloating mercilessly like the spoiled little shit that she was.

From the sound of her high-pitched cackle, it wasn't going well for the boys.

My name is Dwayne Morrow, and I'm feeling more than a little celebratory. At the ripe old age of thirty-five, I have finally graduated from living alone and single to impending wedded bliss, engaged to a woman who's far too good for me and becoming an instant father figure to her twelve-year-old daughter and her daughter's three-year-old half-brother—it's such a long story.

Hopefully, you've been paying attention.

"You don't think the sandbox is too close to the cornhole boards, do you?" asked Melanie as we more or less waddled toward the table under the weight of our burdens. I was carrying a cube of soda in each hand—one Pepsi, the other Diet—while Melanie struggled with the aforementioned potato salad.

"Nah, they're fine," I said, smiling at the scene before me. "Nola's keeping an eye out."

Jordan was having the time of his life with Nola Caudill, one-half of the couple we had all come to think of as our fairy godparents. She had gotten right down into the sandbox with the three-year-old, and they were busily constructing a tiny enclave of sandcastles together. Nola and her husband, Wendell, had been part of my friend, Brady Garrett's life since shortly after his wife died in a tragic car accident, providing support for both Brady and his young son, Billy, in the years since. Little did they know they would collect dependents like tumbleweeds, as all of our lives had become increasingly interconnected over the past year or so.

"That's an illegal throw!" roared Doug Boggs from his position at the cornhole board farthest from us, fists on hips and scowl firmly in place. He gave Brady the evil eye as he rolled one of his disgusting, soggy cigars around in his mouth, scattering tobacco debris along the jagged line of his frown. "You can't *do* it like that! You're cheating!"

Brady, on the other hand, was performing a jubilant dance reminiscent of Snoopy, his dark curls bouncing in the sun while he crowed with laughter. "Oh, but I *can* do it like that, Douglas! There's nothing in the rules about how you throw the beanbag, just from how far. Face it, man—you *suck!*"

"Brady!" admonished Anyssa Williams from where she sat at the table across from Doug's mother, Loretta, and Doug's girlfriend, Lucy Graves. She and Brady had been seeing each other off and on ever since they met during the trial run of a murder mystery weekend Anyssa had hosted at her manor house on a private island in Lake Erie. Lately, they were a lot more on than off; they were practically living together at this point. "Gloating is very unbecoming."

Brady's grin only widened while Doug fumed, tossing his beanbags to the ground.

"Now, Dougie, this is why none of the boys ever wanted to play with you back in school. You've always been a sore loser," said Loretta, as she popped the last half of a deviled egg into her mouth.

She was looking especially festive today. Between her polyester pantsuit and the copious amounts of makeup she wore like face paint, she was completely color-coordinated with the Easter eggs little Brianna was rapidly stockpiling in her woven basket. The fact that she was seated amicably across from Lucy Graves was our Easter miracle. Loretta had been staunchly against her little boy's current relationship until fairly recently, and we weren't exactly sure what had changed.

"I can't believe you'd take his side," muttered Doug, approaching the picnic table to see what Melanie was carrying. "And I am *not* a sore loser. I just believe you should play a game by its rules, and the rules say you have to throw the bags *underhanded*. What that guy was doing was *not* throwing underhanded. It was more like a he was pitching a baseball."

"Oh, *please*," said Brady, waving aside the criticism. "It was really more of a sidearm sort of thing, but close enough, right?"

"I beg to differ," said Lucy, smirking as she consulted her phone. "According to the American Cornhole Association, and I quote, 'bags are to be pitched in an underhand motion.'"

"There's an American Cornhole Association?" I asked, setting the cubes of soda beside the coolers that were already prepped with ice and ready to receive their contents.

"There *is*," confirmed Lucy, setting her phone aside. "Mr. Garrett, you are in clear violation of the rules."

"Oh, geez, *fine*," said Brady, rolling his eyes. *"American Cornhole Association.* I mean, who knew? Okay, let's go again, double or nothing."

"Wait—*what?*" screeched Loretta, stiffening in her seat. "Do *not* tell me you boys are gambling, and on this, the most holy Sabbath day of all—'cept when Christmas falls on a Sunday. I suppose that would trump Easter, wouldn't it?"

Doug's eyes widened as he took a seat beside Lucy and aimed to change the subject. "I was done playing anyhow. How much longer 'til soup's on, Dwayne? You tryin' to starve us or something?"

I sighed. "Patience, my friend. We can't call dinner until the main course arrives, and that's Matt and Sheila's responsibility. They should be here any minute."

Melanie looked back toward the house. "Speak of the devil, I think they're here."

Sure enough, Matt was angling his champagne-colored Honda CR-V around the gaggle of cars already occupying the majority of my driveway. I could only hope Brady wasn't watching as Matt cut it entirely too close to Brady's shiny red Dodge Charger. I would almost believe he loved that car more than his own son.

Melanie and I reversed course to greet them but had only made it as far as the end of my porch before Jasmine burst through the front door, squealing and making a beeline for her favorite uncle. Okay, he wasn't technically her uncle yet, but he'd held the honorary title for some time now, and who was I to stand on a technicality?

"Uncle Matty!" she called, just before leaping into my startled brother's arms. He'd barely had time to stand on his own two feet before she was upon him.

"*Oof!*" Matt grunted, catching her midflight and somehow managing to stay upright. He twirled her around before planting a kiss on the top of her head and setting her down. "Well, Happy Easter, you little hooligan! And just in time to help us unload the car! *Excellent!*"

Jasmine was already peering around my brother, checking inside his car to see if any of the things that needed to be unloaded might be earmarked for her. This wasn't our first rodeo, and we couldn't seem to convince my brother that he was spoiling our little princess with the gifts he always seemed to bring.

"*Jasmine Marie!*" scolded Melanie as we met them at the car.

Jasmine turned, her eyes the picture of innocence. "What? I just wanted a peek at what Abbie was wearing for Easter. Isn't she *adorable?*"

Melanie scowled dubiously at her daughter. "She certainly is." She stepped in for a hug of her own. "Hi, Matt. So glad you all could join us today."

He kissed her on the cheek. "Wouldn't miss it for the world!" He froze as if suddenly remembering something before slowly turning my way, his voice dropping to a monotone. "Dwayne Morrow."

"Matt Morrow," I matched his tone out of habit, fulfilling my half of a lunkheaded greeting we had developed as children and continued to this day. Much like Sheldon Cooper of *The Big Bang Theory*, the tradition wasn't complete until we'd repeated our names at least three times, but midway through the third pass, Sheila interrupted from the passenger side of the car.

"I hate to disturb your lunacy, but I could use a little help here," she said, working to extract Abbie's carrier from its base in the back seat.

"Can I carry her?" asked Jasmine, eagerly racing around to the other side of the car.

The look on Sheila's face was nothing short of a cry for help to Melanie, and one she couldn't possibly miss. "Why don't you let Sheila carry Abbie down to the picnic area and get her settled?" Melanie suggested to Sheila's obvious relief. "It would be a big help if you could carry the diaper bag and any of the other supplies Sheila needs, though."

"Okay," said Jasmine, pausing to hug Sheila. "What would you like me to carry?"

"Well, if you could take the diaper bag and that tote on the other side of Abbie's car seat, I sure would appreciate it," said Sheila. "Thank you, sweetheart."

"Sure," said Jasmine as she loaded up.

Sheila turned her attention to us, brushing a wayward strand of her short, curly brown hair off of her forehead. "If you all can bring the food and the Pack 'n Play, I think we can manage everything in one pass."

"Well, whatever you do, don't set up the Pack 'n Play anywhere close to *Brianna*," said Jasmine, the name falling off her tongue like spoiled milk.

"Jasmine!" Melanie chastised. "Why would you say such a thing?"

"Because, *Mother*—"

"Whoa—how about we drop the tone?" interrupted Melanie. "I'd hate to have to embarrass you in front of our guests."

It was everything Jasmine could do to keep from rolling her eyes. Twelve is really such a *special* age!

"Because, Mother," Jasmine said, taking it down a notch. "That child is demonic. She's spoiled, she's mean, and she can't be trusted. I don't want to see poor Abbie subjected to whatever nastiness that little monster comes up with."

Sheila's eyes widened in alarm as Melanie sputtered, unable to produce a speedy rebuttal. Jasmine may have been exaggerating, but she wasn't exactly wrong. We'd all been subjected to our fill of tantrums and other unpleasantness from a child whose mother didn't seem particularly inclined to discipline a daughter she thought was above reproach. To say our patience had been occasionally challenged was putting it mildly.

"Abbie will be just fine. I'm sure you'll be setting her up where you can keep a close eye on her anyway," I said, aiming to placate Sheila's frazzled nerves while accomplishing the exact opposite.

"Don't you worry, Aunt Sheila," said Jasmine, projecting more confidence than either Melanie or I could muster. "I'll keep that shrieking devil child away from our precious angel. She'll have to get through me first, and I'd just love for her to try."

"*Jasmine!*" Melanie's mortification only grew. She smiled apologetically at Sheila as she took a flimsy foil pan of baked beans from the Honda's cargo hold. "There will be no altercations of any sort on today of all days, do you understand me?"

Sheila shot my brother a wary glance, and he leaned in to kiss his wife on the cheek. "It will be *fine*." Sheila wasn't entirely convinced, but she joined Melanie and Jasmine as they each carried their respective loads toward the picnic area. Matt turned to me. "Which do you want to carry, the ham or the Pack 'n Play?"

"*Pfft*—the Pack 'n Play," I said, reaching for the strap on its carrying case. "*Duh.*"

"Hmm, I figured you'd opt for the food. It's lighter."

"Maybe so, but I'm not going to be responsible for rolling everyone's dinner across the yard if I drop it," I said, setting the playpen aside and preparing to close the hatchback once Matt had retrieved the bag with the HoneyBaked Ham logo on its side. I paused, spotting another large bag in the back. "Should I grab that too?"

7

"Nope, it can stay right there—for now," he said cryptically.

I narrowed my eyes suspiciously. "Please tell me you didn't."

I reached in and grabbed the bag by its handles, pulling it toward me. I peeked inside and found myself staring at the most stylishly appointed moldering cadaver to have graduated from Demon Academy, Valedictoria Appendecta—and not just any version. It was the limited edition featuring human thumb bones for high heels. Jasmine had been pestering us to buy her the doll for months, but to say the cost was prohibitive is an understatement. It's almost as much as my car payment.

"Oh, Matt," I groaned. "Melanie is going to kill you, you know that, right?"

"But Princess Jasmine is going to love her favorite uncle just *that much more!*" His grin went from ear-to-ear, and all I could do was shake my head.

"We've *talked* about this," I said. "You're spoiling that child rotten."

"And I guarantee you'll be doing your own version of the same thing once Abbie embraces material possession. As Jasmine's favorite uncle, it is not only my prerogative, but my sworn duty. But don't worry. I don't want to upset any of the other kids, so I'll wait until after they leave to give it to her."

I sighed, resigning myself to the inevitable. "Well, at least tell me you brought something for Jordan, too."

Matt's face squirreled up. "Jordan? Jordan who?"

My expression had barely shifted to exasperation before he laughed, taking the bag from me and rooting around in its bottom. He retracted a smallish box containing a decent replica of a smartphone.

"I hear the little guy is enamored with his big sister's phone," said Matt, showing me the brightly illuminated graphic on the box. "This way he can have his own. It has some really neat, preprogrammed features, and it's far more durable than the real thing."

I nodded, smiling grudgingly. "He'll love it, and so will she. Thanks."

I tucked the clever gadget back into the bag before placing the whole thing in the cargo hold and closing the hatchback.

Matt took a moment to assess the cars in the drive before scowling. "Mom and Dad aren't here yet? I figured they would have arrived hours ago."

"Yeah, they're not coming," I said. "Mom called a couple of hours ago. Dad was having another one of his spells."

Back in February, we had learned that our father was having some issues related to his mental acuity, disturbing episodes wherein he would momentarily come untethered from the reality around him. During these episodes, he would frequently juxtapose the past with the present, and it was only by accident that I had even learned about them at all. Melanie and I bumped into Mom and my dad's sister, Eunice, in Lymont Memorial's emergency room as we were standing vigil over Melanie's former mother-in-law, Sarah McGregor. Sarah had suffered a heart attack while caring for Jasmine and her little half-brother, Jordan, and although she was continuing to improve, my father was slowly working his way through various specialists' offices, awaiting a definitive diagnosis. All that we currently knew was that he had a "dark spot" on his cerebral cortex, and most of his lapses were brief.

Matt's inhalation whistled through his teeth. "Did she call the squad?"

I shook my head. "She said it wasn't a bad one, but she was reluctant for them to make the long drive so soon after, and I can't say I blame her. She really needs to learn how to drive."

"Never gonna happen," said Matt. "Dad tried to teach her years ago, and he still recalls the experience as something he barely survived."

"Wow, that's saying a lot," I said. "He managed to teach *you* how to drive, and you never even learned how to ride a bike."

"Shut up."

We began a slow amble toward the picnic tables, shuffling under the awkward weight of our cargo.

Matt cleared his throat. "So, have you had a chance to ask Dad about—"

I shook my head and cut him off, anticipating his question. "Huh-unh."

My introduction to Dad's medical issues also included an unrelated but equally startling revelation, thanks to my Aunt Eunice's penchant for good old-fashioned troublemaking. She had let it slip that Dad was confusing our mother, Jo, with Nancy, the first Mrs. Todd Morrow. It was an undisclosed piece of our father's history that had come as a complete shock. Mom wasn't willing to talk about it at all, but it was too much of a burden to carry alone, so I had shared it with my brother at the first opportunity.

After a moment of silence, Matt asked, "Are you *ever* going to talk to him about it?"

"I'm just waiting for the time to be right, you know? Maybe after we get some answers about what's going on. Right now, I'm afraid if I bring it up, I might trigger another event, and I don't want to make anything worse than it already is. Of course, if you're *really* eager to get some answers, there's nothing preventing you from—"

"Oh, no, it can wait," he said, deftly removing himself from the equation. It really came as no surprise. Matt avoided confrontation at all costs, and technically, Dad's secret marriage was a fact we were apparently never supposed to learn.

"If the two of you don't stop yammering and get yourselves down here, I'm coming to meet you with a plate," Doug's voice boomed across the yard. "You've got a yard full of ravenous guests, you know."

I was about to toss off a witty reply when I realized everyone had already seated themselves and were staring at us expectantly.

"We better pick up the pace, bro," I said, doing exactly that. "The crowd is starting to turn on us."

·········•◯◉◯•·········

"I am going to kill that brother of yours if he doesn't knock it off," said Melanie. She sat at her vanity, brushing her honey-blonde hair as I lounged on my side of the bed, watching her graceful movements and grinning in spite of myself. Her satin pajama shorts were showing a whole lot of leg, and I was starting to get all tingly down south.

"He means well," I said, letting the bedsheet fall to my waist while exposing my chest and relatively flat stomach. I was doing my level best to look seductive rather than foolish, but it's a very fine line to negotiate.

"He needs to stop," said Melanie, ignoring my efforts entirely while focusing on her reflection in the mirror. "Lord knows we don't need to create any *other* monsters."

I groaned. "Oh my God, I *know*, right? I've never had to work so hard in all my life to keep from smacking someone else's child. Brianna's like *Lord of the Flies* or something. I really can't imagine Loretta tolerating that sort of behavior for very long."

"I think you're right, but she's trying to mollify her son, and as a direct result, I can't talk to her for more than a few minutes before she's badmouthing Lucy something awful. She probably would have already exploded if she wasn't able to vent to *somebody*, but it isn't easy to listen to. Personally, I *like* Lucy—if not her particular brand of parenting. What was up with Sheila? She didn't seem happy to be here."

I shifted into a position that felt more foolish than sultry before quickly shifting back. "Nah. Matt says she's been fixated on her weight lately. She can't seem to shake the last of the baby pounds."

"Well, that's ridiculous. She looks great!"

"Agreed, but the scales don't lie, and she's determined to get back to her pre-pregnancy number," I said, shifting my legs in an effort to conceal my biological reaction to the rise and fall of Melanie's breasts with each stroke of her hairbrush. It was a losing battle. There was visible tenting in the bedsheets, and I was beginning to feel flushed.

"I'll call Anyssa tomorrow and plot a girls' day out in the near future. Maybe a spa day? Something to boost her self-confidence. I—" She glanced at me and did a double take, her brush frozen in mid-stroke. A slow smile crept across her face as she laid her brush down. "Why, Mr. Morrow, I do believe you are trying to seduce me."

I waggled my eyebrows while attempting to flex my pecs. "Is it working?"

She stood and slowly sauntered over to the bed, pausing just outside of my grasp. "Maybe. Is this?"

She lifted her pajama top over her head and let it fall to the floor while I gaped like a bug-eyed schoolboy. I reached for her hand and pulled her toward me, savoring the sight.

"Most *definitely*."

We were wrenched from sleep by a persistent pounding on the front door.

I groped through the darkness to locate my phone where it was charging on the nightstand. It was only a little past midnight.

"What in the *hell?*" I muttered, pulling my sleep pants on and crossing to the window. My view of the porch was obstructed by its roof, but there was a strange truck parked behind Melanie's silver Mazda.

"Who is it?" Melanie asked, stifling a yawn.

"I don't know," I said, heading for the doorway. "I don't recognize the vehicle, but I better hurry before whoever it is wakes the kids—if they haven't already."

Melanie slipped into her robe, meeting me at the door. "I'll check in on them, but I'll be listening. Don't open the door without seeing who it is first."

"Of course not."

It was a reminder I didn't need. I was tired of getting my ass kicked at my own front door. Dexter came out of nowhere, keeping pace with me as I jogged down the stairs, his black feline shape nearly indistinguishable in the dark. He yowled in dismay as I turned toward the front door instead of the kitchen, operating under the misguided notion that I was on a mission to replenish his food dish.

The relentless pounding stopped as soon as I flipped the switch and flooded the porch with light. I peered through the peephole and gasped, staring at the man currently pacing a short path in front of my door. I immediately unlocked the deadbolt and threw the door open wide.

"Dad?"

My father turned to face me with wild eyes, his mottled skin covered in a sheen of perspiration. He lunged forward and grabbed both of my arms just below the shoulders. "Dwayne, thank goodness you're home."

Trapped in his iron grip, I smiled uneasily. "Where else would I be? It's a little after—"

"There's no time for that, son," he interrupted with renewed urgency. "We have to *go.*"

I shook my head. "I don't understand. Go? Go where?"

His tight-lipped scowl reflected pure frustration. "To bring Gina home. *Come on!*"

CHAPTER TWO

I didn't dare speak, afraid that anything I said might be too much.

I had every reason to be cautious. My father was alluding to a secret I had been keeping for nearly a year. It was a secret I had held so close to the vest it had nearly cost me my relationship with Melanie. I had finally taken her—and *only* her into my confidence, so seeing the urgency on Dad's face, the utter certainty of his convictions was unsettling, especially given his sporadically unpredictable state of mind.

Despite being heavily sedated at the time, I could still clearly see my sister's face hovering above mine as I was being transported by ambulance to a hospital, explaining to me the reasons she had been forced to fake her own death. A clandestine organization was hell-bent on dismantling many of the modern conveniences that had so rapidly changed our daily lives— silly little things like the internet and other technological improvements that made hiding in the shadows while advancing self-serving agendas much more difficult. It was a homegrown effort spearheaded by at least three highly prominent congressional officials, and Gina had managed to capture photographic evidence of their involvement, essentially putting a target on her own back—as well as on the backs of our family. Although they had intercepted the evidence, it still left Gina as an eyewitness, and they had sabotaged her car when she was in town for Matt and Sheila's wedding. What they didn't realize was that Gina wasn't the one driving when the car's steering failed, veering into the path of oncoming traffic. In an effort to protect the rest of us, she had allowed the world to believe that she had perished in the fiery crash. She only shared this information with me as a last resort when I wouldn't leave well enough alone. She made me promise to drop my investigation before anyone else in our family fell victim to another unfortunate 'accident.'

I nearly jumped out of my skin when Melanie's cool hand landed on my bare bicep, nudging me aside. "Todd? Is that you?" She had slipped into a short satin robe that was cinched at her waist.

The urgency in Dad's face dropped in an instant, replaced by a congenial smile. "Hi, Melanie. I'm sorry to drop by without calling first, but I was in the area."

In the area?!?

I glanced at Melanie, and she was doing a much better job of hiding her alarm. She peered out toward the driveway. "Is Jo with you?"

"Um, no, not this time," he said. "As a matter of fact, she thinks I'm bowling."

"At *this* hour?" I was incredulous.

Dad looked at his watch and seemed genuinely surprised to note the time. "I'm sorry, I didn't realize it had gotten so late."

"It's alright," said Melanie, stepping back and motioning for me to do the same. "Why don't you come inside? It's getting pretty chilly out there. We should probably give her a quick call to let her know where you are. She's bound to be worried sick."

Dad hesitated for a few seconds before nodding and crossing the threshold into the living room. "That's probably a good idea," he said with a sigh. "All that woman ever does anymore is worry. I suppose it's not fair to give her a valid reason."

"I don't know, Dad," I said, chuckling uneasily. "I would say her reasons have been plenty valid here lately."

"Pfft—my mind is still just as sharp as it's ever been. All these doctors are interested in is funding their next luxurious vacation at the expense of my insurance company, and—son, do you normally parade around the house like this?" He indicated my bare torso with a raised eyebrow as heat crept into my cheeks.

"We were in bed, Dad," I said. "Where *you* should be. Why don't we set you up in the guest room? It's too late for you to drive all the way back to Lymont tonight. In the morning, we can discuss whatever it is you wanted to talk about. How about that?"

"Oh, I don't know—" hedged Dad, already eyeing the door.

"That's a great idea," said Melanie, coming to my rescue. "The kids are in bed, but they'd love to see you when they get up."

He frowned, considering our offer. "I don't really care for sleeping in a bed that's not my own, but—" His words trailed away as he broke into a yawn. "—it *is* awfully late."

"Then it's settled," said Melanie, smiling as she headed toward the stairs. "I'll make sure the room is ready for you. Dwayne, why don't you help your dad with anything he needs from his car?"

"Yeah, about that," I said, scowling at my father. "That isn't what you were driving last time I saw you. What's up with that?"

His eyes flitted to the window, and his chuckle felt a little forced. "I— sort of borrowed it from a buddy."

My eyes narrowed. *"'Sort of'* borrowed? That doesn't sound good."

He sighed. "It belongs to Tom Wheeler. I worked with him at Pepsi for over twenty years, and I still bowl with the guy. It isn't the first time I've borrowed his truck. He'll be fine with it."

I groaned, rolling my eyes. "Does he even realize you *'borrowed'* it?"

"Well, I'm sure by *now* he does."

"Oh my God, Dad." I began to pace. "You can't just help yourself to someone else's vehicle. That's not borrowing, it's *stealing*."

16

"Oh, nonsense," he said, waving away my escalating concern. "It isn't like I stranded him or anything. I left him a note—along with the keys to my own car. He's fine."

"What was wrong with *your* car?" I asked, the pitch of my voice on an escalator ride to heaven.

"I had my reasons."

"Oh my God," I repeated, hugging myself tightly as nervous laughter bubbled out of me. Melanie continued to hover, following the lunacy from the foot of the stairs. "What were you thinking?"

"I was thinking I could count on my own son to help me, not just pass judgment at the front door!" He was getting a little hot under the collar, unaccustomed to the role-reversal that was currently playing out. "Tom's not going to make a fuss over this!"

"How can you be so sure?"

His arms flailed wildly. "I don't see any police—do *you*, son? You know what? Never mind. I'll do this myself."

He started for the door, but I hurried to intercept him. "Dad, *dad*—stop. Stay. I'm sorry. This is all just a lot to take in, okay?"

He glared at me with his hand on the doorknob, and for a second, I didn't think he was going to stay, but he eventually turned back toward me, stifling another yawn. "There's nothing I need out in the truck. It wasn't like I was planning on staying, so if Melanie could just show me to my room, I'll let you kids get back to sleep."

Melanie looked at me expectantly, unsure of what to do.

"What about Mom?" I asked, and the look he gave me was vacant. "You were going to call her and let her know where you are. Remember?"

That earned me another scowl. "Of course, I remember. Do me a favor and take care of that for me, will you? I don't feel like explaining myself all over again. I'd like to talk to you more in the morning about why I came in the first place—after you've had enough time to *'take it all in,'*" he said, flying air quotes around that last bit. "Right now, I've had about enough of you."

He shuffled across the floor to where Melanie waited, and all I could do was shrug before heading to my office to make what promised to be a most interesting phone call.

······•••••●◯◯●•••••·····

A new favorite thing of mine is waking to the sound of children's laughter wafting up the stairs in the morning, and ain't *that* some decidedly unexpected shit? Melanie, Jasmine, Jordan, and I have only been living as a family for a little over a month, but I've already acclimated to the soundtrack of my new life. Everyone gets up earlier than I do, which should come as a surprise to no one, if you've been paying any attention whatsoever. Dexter has also gleefully adapted to this new normal as it comes with the tacit understanding that his morning nibbles arrive more than an hour earlier than his customary breakfast time.

A cat has very little loyalty; ultimately, it's all about the food.

It took me a moment to pick out this morning's acoustic difference. Dad's modulated timbre was in the mix, and it sounded like the kids were thoroughly enjoying his company. The mouthwatering aroma of breakfasts long past wafted up the stairs and urged me to my feet as I recognized the unmistakably buttery scent of Dad's signature fried potatoes. Healthy? No. Delicious? Oh, *God*, yes, and it had been years since I'd had the pleasure.

I slipped a white T-shirt over my head as the events of the previous evening came rushing back to me. Mom had been surprisingly calm about the entire affair. She had dozed off on the family room sofa and hadn't quite realized that Dad wasn't home from his bowling league when I called. Apparently, his buddy, Tom Wheeler, wasn't too bothered by Dad's automotive switcheroo, because he had neither notified Mom nor called the police. Of course, if my memory served me correctly, Dad's car would have been a real upgrade from the ancient truck I had spotted in the drive. Honestly, she seemed a little relieved that this was a problem that someone else was going to have to deal with, and while I wasn't exactly thrilled to *be* that someone, Mom certainly deserved a reprieve. After I assured her that he was in no immediate medical distress, I promised I would see him home safely.

I descended the stairs on my bare feet, amused by the sight of my father engaging in an animated game of 'Thumb Wars' with Jasmine at our cozy little dinette table. Jordan was giggling himself silly while hanging on Dad's arm.

"Ha!" crowed Jasmine. "That's two out of three! I win!"

"Well, you clearly cheated," groused Dad, trying to shake Jordan loose—but not really. "You've got your trained little minion here distracting me."

Jasmine's exaggerated gasp was followed by fingers splayed over her heart. *"Me?* I would never cheat *you,* Mr. Morrow."

Dad's face squirreled up in mock indignation. "Mr. Morrow? *Mr. Morrow?* What kind of way is that to address me, young lady?"

"Well, what do you want me to call you?"

Dad took a moment to ponder the question quite seriously before saying, "In the service, I was called Sir, but that seems a little bit formal, doesn't it? Seeing as how your lovely mother and my slow-witted boy over there have finally agreed to tie the knot, do you think it would be premature to go with Grandpa? *No*—wait. I don't care for the sound of that. It makes me feel a hundred years old."

"How about Gramps?" suggested Jasmine, but Dad's face only soured.

"Worse," he said, returning to serious contemplation before his face finally lit up, and he snapped his fingers. *"I've got it!* How about—Peepaw?"

Jordan collapsed into hysterics, snorting the observation, "He said *Pee-paw!"*

Jasmine's grin couldn't have been wider. "Done. *Peepaw.*"

Melanie exited the kitchen as I reached the foot of the stairs and raised to her tiptoes to plant a quick kiss on my lips. "Morning, sweetheart. Breakfast's waiting for you in the kitchen."

"So I smelled," I said with a grin. I glanced at my watch and noticed it was nearly half past eight. "Isn't Jasmine going to miss the bus?"

"I told her I'd drive her to school this morning," she said, crossing to the table and collecting a round of dirty dishes. "It gives her a little more time with your dad, and I have to head that way with Jordan anyhow. He's got his first appointment with his new pediatrician at ten, and he's due for a couple of S-H-O-T-S." She whispered the last bit, unsure if simple spelling provided sufficient obfuscation. "Plus, I thought it would give you some quality time to catch up with your dad without me underfoot."

"Don't be silly," Dad interjected. "You could never be underfoot."

She leaned down and kissed him on the top of his bald head. "You're sweet."

Dad shot me a knowing look that belied his actual words, and I sensed he was eager to continue the conversation we had only just begun before Melanie interrupted us the previous evening at the front door. Honestly, I was hoping it had been delusional rambling. I wasn't in any hurry to discuss Gina and whatever fantastical theories might have hatched in his malfunctioning mind. It was an awfully slippery slope to tackle first thing in the morning.

"After Jordan's appointment, we're going into the office for a little training with Loretta," Melanie called over the running water in the sink. "Do you have anything on your calendar for today?"

"Just the three o'clock touchpoint with Doug, but I might have to take a raincheck. I promised Mom I'd see to it that Dad makes it home safely."

Dad sputtered on the coffee he was sipping and scowled at us. "I am *not* an invalid, and I would surely appreciate it if everyone would stop treating me like one! I've been driving for more years than you've been alive, son, and I can promise you this—I don't need or want an escort."

I sighed, deciding what the hell? I may as well throw Mom all the way under the bus since she wasn't here to face Dad's escalating irritation. "I didn't say you needed one, Dad, but Mom made me promise. I don't want her crawling all over me if I don't follow through."

Strictly speaking, I wasn't lying, but Dad seemed ready to take his keys and bolt, and I didn't think losing track of him while in a state of agitation was a particularly good idea.

He stared at me long and hard, deciding whether to take me at my word but finally, he nodded stiffly. "I suppose you're right. Knowing your mother, you'd never hear the end of it. I suppose I owe you an apology for hijacking your day."

"*Pfft,*" I waved his apology away with a smile. "You've given me a legitimate excuse for avoiding Doug and Loretta Boggs for a day. I should be thanking you. And hey, it's not every day I get the chance to spend a little quality time with my old man."

Dad clapped his hands and pushed away from the table, heading through the open archway into the kitchen where he paused and turned toward me, his eyes practically twinkling. "It's settled then. But first, let me fry you up some eggs over medium to go with the potatoes and bacon. I held off on making 'em until you finally dragged your lazy backside out of bed. Nobody wants cold eggs, am I right? Now, how many? Two or three?"

I laughed. "Three, please. Thank you."

Dad turned on his heel, whistling a nameless tune as he grabbed what he needed from the refrigerator and headed to the stovetop, igniting the fire under the cast iron skillet resting on one of its front burners.

"Jasmine, would you please help Jordan into his coat? We need to head out," said Melanie, as she took my arm and pulled me aside. Keeping an eye on Dad as he cracked eggs into the skillet, she leaned in and lowered her voice. "Am I missing something here? Are you really planning to follow your father all the way to Lymont? What if he decides to make a run for it?"

I blinked. "Do you really think he'd do something like that?" I asked, matching her volume.

"I wish I could say I didn't, but I wouldn't have expected him to show up like he did last night, either. From what you shared, it sounds like he's got some sort of rescue mission on his mind. Do you think he actually knows something about Gina that you don't?"

"I don't see how he possibly could, but I guess I'll find out shortly."

"I can't imagine he'll go home willingly if he's got something in mind," she said. "You know how stubborn he can be once he gets an idea stuck in his head. The apple didn't fall very far from the tree on *that* one." She looked at me pointedly.

"Hey!" I protested, but she was absolutely correct.

"You should offer to ride down with him. At least that way you can keep tabs on him if you can't get this crazy notion out of his head," she suggested.

"How would I get home?"

"We can come get you after Jasmine gets out of school," she said. "It'll make for a long evening, but it's preferable to the thought of your dad trying to shake you off his tail in a vehicle that's already technically stolen. I imagine Mr. Wheeler might just change his tune on that whole subject if Todd totals his truck."

I groaned as the scenario felt all too probable. "Alright, but don't leave for Lymont until we touch base. I have no idea where he's going with all of this, and I wouldn't want you to waste your time until I know for sure what's going on."

"Sounds like a plan," she said, pulling me down to her level by my t-shirt to seal the deal with another kiss. It was promptly greeted by a chorus of mortification from the children who had appeared at our feet, bundled in their outerwear and ready to go. Overtop of their cacophony of *'eeews'* and *'gross,'* Dad cleared his throat loudly from the entrance to the kitchen, where he stood wielding a spatula.

"How many slices of toast?" he asked with a grin.

······•••●◎◉●•••·····

"Oh my God, this is *delicious*," I said, dragging a piece of toast through the ruptured yolk of an egg that had been fried to perfection in pure bacon grease. Seasoned with just the perfect amount of salt and pepper, I could feel my arteries hardening as the seconds passed, and I had no idea how Dad managed to maintain his trim physique. As it was, my three-mile morning run was becoming less and less of a daily occurrence, and if interruptions like this were to become commonplace, I'd be shopping in the 'Big and Tall' section before long.

Dad sat across from me at the dinette table nursing another cup of coffee. "It's been a minute since I've made breakfast on this sort of scale, but it was a pleasure. Those kids are something else. Are you and Melanie any closer to setting a date?"

"Not yet," I said. "Although Melanie is on the phone almost every other day, plotting with her sister, Cheryl. I'm lying low. I'm sure I'll get a heads-up when I'm supposed to show up and do my part."

Dad snorted. "Sounds safe."

I shot a finger pistol at him and nodded, scooping up another forkful of fried potatoes. Dexter hovered near my feet with the fervent hopes of something delicious missing my mouth and falling to the floor, but I wasn't letting any of this get past me. I was running out of food, and it was getting awkward avoiding the elephant in the room, so I decided to provide an opening.

"So, Dad," I said, clearing my mouth with a sip of my own coffee. "About last night—"

He immediately stood and peered out the window into my side yard and driveway, almost as if he expected someone. "Are you sure they're gone?" he asked, scanning the horizon.

"They better be, or Jasmine's gonna be late for school," I said, wiping my mouth with a napkin. "What's up?"

He sighed, settling back into his chair and struggling for words. "I—I don't really know how to begin," he finally said, his eyes darting around the room before landing on me in earnest. "With everything that's been going on lately with—"

He indicated the general vicinity of his shiny, bald cranium, and I nodded my understanding, steepling my fingers underneath my nose and leaning forward on my elbows while waiting for him to continue.

"I'm not crazy, son," he blurted, his cheeks reddening. "But it's sure going to sound like I am. I haven't even shared this with your mother because I don't want to upset her. I need you to promise you'll keep an open mind and hear me out, alright?"

"*Um*, of course I will—"

"I need you to *promise* me, because there's a whole lot riding on this, and I can't afford to fuck this up." His eyes were earnest and unblinking, and I flinched from his rare use of one of my own favorite pejoratives.

"Okay," I said. "I promise."

Dad took a deep breath before saying, "Your sister's life is at stake."

Oh, boy. Here we go.

"Dad? You know Gina's gone. We—"

"*Shhh!*" His agitation was immediate, and he shot me a look I hadn't seen since I got busted 'borrowing' the family car at fourteen for a little late night neighborhood joyride. I blanched, my mouth snapping shut for fear he'd shut it for me. "You promised you'd hear me out. You *promised*."

"Alright," I said, nodding for him to proceed. I concentrated on keeping my expression neutral, which was no small feat considering I didn't know where he was going with this, but I knew he would sense any disbelief that crossed my face, and that would likely be the end of his confiding in me. "Go on."

The muscles in his jawline flexed as he stared me into discomfort, and I was beginning to think I'd already blown it when he finally said, "You think I don't remember burying my own daughter? *Of course* I do, and let me tell you something, son, it's a pain I wouldn't wish on anyone, not even my worst enemy. These past several months have been sheer hell, and there are days I have to make myself get out of bed in the morning."

I returned his even stare, impatiently waiting for more.

His gaze abruptly fell away, coming to rest on his fidgeting fingers. "She's not dead, son. I'm sure of it. She's out there—just waiting for us to find her and bring her back home."

I silently counted to ten.

Then twenty.

By thirty, I realized I was going to have to resort to cautious interrogation to hear any more of his story without spilling any of my truth in the process. It was like tiptoeing through a minefield with extra-large feet. I decided to keep it simple.

"What makes you think that?" I asked, keeping my tone flat.

His sigh was even more drawn out than the last one, and he still couldn't look me in the eye. He chuckled mirthlessly. "This is where we enter *The Twilight Zone*. I've been having these dreams—"

"*Dreams?* Oh, *Dad*—" It slipped out of its own accord, and he slammed his hands down on the table, jumping to his feet.

"Never mind. I guess I should have gone to Matt. He would have at least had the courtesy to let me finish," he said, his mottled face reflecting white-hot anger. "I just thought that with your experience in private investigation, you might be more willing to help, but I guess I overestimated—"

"Whoa, whoa, whoa!" I said, throwing my hands up in surrender. "I'm sorry. I'm listening. Tell me about these dreams you've been having."

"Do not patronize me, son," he warned, waggling a forefinger in my face. "I will not tolerate it."

"I'm not," I said, aiming to assure him. "This is all just a little out of the clear blue nowhere, you know? I'll do my very best to reserve judgment, I promise. *Please.* Go on."

He was eyeing his coat where it hung by the door, and I was nearly certain he was about to storm off. Instead, he dropped back into the chair, taking another deep breath. "She's gone off the grid. She thinks she's protecting us, but she's still in danger."

My breath hitched as he skimmed the truth as I knew it. "And you know this—from a dream," I said, more careful than ever to sound neutral. "Do you have any idea where she might be?"

His face tightened as he shook his head. "Not exactly. The dreams are only giving me flashes of information in no particular order, and I haven't been able to put them together—at least not yet. That's why I was hoping you could help me. I'm sure she's in a small town, maybe somewhere in Kentucky or West Virginia."

Every hair on my body stood on end as I stared at him dumbly.

"That's a lot of ground to cover," I noted absently, my voice sounding far away in my own head.

"But I've seen something else that might narrow it down a bit," he said, excitement creeping into his voice. "Wherever she is, there was a celebration going on."

"A celebration? What kind of celebration?"

His eyes were practically shining now. "It was some kind of street fair or jamboree that was held in an old-timey town square. Maybe a blackberry festival?"

My mouth fell open as my coffee cup dropped to the floor, splintering into pieces.

CHAPTER THREE

I don't know how long I stood beneath the warm spray of the shower head, processing Dad's words and trying to find a logical explanation for them. There wasn't one. While he didn't have the facts exactly right, he was close enough to send me spiraling into a panic. Where was all of this coming from? I rinsed the last of the shampoo out of my hair and stepped out of the tub to dry myself off.

I had tried calling Melanie just as soon as I excused myself from breakfast, but she shuttled the call off to voicemail, and a quick time check told me she was probably in the pediatrician's office, filling out all of the endless paperwork required of new patients, regardless of their age. I started to send her a quick text asking her to call me when she was free, but then realized I'd probably be sitting right beside Dad when she did and wouldn't be able to speak freely. I considered calling Matt, but I didn't see the point in worrying him, or at least not yet. He worked for a company that ensured security features used in most credit and debit cards worked as expected, and he didn't have the same flexibility with his work schedule that I enjoyed. I had purposefully left this week open from my IT consulting business, intending to make myself more available to Melanie and the kids as she more fully integrated herself into a routine at Boggs Investigations, but it looked like that was going out the window in a hurry.

After sliding on a pair of jeans and an OSU t-shirt, I headed back downstairs to face Act Two of *The Outer Limits*. Part of me almost hoped that Dad might have used the opportunity to escape, heading off to who-knows-where in his stolen transportation, but it didn't take long for shame to get the better of me. Despite my growing sense of dread, I couldn't help the curiosity that had slowly started to eat away at me.

As I rounded the bend at the midpoint landing to descend the final run of stairs, I was relieved to see Dad lounging on one of my two brown leather sofas, holding the TV remote in front of him. I would've recognized Brady Garrett's voice even without the unnecessarily loud volume Dad had set on my surround sound.

"—in a multi-state initiative designed to slow the influx of illegal immigrants into the tri-state area and spearheaded by long-term senator from Pennsylvania, Amelia Gorham," said Brady as another shoe dropped, and I froze where I stood, staring at the television. The image shifted from what I've come to think of as Brady's 'reporter face' to that of an impeccably dressed senator with flaming locks of auburn hair piled high in a French twist at the top of her head. She stood behind a podium with steely resolve, ready to deliver a prepared statement that lay before her, but she never once consulted; it was a crutch she was too seasoned to need.

She had only begun to speak when Dad snapped the television off. "God, I *hate* that woman!"

"Huh?" I mumbled, hovering somewhere between startled and dazed.

"Any opportunity to put her smug face in front of the masses. She pretends to have the interests of the common man at heart, but I'm telling you, she's in love with the sound of her own voice. I wouldn't trust her any farther than I could throw her."

Yeah, me neither—but I kept the thought from racing out of my mouth. Senator Amelia Gorham was the last surviving member of the trio of congressional officials behind Gina's current circumstance, and this felt more than coincidental. It practically knocked the breath out of me.

Dad got to his feet and headed for the door, snagging his coat from where it hung on the wall. "Well, if you're finally ready, son, let's get this show on the road. I swear, you're slower than your mother. I've got some places to see before we head south."

· · • • • • ● ◌ ◌ ● • • • • • · ·

Approximately forty-five minutes later, I sat stock-still in the passenger seat of the ancient Toyota Tacoma truck Dad had "borrowed" from his buddy, almost wishing I could just drop through the rusting floorboard that seemed unlikely to support my weight for much longer anyway. A curious peek at the odometer had revealed it was well over 300K miles, and noxious exhaust fumes seeped up from the undercarriage, turning this morning's breakfast into a roiling mass of potential upchuck in my stomach. If I'm to be completely honest, it wasn't the only thing making me sick.

This was the site of Gina's supposed death.

We idled on the berm of U.S. Route 33, just a handful of miles west of Lancaster as Dad stared out the driver's side window at a median that no longer bore the twin tracks of rutted earth that had once signified where my sister's car had careened into the oncoming path of a gasoline tanker.

I wasn't sure why we were here, but it wasn't exactly my idea.

I had offered to drive, but Dad wasn't willing to cede responsibility for Mr. Wheeler's truck to me, and I had spent the past forty-five minutes working imaginary pedals to little effect, although I'd nearly succeeded in punching through the aforementioned rust of the floorboard more than once. I didn't recall Dad being such an erratic driver, but I suppose it's possible our perception of such things changes as our own experience behind the wheel grows. As it was, every time a sight caught his eye, his

30

speed stumbled, and the truck drifted toward wherever he was looking. My nerves were actively shredding with each angry honk from passersby, some of whom actually punctuated their frustration with a good ol' fashioned middle finger salute.

Dad remained oblivious to it all, focused on whatever inner voice was currently guiding him and jerking back into his own lane whenever the rumble strips bordering the road signaled he had gone too far astray. I had pit stains down to my waist.

And now we were here, staring at the scene of a crime that wasn't at all what he imagined it to be.

Gina hadn't been traveling in her car at the time of the accident. An agent from Homeland Security named Chloe Devereaux was, and she had given her life in an effort to help dismantle the shadowy organization known as The Academy. None of this was public knowledge, and I had been sworn to secrecy by a sister who was presumed to be dead—at least until now.

After what felt like an eternity, I said, "Why are we here, Dad?"

He continued to stare through the driver's side window, tugging at his bottom lip.

"Dad?"

He started, looking at me. "Hmm?"

"What are we *doing* here?" I repeated. "It's not exactly my favorite place to be."

He shook his head and straightened in his seat. "No—I'm sure it's not. I'm sorry, son. I just had to know."

"Know what?"

His lips pressed together as he slowly shook his head. "I thought I would *feel* something, but—" His voice trailed away before his eyes found mine. "Nothing. I feel nothing. Do you?"

I blinked. "Do I *feel* anything? Of course, I *feel* something. I'm angry, and I don't want to be here. Why would you want to be?"

He sighed, closing his eyes and leaning back against the headrest. "I think whatever is—you know—*wrong* with my head is why I'm seeing these things. So far, everything I've seen has come to me in a dream, but I thought that maybe—just *maybe*, if I got close enough to where—to where—"

He swallowed hard, and I knew he was fighting back tears. Public displays of emotion weren't an indulgence he allowed himself, and he didn't give two shits if 'real men' were supposed to express themselves openly these days. After a moment, he cleared his throat.

"You're very lucky, son. I hope you realize that," he said, returning his vacant gaze to the empty median where tragedy had torn our family into pieces.

"I suppose so," I said, eyeing him curiously.

When he turned back, he was almost angry. "I'm serious, Dwayne. You're starting an exciting new chapter in your life, even if you are a little behind schedule, but you're even making up for lost time."

I just stared at him, waiting for him to make a point that wasn't readily apparent to me.

Another heavy sigh, and he pinched the bridge of his nose between his thumb and forefinger. "Your mother and I had pretty much given up hope that you were ever going to find a nice young lady and settle down. I'm sure I don't need to tell you this, but Melanie's a real treasure, and we adore her, but those *kids!*"

I scowled. "Jaz and Jordan? You've got a problem with her kids?"

He returned my scowl, rolling his eyes. "Don't be dense! Of course not. The kids are great! The point I'm trying to make is that you went from living alone to having a ready-made family, practically overnight. It's not going to be without its challenges, but let me tell you son, you're only just beginning to understand the rewards. Those rotten little kids are gonna worm their way into your heart in ways I can't even begin to describe, but you'll never be the same, and I mean that in the best way possible."

I nodded as he patted my arm, his smile slowly fading as his eyes darkened.

"I can only pray you never know the pain of losing one of your children," he said, his voice barely audible. "No parent should have to go through that."

"Oh, *Dad*—"

He held up a forefinger to silence me, struggling once more to get his emotions in check. After a moment, his expression brightened. "There's nothing more to see here," he said. "Why don't we get underway? Your mother's probably coming up out of her hair with worry."

He put the truck in gear and eased back out onto the highway heading east.

We cut over to SR 159 and traveled southwest to Chillicothe where we would pick up US 23 and head south toward home. The Toyota's radio was busted, and the only thing interrupting the awkward silence was the steady growl of exhaust leaking through a rust-riddled muffler. There wasn't much traffic along the two-lane road, and Dad remained absorbed in his thoughts, keeping his focus on the road ahead while keeping the truck in its proper lane—for the most part. I was working my imaginary pedals less, and my jangling nerves were a little less noisy.

I discreetly eyed him from the side. Was this the opportunity I'd been looking for to ask him about the bombshell Aunt Eunice had dropped at Lymont Memorial? We still had over an hour of travel ahead of us, and it had been on my mind for months. My approach would require a little delicacy and tact, and I wasn't really known for either. Several more miles passed as I considered a point of ingress to a topic that had always been guarded like Fort Knox.

"Dad?"

He glanced at me. "Yes, son?"

"Earlier, you made the comment that I was 'a little behind schedule,'" I said. "You weren't that much younger than me when you and Mom got married, were you?"

He pursed his lips, doing the math. "I guess not. I was thirty-one when your Mom and I tied the knot."

"Was it a big wedding?"

He snorted. "Hardly. We eloped."

Well, *fuck*. The surprises just kept on coming. "You *eloped*? Why?"

He shrugged. "We had our reasons."

I tried to keep from gaping as his non-answer only served to pull me further off balance. I focused on my breathing, trying to restore a sense of calm that might allow me to get my line of inquiry back on track. I took another deep breath and plunged ahead.

"Did you have any other serious relationships?" I asked, trying to keep my eyes on the road ahead. "I mean, *before* Mom?"

The corners of his mouth dipped down as he considered my question, and he slowly began to shake his head. "No, I can't say that I did."

I nearly gasped out loud at his bold-faced lie, and while I managed to contain most of my outrage, I could feel heat creeping into my cheeks.

It was back to controlled breathing.

Once I felt sufficiently capable of controlling the tone of my voice, I tried again. "Surely, you had some girlfriends in high school," I prompted. "Or in any of the many years that followed."

"Well, sure," he acknowledged with a little curious side-eye. "I *was* in the service, after all."

Wow, was he *good!*

His ability to selectively divulge truth was a gift I'd nearly kill for. I can't even *skirt* the truth without breaking into a clammy sweat, my facial expression spilling all the tea. I could feel the heat rising in my cheeks again, and this time, I couldn't keep a lid on my indignation.

"Nancy," I said, a little louder than intended.

Dad's head whipped toward me at lightning speed. "What did you just say?"

"*Nancy*," I repeated, glaring right back at him.

For the first time in the history of ever, I had knocked him off his game. His lips worked soundlessly as the truck began a slow drift across the center lane.

"*Dad, Dad, Dad,*" I said, grabbing the wheel and pulling us out of the path of a compact sedan approaching from the opposite direction. I waved apologetically at the poor, elderly woman behind its wheel. All the color had drained from her face, her mouth frozen in a perfect 'O'. "Let's focus on the road before someone calls the cops, okay?"

It took a little longer than it should have, but Dad finally returned his attention to the road ahead. "Where did you hear that name?" he finally asked.

"Aunt Eunice," I said, prompting an uncharacteristically crude string of swear words to fall from my father's lips.

"Why in the *world* would that old busybody be talking about *her?*" he finally spat.

"Does it really matter?" I asked. "She said you were married to this 'Nancy' woman before Mom. That sounds pretty serious to me."

His lips only tightened as the color in his own cheeks began creeping to the top of his bald head. He exhausted my patience as I waited for something—*anything* more, but it soon became apparent he was done talking.

I sighed. "Will you at least tell me if Matt and I have any other half-siblings running around out there?"

Ugly laughter erupted from his throat as his eyes rolled to the heavens. "Oh, boy," he muttered, shaking his head. "No. You, Matt, and Gina are my only children."

"And I'm just supposed to take your word?"

"Of course you are!" he roared. "I am your *father*. When have I ever—" His voice dropped off as he suddenly realized the utter hypocrisy of what he was about to say.

I'll give him credit for at least looking thoroughly mortified as silence descended on us like an anvil. We had somehow managed to elevate awkwardness to as-of-yet undiscovered heights.

We Morrows have a curious way of dealing with conflict.

Mostly, we just ignore it and pretend it never happened, finding a neutral topic of conversation once the anger has safely left our voices. As we passed the Kenworth Truck Company on our left, signs announcing the exit to US 23 appeared, and Dad cleared his throat, startling me.

"It's almost lunchtime, and I'm starting to feel a little peckish. How about you? My treat."

"I suppose I could find something," I said, although I wasn't all that hungry. "What did you have in mind?"

"There's a Wendy's right off the Main Street exit," he said. "We could just grab something through the drive-thru. I don't want to keep you any longer than necessary."

He added that last little bit sullenly in a not-so-subtle attempt to make me feel guilty for kicking a hornet's nest I wasn't even supposed to know about.

"That's fine," I said, staring through the passenger window and refusing to take the bait.

We merged onto the two-lane southbound thoroughfare where traffic was much thicker, and it wasn't long before I was back to working my imaginary pedals on the floor. A heavy sigh from my father indicated it hadn't gone unnoticed, and he made a spectacle of changing to the outermost lane after US 35 swooped in and merged from our right. He was purposefully riding the bumper of the SUV in front of us, and I sat on my hands to fight the urge to clasp them in urgent prayer. I wouldn't give him the satisfaction of reacting. I fervently sought out the same 'happy place' in my mind where I retreated during invasive dental work, but the sheer proximity of the SUV ahead made it impossible to focus, and closing my eyes only made it worse.

I breathed a sigh of relief as we approached Main Street, and Dad was forced to slow in order to take the exit. He feigned nonchalance as he turned right and drove the short distance to Wendy's parking lot, hooking another right to join the line of cars waiting in the drive-thru.

Almost immediately, he was up to his old tricks, nibbling away at the distance between the Toyota's front bumper and the rear bumper of the Chrysler minivan in front of us.

"Do you know what you want?" he asked, fishing his wallet out of his back pocket while inching even closer to the Chrysler.

"Just some chicken nuggets," I said, regulating my tone as the line moved forward, and we lurched along with it. My foot was twitching, itching to work the imaginary brake pedal, but I managed to suppress the urge. "No sauce."

"I think I feel like a burger," he said, eyeing the menu board as we crept forward, and I could read the fine print on the Chrysler's registration sticker. "The question is, how much of a burger do I feel like?"

I was vaguely rocking in the passenger seat now, unable to sit still, and he caught my movement from the corner of his eye.

"Do you need to pee, son?"

"No," I said, clasping my arms tightly around me as the line moved forward. We had reached the speaker, and Dad cranked down the window as he approached. It was my only hope that the handful of cars ahead of us would clear the line before Dad finished relaying our order.

"Welcome to Wendy's, may I help you?" inquired a bright female voice from the speaker, competing to be heard above the grumble of the Toyota's noisy exhaust.

"Um, yeah," Dad began, projecting his voice like he needed to reach the ears of the employee inside the store. "Gimme a double with cheese, everything on it."

"Would you like that in a combo, sir?"

"Um, yeah—no, wait. You're not a Pepsi store anymore, are you?" he asked, scowling. Inwardly, I groaned. He already knew the answer. Pepsi hadn't been served at Wendy's since the late 80s, but he always felt compelled to register a complaint. He may have retired, but he still served his former employer well at every conceivable opportunity, and I wasn't about to stop him. It gave the other cars in front of us more time to conclude their business in the drive-thru lane.

"No, sir, but we have Coke Freestyle, which has about every flavor you could imagine—"

"Except Pepsi," he interjected sourly.

"Um, yes, sir. We also have several flavors of lemonade and tea, both sweetened and unsweetened," our gracious host suggested.

Dad ensured his sigh was loud enough to be heard over the exhaust. "Just make it a sweet tea, I guess."

"Does that complete your order?"

"No—gimme chicken nuggets," he barked, never failing to use 'gimme' instead of just asking politely.

"Four, six, ten, or our party pack of twenty-five?"

He looked at me for guidance. "Six," I muttered before dropping my face into my open hands.

"Six!" he shouted, following up with, "No sauce!"

"Would you like that in a combo?"

"Sure," I said, my spirits lifting as another vehicle exited the drive-thru lane. "And water's fine."

"Yes!" boomed Dad. "And just water for that one. *No one* wants your lousy Coke."

"Um, yes, sir. Spicy or original?"

"Original! Original! Original!" I cried overtop of Dad and directly into the speaker, wondering if this fresh hell might ever end.

"Does that complete your order?"

"I believe so," Dad said, giving me serious side eye as he listened to the total and cranked his window back up. "You need to calm yourself, son. There's no reason to shout at that poor kid. She's only doing her job."

I practically choked on my exasperation as he shifted the truck back into gear and lurched forward, targeting the back end of the Chrysler minivan that hadn't quite managed to escape us. I closed my eyes as he braked, bringing us close enough that I could see the short hairs on the thick neck of the soccer mom piloting the thing. My terror was reflected in the face of a young boy in the back seat, his own eyes glued to the microscopic space separating our bumpers. He nudged a girl in the seat beside him, adding her terrified gawking to his own.

As the driver collected bag after endless bag from the window, Dad allowed the truck another inch, and I couldn't help it—my right foot urgently pumped my imaginary brake pedal.

"Da-*a-a-d*," I warned in little more than a hiss, earning myself a hearty chuckle in the process.

"What's the matter with you, son? I've got *plenty* of room," he crowed, lifting his foot and promptly hitting the car in front of us.

"Are you *serious?*" I demanded.

"I'm sorry, son, but I'm fairly certain Tom would have a problem with me letting someone else drive his truck," said Dad, sliding back behind the wheel while I gaped at him from the parking lot.

After nearly twenty minutes of begging and pleading and a quick race across the street to an ATM, I was able to convince the soccer mom to leave the police out of it. No one had been hurt, and there was no visible damage to either car, although it would have been admittedly difficult to tell with Mr. Wheeler's Toyota.

And I *still* couldn't talk Dad out of the goddamn keys.

Dad leaned on the horn. "Get in, Dwayne. Your food's getting cold."

Getting cold, indeed. My nuggets were officially in rigor mortis.

I strapped myself back into the passenger seat, and Dad handed me our bag of food. "Once I get back on the highway, unwrap my burger and hand it to me, okay?"

"Fine," I said, foraging through the bag and snagging a limp fry. Dad saw a break and seized the opportunity to launch us back into traffic, turning left on Main Street and causing me to be clotheslined by my own seatbelt.

"For Pete's sake, Dad! I'm gonna spill your lunch into the floorboard! Slow it down, will ya?"

He didn't respond, his attention rooted to the rearview mirror. "Damn," he muttered.

I watched helplessly as the entrance ramp back onto US 23 sailed by. *"Dad!* You missed our exit! Eyes on the road! *Eyes on the road!"*

"I didn't miss anything, son," he said, his voice oddly calm. "Do you see what I see?"

I blinked, utterly flummoxed. "It's a little late for Christmas carols, Dad. What are we doing here?"

"The car that's behind us," he said, grabbing my arm as I started to turn around. *"Don't look directly at it!"*

I casually leaned to my right, using the passenger side mirror to scope the nondescript Honda sedan that followed us at what I considered an assured clear distance. "Yeah? What about it?"

"It's been following us since before we got onto 23," he said, his knuckles tightening on the wheel. "I think we might be in a little bit of trouble here."

CHAPTER FOUR

"What do you mean, it's been following us?" I asked. "We practically spent a half hour at Wendy's."

"It followed us into the drive-thru and pulled off while you dealt with that hysterical woman driver."

I sighed. "She wasn't hysterical. You hit her car."

He scowled. "I barely bumped her car, but that's neither here nor there. Point is, as soon as we were back underway, this joker fell in line behind us again."

The stretches between residences lengthened the farther we went along Charleston Pike, and as ridiculous as it seemed, I was beginning to allow paranoia to creep in. I couldn't tell much about the Honda's driver from my view in the side mirror, but I swear, the outline was reminiscent of Michael Myers from the *Halloween* movies, and he appeared to be traveling alone.

"Well—driving away from civilization seems counterintuitive," I said. "Do you have an actual plan, or are we just hoping they run out of gas before we do?"

"Well, *crap*," said Dad, glancing at the dashboard before returning his attention to the road. "We forgot to gas up before we headed out."

"*We?*" I was incredulous. "I've never been close enough to the driver's seat to even *see* the gauge! How much gas do we have left?"

A thin whistle escaped his lips. "Not much."

"Dad!"

He sputtered. "One problem at a time, son! Let's keep our priorities straight. Are you carrying your gun?"

I gaped at him. *"No!* Why would I be carrying my gun?"

He quickly shook his head. "Never mind. If you reach into the glove box, I tucked my little peashooter behind the registration and all those napkins."

I continued to stare. "You've *got* to be kidding me. You stole your buddy's truck *and* brought a gun?"

His agitation was beginning to show as his attention was firmly divided between the rearview mirror and the winding two-lane road in front of us. Alarmingly, it was more to the former than the latter. "Just get it! I swear to goodness, with everything you've been through since trying your hand at this whole PI thing, I would think you'd keep yours on you at all times. You really should, you know."

I sighed, and I could practically hear Melanie agreeing with him in my head. I opened the glove box only to have all of its contents spill out into the floorboard, Dad's tiny handgun landing on my foot. I froze, half-expecting it to discharge and put me out of my misery. When that didn't happen, I unfastened my seatbelt and leaned forward, picking up the gun and putting it into the pocket of my jacket while I scooped all of the other junk together and shoved it back inside the glove box, barely able to force it closed. I buckled myself back in and tried to get a better look at our pursuer, but whoever it was kept their distance, denying me the privilege.

"Okay, I've got it," I said. "Surely, you don't expect me to just open fire at them through the window?"

"Of course not!" he snapped. "I just want you to be ready. Do you see that road coming up on our right?"

I eyed him dubiously. "Yeah."

"I'm going to see if I can lose them, but son? If they follow us, there's no *way* this a coincidence, do you understand what I'm saying?"

Unfortunately, I did. I nodded, putting my hand around the grip of the pistol in my pocket and bracing myself for whatever came next. My anxiety started to spike as the turnoff neared, and Dad showed no sign of slowing.

"Um, Dad," I said. "I thought you said we—"

"*Shhh!* I'm concentrating."

"Well, *sure*, but—"

"*Shhh!*"

My mouth snapped shut as I double-checked my seatbelt. I could understand why he wasn't signaling his intention to turn, but making the turn at our current velocity would challenge the laws of physics, and it didn't take much imagination to picture us rolling across the vast expanse of plowed farmland that stretched for miles beyond the adjoining road.

"Okay, brace yourself," he warned, his knuckles tightening on the steering wheel.

"Oh, shit," I mumbled, closing my eyes and clinging to my seatbelt. I was fairly certain this rusty bucket of bolts predated passenger side airbags by about a decade.

The tires barked as Dad jerked the wheel hard to the right, the truck's springs groaning in protest as its load shifted to the left, and I might have peed myself a little. Dad fought to keep the truck from fishtailing as our center of gravity stabilized, and I wondered whose nervous tittering was filling the cabin.

Oh. It was mine.

With subtlety already out the window, I craned my neck to look behind us where the Honda was in the process of making the turn a lot more casually. The driver even used the turn signal, utterly unconcerned with forecasting his intent.

"They're still following," I noted, and Dad responded by flooring it, our momentum pinning me back in my seat.

For the moment, it was working.

The distance between us rapidly grew. Thankfully, there was no other traffic on the two-lane road as Dad paid little attention to the center line and used whatever part of the road he deemed necessary. On the horizon, the road curved to our left, cutting deeper into the farmland surrounding us.

"So, our plan is to outrun them?" I asked.

"I'm hoping for another turn, one we can take without being noticed," he said.

"We're going to need a little more distance," I said as the Honda rounded the curve far in the distance. Its driver seemed unconcerned with our escape, and it suddenly occurred to me that maybe he had a partner waiting to intercept us somewhere ahead. My lousy chicken nugget lunch sat like lead in my stomach as I considered sharing my concern with Dad, but for the moment, I decided to keep the thought to myself. I wouldn't worry him unless it became absolutely necessary. It felt wisest to keep his focus on negotiating the road.

"Hang tight," he warned. "There's another curve ahead."

The road bent left once more, and Dad chuckled as the Honda disappeared from our rearview.

"*Dad!* There's another road straight ahead on the left," I said, pointing as the truck sputtered. Startled by our sudden reduction in speed, I figured it was just our luck to run out of gas at such an inopportune moment, but the engine continued to idle grumpily, and I could see that Dad had lifted his foot from the gas pedal. I turned to him, alarmed. "What are you *doing?* This is our opportunity to—"

My voice trailed off as I noted the vacant look that had settled over his face. Although he continued to stare through the windshield, his actual focus was anyone's guess.

"Dad?"

"I—uh," he cleared his throat, smiling apologetically as the truck continued to slow. "I'm—uh, I'm not sure—"

"Dad!" I couldn't keep the panic out of my voice as I watched the Toyota drift into the other lane while he did nothing to correct our course. There still wasn't any traffic headed our way, but we were on a steady path toward the low ditch running parallel to the road.

He looked at me, surprise competing with confusion for control of his features. "Dwayne? When did you get here? And which way takes us home? Nancy won't be happy if we're late for dinner."

Nancy.

Oh, shit. I was witnessing my first of his 'spells.'

"Dad, you need to watch where you're going," I said as we drifted toward the turnoff I had pointed out, but Dad was busy studying his surroundings, seemingly oblivious to the fact that he was even behind the wheel.

"Is this a new development in Lymont?" he asked, scanning everything but the road. "I don't ever recall—"

"Dad!" I urged, grabbing for the wheel to try and coax us left. He smacked my hands away.

"What do you think you're doing, son?" he snapped, jerking the wheel back to the right. "Don't you *ever* mess with me when I'm driving! You could have—"

His words fell away as we dropped off the side of the road. There was a horrific metallic grinding as we lurched to a stop, the truck's front end embedded in the trunk of an old oak tree that stood guard over the intersection.

⋯⋅•••••◉◎○◉••••••⋯⋅

"Are you sure you don't want me to call someone?" asked the woman who had been driving the Honda. Clutching her long, tan housecoat tight to her chest, she hovered near the door of her idling car where she could keep an eye on her infant son who slept in his car seat in the back. Her name was Patty Dawes.

I flashed my phone at her and aimed for a reassuring smile while Dad continued to examine the mangled front end of his friend's truck. "Thanks, but I've got someone I can call."

She nodded but looked a little less than convinced. "Is your father alright?"

Good question! Physically—yes, but mentally? I had no fucking idea.

"Yeah, he's just not familiar with either the truck or the area. I should have been the one behind the wheel, but he's kind of a control freak about the whole driving thing."

"I have to say, after he bumped that car in the drive-thru at Wendy's and then started drifting all over Charleston Pike, I nearly called the police. I thought he must be drunk or something," she said, not-so-subtly sniffing the air around me to see if maybe we were both sauced. I held my smile, wishing she would just move along. I wasn't about to fess up to our ludicrous suspicions about her intentions and how that had prompted all of the erratic behavior—well, until Dad checked out for a minute and referenced his former wife. I had no idea what prompted *that*. His buddy's truck was probably totaled based on age alone, but the last thing I wanted was police involvement. I needed time to find a way to soften the blow for poor Mr. Wheeler.

"Well, if you're sure," said Mrs. Dawes, and she was already reaching for her door handle. "I've got groceries in the car, and my little Stanley won't stay down for long. I really need to get home."

"Yes, I'm sure," I said, nodding. "Thank you anyway, though."

She got behind the wheel of her car and pulled away, continuing past the road we had intended to use to evade her and waving uncertainly as she passed. My smile faded as I turned back toward Dad, who was inspecting the truck from all angles.

"So, she was following us, huh?" I couldn't keep the sarcasm out of my voice, but Dad just looked at me and shrugged.

"How was I to know?" he asked irritably. "She certainly was *acting* suspicious. I mean, what was that business pulling out of the drive-thru and just sitting there?"

"She was nursing her child!" I said, joining him down by the wreckage to evaluate the damage for myself.

The front tires appeared somewhat pigeon-toed, but that might have been because one had blown, its shredded remains embedded in the soft, muddy earth. Even if we were able to separate truck from tree, this baby wasn't going anywhere on its own. Fluorescent green antifreeze dribbled onto the ground from its ruptured radiator. We were stuck, and I couldn't help but notice Dad beginning to shiver, his lightweight jacket not quite warm enough to counter the briskness of the overcast spring afternoon.

"Here, Dad, trade me coats," I said, beginning to slide my heavier insulated coat off.

"Would you stop fussing over me?" he groused, waving my offer away. "I've seen worse weather than this when I was overseas. Did I hear you tell that woman you had someone you could call?"

I nodded, fishing my phone out of my pocket and swiping through my contacts. Someone owed me a big favor, and I was about to collect.

"Welp," I said, pocketing my phone after disconnecting. "I've got some good news and some bad. Which do you want first?"

Dad shrugged, rolling his hand to encourage me to get on with it.

"I've got a tow truck on the way. My guy is making no promises until he sees what you've done, but with any luck at all, we might be able to get your buddy's truck back up and running," I said.

"Well, that's something," said Dad, nodding appreciatively. "What's the bad news?"

"It'll be at least a couple of hours before he can get here," I said, watching my frosty breath float away. "We can wait inside the truck's cabin, but with the radiator leaking antifreeze like a sieve, we won't be able to run the engine for heat."

Dad scowled, rubbing his hands together to generate a little warmth.

"I've got a better idea," he said, crossing to the truck's tailgate and releasing its gate with a rusty screech. I had failed to notice the rolling bowling ball bag he had stowed in the truck bed. I suppose it made a perverse sort of sense; he was bowling when he helped himself to his buddy's truck, so why wouldn't he have his equipment with him? He pulled it out, setting its wheels in the spongy mud at his feet as he slammed the tailgate back into place.

I scoffed. "Bowling? You want to go *bowling?*"

He raised an eyebrow. "You've got something better to do?"

I sputtered out a chuckle. "Well, *no*, but we're kind of stuck in the middle of nowhere," I said, indicating the relative desolation that surrounded us.

"*Pfft*," he said, and he was already lugging his bowling bag across the lumpy terrain toward the road. "This is practically a metropolis compared to the Saudi Arabian deserts. I say we make our way back to Charleston

Pike and then put our thumbs in the air. Shawnee Lanes isn't too far from here."

I blinked. "You want to hitchhike? You always told us we should *never* hitchhike."

"*Pfft*," he repeated, waving my concern away. "That was for your mother's benefit. She worries about anything and everything, but she's never really had to be resourceful, has she? But we both know that sometimes you do what you gotta do, am I right? I don't know about you, but I can hold my own in the off chance we get picked up by some psycho."

He pulled his bag up onto the gravel berm before turning back toward me.

"Are you coming?" he asked expectantly.

I stared at him in raw disbelief. Who *was* this man, and what had he done with my father?

He sighed, weary of justifying his every thought. "Don't be such a pantywaist, son. For heaven's sake, if you're scared, you've still got my pistol in your pocket, right?"

Oh, shit. I did. I had already forgotten about it.

"Fine," I grumbled, following his lead while mentally prioritizing all of the calls I would need to make.

I glanced at my watch and sighed. It wasn't even one o'clock.

"Jeb, I can't thank you enough for giving me and my boy a lift," said Dad, sliding down from the passenger seat of the monster truck that had picked us up in surprisingly short order. It was a dark gray Ford F-150 SuperCrew, and I shared its cavernous rear seat with Dad's bowling bag.

"Always happy to help a fellow Vet," boomed Jeb Blevins, his voice unnaturally loud due to hearing loss he had sustained during his own tour of duty. He was a big, barrel-chested guy with thick arms and a pot gut, his hair a wiry tangle of gray peeking out from beneath a John Deere ballcap and deep smile lines that radiated from the corners of his eyes.

On the short jaunt back into Chillicothe, he and Dad found an easy rapport from their shared experiences overseas, and they filled the empty air chuckling over recollections from days gone by. I, on the other hand, used the time to text vague updates on our progress to all interested parties since it was painfully obvious our schedule had derailed like a runaway train. I didn't want Melanie to make the trip for nothing, and at this point, I didn't know when or if I would feel comfortable returning Dad to Mom's care. I kept it simple, relaying that we were running behind without going into any details that would only invite unnecessary concern. As unnerved as I was by the content of Dad's dreams, I would have to find a way to broach that topic again and try to talk him down. Otherwise, he was liable to just steal someone else's car and disappear into the night, and in good conscience, I couldn't do that to Mom.

Dad passed Jeb one of his old business cards as I fumbled my way out of the back seat, dragging his bowling bag after me. "I'm retired, but my home phone is written on the back," he said. "If you ever find yourself near Lymont and in need of anything, look me up, my friend. I owe you one."

Jeb pocketed the card with a tip of his head.

Dad nudged me with his elbow. "Son—thank the good man for giving us a ride," he urged from the corner of his mouth, using a bit more volume than was necessary.

Oh, my God, I was ten all over again.

I leaned in and sheepishly said, "Thank you, Mr. Blevins."

Dad rolled his eyes at his new friend and grinned, hooking a thumb in my direction. "Kids these days. What's the world coming to? I blame his mother."

They shared a hardy guffaw at my expense while I shuffled awkwardly from one foot to the other. Dad closed the passenger door, and after one last wave, Jeb was on his way.

"Now, see? That wasn't so bad," said Dad, taking the handle of his bag from me as we ambled toward the entrance to the bowling alley.

We had no sooner cleared the foyer when a loud voice greeted us from somewhere behind the counter. "Well, if it isn't Todd Morrow! For heaven's sake! I haven't seen *you* in a minute!"

"Howdy, Roy!" Dad responded in kind, greeting his friend with a quick bro hug as he emerged from behind the counter. "Long time no see. Don't make it up this way nearly as often since I retired."

"Don't remind me," said Roy. He was rail-thin with prominent teeth that were most likely false. "Our service here just ain't been the same since you stopped runnin' the show down there at Pepsi."

Dad turned deadly serious on a dime. "What kind of issues are you having, Roy? Don't think I won't call and raise some serious hell on your behalf. I may be gone, but I've still got connections."

Roy's laugh came from deep within a belly he didn't have, and for a moment, I worried he was going to shoot those choppers clear across the room. "I'm just razzin' ya, Todd. The new folks are doin' fine, but they're nothing like the old guard."

"*Awww*, that's good of you to say," said Dad, clearly pleased.

"Is that Todd Morrow?" A husky female voice inquired from behind me.

I turned to find a woman with identically false teeth approaching us from the direction of the snack bar. Maybe there was a two-for-one special at Dentures "R" Us. Other than the teeth, she was the polar opposite of Roy, with pendulous breasts riding atop her ample midsection, all of which was shored up by skinny jeans that accentuated her utter lack of derriere.

"Virginia!" Dad smiled as he pulled her in for a hug. "Here I thought you would have left this loser by now." He winked and nodded toward Roy.

"I've just been waiting for the right man to come along," she said, slipping into a perfectly awful imitation of Mae West before pinching my dad's ass.

All three turned toward me when I gasped in horror.

"This is my son, Dwayne," said Dad, an edge of mortification tainting the look he shot my way.

"Oh, my goodness, *no!*" said Virginia, leaning in and cupping my face in her withered hands. I froze in place, afraid to move. "I haven't seen this one since he was just a little boy! Look at how *handsome* he is!"

I had no response. I had exactly *zero* recollection of this woman who was mooning over me.

"He takes after his mother," Dad said, and if I'm not mistaken, I detected a hint of pride.

"Well, he sure as hell doesn't take after *you*," ribbed Roy, throwing an elbow before unleashing another unsettlingly amplified guffaw that shook his entire frame. "So, what can I do ya for?"

"Well, we're killing some time waiting for a tow truck, and we thought we might bowl a few games."

Roy scanned the thirty-nine lanes, only a handful of which were in use, before shaking his head and tsking. "I don't know if we can squeeze you in." He stepped back behind the counter and slipped on an oversized pair of reading glasses. "I'm assuming you want me to set you up for league play."

"Of course," said Dad.

"How many games?"

Dad looked at me. "You good for three?"

I hesitated, realizing I was completely unprepared for this. "I don't have my ball or my shoes."

"Got plenty of balls over on the racks," said Roy, indicating a multi-colored variety of loaner balls of varying weights. "I'll throw the shoe rental in for free." He waggled his bushy eyebrows at me.

"Oh, I don't know, Dad." I continued to hedge. "I won't be any competition if I use a house ball."

"You wouldn't be any competition if you *had* your own ball," Dad countered, goading me.

I scowled at him before delivering a shot that was completely below the belt. "Really? I seem to recall Matt telling me he swept the floor with you at Thanksgiving."

His face fell, and I almost felt remorse before he suddenly rallied, throwing down the gauntlet. "Tell you what, son—I wouldn't want you to blame the way I'm going to bury you on the fact that you had to use a *'house ball'*," he said, before turning to Roy, who was watching our exchange with entirely too much interest. "Have you got time to prep a ball, Roy?"

"I surely do, Todd," he said, his grin widening.

"Time to—what?" I was lost.

"C'mon, son," said Dad, taking me by the arm and following Roy as he once more stepped out from behind the counter and headed toward the pro shop. "You're about to get a new bowling ball."

"Dad! I've already got one at home," I protested.

"Consider it an early birthday present."

"My birthday isn't until December!"

"Then consider it a late Christmas present," he said with an ornery smile. "That is—unless you're *afraid?"*

Roy and Virginia stared at me expectantly, and I felt a smile slowly creep across my face. "Oh, it is *on*, old man!"

CHAPTER FIVE

Okay, *fine*—it was a clean sweep, but don't you dare tell Matt.

I would never hear the end of it after my brother had somehow managed to best Dad not only once but *twice* over the Thanksgiving holiday. Still, other than the first game—when I was acclimating to the new ball I hadn't asked for, I managed to at least give the old man a run for his money, and the vindication on his face was strangely satisfying.

This was the dad I remembered—self-assured and affable, radiating confidence. I could almost forget his momentary frightening lapse that had landed us in this pickle when he was so thoroughly in his element. What I *had* completely forgotten was the man's extraordinary network of acquaintances, both personal and professional. As a teen, he was practically a local basketball legend for Midland High, shattering several long-standing records set by former alumni. As an adult, he had cultivated long and meaningful relationships as the sales manager for Pepsi, effortlessly ingratiating himself to his tri-state customer base by knowing his clients by name, including trivial shit that wouldn't stand a chance taking root in my memory. By the time we were wrapping up the third game, he had stopped to shoot the shit with no less than ten other patrons who were complete strangers to me but knew my dad on a first-name basis. They were all delighted by the chance encounter, and by all appearances, the feeling was entirely mutual as hearty handshakes, back slaps, and jovial reminiscences abounded. I attempted to fade into the background, enjoying the spectacle of watching my dad in action—although once or twice, he *did* introduce me, almost as an afterthought. It was an unexpected reminder of my teenage years and why I could never get away with anything too ornery. The man knew *everybody*; he had eyes and ears *everywhere*. Literally anything I might say or do had an inexplicable way of making it back to him—trust me, it was a lesson I was painfully slow to learn.

I was waiting for him to finish holding court with another couple of his cronies a few lanes down when I sensed someone approaching me from behind.

"Hey, Dwayne."

I turned to find Craig Mullins, my future brother-in-law, smiling sheepishly, his thick arms crossed in front of his broad chest. Dressed in red and black flannel and faded jeans, he was wearing his ever-present ballcap to cover his thinning sandy hair and looked more like a lumberjack than an auto mechanic. "Sorry it took so long, but I got here as fast as I could."

I nodded, extending a hand for him to shake. "Yeah, well, I'm sorry I had to play the favor card. I honestly didn't ever plan to use it, but I didn't know who else to call. At least now we're even."

During our Thanksgiving stay with Melanie's sister, Cheryl, and her husband, Craig, I had inadvertently uncovered—let's just call it a transgression of propriety on Craig's part. He had pleaded with me to keep my big yapper shut, and I had grudgingly agreed, adding to a teetering pile of secrets that had nearly been the end of me and Melanie. It would be fair to say I was more than a little salty about the whole thing. But Craig operated an automotive repair shop next door to his home in Ironton, and his expertise with vehicles of all makes and models was exactly what Dad and I needed, so I had called in my marker.

His grin became even more sheepish. "I would've come even without the blackmail. It's what families do, but I suppose I deserved that. I put you in an awful position, and I'm truly sorry about that. Cheryl knows."

My double take was undoubtedly priceless. "Cheryl *what?*"

His shoulders relaxed, along with this smile. "She knows," he repeated. "The guilt was eating away at me, and I realized it would stain our entire future together if I didn't come clean."

I was stunned. I'm unaccustomed to people doing the right thing, and I'm ashamed to admit it suddenly became all about me and what this might do to my newfound happiness with Melanie. "Does she know I knew? Please tell me you left me out of this. If Mel catches wind that I knew—"

He raised a hand to stop my avalanche of words. "I kept you out of it," he assured.

Suddenly, I could breathe again, and with that rush of oxygen came a wave of shame as I realized the question that should have been my first. "Are the two of you, um, still—"

"Together?" His nod was slow. "It's a work in progress, but yeah. We've got a weekly standing appointment with a couples' counselor that's a bit like putting a fork in my eye, but I'll do whatever it takes to save our family. Cheryl and our girls are my whole world."

An involuntary shudder rippled through me at the mere mention of couples counseling. It hadn't been so very long since Melanie insisted we seek professional help sorting through our own difficulties. I had found the entire experience to be awkward and invasive, not to mention entirely unsettling when our counselor vanished off the face of the earth before I had the satisfaction of discontinuing her services once Mel and I had reconciled. I didn't envy Craig the long and arduous path that lie ahead; he was going to be swinging on this hook for quite some time, and sharing my disdain for the process wouldn't be particularly helpful. Instead, I offered what I hoped would be an encouraging smile.

"That's great, man," I said. "I'm really rooting for you."

"Thanks," he said, clasping his hands together and scanning the alley. "Maybe we should get this show on the road. Where's your dad?"

Laughter erupted from where Dad stood, and he was surrounded by even more strangers than before. Whatever Dad was saying had them all in stitches, and Craig followed the sound, his eyes lighting up as they landed on the group.

"Oh, my *Lord!*" he said, a wide grin spreading across his face. "Is Todd Morrow your *dad?*"

I blinked. "You know my dad?"

He laughed. "Hell, *yeah!* I played slow pitch softball with him before he gave it up last year. My cousin, Andy, drives a truck for Pepsi, and he recruited me onto their team when they were down a man a few years back. This is *unbelievable!* Your dad's one helluva good pitcher! How did I not know this about you?" His arm flew into the air, and he waved it with wild abandon. "Hey, Todd! *Todd!*"

Recognition dawned on Dad's face as he enthusiastically returned the wave, and Craig was off, leaving me to gape as he was welcomed into the fold.

Of *course* Craig knew my dad. Everybody does.

"Well, it could be a lot worse," said Craig as he knelt in front of the Toyota to inspect the damage. "It's a good thing you weren't going very fast."

"You don't think it's totaled?" I asked dubiously.

"Oh, sure it is," said Craig, his knees cracking audibly as he stood. "This truck hasn't been manufactured for decades. But that doesn't mean I can't fix it."

"Aw, that's just tremendous!" said Dad, enthusiastically clapping Craig on the shoulder.

"Now, Todd, before you get *too* excited," Craig said, holding up a hand. "I'm just talking about making it run. There's only so much I can do to make it look better before you're just throwing good money after bad. I got a buddy that owns a pretty big salvage yard over in Greenup, and if he doesn't have the parts we need on hand, I'm pretty sure he can get them through the internet, but let's face it—the clearcoat was already shot all too hell, and the blue paint underneath has faded and chipped. Our chances ain't all that great that any replacement parts we find will match each other, much less what's left of the paint on the truck."

"*Pfft,*" Dad blew out, as if it were no big deal returning his friend's truck a day late and a dollar short with a full-on Frankenstein facelift. "Tom only uses this old truck when he's out junking. He gives it a beating on a daily basis. He doesn't care how it looks, just so long as it runs. It'll be fine."

Hmm. Apparently, it *was* no big deal.

"Alright, then," said Craig, heading back to his flatbed tow truck that sat idling along the berm. "Let's get 'er hooked up and hauled outta here. If you'd like, I can drop you and Dwayne off at your place in Lymont before taking everything back to the shop in Ironton."

"Oh, I don't want you to go out of your way," said Dad. "You can just put me and the boy out on the road by 823. We can hitch the rest of the way to—"

"*Dad!*" I interjected loudly. "Are you really going to put me through that *again?*"

"*Pfft,*" he sputtered, and I was really beginning to hate that sound. "We got where we needed to go, didn't we?"

"Well, yes, but if—"

"Nobody tried to kill or kidnap us, did they?"

"Well—*no,* but—"

"And you've still got my gun in your pocket, right?"

He looked at me expectantly, and my eyes went wide. For a fleeting second, I thought I might have lost the damned thing somewhere between Lanes 11 and 12. I conducted a frantic self-pat down, only allowing myself to breathe once I found the tiny pistol nestled safely in my right coat pocket. The tension squeezing the mobility out of my neck wasn't so quick to dissipate, and I could only manage a stiff nod as confirmation.

Craig wasn't quite able to shield his amusement behind a gloved hand. "Really, Todd—it's no trouble. It's barely out of my way, and I'm not about to put you and Dwayne out on the side of the road."

"Well, now, only if you're sure."

Dad was being deadly serious, and I could already envision us thumbing our way through Lucasville as the sun set and the ambient nighttime temperature approached that of a beverage cooler at Sheetz. I silently mouthed, *"Thank you!"* to Craig over Dad's shoulder, and his grin widened.

"Not only am I positive, I ain't takin' no for an answer. Now, get out of my way and let me do my job here," he said, continuing to the cab of his truck and hopping up into the driver's seat. Before pulling the door closed, he turned and pointed at me. "Dwayne? Be my eyes and guide me in, will ya?"

I nodded, taking position and shooing Dad out of the only path Craig had from the road to the back of the truck without getting stuck in the soft mud proliferating the area. I launched into my own version of semaphore to guide the tow truck into place, and before long, the truck was securely loaded, and we were back on the road. We were shattering the very concept of personal space and boundaries, squeezed side-by-side in the truck's tight cab—but at least we were on our way.

· · · • • • ● ⊖ ◯ ● • • • · · ·

I was taller than either of these chuckleheads, and yet somehow, *I* got stuck in the middle riding the goddamn hump.

I wasn't happy.

My knees were pinned to the dash in such a way that every time we hit a bump, I changed the radio station. After a few miserable miles of *Name that Tune*, Craig switched the radio off. Unfortunately, there was little he could do about the hard plastic controls digging their way through my jeans and into the thin flesh covering my shins. You'd think it couldn't get worse, but it most certainly did. Dad and Craig kept a steady stream of conversation afloat over top of me, covering such fascinating topics as hunting, predictions about who would take the NBA playoffs, and reminiscences of their own greatest hits playing slow-pitch softball together. I didn't have a horse in any of those races, so I just kept my mouth shut and tried to make peace with the constant contact of thighs that were not my own, pressing against me from both sides as we wound our way through the southern hills of Ohio on US 23.

"Who was that one guy who played for Coke?" Craig asked, and he was already chuckling. "You know the one I mean. Short, stocky, and completely full of himself. He was a pitcher, too, but nowhere near as good as you, not that he'd ever admit it. He was, like, your arch-nemesis or something."

"You're talking about Neto," Dad said, grinning and nodding his head. "Robert Neto didn't just play for their team, he was Coke's regional sales manager, and we didn't just compete on the playing field. We were always after the same local restaurants for their soft drink business. I was just better at my job, that's all."

"I swear, we always seemed to face off with those losers in the playoffs," said Craig, and I'm pretty sure he was talking to me. It was difficult to tell since everything he said pervaded my airspace, and by this point, it was obvious that whatever he'd eaten for lunch had been seasoned with a heady blend of garlic and onion. "While we didn't always win the championship, his team was never the one to bring us down. I will *never* forget the time that your dad put that blowhard in his place but good."

"Son-of-a-gun deserved that," said Dad, jabbing the air with this forefinger to punctuate the point before he and Craig dissolved into bawdy laughter at whatever shared memory had washed ashore.

I, without my trusty crystal ball, remained firmly in the dark.

"Would either of you care to elaborate?" I ventured, not really interested but irritated at being left out. I was a captive audience. The least they could do was entertain me.

"You tell, you tell." Craig barely managed to squeeze the words out before succumbing to the guffaw that shook his entire frame.

Dad was only too happy to take up the mantle. "I'd spent the better part of the month in a back-and-forth negotiation trying to secure a deal with Grandma's Biscuits and More. You remember the place, don't you son?"

I cast a mental line back a couple of decades but came up empty. Let's face it—I've eaten a lot of biscuits over the years. I shook my head and shrugged while Dad rolled his eyes.

"Oh, *sure* you do!" he insisted. "It was that little hole in the wall on Front Street in Ashland where you got lost coming back from the bathroom and got all hysterical."

Okay, *that* I remembered. "I was seven."

The recollection brought a fresh twinkle to Dad's eyes, and he looked past me and at Craig. "You should have seen him. All red-faced and blubbering like it was the end of the world."

"I was *seven!*" I protested, reenacting the whole red-faced thing. "I couldn't *find* you!"

"It was a one-room diner. There weren't even tables, just a U-shaped counter that sat between the kitchen and the plate glass storefront. All you had to do was keep walking. You would have found me eventually."

"The place was *packed!* I got all turned around, and you didn't answer me when I called out for you!"

"Called? *Pfft*…more like *cried*," he said, the corners of his mouth twitching. He winked at Craig who at least had the decency to look uncomfortable. "Eventually, Grandma herself came bustling out of the kitchen to settle him down."

I scoffed. "And when she did, you refused to acknowledge that you were my dad! You said, and I quote, 'Stop bothering me, boy! I have enough kids of my own at home.' You shooed me away and suggested she drop me off at the fire department!"

"You called her Mommy."

"I was seven!"

I wasn't enjoying this particular trip down memory lane, but Dad was clearly having a ball. Tears streamed down his face as he struggled to suppress his laughter. "Oh, it's not like I left you there."

"You know what? Never mind. You've gotten *way* off track here," I said. "I believe you were talking about humiliating some *other* poor soul."

"Ah, yes. Rob Neto. Now, where was I?"

"Grandma's Biscuits," I prompted, rolling my hand impatiently.

"Of course. Well, I had it on good authority that Grandma's bustling little biscuit joint was on the verge of a rapid expansion and looking to add two more locations—one in Huntington and another in New Boston. Neto thought they were only moving the mothership to a bigger and better location in Ashland. He went in prepared to offer a token discount for re-upping with Coke, and I went in and completely undercut him, securing the exclusive rights for Pepsi for at least a decade that would eventually include the opening of seven more locations in the tri-state area. He got word of the deal on the day our teams were due to face off in the championships, and he was *steamed*." Dad's eyes were practically gleaming.

"He tried every trick in the book to throw your dad off his game," said Craig, grinning and looking across me at Dad. "For a minute, I really thought he was trying to hit you when you were up to bat, and he was throwing awfully hard for slow pitch."

"He *was* trying to hit me!" Dad agreed. "He got his backside chewed out royally for bungling that deal and ended up on probation at Coke. He eventually went to work for RC Cola, and I heard it wasn't exactly a mutual decision."

"This sounds completely cliché, but it was the bottom of the seventh, and we were all tied up with runners on first and third, two outs," said Craig.

"The *seventh?*" I interjected. "I thought there were nine innings."

I couldn't miss the disappointment on Dad's face. "Not in slow pitch, son. Seven's the limit unless time runs out. How could you not know this? You and your brother tagged along with me every week."

I scowled. "Matt was the geeky statistician. Of course, *he* would know. I had better things to do."

"Oh, that's right," Dad said, tapping a finger to his chin as he reflected. "I seem to recall you and Mike Perry's daughter getting caught in one of the empty dugouts with your shirts off, comparing the size of your nipples or something—"

"Dad!" My ears were on fire, and I couldn't believe he went there. I stole a mortified glance at Craig, who wasn't even trying to hide his amusement. "It wasn't like *that*. We were only ten. We were just curious what was different about boys' and girls'—"

"Boobies?" Dad suggested, and I dropped my blazing hot face into my open palms.

"We were only ten!" I suffered through as much of their laughter as I could before attempting to pull this conversation back on track. "It was the bottom of the seventh, runners on first and third, two outs—"

Craig finally came to my rescue, even if it was a pity save. "Neto threw two screamers that nearly nailed your dad. He never in a million years expected your dad to actually hit the third ball he threw, but Todd nailed it—a line drive straight back to the pitcher's mound. Neto was so stunned, he barely had time to put up a hand to catch it. Problem was, it was the wrong hand."

The two collapsed into giggles, jostling me from both sides.

"Th-th-the look on his *face*," Dad barely managed, and okay—I guess it was sort of funny, but not *that* funny. Then he got a second wind. "His thumb was just hanging there by a tiny strip of skin."

My eyes widened. "His thumb was *what?*"

"He tried to catch the ball with his bare hand," said Craig, feeling the need to paint a graphic picture for me. "Ended up with a compound fracture of his thumb, jagged bits of bone poking right through the flesh."

"His eyes rolled back in his head, and he hit the ground just as soon as he saw the blood pouring down his arm," said Dad, and he was practically wheezing.

"And that was the end of Neto's pitching days," added Craig before joining in Dad's celebratory chortling.

I was appalled. Sandwiched between these ghoulishly cackling hyenas and with no easy means of escape, it was everything I could do to hold on to my paltry Wendy's lunch.

The single saving grace of our own version of *Tales from the Darkside* came in the lull that mercifully followed the mirth. We traveled for several miles in what passed for companiable silence, breezing through Waverly and Piketon without any further shared 'frivolity.' We were nearing Lucasville when Craig cleared his throat.

"So, one thing's been puzzling me, Todd," he said.

"What's that?" Dad asked.

"What were you doing in your buddy's truck? Don't you have the Corolla anymore?"

"Oh, sure," said Dad, staring out the passenger window to watch the mile markers whip by. "I just needed—something different."

Craig tossed him a puzzled glance. "Different? How so?"

Dad continued to stare through the window for a long moment before turning to me. "I believe I can be straight with Craig and trust him to keep this to himself. What do you think, son?"

I froze, unsure of exactly where he was going with this while put completely on the spot. No, I *didn't* think he should be straight with Craig, especially if it had anything whatsoever to do with Gina, but how could I possibly indicate disagreement when the man who had just rescued us was sitting right beside me, his beefy thigh pressed uncomfortably close to mine? I tried to telegraph my reservations with my eyes, but Dad wasn't really looking at me anymore.

"I suppose you heard about my daughter, Gina," said Dad, turning toward the window again.

Craig sucked air through his teeth. "I did. I'm so sorry, man. Both of you—"

Dad shook his head. "It's alright. She's not really gone."

Craig looked at me uncertainly. *"Umm*, okay—of course not. She'll always be with you, *um*, in your hearts—?"

Dad looked at him and winced. "No, not like that. She's not dead."

I wasn't even sure I was breathing anymore. Craig looked from Dad to me, and the best I could do was shrug.

"There's some big conspiracy at work here," said Dad. "And I've enlisted my boy's help to get to the bottom of things. We're gonna bring my girl home, aren't we son?"

I was a deer in headlights, but Dad was on a roll and didn't notice.

"I'm trying to stay off the grid, and that's just something we can't do if we're in a car that's been made in the last decade or so." He fixed Craig with a somber, knowing look. "As you know, they've all got these GPS tracking thingies these days."

"Ah—I see," said Craig, nodding slowly. "But your buddy's truck is too old for that."

Dad shot a pistol finger at him. "Precisely. Now, I've got to find another mode of transportation that fits the bill. We'd only just started our investigation when we got waylaid."

"You thought a soccer mom was an assassin, Dad," I said, massaging the bridge of my nose.

"She drove like an assassin!" he hissed.

"Well, I don't mean to get in the middle of all this," said Craig. "But I might just be able to help you out. I've got a couple of old beaters in my garage that might just fit the bill. I'd be happy to give you a loaner while I work on your friend's truck."

I couldn't contain the dread on my face as I stared at Craig in disbelief, but Dad latched onto the idea immediately, his excitement spiking.

"That would be fantastic, Craig! And you know I'll take responsibility for anything that might happen along the way."

Craig's smile was wide. "No worries. Anything I can do to help an old friend."

Help an old friend, indeed.

I saw the light at the end of my tunnel face as we approached SR-823, and Craig activated his turn signal, indicating our endpoint was no longer Lymont, but Craig's Automotive in Ironton.

I had no say in the matter whatsoever; our road trip had just been extended.

CHAPTER SIX

"Well, as I live and breathe!" exclaimed Cheryl, throwing open the screen door and stepping out onto the Mullinses' covered back porch. "If it isn't my favorite brother-in-law-to-be! Get your handsome face over here where I can see you better!"

Melanie's sister greeted me in the wide gravel drive that separated their two-story dwelling from Craig's Automotive garage at the rear of the property and the small trailer nestled into the woods along the northern edge. Her shoulder-length blonde hair had been layered and streaked with neon pink highlights since I had last seen her, but I had already learned to never expect the same look twice from Cheryl. She worked as a cosmetologist and was always trying something bold and new. She wore denim capris and a flowered spaghetti strap halter that accentuated her enviable assets with an easy confidence that would be utterly foreign to Mel. She was comfortable in Dollar Tree flip-flops that showed off her bright red toenail polish, and she threw her arms around my neck, planting a sloppy kiss on my cheek with a wet smack.

"Hey, Cheryl," I said, the tips of my ears matching the paint on her toes. I awkwardly leaned in to return her kiss at the same time she turned her head and almost planted one right on her mouth.

"Whoa, there, partner," said Craig as he and Dad approached from behind me. "That's my woman you're messin' with, there."

"Hey, babe," said Cheryl, giving Craig a quick peck before turning back to us. "I didn't realize we were having company tonight, not that I mind. What's the occasion?"

"Turns out Dwayne's dad is an old friend of mine," said Craig, clapping Dad on the shoulder. "I've played softball with Todd for years, but the last name went right over my head when I met Dwayne at Thanksgiving. Todd, this is my wife, Cheryl."

"Nice to meet you," said Dad, gently taking her hand and bowing ever-so-chivalrously.

"My, oh my," said Cheryl, grinning broadly. "I can see why. They don't look a thing alike."

"Nope, I can't say that we do," agreed Dad. "My other kids favor my side of the family. I'm not really sure if this one is actually mine."

"Oh, God," I groaned, dropping my face into my hands while Cheryl giggled.

"Are you fellas hungry?" asked Cheryl. "I've had a pot of beef stew on the stove all day, and there's *puh*-lenty." She turned to her husband. "Maggie took the girls clothes shopping in Ashland, and they're grabbing dinner while they're out." She referred to her two daughters, Amanda and Mackenzie, as well as her and Melanie's younger sister who lived in the trailer across the way.

"Oh, we wouldn't want to intrude," I hedged, not wanting to involve Craig and Cheryl any more than we already had. I looked at my watch and saw that it was nearly six o'clock. I just wanted to collect the ill-advised loaner vehicle from Craig and get Dad safely home. It was already too late to ask Melanie to make the round trip tonight, so I was resigned to spending the night in my childhood bed. I'd figure out how to get home in the morning.

Cheryl scowled. "Are you afraid to eat my cooked food?"

"Of course not!" I sputtered, still retaining the heat in my cheeks. Cheryl thoroughly enjoyed deviling me, so why should tonight be any different than any other night? "I've just got to get Dad home, and—"

"*Get Dad home?*" Dad interrupted, arching an eyebrow. "I wasn't aware I had a curfew."

"I didn't mean it like *that*," I said. "I just figured we—"

"You just figured nothing," said Craig, grinning. "You haven't tasted beef stew until you've had Cheryl's. Paula Deen could take notes. Besides, I've got a few things I need to double-check before I turn you loose in the Monza, so you're going to be here a little while longer anyway. You may as well top off your tanks before you go."

Dad looked at me and shrugged. "It sounds good to me. I'm sure your mother would be relieved to have me out of her hair for just a little longer."

Cheryl clapped her hands. "Then it's all settled. You boys go play with your cars while I get the table set. I'll call you just as soon as soup's on." She turned on her heel and marched back into the house before I could think of another excuse to get us back on the road.

I sighed as Dad and Craig walked toward the five-bay garage at the rear of the drive, already deep in discussion. It was time for me to face facts—I had zero say in whatever it was that we were doing.

I was merely along for the ride.

Rather than follow Craig and Dad to the garage, I decided it made more sense to use my time catching everyone up on our current status. I followed Cheryl into the house, and the rich, sumptuous scent of her beef stew hit me like a wave as soon as I stepped inside. I swooned visibly, and she winked at me before I passed through the kitchen into the living room, pulling my phone from my pocket and unlocking its screen on the way.

I started with Mom, assuming she would be on the verge of panic by now. Imagine my surprise when she answered with a bright, "Well, hey babe! Did your father decide to stay over another night?" If I wasn't mistaken, she sounded hopeful.

"*Umm*, no," I said. "We're just running a little late. We should be home in about an hour or so."

"Oh," she said and this time, there was no mistaking it—she was disappointed.

"Is there a problem?"

"No," she replied, quick to recover. "It's fine."

"*Umm*, Mom?"

She sighed. "Okay, *fine*. It's been nice to catch a little break from all of the uncertainty we've been going through the past several months. After you called last night to let me know that your father's latest madness had taken him all the way to Grove City and that he would be spending the night, I had the most glorious night of sleep I've had in months. I didn't wake up once, wondering where he might have wandered off to when his side of the bed was empty."

"Oh, *Mom*. I had no idea it had gotten so bad," I said. "Why didn't you say something? Matt or I could have helped with—"

Her chuckle was perfunctory. "This isn't a problem for you or Matt to handle. You've both got your own responsibilities and families, and even if you didn't, you live too far away. This is part of the wedding vows you never really think about—you know? In sickness and in health, until death do us part."

Well, that got dark fast. I couldn't find adequate words to respond.

"I'm sorry," Mom continued. "I really shouldn't have said anything. Sooner or later, we'll have an answer to what's going on with your father. It's the not knowing that's getting to me more than anything else. As it is, I feel guilty enough for being relieved that he's currently in your care. It's not like he's out there endangering himself or others."

I inhaled through my teeth. *"We-e-ll—"*

"Oh, good Lord," she said, instantly on alert. "What happened?"

I took a deep breath and gave her a summary of our day, leaving out any of the parts related to Gina. This was enough of a dumpster fire without tossing gasoline onto it, but I had a couple of other good reasons to be selective, as well. As it was, I suffered my own paranoia about discussing my sister through any means that could be hacked or traced because of what I believed to be true, but Dad had also said he hadn't shared the content of his spooky dreams with Mom to protect her feelings. All of that was reason enough for me to keep my big mouth shut. It was bad enough having to explain that he had wrecked his friend's stolen truck on our way home, leading us to our current circumstance. Eventually, I ran out of words, and there was nothing but empty air to greet me on the other side.

"Mom?" I asked. "Are you still there?"

"Ugh," she groaned. "Yeah—still here. I may not be once you all get back to Lymont—"

"Mom—"

"Kidding, kidding," she said, albeit rather unconvincingly. "Just be careful coming home."

"Will do," I said. "Love you, Mom."

"Love you, too, babe."

My call to Melanie was brief; I had caught her in the middle of overseeing Jordan's bath, and I knew from experience you couldn't leave the little guy alone for very long in the bathtub unless you were willing to mop up the aftermath of his enthusiastic water play. I told her where we were and wasn't all that surprised to discover that she already knew—of *course*, Cheryl had already texted her. To say the two were tight was a complete understatement. They practically shared everything. I told Melanie I would be spending the night with my parents and that I'd call her once I arrived to fill her in on all the details of my eventful day, figuring the kids would probably be in bed by then.

The kids.

The newness of our situation had yet to wear off, and I couldn't help but smile at how nicely things were coming together. We hadn't set a wedding date yet, but I was leaving all of that up to Melanie, Cheryl, and whoever else they decided to enlist for help. In the meanwhile, I would do my level best not to fuck anything up and make sure to show up on time— for once—whenever she finally picked a date, time, and place.

I followed my nose back into the kitchen, groaning appreciably at the enticing aroma emanating from the stovetop. My stomach grumbled in agreement, my lunch barely a distant memory. "That smells *so* good. Thanks for inviting us to stay."

The corners of Cheryl's mouth quirked up. "Of course. You know you're always welcome here. Besides, I figure I owe you one."

I lifted an eyebrow. "Yeah? How so?"

She put her hands on her hips, a knowing look on her face. "I have good reason to suspect that I owe my upcoming Caribbean cruise with my philandering but repentant husband to you."

I blinked back my surprise and tried to keep my expression neutral.

"I don't know what you're—"

"Oh, stop it," she said, shooing my words away. "All that nonsense at Thanksgiving about how much Craig spent on my Christmas gift. You knew."

I deflated like a week-old birthday balloon. "I'm sorry. I only found out while investigating the McAlister case, and I—"

"It's alright," she said, holding up a hand to stop whatever feeble excuse I had yet to manufacture. "The problem wasn't yours to navigate, and I'm glad everything is out in the open. In fact, I'm not sure that Craig would have fessed up if it weren't for you. Whatever you said to him was like fertilizer to the seed of guilt he was already carrying. It was a cancer that would have eventually eaten through our marriage, and while we're still finding our way back to a good place, I'm willing to give him the chance to make things right. We've been through too much together not to try."

"Does Melanie know?" I asked, nearly dreading the answer. After finally resolving our own issues with trust and honesty, this was the one secret I had never divulged. I may have accidentally uncovered Craig's illicit one-night stand with Maggie's best friend, Katie, but I refused to put myself in the middle of someone else's family drama. I wasn't sure that Melanie would agree, considering her sister was an integral part of that family.

"Of course," she said. "She's my big sister and best friend. I share everything with her."

I felt my face fall.

She smirked. "Don't worry. I left your name out of it. It felt like the least I could do after you put Craig on the hook for a gift I've been after for *years*."

I exhaled in a whoosh. "Thank you. I wasn't sure if she would understand."

"It's all good. And in a way, we're already sort of even," she said, pulling placemats from a drawer to the right of the sink. "I was the one who suggested couples' counseling when the two of you were having issues. Seemed to work out pretty well for you guys, huh?"

I could only nod. Our few counseling sessions had been torturous at best, and while we had found our way back to each other on our own, our counselor had vanished into thin air before we had the opportunity to release ourselves from her care. I was still unsettled by the experience, but

I guess I couldn't discount the whole profession based on one dubious doctor.

"You wanna let the other fellas know I'm taking the food up?" Cheryl asked as I drifted back into the kitchen. She had set the placemats at the small table to my right and was in the process of collecting soup bowls from the cabinets beside the sink.

"Sure," I said, stepping out onto the porch. It was a relief to know everything was finally out in the open—well, *mostly*, but I had already found another skeleton to take its place in the closet. I wasn't sure what else Dad might have disclosed to Craig in my absence, nor could I predict what he might share with Cheryl over dinner. As much as I loved Cheryl, I knew she enjoyed gossip, both receiving and sharing. I could already imagine her sharing the story about a sad old geezer whose dreams had him questing after his not-so-dead daughter to her clients and co-workers at the beauty salon. It was an amusing story that could have serious ramifications if it were to hit the wrong ears. I had practically worked myself into a panic by the time I reached the garage, where I found Dad and Craig peering underneath the long hood of a two-door coupe that was the color of a burnt sienna crayon.

"Hey, guys, dinner's ready," I called out, before adding, "Dad, can I speak to you for a moment?"

"What's up, son?" he asked without bothering to move a muscle.

"Privately?" Why, oh, why couldn't Dad respond to my simple request with subtlety instead of forcing me to awkwardly spell it out in mile-high letters? I smiled at Craig apologetically.

Dad glanced at Craig and shrugged. "I suppose. Craig, do you mind?"

Craig lifted the hood off of its prop rod and snapped it into place before dropping the hood with a thud. "No worries. I'll head to the house to get washed up. You gents take your time."

He sauntered toward the house while Dad stayed back with me, giving Craig time to enter the house. "What's on your mind? Is it your mother? Is something wrong?"

"No, nothing like that," I said. "I just wanted to suggest that we keep the dinner conversation light, you know?"

"So, what—my hemorrhoids are off limits?"

"Dad!"

He sighed. "Would you *relax*, son? This may come as a complete surprise to you, but I've been conducting myself in public without incident for years—long before you were even born, in fact. I think I can manage a dinner with Craig and his lovely wife without embarrassing myself—or even *you*, for that matter."

It was my turn to sigh. "You told Craig about Gina."

"Only the bare minimum, which I felt he was entitled to, and I asked him to keep it to himself, which I'm sure he will. It's not like I'm running door-to-door sharing my every thought. What are you so worried about?"

We didn't have that kind of time.

"Nothing, I guess," I said. "I'm sorry. It's been a long day."

"Agreed," he said, clapping his grease-stained hands together before looking at me expectantly. "Now, I'm starving. Can we eat?"

The stew was even better than it smelled.

Cheryl made a basket of drop biscuits to break into the rich broth laden with chunks of beef, potato, carrot, and turnip, and polite conversation carried us through enough of the meal that I actually began to relax.

That was my first mistake.

After Cheryl and Craig regaled Dad with information about their upcoming Caribbean cruise which included stops in Cozumel, Barbados, and Belize, he seized the opportunity to steer the conversation back toward our own family.

"It sounds like lots of fun," he said, setting his spoon in his empty soup bowl and pushing it toward the center of the table. "Jo would never agree to anything like that. Saw *The Poseidon Adventure* and *Jaws* in a double feature at the drive-in, and that was all she wrote. She wants nothing to do with the ocean."

"That's too bad," said Cheryl. "She's really missing out. We try to take our girls to Myrtle Beach at least every other year. Seeing the water stretch all the way to the horizon kind of puts our little corner of the world into perspective, you know? So, what did your family do for vacation?"

Nothing. That's what we did. Dad didn't care much for sleeping away from home, and vacations were expensive. An occasional afternoon at Shawnee State Park avoiding whatever lurked within the murky waters of Turkey Creek Lake was about as good as it got.

Instead, he said, "We stayed closer to home, but my job with Pepsi got us into any number of county fairs and small-town festivals. We were all over the tri-state area. The family would tag along to enjoy the attractions while I checked in with my customers to make sure their needs were being met. It was a lot of fun, wasn't it, son?"

I looked at him dubiously. I remembered me and Matt tagging along with him to the Scioto County Fair maybe once or twice, but I wouldn't exactly call it fun. He never wanted to spring for the cost of tickets so we could enjoy the rides, calling them death traps assembled by, and I quote, 'day drunk carny convicts.' Still, I had just emptied my own bowl of stew, and the finish line was in sight, so I simply nodded.

"I think my favorite were the small-town festivals," he continued, sitting back in his chair. "All the townsfolk coming together to celebrate the fruit of their labor, and I mean that literally. There's the Pumpkin Show in Circleville and the Jackson Apple Festival—"

"Oh, *wow*, that takes me back," interjected Craig, wiping his mouth and pushing away from the table. "When I was a little kid, me and my sister, Julie, always spent a couple weeks each summer with our grandmother in this little Podunk town in the boonies of West Virginia. It was always during their annual Apple Festival in July."

Gooseflesh lifted the tiny hairs all over my body, and I sat visibly straighter in my chair, which would have gone unnoticed if Dad hadn't chosen that exact moment to kick me under the table.

"Owww!" I yelped, tossing Dad a dirty look as I stooped to massage my throbbing shin.

"I'm sorry, son. Was that your leg?" he asked, sounding reasonably apologetic and concerned but his eyebrows were waggling up and down like Groucho Marx's. Craig's comment hadn't gotten past him, either, although he had no way of understanding the sense of dread and foreboding that washed over me. He didn't wait for my reply before turning back to Craig. "Well, how about that? Another Apple Festival. The one in Jackson is the only one I've heard of. Where did you say this was?"

"Little town called Briarstaff," Craig said, carrying his bowl into the kitchen and rinsing it out in the sink. "It's a couple hours east of Charleston, almost smack dab in the middle of the state."

"Hmm, can't say I've ever heard of it," said Dad, his eyebrows still twitching as he shot me a knowing look.

"Can't say I'm surprised," said Craig, carrying a rectangular baking dish that looked to be full of some sort of cobbler back to the table and placing it in the middle. "Once upon a time, it was a mining town, but those days are long gone. If you were driving through, you could pretty much blink and miss it. I was maybe fourteen last time we went, and that was for Granny's funeral. Not much reason to go back after that. The rest of my family moved away a long time ago. Anyone care for a piece of cherry cobbler?"

I blanched at the thought. My stomach had already soured to the point I feared my dinner might be on the verge of making an ugly encore. "No, thanks," I said, patting my belly. "I couldn't eat another bite."

Dad eyed the golden-brown crust, practically salivating. "Oh my, that does look good, I—"

"Dad," I interrupted, contemplating the idea of returning his under-the-table kick before settling on a subtler version of eyebrow waggling. "Don't you think we've taken up enough of Craig and Cheryl's time? We've still got a long drive ahead of us, and I'm sure Mom is getting pretty anxious to see you."

He opened his mouth to argue but held his tongue once I widened my eyes and shook my head slightly. His eyes ventured to the cobbler, the corners of his mouth dipping. "I suppose you're right, son."

"Please, don't hurry yourselves on our account," said Cheryl, collecting mine and Dad's bowls and depositing them in the sink before grabbing a container of French vanilla ice cream from the freezer and returning to the table. "My cobbler's even better than my beef stew, if I do say so myself."

"Thanks, Cheryl," I said, standing. "It looks delicious, but I'm stuffed, and we've really got to get going. Dad?"

He gave the dessert one last longing look before standing, and Cheryl laughed. "How about I give you some to go?"

Dad's face brightened. "Aren't you a sweetheart? Thank you, ma'am." He turned to Craig. "You've got yourself a real gem here."

Craig smiled, winking at his wife. "Don't I know it?"

The sun had completely set while we were eating dinner, and the motion-activated security light sprang to life as we stepped off of the porch, illuminating our path. Dad took a detour to the back of the tow truck to retrieve his bowling bag while Craig and I continued across the driveway toward his garage.

"Listen, Craig," I said, seizing the opportunity to talk privately while keeping my voice low. "All that nonsense Dad was spouting about my sister—I'd appreciate it if you could keep that to yourself. Dad's currently being evaluated for a brain lesion, and he's been having these episodes where he's prone to tell some fantastically tall tales."

"Oh, no," said Craig. "To look at him, he seems so healthy. I hope it's nothing serious."

"Thank you," I said, picking up the pace as Dad raised the handle on the bag and started trudging toward us. "He's not really talking about it until we know what it is, so please—"

Craig held up a hand before simulating locking his lips with an imaginary key. "Got it." He held the door open for us, and we entered his workspace, crossing to the ancient Chevy Monza in the last bay. "First thing, you'll need to get some gas. She's a little throaty, and her clutch plate slips a little, but I'm confident she'll get you where you're going."

"Clutch plate?" I repeated, making for the driver's door while Dad loaded his bowling bag into the back seat.

"Mmm-hmm. She's four-on-the-floor. Ever drive a stick?" He dangled the keys to the car in front of me.

Dad's laughter was a short, sharp bark as he returned the passenger seat to its upright position. "You better let me handle this, son."

I snatched the keys from Craig before he could. "I've got this," I said, sliding behind the wheel. I had been subjected to enough of Dad's driving for one day.

"If you so say." Dad was less than convinced as he got in on the passenger side and made a show of buckling his seat belt.

Craig flipped a switch beside the garage door, and it began its slow ascent along its motorized track. I depressed the clutch and the brake pedal before turning the key in the ignition. The engine cranked several times but wouldn't stay running. Craig rapped a knuckle on the driver's side window, and I cranked it down.

"You've gotta give it a little gas," he said. "This baby's got a carburetor, not fuel-injection."

I smiled tightly and tried again, and the engine came to life. I disengaged the parking brake and slowly lurched out of the garage. It had been a while since I'd driven a car with a manual transmission, and Dad wasn't entirely successful in hiding his amusement. I stuck my arm through the window and waved to Craig as we pulled out of the driveway and turned right.

If I wasn't so irritated by Dad's silent mockery, I might have noticed the nondescript black sedan that pulled into Craig's driveway as we rounded the bend and lost sight of the house.

CHAPTER SEVEN

I followed S.R. 93 into Ironton and pulled into a Speedway along Park Avenue to gas up. Craig wasn't kidding; the needle was practically flat on 'E,' which only heightened my mounting anxiety. I had been reeling ever since Craig mentioned his youthful stays in Briarstaff, and *seriously*, what were the odds? I couldn't help but marvel at how very small this great big planet can be at times. It felt like fate was doing its damnedest to pull me back to a place I'd hoped to never see again, and I was fighting a losing battle.

Dad had gone inside the convenience store to pay for the gas I was currently pumping and to make use of the facilities. It gave me a little time to fret about how I might dissuade Dad from pursuing the vision he had come to believe was prophetic, a task made infinitely more difficult once Craig had shared his childhood recollection. I honestly wasn't sure how to redirect his focus and get him safely back into Mom's care. Once that man has set his mind on something, his obstinance is a force of nature. I should know; we're very much alike in that regard. And I'd be lying if I said my own Spidey sense wasn't going off like a car alarm. I mean, there's only so much you can chalk up to coincidence before wondering if the universe is trying to tell you something, and with stakes like these, I'd hate to be too dense to listen.

I wasn't any closer to devising a diversionary tactic when Dad pushed through the doors of the Speedway loaded for bear. He shuffled back to the car carrying a six-pack of Milwaukee's Best, another six-pack of some sort of bottled beverage, and two plastic bags straining with God only knows what.

"Did you know they don't sell maps here anymore?" he asked as he fumbled with the handle of the passenger door.

I reached over and opened the door for him. "It's not really all that surprising. People don't use paper maps. They use Google Maps and GPS on their phones. What in the world have you got there?"

"I figured we could use some snacks, and if you're anything like me, I like to kick back with a beer or two before I call it an evening, especially if I'm not sleeping in my own bed. Now, I know you don't care so much for beer, so I picked up a pack of Mike's Hard Lemonade for you. They remind me of those fruity little wine coolers I used to catch you and the McGregor boy drinking way back when you were in high school, and—"

"Whoa, whoa," I said as the nozzle of the pump shut itself off. "Back up a sec. What do you mean, 'if I'm not sleeping in my own bed?' Where, exactly, do you think you're going to be sleeping?"

Disappointment was evident on his face as he straightened and pushed the passenger seat back into its upright position. *"Son."*

I offered him a vacant look, reattaching the nozzle to the pump and replacing the gas cap. "What?"

He sighed. "You can't tell me you aren't intrigued by what Craig said. It's just too close to what I've been dreaming. That's why I mentioned the lack of maps here. You're gonna need to look this Briarstaff up on your phone, and we can—"

"Oh, no," I said, already shaking my head. "Mom is expecting us back at home, and I'm sure Doug needs my help at the office. I can't just—"

"Dwayne. This is your sister we're talking about," he said. "Doug Boggs will surely understand if you need to take a little extra time."

I scoffed. "Have you met Doug? Understanding doesn't come easily for him or that mother of his. Loretta's always looking for reasons to get me fired, and I can't really afford to give her any extra ammunition."

"Okay, fine," he said. "You can drop yourself off at the house, and I'll just come back on my own. It'll add a couple of unnecessary hours to my trip, but if you're not willing to help your old man out—"

"Aww, Dad, that's not fair! I—" My phone launched into my ringtone which was the chorus of Tom Petty's *Runnin' Down a Dream.* I fished it out of my pocket and was surprised to see 'Craig Mullins' on the caller ID. I held up a finger to pause our discussion and slid a thumb across my screen to take the call. "Hey, Craig. What's up? Did we leave something behind?"

Craig's voice was subdued. "Um, no, but I thought maybe I ought to give you a little heads-up. We just received a visit from a guy who could have walked straight off the set of *Men in Black.* He was looking for Todd."

"He was looking for Dad?" I repeated numbly, and Dad instantly tuned in. "Did he say what for?"

"Huh-unh. He was very close-lipped."

"What did you tell him?"

He chuckled. "Not a lot. He never mentioned you, so I didn't either. I don't tend to volunteer information if I can help it, but since Todd's truck was still loaded onto the flatbed of my tow truck and was right there in plain sight, I couldn't exactly claim total ignorance. I told him that I hauled the Toyota back for Todd, but I kept it vague. I didn't tell him when you left, where you were going, or that I'd loaned you a car, but he seemed pretty determined to find Todd when he left."

I furtively scanned the Speedway parking lot, looking for anyone who might be closing in, but there was nothing to see. The only other car at the pumps was being fueled up by a skinny teenaged boy who was intensely focused on pumping exactly five dollars' worth of gasoline into his tricked-out lowrider and not a single penny more.

"You didn't mention anything about my, uh—" *Sister.* My tongue was sticking to the roof my mouth as dread and paranoia washed over me. I was reluctant to say anything more specific over the phone and could only hope Craig might pick up what I was putting down.

Thankfully, he did.

"No," he said firmly. "Like I said before, if he didn't ask, I didn't offer. But I thought you might want to keep your eyes open. Maybe it's nothing, but it kinda gave me the willies."

"Thanks, man," I said absently as I continued to scan the incoming traffic on Park Avenue. "I appreciate it." I disconnected the call and pocketed my phone.

"What did Craig want?" Dad asked as I hustled to the driver's door and opened it.

"Get in," I said. "We need to get out of here."

I took US 52 east instead of going west toward Lymont.

There wasn't any real way to downplay what Craig had told me, and Dad felt immediately vindicated, asserting with certainty that his beliefs weren't mere conjecture borne of some biological misfire which may or may not be occurring within his brain. All I wanted was a moment to think, but I could barely focus on the road ahead while keeping as much of an eye on the rearview mirror as the dark ribbon of highway in front of me. Dad's constant yammering certainly wasn't helping.

"I'm glad you've come around to my way of thinking," he said, as I merged with the eastbound traffic.

I snorted. "I wouldn't go *that* far."

"Oh, come *on*, Dwayne! Somebody doesn't want us looking for your sister. What else could it be?"

"Oh, I don't know," I said absently, squinting at a vehicle that seemed a little too close to our rear bumper. "Maybe your buddy Tom Wheeler finally reported you for stealing his truck?"

"Pfft! He'd never do that." He turned to stare out the window, dejected that I wasn't ready to board his crazy train quite yet.

I didn't really believe Tom would phone the police either, but I left it alone, thankful for the sudden silence that might just allow me to figure out what in the hell we might do from here. It wasn't like I could just ignore my own beliefs at this point. I had already powered down my cell phone, afraid that whoever was looking for Dad might just use its location to track us, and that gave us a whole new set of considerations to fret over. Mom would be expecting us back home at any minute, and Melanie would be looking for an update, too. If either one tried to reach my cell phone, it would go straight to voicemail, and I was generally pretty good about keeping my phone charged. It would only invite more worry to join the party.

As we approached Chesapeake, I took the West Huntington Bridge across the Ohio River and into West Virginia. Dad looked at me with an eyebrow raised.

"So, if you don't believe me, where exactly are we going?" he asked.

I was busy smiling into the rearview mirror, relieved to see the car that had been trailing us continue on toward Chesapeake. "I'm not sure yet," I admitted.

He tapped the darkened screen of my cell phone where I had stowed it under the parking brake in the center console. "You turned your cell off." It wasn't a question.

"I did."

He slowly grinned. "You believe me."

I sighed. "I don't *disbelieve* you. I just think we should exercise some— *caution* until we know what's going on. I'm taking things one step at a time." I don't know why I was so reluctant to spill what I knew. Maybe it was just muscle memory from keeping this horrific secret for so goddamned long. Maybe it was because I had promised Gina that I wouldn't say a word to anyone, especially our parents. Either way, it was a bell I couldn't unring, so at the bare minimum, careful deliberation on my part was in order.

"What's our next step, then?"

"I want to find another Speedway or somewhere like it. It's probably a total waste of money, but I want to pick up a burner phone. I've got to call Mom and Melanie and tell them *something*." I signaled for the exit to US 60 that would deliver us into the western neighborhoods of Huntington.

Dad sat back in his seat, smiling smugly. "You *believe* me."

I rolled my eyes. "Whatever."

"I almost didn't answer," said Melanie, after finally accepting my call. "I didn't recognize the number, and those calls are almost always spam."

"I had to call Mom twice before she finally did," I said, my eyes constantly sweeping the Kroger parking lot from my vantage point just inside the entrance and beside a row of nested shopping carts that lined the interior wall.

We had already tried both Sheetz and Speedway to no avail. Speedway only sold prepaid phone cards but not the phones themselves, and Sheetz didn't carry either one. I was starting to think we weren't going to be able to get one when it occurred to me that I had seen them at my local Kroger, so I got directions to the nearest location before I left Speedway. I had left Dad in the car with the engine running at each stop, paranoid about the electronic surveillance all of these places were bound to have. I knew Craig's visitors were looking for him. I could only hope they weren't looking for me—at least, not yet.

"This is all getting very weird," I continued.

"I'll say," said Melanie. "Cheryl called and told me they had a visitor after you left."

"*Shit.* Well, so much for keeping myself off the radar," I said. "I should've known she'd call you first thing."

"You seriously think my phone could be—" Melanie began before I stopped her in her tracks.

"Do I really have to explain this again? Because I feel a little less than free to talk, and you know what I mean."

"Alright, sure, I do," she acknowledged. "We didn't talk for long, though. I had just gotten Jordan to bed and was in the middle of helping Jasmine with her homework. So, when do you think you'll be home?"

I exhaled in a whoosh. "I wish I knew. I've got some thinking to do. A lot of what Dad said lines up eerily with things I've told you about my own time in West Virginia. And then Craig added more fuel to the fire when he told us where he and his sister spent a couple of weeks out of their summer vacations when they were growing up. Care to guess? I'll bet you'll only need one."

"*No!*" she gasped. "Well, that seems awfully coincidental, doesn't it?"

"I don't know what to think."

A moment of silence stretched out before Melanie finally asked, "Have you shared any of this with your dad?"

"No," I said. "At least not yet, but I'm not sure how much longer I can hold out."

She sighed. "I swear, Dwayne, sometimes a house *does* have to fall on you. Doesn't it feel like maybe the universe is trying to tell you something here?"

"Maybe. But I witnessed one of Dad's little 'episodes' earlier, right before he ran us off the road and wrecked his buddy's truck. He was talking about his first wife again. It didn't last long, but long enough to spook me. I'm worried about confusing him even more." I shifted to my left as an exiting customer returned a cart a little too close to my position for my liking.

"I think you worry too much. Whatever is going on with him, it started long after you came home from West Virginia. This feels like the opportunity you've been looking for to—um, you know. Resolve things once and for all."

"I know," I said. "I'm just trying to be cautious."

"Make no mistake, I'm a big fan of that idea," she said. "But you don't want to be so careful that you miss the chance that is practically throwing itself at you. You'll drive yourself crazy wondering what might have been, and you know I'm right."

It was my turn to sigh. She knew me too well. "Yeah, you are."

"Just promise me you'll proceed with caution and keep me posted when you can," she said. "We've got ourselves a wedding to plan when you get home, mister."

Before returning to the car, I took a quick moment to access Google Maps on the prepaid phone to get my bearings. Briarstaff was a solid three-and-a-half-hour drive from Huntington, and it was already past eight o'clock.

After the day I'd had, it felt like midnight, and I was dead on my feet— what a stupid expression!

I couldn't see making the drive in its entirety without stopping somewhere for the night. I certainly didn't want to pull into Briarstaff in the dead of night where our only choice of accommodations was likely to be Fred's Beds, another place I hoped to never see again. Let's face it, the thought of returning to Briarstaff at all filled me with unspeakable anxiety and dread, despite the fact that all of the bad guys had been rounded up and taken away. Nevertheless, all signs were pointing toward revisiting a place that had nearly been my undoing, and to paraphrase a line from *Star Trek: The Next Generation*, resistance was seemingly futile. It was only an hour to Charleston, and I figured we could find lodging for the night there.

I quickened my pace as I approached the Monza, which I had parked toward the back of the lot. Dad sprawled in the passenger seat with his eyes closed and his mouth hanging open, and an icy dagger pierced my heart.

He looked like he was dead.

I broke into a run in the last few feet, jerking the driver's door open and leaning into the car. "Dad? *Dad?*" I couldn't keep the panic out of my voice, and my heartbeat was thunderous in my own ears. "Aww, *no*—"

I reached over and placed my fingertips on the side of his throat, feeling for a pulse. I nearly jumped out of my skin when he suddenly gasped and pulled away from me with a snort.

"What in the hell are you *doing*, son?" he asked, staring at me with alarm. "Your fingers are ice cold!"

Nervous laughter burbled out of me, and I slumped back into the driver's seat. "I thought you were—"

"I was trying to catch a couple of Zs," he said irritably. "My belly's full, and it's been a long day. Do you mind?"

I was still giggling like an idiot. "Not at all. It doesn't matter what I thought. You go right ahead and get some sleep. I'll let you know when we arrive."

"Arrive? You finally decided where we're going?"

I nodded. "We're heading to Briarstaff, just like you wanted, but I think we should spend the night in Charleston. Briarstaff is too far away to make the full drive tonight. We've both been going for hours, and we should be fresh and sharp when we finally get there."

"That's the first sensible thing you've said all day," he grumbled. He scowled for a long moment, but his eyes continued to droop, and next thing I knew, he had dropped off once again, a soft, rhythmic snore fluttering through his lips. I took a deep breath to steady myself before buckling in and depressing the clutch. The gears ground in protest as the clutch slipped before finally engaging, and we lurched out of our parking spot toward the lot's exit. I turned left in a series of herky-jerky movements as the car's transmission continued to complain. Everything smoothed out once I accelerated, heading back toward I-64 which would take us into Charleston.

Dad smacked his lips without opening his eyes. "I see you *still* haven't learned how to drive a stick," he muttered before turning toward the window and fully surrendering himself to sleep.

·····•••●◌⊙●•••·····

After a slow runup traversing the mountainous terrain that is West Virginia, the city of Charleston finally sprang into sight across the Kanawha River, its imminent appearance foreshadowed by the numerous suburbs leading into it. The interstates were a webwork of elevated throughways, often coiling in and converging on one another before eventually branching off in their own separate directions. Exits frequently offered descending access into a city that felt as if it had been constructed almost entirely beneath bridges. Once we had crossed the river along the Virginia Street Bridge, I followed exit 58B into a checkerboard of one-way streets traversing the city in a straight albeit southeasterly direction. This neighborhood was home to the Charleston Coliseum & Convention Center where concerts and other live events would frequently congest the surrounding streets, but this was a Monday evening, and thankfully there was nothing on their calendar for tonight. It also afforded a decent choice of lodging, but after passing a Hampton Inn followed by a Holiday Inn Express, I started questioning the wisdom of choosing a national chain for our overnight accommodation. Any one of them would require a driver's license and credit card in exchange for a room.

I turned left on Court Street and traveled north a block to Quarrier, where I took another left, heading west and away from the center of town. Quarrier eventually terminated into Randolph Street, and as the neighborhoods became exceedingly residential, I widened my approach, bobbing and weaving through blocks while fairly certain I wouldn't lose my way entirely. It was laid out in a precise grid that would be hard to get lost in.

After twenty minutes or so of aimless rambling, Dad startled me by clearing his throat. "Do you have an eventual destination in mind, son, or are we just running out our gas?"

"I'm not really sure where to stop," I said, scouring my surroundings. "I'm thinking that one of the big box hotels isn't such a great idea. They're going to require ID and a credit card at a minimum. Now that I think about it, just about any place we stop is going to ask for that, and if we're trying to stay off the radar...maybe we'd just be better off to find a rest stop and—"

"That might be worse," he said. "Too easy to picture state police checking in on us while we're fast asleep in the car. Once they phone in our info, we're busted. What's that place up there?" He pointed toward a squat cinderblock double-decker building in the distance and off to our right.

I squinted my eyes at the flickering neon of its barely functional sign. "Sleepytime Motel," I said. "Well, it's certainly no Hilton."

As I neared the painted concrete rectangle, I noted its relative vacancy, with only a few cars parked in an otherwise empty lot that circled the building in its entirety. Rooms faced out onto cement walkways on both levels, the upper one protected by a wrought-iron rail running the full length of the building. At the midpoint, a passageway led through to the other side where ice machines and other vending lined the interior walls. A 'Rooms for Rent' sign flickered in the office window, one of the few through which any illumination showed at all.

"Take her around back, son. This may just be the answer to our prayers."

I followed his instructions, still dubious about the wisdom of this maneuver. We circled around to the back of the lot, which was virtually empty and offered only half of the security lighting afforded by the front.

"*Perfect!*" Dad exclaimed. "You can't even see the road from back here, so anyone looking for us would have a hell of a time finding us easily. Pull in."

"I don't know, Dad," I said, reluctantly nosing into one the empty slots, nevertheless. "I don't usually carry much cash on me, so I'd need to use a credit card to get us a room. If anyone's monitoring us, it would be a dead giveaway."

"*Pfft*," he exhaled, and if I never heard that ridiculous, self-confident sputter again, it would be too soon. "You worry too much, son. Let your old man handle this."

With that, he pivoted around and grabbed the zippered handle to the front of his bowling bag which was reclining in the back seat. He opened the front compartment and reached in, extracting an enormous wad of cash and fanning my face with it.

"Where did *that* come from?" I asked, alarmed.

"I came prepared," he said simply as he unfastened his seatbelt and opened the passenger door. "Just stay put. I'll be right back."

I continued to sputter, but he was already crossing the sidewalk, approaching the passageway through to the motel's front. There was nothing tentative about his movement; he carried himself like a man on a mission, and all I could do was pray that the next sounds I heard wouldn't be the incoming wail of police sirens.

The clock on the dash of the Monza was forever frozen at four o'clock, so I monitored the passage of time on my wristwatch, and as the second hand ticked off fifteen minutes, I was well on my way to Panic Town. I was just about to ease the car around to the front of the building to determine whether I needed to stage a getaway when Dad came strolling back through the enclave through which he had earlier disappeared, a spring in his step and an old-fashioned room key swiveling on his forefinger. He strode up to the passenger door and opened it, leaning the seat forward to retrieve his bowling bag.

I killed the engine.

"You got a room?" I asked incredulously, earning myself a scowl.

"Of course, I got a room," he said. "Not only did I get a room, but I was able to persuade the desk clerk—a delightfully helpful lady by the name of Carol Nauss—to give us a room facing away from the main drag."

"But how did you—?"

Dad waggled a finger in my face, interrupting my inquiry while offering a smug grin. "Son, if there's one thing you should never *ever* underestimate, it's the charm of Todd Morrow. Now, let's go to our room."

CHAPTER EIGHT

I stood underneath the surprisingly robust shower head until the hot water began a slow slide into tepidity. I felt sticky from decades' worth of grime infesting the Monza's well-worn interior, but more to the point, I needed time to collect my thoughts before I trotted them out to Dad all willy-nilly. I was worried about how he might receive the news that I had been withholding from him—from *everyone*—for all of these months. As I stood in front of the mirror in the tiny motel bathroom, continuing to towel hair that was already well on its way to dry, I tried to convince myself I wasn't just stalling, but even my own reflection wasn't buying that. More than a tiny part of me hoped I would emerge from the bathroom to find Dad asleep, giving me another full night to ponder an approach to the unapproachable. I slipped back into the only clothing I had and eased the door open a crack to covertly peek out and see if my wish had, by some miracle, been granted.

It hadn't.

Dad had rolled the rickety task chair away from the small writing desk that was across from the foot of the room's matching double beds and had aimed it toward the ancient television sitting on its neighboring TV cart. Every single furnishing in our room looked as if it had been manufactured while I was in elementary school, but I had to give management *some* credit. It was very clean.

Dad leaned back in the chair with his shoes kicked aside and his stockinged feet propped up onto the mattress closest to the door. He had already popped the tab on one of his beers and was giggling himself silly at what looked like *The Benny Hill Show* playing on the tiny 13" TV screen. I paused, the corners of my mouth quirking upward. I hadn't seen *Benny Hill* in years, maybe not since I had lived at home. The legendary British comedian's bawdy yet completely sexist humor hadn't aged well at all, and it was no longer shown in syndication like it once was, but there was no mistaking "Yakety Sax," nor the rotund little man who was busily chasing an ever-expanding legion of busty babes through a neighborhood park in double time.

"I was about to send in a search party," said Dad, sitting up and lowering his feet to the floor. He leaned forward and switched the TV off before opening the small dorm fridge tucked underneath the writing desk and snagged a Mike's Hard Lemonade, tossing it to me. "Sit down, son. It's about time we had ourselves a talk."

Shit.

Apparently, my time to hedge was over. I perched on the edge of the other bed and twisted the cap off the malt beverage, tossing back a mouthful and wincing at the unexpected burn. Its flavor was strawberry lemonade, and I could almost guarantee the heartburn that would inevitably follow.

"Sure," I said. "What did you want to—" My voice trailed away as I sniffed the air around me, my expression souring. "*Uck*—what is *that?*"

Dad's eyebrows shot to the ceiling as he reclined and put his feet back up on the bed. "What? I don't smell anything." He leaned to the side and nabbed a box of Cheez-Its he had pulled from his bag of convenience store snacks, and my entire childhood came racing back to me like a foul thunderclap.

It was his feet.

Well—his feet combined with the unmistakably sharp aroma of the cheese crackers. He had cleared our living room on a fairly regular basis with this particular one-two punch. Mom seemed to have developed an immunity to it over time, but Gina, Matt, and I could only take so much before we found another part of the house to occupy. This was a ghost from the past that I would have been absolutely fine leaving behind. To this day, I can't fathom putting one of those artificially orange crackers into my mouth.

I sighed. "So, what do you want to talk about? I've been thinking about our plan for tomorrow. I thought we'd get started early, maybe nine—"

He laughed. "Nine? You certainly *are* your mother's son when it comes to the concept of morning. But no, that isn't what I want to discuss."

I blinked. "Okay. So, what *did* you want to talk about?"

"I want to know what changed your mind," he said, tossing a handful of crackers into his mouth and washing them down with his beer. "You've been all ready to chalk everything I've told you up to this, this—" He motioned toward his own head. "—whatever this thing is. How come you suddenly believe me?"

"I never said I *didn't* believe you. It's just—"

"What? It's just *what?*"

I looked away. This was going to be *tough.*

"I don't want to make anything—*worse.*"

He nodded slowly. "That would be a real trick, son. There's nothing quite like losing the faith of your entire family, and I hope to God you never find out what I mean by that."

Ouch.

His tone was conversational, but his words landed like physical blows.

"I'm sorry, Dad," I said, shifting uncomfortably in my seat. "It's just a lot to take in. You're telling me you think Gina is alive based on dreams—"

"Do you think I'm just making them up? Do you think I'm losing my mind?" There was nothing defiant about his questions, only simple curiosity.

I stared at him evenly. "I don't know what to think. What happens to you during these little episodes? I'm not talking about your dreams. I'm talking about when you confuse Mom with—with your—"

"Nancy," he supplied, and I nodded. He sighed. "I honestly don't know. I have no recollection of speaking that woman's name in nearly four decades. I guess I'm almost as shocked as you to find out I've been doing it. These spells sneak up without any warning. I feel just fine. One minute, I'm just going about my business—like now. I'm sitting here talking to you. Next thing I know, I'm no longer where I was, and I can't even remember what I was just talking about. It's jarring, like a needle skipping across the groove in a record. It's not so bad when I'm alone, but when I'm with your mother—or like earlier this afternoon when it happened with you in the truck—I just blink, and I'm suddenly surrounded by so much concern it's unsettling, especially considering that I don't feel any different than I've ever felt."

He shook his head, and I saw something in his eyes that I had never seen before. I'm pretty sure it was fear.

"But that isn't what's happening with these dreams about Gina," he continued. "Those are different, and I'm pretty sure you think they are, too. What is it you're not telling me?"

I opened my mouth to speak but took another long pull from my hard lemonade instead. I had kept this secret for so long. I wasn't sure I could actually *do* this.

Dad's disappointment was growing while his patience was running thin. "Don't you dare hold back because you think you're protecting me. It's not up to you to protect *me*. I protect *you*. I protect *all* of my family. It's what I do. It's what I've always done." His eyes darted around the room as the tension filled the space between us. "Okay, *fine*. You wanna know about Nancy? Let's talk about Nancy."

"Dad. You don't have to talk about her if you don't want to."

I couldn't believe the words that were coming out of my own mouth. He was finally willing to spill the tea I'd been desperate to drink for months, and I was encouraging him to stop. I couldn't help myself. He was getting increasingly agitated, and this wasn't the way I wanted to learn anything.

"No, no—it's fine. It's been so long ago, I can't even tell you why it should matter to me anymore. Nancy Bailey was my high school sweetheart. My mom and dad were crazy about her, and she fit right in with all my brothers and sisters—not an easy feat when considering there were thirteen of us. Even Eunice loved her, and Eunice can find fault with *anybody*."

He paused to swap his empty can for another one from the fridge, his eyes clouding over as an unwelcome past took center stage in his mind.

"After high school, I'd had my fill of book learning. I've always been more of hands-on sort of guy, and the Army seemed like a better option for developing some practical skills while seeing parts of the world I'd probably never see otherwise. Once I enlisted, I learned that I'd be spending time in the Middle East after I finished basic training. I asked Nancy to marry me before I was scheduled to leave. It gave me something to hold on to during those long, dark nights when I sometimes thought I'd never see home again. I should've known something was wrong when her letters became less frequent. Four years seems a lot longer when you're only nineteen. She was a young, vibrant woman with needs of her own, and I should have known that more than anyone else." The corner of his mouth inched upward, and I hoped he wouldn't feel compelled to add details to a picture that was already quite clear enough. No one wants to hear about their parents' sexcapades. No one.

"After four long years, I expected to come home and begin the life I had put on pause while serving our country. I had some promising interviews lined up, and I was eager to start my own family with the woman who felt like my other half. You can't even imagine my surprise when I walked in on Nancy in bed with my best friend, Greg Dixon. They had been carrying on for months behind everyone's back, somehow avoiding a gossip mill that thrives on such things. In one short minute, I lost two of the most important people in my life, and that was the new reality of my homecoming. Complete and utter betrayal."

"Oh, Dad," I said. "I'm so sorry. I—"

He cut me short with a flash of his hand, a pained expression pinching his features. "Let me finish, okay? This is hard enough, and I don't ever want to talk about it again."

He cleared his throat and took another pull from his beer before chuckling softly.

"I was such an idiot," he said. "There was no question we would divorce, but I let her be the one to file. I let her claim irreconcilable differences, allowing everyone to believe that whatever went wrong was my doing and not hers. I didn't want to brand her with the reputation she completely deserved. I was humiliated and just wanted to be done. I told her I'd keep the facts to myself, but she would have to pack her things and leave our house in Lucasville. It was a small split-level that was a gift from my dad and older brothers. They had built it from the ground up while I was overseas, a sort-of 'welcome home' present that I wasn't willing to surrender. I mean, I'd already lost everything else. I wasn't about to move back in with my parents who were already blaming me for the failure of my marriage."

I guess that answered my question about half-siblings. They hadn't married because she was pregnant, and Dad's four years overseas pretty much precluded anything short of immaculate conception. Enough silence stretched between us that I thought he was done, but he still had an epilogue to add to his story.

"Nancy stalked me for years, begging for another chance, but it wasn't a chance I was willing to take. In fact, I seriously doubted if I'd ever date again. A betrayal like that does something to your ability to trust, and I couldn't ever imagine putting myself in such a vulnerable position again. I met your mother at Sunset Lanes in Portsmouth. I was bowling for a team sponsored by Pepsi, and she was killing a Friday night with her sister, Jane, on the handful of lanes that were available for open bowling. She wasn't paying a bit of attention to what she was doing and ran right into me, dropping her pretty pink ball on my foot."

Finally, a smile broke through the storm collecting on his face.

"Love at first sight?" I ventured hopefully.

He shook his head. "Nah, I don't believe in that kind of stuff. But she sure was persistent with her apologies. She sent a whole pizza over to my team by way of apology, and I kept catching her watching me from across the lanes, turning away any time she caught me looking back. She and Jane had finished their game long before we finished ours, but they continued to find reasons to stay for just a little bit longer. I knew she was interested, and she was very easy on the eyes."

"So, you asked her out?"

He chuckled. "Nope. Before the end of the evening, she worked up the courage to ask me out. She was raving over some double feature playing at the Scioto Breeze and wondered if I might be interested in taking her. I told her thanks, but no thanks."

"Dad!" I was more than a little surprised by this turn of events.

"Yeah, I know," he said, grinning. "But what can I say? I was still feeling bruised and wasn't completely sure I wanted to run the risk of getting myself hurt again. I could tell I hurt her feelings, and even though I felt awful, I just let her and Jane go, figuring I'd never see them again."

"But clearly you did."

He nodded, smiling again at the recollection. "Oh, yes. You see, I completely underestimated your mother and her obstinance when she's set her mind to something. Maybe three days later, my supervisor at Pepsi, Bud Kitchen—you remember him?" I nodded. "Bud stopped by while I was loading my truck with product. He said the prettiest girl he'd ever seen was sitting on the hood of my car in the employee parking lot, and I might want to find out why."

"It was Mom?" I asked incredulously, having a most difficult time picturing Mom perched on the hood of any car.

"It was, and she was *pissed*. She said she wouldn't be able to rest until she got a few things straight with me, beginning with how much I had embarrassed her in front of her sister. She had a bunch of other choice words for me, too, but I'll spare you the details. It was my turn to apologize, and I did so by asking her to the movies that weekend. We've been together ever since."

I smiled. "Well, see? That wasn't so awful. All's well that ends well, right?"

He teetered his head side to side. "Mostly. But that isn't exactly the end of the story."

I blinked. "It isn't?"

"Once Nancy caught word that Jo and I were dating, she started making a real nuisance of herself. She mostly stayed clear of me, but she could turn up at any given moment during Jo's day. At the time, your mother was working for *The Portsmouth Times* doing clerical work."

Another surprise. In my lifetime, Jo Morrow had always been a stay-at-home mom. It was difficult to imagine her in a nine-to-five position, but I can't exactly say I've invested much time learning about her exploits prior to bringing me into this world.

"What happened?" I asked.

"Nancy deluged her with harassing phone calls, both while she was working and while she was at home, warning Jo to stay away from me. Nancy could be physically intimidating when she wanted to be, and she was really going all out. It didn't help anything that my family didn't really care for your mother all that much."

"You're kidding," I said, stunned that anyone could find fault with Mom. My dad's parents had died when I was very young, so I really didn't remember much about them at all, but I had never detected any animosity between Mom and Dad's surviving handful of siblings. Well—maybe a little with Aunt Eunice, but everyone got a little tired of Aunt Eunice's shenanigans here and there, including me.

"It had gotten so bad that by the time I finally realized that I was ready to give marriage another chance, I asked your mother to elope with me. It broke your grandmother's heart, but I couldn't run the risk of Nancy turning up and ruining our big day, because believe you me, she would've. Even after we were married, she kept trying to cause trouble."

I finished off my hard lemonade and motioned for another, setting the empty bottle on the floor at my feet. "So, when did she finally get it through her thick head that you had moved on?" I asked, taking the frosty cold bottle from Dad's outstretched hand.

"It wasn't until Gina came along," he said, crumpling his empty can. "Your mom was only six months along when her water broke. I thought I knew fear when I was overseas, but it was nothing compared to what we went through when your sister was born. She was just so damn small and fragile. She barely weighed a pound, and her odds for survival weren't all that great, but my God, was that little girl a fighter! Your mom and I practically lived at the hospital, taking each day as the gift that it was. Everything else was just irrelevant at that point, and when Nancy turned up at the hospital, I was fully prepared to physically remove her myself."

"You've got to be *kidding* me!" I said, freshly outraged by actions that had taken place before I had ever even taken my own first breath.

Dad's smile was wistful. "She wasn't there to make trouble. In fact, she was there to offer her sympathy and support. She promised she was done making our lives a living hell and apologized that it took something so serious for her to get her own priorities in order. It doesn't change what happened, but it gave us the closure we desperately needed. Maybe you can understand why it isn't a subject your mother and I care to revisit?"

I felt like such a heel. Of *course*, there was a logical explanation for why this subject had remained buried for all of these years, and I almost found the news regarding Gina's premature birth as startling as the facts of Dad's first ill-fated marriage. Neither were topics for casual conversation, and the fact that I had felt deceived by this simple act of omission made me feel petty and small.

"I'm sorry, Dad," I said, and I couldn't have meant it more.

"I know you are son," he said, letting me off the hook just like that. Well—almost. "Now, it's your turn. Start talking."

I chewed on my bottom lip and took a deep breath. "It was last July, just after the funeral," I began, determined to get through this before I lost my nerve.

I started with Michael Arthur's unexpected appearance at my door and soon enough, I was reliving some of the most frightening days I had ever survived in the very same little West Virginia town we planned to visit in the morning. He listened intently as I told him what I knew about The Academy and their ridiculous agenda designed to take the internet out of the hands of the public, rolling us back into the Dark Ages by restricting use of such technology to a select few governmental entities who would use it however they saw fit. I told him about being victimized and nearly killed by the only lawman in town, Sheriff Charley Daniel. I did my best to describe my otherworldly experience with Madame Phalange, whose actual name was Delphine Bartlett, as well as the incredible group of local teens who had come to my rescue when I couldn't reach out to anyone else. My throat nearly closed up when I told him about Hattie, and I'm not gonna lie—I was a blubbering mess for a long minute getting through all that. As I relayed the final harrowing minutes near the mouth of the abandoned mine whose tunnels were key to bringing down the whole operation, Dad sat back in the task chair, blowing out a long breath.

"My Lord, son, I guess I didn't realize that what you were doing was so dangerous," he said, and I was pleased to detect a note of pride in his voice. "So, you're telling me Gina was killed because she was an eyewitness to the congressional officials involved in this?"

I squirmed a bit. "Yes, but that's not everything," I said. "When I was on my way to the hospital in an ambulance, I, um—I saw her."

Dad was confused. "I'm not catching your meaning. You saw her? Saw who?"

"Gina," I said, and his mouth snapped into a tight line. "She was inside the ambulance. She made me promise not to investigate any further. She said these people were threatening you, Mom, Matt—all of us, and she had every reason to believe they meant what they said. As long as they continued to believe she was dead, we were safe."

His glare was withering. I watched the muscles of his jaw tighten, and for a moment, I thought he was going to smack me. Instead, he abruptly stood, pushing the open box of Cheez-Its away and tucking the task chair back underneath the writing desk. He crossed to the bed nearest the door and turned off the tabletop lamp.

"Dad?" I ventured nervously, and the look he shot me offered no relief.

"All this time," he said, his voice scarily even and low. "You've known this *all this time*, and yet you've let me and your mother go through—" His voice dropped away, and he shook his head. "I can't talk to you anymore tonight. I'm afraid of what might come out of my mouth."

"But *Dad*—"

"*No.*"

He lay down and turned his back to me, pulling the blankets up over his shoulders. I sighed, turning off my own bedside lamp. I crawled beneath the covers of the bed I had been sitting on and stared at the ceiling, worried that things might never be the same between Dad and me again.

I tugged the gearshift from first to second as gears ground and the little car lurched in response, the engine faltering and almost stopping before the clutch fully engaged. Something was different, but it took me a minute to recognize the black vinyl interior of my M&M green Ford Fiesta, vintage 1979. It was my first car, and I realized that this was a dream. I was working my ass off to pay for it by shoving carts around and cleaning restrooms at Lymont Sundries after school. I was desperate for wheels, and when Dad brought this little guy home, I was too impatient to wait for a car that I could afford featuring an automatic transmission. Dad offered to teach me how to drive a stick, but his idea of teaching was restricted to a single Sunday session looping around Spartan Stadium in nearby Portsmouth, explaining the rudimentary concepts before tossing me the keys and telling me to drive home.

It was a miracle we ever arrived.

Never in the history of ever has a car been manufactured with such a touchy clutch, and I killed that engine time and again trying to get us home. I made an entire line of cars in my rearview back away for their own safety when I couldn't get the hang of keeping the car from rolling backwards after stopping on a hill. Dad hid his amusement behind a hand while insisting he had already explained the concept to me.

He most certainly did *not*.

Over time, I gradually got the hang of driving a stick, and that car was my most treasured possession in those days. I was completely comfortable behind the wheel with the exception of my monthly assessments from Dad that always landed like pop quizzes. Out of nowhere, he would ask me to drive him somewhere so he could gauge my progress, and I immediately tensed up as soon as his seatbelt clicked. In retrospect, it was my own nerves that were the problem. It wasn't like he yelled or made exaggerated gestures like he was afraid for his own life. Inevitably, at some point along our short trip, he'd sigh, muttering, "I see you *still* haven't learned how to drive a stick."

I would be thoroughly mortified, and his work there would be done.

It was a sunny afternoon in Dreamland, and from what I could see, I was in a neighborhood in Lymont known as Flaugher's Ridge. I wasn't surprised to find Dad sitting in the passenger seat beside me. As I fumbled the shift into third, his sigh was exaggerated. "I can't believe you've been lying to us this whole time. You've known she was alive this *whole time*, and you just sat back and watched us suffer. What is *wrong* with you? I cannot *believe* we raised such a deceitful, lying, *horrible*—"

My eyes snapped open, and I immediately sensed there was something amiss. I looked around furtively to get my bearings, chilled by the breeze that blew in through the open motel door.

Dad's bed was empty.

"Aww, *fuck*," I said, fighting to free myself from the tangle of bedclothes and racing to the door.

I stuck my head out and looked to my left, finding nothing but the concrete walkway that stretched to the end of the building. A startled cry sounded behind me, and I turned to discover Dad duking it out with a man who was significantly larger than him near the entrance to the vending machines at the motel's midpoint. Fists were flying, and the scuffle was punctuated by disembodied grunts from both men. Dad was like a cage fighter, keeping his center of gravity low as he circled his opponent. He darted forward with surprising speed and agility to deliver a rapid-fire volley of punches into the man's abdomen with his bare fists, pulling back just in time to avoid a sloppy roundhouse punch the man attempted in desperation. I glanced over my shoulder into our room where my coat was hanging too far from easy reach, the gun in its pocket entirely useless from this distance.

Without any other feasible option, I charged down the walkway on my bare feet, adrenaline deciding my next moves. *"Get the fuck away from my dad, you ass—"*

But before I could articulate a threat I fully intended to fulfill, Dad had boosted the man up and over the wrought iron railing, sending him sailing through the night air before he landed with a sickening *thunk* on the asphalt below.

CHAPTER NINE

I couldn't move, my jaw gawping in disbelief as my fists hung uselessly in the air. My stuttering heartbeat roared in my ears, temporarily deafening me to the sounds of the night, and yet I could swear I heard sirens approaching from all directions.

"Oh, my *God!* Oh, my *God!* Oh, my *God!*"

Someone was chanting in the distance, frantic words drawing attention to our developing plight, and as the roar in my ears slowly diminished, I realized it was me. I couldn't seem to stop myself—just those same three words over and over. I inched forward on unsteady feet to where Dad leaned over the safety rail, staring at the parking lot below. I peered over the edge and inhaled sharply.

Dad's boxing partner stared up at us with the most ridiculous look of surprise on his face, his eyes wide open, his jaw slackened, and a pool of crimson blood blossoming beneath a skull that had been structurally compromised due to rapid deceleration. His arms and legs were splayed out at odd angles, his left arm clearly broken. Underneath the flickering, failing light of the motel's rear lot, the scene was garish and surreal.

"Oh, my God—*Dad!* What have you *done?*" I demanded, scanning the area for witnesses or, heaven forbid, security cameras. None were apparent, but it did little to ease my adrenalized nerves. The only difference I saw was a black Dodge Challenger that was parked one space over from the Monza. I assumed it was our dead guy's ride.

Dad turned toward me, the shock on his own face somehow surpassing that of the dead guy below. "I was just—I was just protecting us," he said. "I didn't mean to—"

"Oh, my *God*, Dad!" I was just shy of freaking the fuck out, struggling for a rational explanation for the horrific thing I had just witnessed, preferably one that wouldn't end with both of us behind bars. "What were you even doing outside the room? Was this guy one of the other guests? Please tell me you weren't having one of your episodes—or better yet, tell me you were. Maybe we can use temporary insanity as a defense—"

"*Son!*" he hissed, grabbing me by the shoulders and giving me a good, hard shake. "Get hold of yourself! I didn't mean to kill the guy, but this wasn't just some accident. I woke up to find the guy letting himself into our room."

I couldn't stop blinking, trying to unsee everything I had just seen, but his words slowly worked their way through the panic that was hobbling me. "He was—breaking into our room?"

Dad nodded, and there was no doubt he believed what he was saying. "I heard him working at the lock, but I was able to get to the door just before he managed to open it. He wasn't expecting me to be right there waiting for him, and I sucker punched that bastard before he even knew what hit him. I chased him out onto the walkway, and I think you pretty much saw what happened after that. Now, come *on!*"

"Come *on?*" I repeated numbly. "Where are we going?"

"Anywhere but here," he said, and he was already moving toward our room. "We have to get out of here before someone stumbles across him and calls the police. It's a good thing our room isn't facing the street. It might just give us the time we need, but we have to hustle. *Move!*"

I stumbled along, following Dad into the room, and we began to gather our meager belongings as quickly as possible. For once, I was grateful we hadn't planned for an overnight stay. There wasn't much to collect.

"Grab a wet washcloth from the bathroom and wipe down anything we might have touched," said Dad, and I was more than happy to follow his lead. My brain was stalled, flooded with far too much to process. He was busily stuffing his assorted Speedway snacks back into the plastic bags from which they came, and I headed to the bathroom to dampen a washcloth. He pulled the liner from the small trashcan and tied it off, carrying it and the Speedway bag toward the open door while I quickly hit every surface we could have possibly laid hands on. From the door, he asked, "Can you get my bowling bag?"

"Got it," I said, tossing the washcloth into the tub. I crossed to the closet, pulling my coat free from its hanger and slipping it on, momentarily startled but then relieved to feel the extra heft from Dad's handgun in its right front pocket. I snagged our only real baggage from the closet and rolled it toward the door. "Is that everything? Should I make the beds?"

"No time," he said, taking a quick look around the room. "Let's go."

I pulled the door shut behind me, realizing immediately that I had just left fingerprints as a parting gift. I stuffed my hand into my coat pocket and used it to thoroughly wipe the knob down as Dad urged me to hurry. We turned left, hustling to the switchback stairs where I hoisted Dad's bowling bag off the ground to prevent it from thunking against each riser as I descended. I felt certain that by the time we reached the parking lot, our mysterious intruder would have vanished like Michael Myers at the end of any number of *Halloween* films, but no—he hadn't moved a muscle. We paused for one last look on our way to the car, his sightless eyes already beginning to cloud over.

"Look," Dad said, pointing.

"I did." I had already seen more than enough and was getting a little queasy.

"*Dwayne*," he snapped, and this time, I followed his gesture. Resting against the man's torso and almost entirely obscured by shadow was a much larger gun than the one I cradled in my coat pocket. "Do you see what I see?"

We needed to leave, and it was everything I could do to keep from racing ahead to the car. This wasn't the time for a 'teaching moment.' "Yes, Dad. It's a gun. Now, can we—"

"Look closer."

I sighed, taking another quick glance before doing a double take. The barrel was oddly elongated. "Is that a—is that a silencer?" I asked, stooping to take a closer look.

"It is. This guy wasn't just some run of the mill thief tossing motel rooms. He was here to carry out a hit, and we were his intended targets."

My mouth went dry while nervous perspiration crept down the small of my back. I hooked a finger into the pockets of my jeans and fished the burner phone out, unlocking its screen. I pulled up the camera app and leaned in, snapping a few closeups of the man's face.

"What are you doing?" asked Dad.

"I want to know if this is the same guy who showed up at Craig and Cheryl's house earlier," I said, slipping the phone back into my pocket. "Now, let's get the hell out of here while we still can."

As we got back onto I-64 and headed east, awkward silence enveloped us. It was painfully clear from Dad's body language that all was not forgiven from my earlier revelation. He stared through the passenger window into the clear West Virginia night as the exits came with less frequency, and I was surprised to realize how much gasoline we had used since filling up in Ironton. While the Chevrolet Monza might have been considered fuel efficient in its heyday, it felt like it was gulping the stuff now, and I was afraid to get too far beyond civilization without topping off first. My adrenaline buzz was ebbing, and I wouldn't mind a cup of coffee either.

"I'm going to stop for gas," I said, signaling at Exit 89 where yet another Sheetz stood ready to serve our every need. "Do you need anything? I'm going to grab some coffee."

He continued to stare through the window as if I hadn't said a word. I sighed. I didn't know how to fix this, and it was frustrating to be on the run with someone who wasn't even talking to me—especially when that someone was my dad. I would have thought that he more than anyone else would have understood my obligation to honor my sister's wishes. After all, he was the one who had always taught me the value of keeping your own word, worth so much more than any amount of material possessions. It was the sort of thing a person would be remembered for, and I had taken that lesson to heart. It certainly hadn't made my choice any easier—and honestly, even if I *could* have gone back and done things differently, I don't think I would have. All I could do now was stay the course and hope that Dad would eventually come around.

I pulled underneath the lighted canopy, one of only two passenger cars in a lot bordered by semi-trucks whose drivers were either sleeping in the back of their cabs or grabbing a bite to eat inside the store. I checked my watch to find that it was only three-thirty in the morning, and I automatically yawned, my need for sleep unsatiated by the tiny, nightmare-filled slice I had managed to grab thus far. Driving straight through to Briarstaff would put us in town before sunrise, and I wasn't really ready to face that place under the cover of darkness, especially when I was too tired to think clearly.

First things first—gas. I switched off the engine and unfastened my seatbelt.

"Umm, do you have any more cash on you, or should I get into the bowling bag?" I asked, and it felt like I was asking for an advance on my allowance. Without a word, Dad reached into his pocket and pulled out a wad of twenties and handed them to me.

I went inside and poured myself a large cup of black coffee, paying for it as well as thirty dollars' worth of fuel, keeping my face down to avoid the cameras as best as I could. I was struggling with a dueling motivation that demanded we keep moving even though I dreaded the thought of arriving in Briarstaff too early. As the pump clicked off a little short of the thirty dollars I'd left on deposit, I briefly considered leaving the change and driving away, the urge to flee almost overpowering. I decided it would make a more lasting impression on the clerk if I walked away from nearly five dollars in change, so I forced myself to go back inside, trying not to let my anxiety quicken my pace. I almost groaned out loud when I found myself behind a barrel-chested truck driver who was in no real hurry to conclude his business at the register, which included more items than I usually buy in a regular grocery run. I guess all those hours out on the open road leaves a guy starved for a little human interaction, and rosy-cheeked Janice was making the same wage whether she waited on one guy or a hundred. It took everything I had to suppress my impatience, knowing that it would only draw unwanted attention, and after what felt like an eternity, I finally had my change and was sliding back into the driver's seat. I was startled when Dad abruptly turned to face me.

"Something's bothering me," he said.

"I know, Dad, I know," I said. "And I'm sorry. If there had been any other way—"

"No, no—not *that*," he interrupted, waving my words away. "How did that guy know where we would be? Craig called you right after he left their place, right?"

"I think so."

"We would have been long gone before he ever caught up with us at the gas station. I don't carry a cell phone, and you turned yours off. The whole point to borrowing this heap was that it's too old to have any of that tracking stuff in it. How did he find us?"

"I don't know," I said, giving the matter some thought.

"You didn't have to use any sort of identification when you bought that prepaid phone?"

"Huh-unh. I paid for it with cash along with a prepaid card to load minutes onto it. No credit card or ID required."

He narrowed his eyes. "And you're *sure* there's no way you can be tracked with one of those prepaid things?"

"I'm sure it's not nearly as easy, but as a precaution, I turned it off after I made my calls."

"And you haven't powered up your own cell phone?"

I sighed. "No, Dad. See for yourself. It's right there."

I pointed to the darkened screen tucked underneath the car's hand brake, but I couldn't shake the feeling of unease that was settling in. We needed to get moving sooner rather than later.

He slipped his hand under the handle of the brake and plucked my phone out with his fingers, tentatively poking at its screen like it might poke back.

"See? It's off," I said.

"O-o-kay," he said, sounding less than convinced. "Then tell me this— if your phone is off, why is it so warm?"

He tossed it to me, and I caught it with both hands. He was right. It was noticeably warm to the touch. I stuck my fingers underneath the hand brake to feel the temperature of the molding around it. It was markedly cooler. As understanding slowly dawned, Dad snatched the phone out of my hand and unfastened his seatbelt.

"What are you doing?" I asked.

"I'm going to stomp the hell out of this damned thing," he said, and as he reached for his door handle, I grabbed his arm.

"Hold up, Dad," I said, focusing on a dump truck parked toward the front edge of the parking lot. It was one of those loathsome types with nothing to cover and contain whatever hazardous cargo it carried, but a big ol' sign on its tailgate denying responsibility for a payload that just might turn your windshield into a webwork of laminated safety glass. Its lights were on, and its engine was idling, and if I wasn't mistaken, the same barrel-chested fella who had tried my patience at the counter was behind the wheel, stuffing his face with a roller dog.

I snagged the phone from Dad's hand and was out of the car before he could question my intention. Time was still of the essence, and I was through screwing around. I hurried past the front of the store to the edge of the parking lot and cut a wide path, staying within the shadowy footprint of the trucks lined up behind my intended target. I swung my arm low and lobbed the phone underhanded toward the bed of the dump truck, nearly jumping out of my skin as my target suddenly began inching forward. I chewed on my bottom lip as I followed the phone's lazy arc through the air, hoping the driver wouldn't accelerate out of range before it found its destination. The phone glanced off the top of the tailgate, and for a scary moment, I thought it was going to bounce back out and land on the pavement. Instead, it dropped into the truck bed, and after one last whoosh and a plume of diesel exhaust, the truck pulled ahead to the end of the lot where it turned left on McCorkle Avenue and disappeared from sight.

Track that, *you motherfuckers*, I thought with a self-satisfied smirk.

Despite my ingenuity, it really wasn't the time to get cocky. We had already been in one place for far too long with that phone in tow. If someone were truly using it to track our whereabouts, they could be moments away. We really needed to be anywhere but here.

I aimed for nonchalance as I walked purposefully back to the Monza, averting my gaze from the storefront as I was sure that I'd find Janice staring directly at me, phone in hand. Another car swept into the lot and pulled to a stop along the opposite side of the pump we had used. Heavy bass from its premium sound system was distorted and discordant in my ears, but at least I didn't have to look up to know it wasn't a threat. Nobody performing stealth surveillance would announce themselves so loudly. I opened the driver's door to the Monza and started to get in when I realized something else was amiss.

The car was empty, the passenger door standing wide open.

A fresh wave of panic pushed the air out of my lungs, and I cracked my head against the doorframe as I stood back up, frantically searching the parking lot for any sign of Dad. He was nowhere to be seen. The kid with the sonic audio was staring openly as he pumped gas, a lit cigarette dangling from the corner of his foolish mouth.

"S'up, dude?" he asked cautiously, and I scowled in response.

"Probably all of us if you don't put that damned thing out," I said. "Can't you read?"

I pointed at the sizable 'NO SMOKING' sign mounted on a post near the pump and caught sight of Dad milling about inside the store. From the corner of my eye, the kid was challenging me with his middle finger, but I didn't have time to argue. I could see the confusion clouding Dad's features from where I stood, and any shot of passing through discreetly was about to go up in smoke. I shut my door and circled around to do the same on the passenger side before racing back to the entrance and pushing my way into the store.

117

"Nancy?" Dad called out from beside an endcap featuring a display of ridiculously overpriced sunglasses. *"Nancy?"*

There were only a handful of customers inside the store, but every single one had stopped to witness the forlorn man wandering aimlessly through its middle, including Janice, who had stepped around the counter and was tentatively approaching Dad quicker than I could intercede.

"Are you alright, sir?" she asked, enunciating each word loud and clear as if Dad's distress might also be compounded by hearing loss. Genuine concern played across her face as she reached out to place a hand on Dad's arm.

He slowly turned, his perplexity heartbreakingly evident. "I'm looking for my wife," he said. "She was here just a minute ago, but I—"

His voice fell away as he caught sight of himself in a mirror nested in the center of the sunglass display.

"Who is *that?*" he asked, terror creeping into his voice as he stared at his own reflection. He lifted his fingers to his cheeks and gasped as his unrecognized likeness did the same. A low, guttural groan began to creep out of his mouth as I finally reached him, more than a little out of breath.

"Dad," I said, pulling his attention away from the mirror and toward me. "It's me, Dwayne."

He shrank away, his eyes widening as exactly zero bells of recognition rang. "We don't *have* kids," he sputtered, and Janice looked to me with alarm.

I tried to give her a reassuring smile, but I can only imagine what it must have looked like. This was beyond anything I had seen before, and I wasn't entirely sure what to do. All I wanted was to extricate us from this public place before we drew any more of an audience than we already had.

"He'll be fine," I said, and my tone was apologetic. "He's been having these spells lately, but he's under a doctor's care. In fact, we're on our way to a specialist in the morning. He'll come out of it any moment now."

He scowled at me. "What in the hell are you talking about, young man? I'm not going anywhere until I've found my Nancy. I'm not sick, I don't need a doctor, and what kind of parlor trick is this funhouse mirror, anyway? I look like old enough to be my *father* in that—"

He gasped sharply and clapped a hand over his left eye, wincing.

"Dad? *Dad?*" I leaned in and looked up into his pained expression, but his eyes were pinched tight.

"Should I call someone?" Janice asked, already moving back toward the counter and reaching for the phone. I honestly wasn't sure what to tell her. For all I knew, Dad could be stroking out right in front of me. I was just about to nod when Dad took another deep breath and suddenly straightened up, a shudder rippling across his shoulders.

"I'm alright," he said, offering a weak smile. "I'm sorry."

"Dad?" I looked at him pensively, terrified of getting another glimpse of the utter lack of recognition he had shown me before.

He exhaled shakily. "It's okay, Dwayne. Let's just get out of here."

"Are you sure?" I asked.

He nodded, gently touching his left eye again. "Just a little bit of a headache, that's all."

Janice stood with her phone at the ready. "Should I call or not?"

"No, thank you," said Dad, turning his smile to her. "I don't suppose you have some Excedrin for sale?"

"Of course," she said, bustling over to a well-stocked display of single-dose packets of every over-the-counter medicine known to man. She plucked a packet of Excedrin off its peg and handed it to Dad. I stepped away long enough to snag a bottle of water from a nearby cooler and was digging into my pocket for cash when she said, "They're on the house."

I looked up, surprised by her offer. "Are you sure? I wouldn't want you to get in trouble. I've got money—"

She chuckled. "It's fine, sweetheart. Ain't nobody going to say nothing to me—I'm the night manager. You just help make your dad comfortable and get him to that specialist in one piece, you hear?"

I nodded numbly, taking Dad by the arm and leading him toward the exit. The other customers were already losing interest, and we were nearly home free. Dad was growing steadier with each step, and soon enough, he pulled his arm free, embarrassed to appear dependent on my support to get him outside.

I was glad to see that the smoking teen had concluded his business at the pump where we were parked, and as I moved to open the passenger door for Dad, he stopped me cold with a withering look.

"I'm not a complete invalid, son," he said, reaching for the handle and pulling the door open. He fastened himself in as I crossed around the front of the hood and got behind the wheel. He ripped the top off the pack of Excedrin and tossed them back, washing them down with almost half the bottle of water we'd been given.

I started the car and looked at him sideways. "Are you sure you're okay?"

He nodded, wiping his mouth with the back of his hand.

"What—happened?" I was almost afraid to ask.

He shook his head slowly. "I don't know. It's like all the other times I told you about. One minute, I was sitting here wondering what in the hell you were doing with that phone, and the next thing I know, I was inside the store, and everyone was staring at me. It was damned unsettling."

A high-pitched chuckle spilled out of my mouth. "Yeah, that's one way of putting it. You scared the *shit* out of me, Dad."

He scowled, wincing at the movement. "So sorry to inconvenience you, son," he muttered dryly. "Let's get out of here, huh?"

I shifted into first and started to ease up on the clutch when I spied something out of the corner of my eye that stopped me cold. "Oh, shit."

"What's with all the cursing, son? You know I don't care for language like that. I—"

"Look," I said, ever-so-slightly nodding my head toward a new arrival at the far end of the lot. It was another black Dodge Challenger, identical to the one we had left behind at the Sleepytime Motel. "It looks like we've got company."

This was bad. Parked underneath the brightly lit canopy, we might as well have been on stage. It was only a matter of time until we were spotted.

"Should I try and make a break for it?" I asked, slightly revving the engine in anticipation.

"Are you *insane?*" Dad was incredulous. "We wouldn't make it thirty feet before they'd be on us. We couldn't begin to outrun a Challenger in this thing. Give me my gun."

"What?"

"You heard me. Give me my gun. I'm not going down without a fight."

"Dad! You can't just open fire in a public place! You wanna talk about insane? *That* would be insane!" I countered.

Suddenly he was reaching for my pockets, trying to retrieve the gun with or without my cooperation. I tried my best to block him, but his determination had me squirming in the driver's seat like I'd spilled hot coffee in my lap. My foot slipped off the clutch and the car lurched forward before the engine died.

"Would you stop it, please?" I begged, trying to hold onto the gun while sneaking a peek to see if we'd been spotted yet.

The Challenger was slowly creeping toward us, and there was no way its driver could possibly miss the sideshow we were putting on. My mind raced through a neighborhood of possibilities, all of which terminated in dead ends.

"Ha!" Dad proclaimed, pulling the handgun free from my pocket. All I could do was watch in horror as he released the safety and unfastened his seatbelt. "Just keep yourself down, son, and let me—"

His voice abruptly trailed away as he stared over my shoulder.

I turned to follow his gaze, nearly certain I'd be staring down the barrel of yet another gun but was surprised to see that the Challenger had turned away, racing toward the exit as if it were on a mission. It turned left on McCorkle and rocketed away toward the interstate.

"I think they got a new fix on your phone, son," said Dad, reengaging the safety on his gun and slipping it into his own jacket pocket.

We looked at each other for a long moment before I got a case of the giggles, and they were contagious. Before anything else could go wrong, I restarted the engine and pulled to the edge of the lot, opting to turn right on McCorkle. It wasn't part of the original plan, but at this point, *anything* felt smarter than turning left.

CHAPTER TEN

We had only been traveling south on WV-61 for maybe ten minutes when an obnoxious snort from the passenger seat startled me, removing any lingering doubt I may have had that Dad had finally nodded off. I'd be lying if I said I wasn't more than a little relieved. His latest episode in Sheetz really frightened me. It was looking increasingly likely that we were being followed, and the thought of him flaking out at an inopportune moment was worrisome, especially if it happened while he was brandishing his gun. He might just shoot me without realizing who I was, and it was a recipe for disaster that felt only too plausible. I was hoping that a little sleep might anchor him to reality a little better, but I knew it was only wishful thinking on my part. Whatever was afflicting Dad was an unpredictable wildcard I couldn't discount, and I would have to find a way to mitigate its risk to our ultimate objective—whenever we finally landed on one. This unexpected detour had me navigating uncharted territory with only the guidance of an aftermarket compass that was barely attached to the dash by two-sided tape that had lost most of its potency. It jumped with every little bump in the road, sending its directional indicator dancing like a bobblehead. Eventually, I'd have to pull off and consult the internet on my prepaid phone to determine a step-by-step path that would eventually lead us to Briarstaff. This Boy Scout shit was for the birds.

The highway meandered alongside the Kanawha River, taking us through a series of small towns nestled within the increasingly mountainous terrain, and the Monza's four-cylinder engine groaned as it labored to maintain speed on the steeper grades. It was more than a little troubling, but no more so than the fact the steady drone of the engine was doing its best to lull me to sleep. There was no way I was going to make it much longer without catching some Z's. While I wasn't keen on revisiting Briarstaff at all, it felt pointless to arrive while I was functioning about as well as a zombie and everyone in town was still in bed. I was only just beginning to formulate a game plan, and it involved consulting a woman who probably wouldn't be too happy to see me. It would be in our best interests to keep it surgical—get in and get out, preferably without attracting any unwanted attention. I wasn't exactly popular with the locals during my earlier stay.

At some point, Dad had entered a deeper level of sleep, and his abrasive snoring was now punctuated with short bursts of nonsensical gibberish. At no point did he utter the name, 'Nancy,' so I thought he was still with me— or at least as much as a sleeping man could be. We mostly had the highway to ourselves, save for the occasional semi or logging truck attempting to pull us into its vacuum as it whipped by. I started to get antsy as the little patches of civilization became increasingly less frequent. I didn't want to lose cell reception before I had a chance to consult Google Maps and get us back on course. Once we cleared Mt. Carbon, I began scoping for a place to pull over.

It wasn't long before I spotted a teetering, dilapidated barn off to our right, nestled in a field of overgrowth but accessible via an equally overgrown lane that ran alongside it before being completely overrun by dense encroaching foliage. I suspect a farmhouse once sat somewhere nearby, and this was its long-forgotten orphan. The structure was clearly abandoned, its weatherworn, skeletal walls anything but plumb and its corrugated tin roof rusted through in multiple places. While I wouldn't want to be in its shadow during high winds, it should provide sufficient cover to satisfy our immediate needs. The frame of the Monza screeched in protest as the passenger front tire dipped off the pavement at an angle, and I thought I might just lose our muffler before it was all said and done, but the car managed to hold onto all its essential parts as the rear dropped down onto the hard-packed dirt and leveled off. Dad mumbled something incoherent, shifting in his seat while clinging to sleep, and that was just fine with me. I pulled far enough behind the barn to be concealed from the highway before switching off the headlights and setting the parking brake, shifting the car into neutral and leaving the engine running. Sure, it would use some gas, but the night was too cold to go without heat for very long. It would be hard enough to find sleep while sitting behind the wheel—absolutely futile if my teeth were chattering, too.

I pulled the prepaid phone from my pocket and while it powered up, I stretched across Dad's supine form to rifle through the glove box in front of his knees, using the illumination from the phone's screen to search for what I needed to transcribe some basic directions. I lucked into a chewed-up golf pencil that was little more than a nub but was shit out of luck for something to write on. I was getting a little desperate when I remembered Dad's bag of snacks in the back seat and retrieved the box of Cheez-Its. There was just enough white space around the Nutrition Facts to make notes. I pulled up Google Maps on the phone and retrieved step-by-step directions from our current location to Briarstaff, avoiding interstates whenever possible. The pencil lead snapped just before I finished, but it was only a few words, and I was pretty sure I could remember them. I powered the phone back down and adjusted the driver's seat as far back as it would go. I closed my eyes and tried to find a comfortable position for sleep.

Dammit. My large coffee from earlier was coming back to haunt me. I really had to pee.

I winced at the sudden wash of illumination from the overhead light as I eased my door open, but Dad didn't even flinch. His face remained tilted toward the passenger window, his breathing a steady buzz that vibrated softly through his lips. I slipped out into the darkness and closed the door carefully behind me.

Once outside, I shivered against an unexpected breeze. It was difficult to see where I was going, and I briefly worried about snakes or other nocturnal critters that might be lurking in the tall grass, but once I convinced myself that it was really too cold for reptiles, I was able to talk myself into a few tentative steps away from the vehicle. I unfastened my jeans and exhaled a cloud of pure relief into the night sky as my bladder began to empty.

"Son?"

"Gah!" I jumped at the sound of Dad's voice, dribbling on my own shoes before drying up completely. *"Dad!* What are you *doing* out here?"

"Same as you," he said. "Nature called, but I think I'll just step over this way a bit. It's been over thirty years since you last peed on me, and I'd really like to keep it that way."

He shifted a few feet to my left, and we lapsed into mandatory silence until we had finished conducting the business at hand. According to The Big Book of Man, there's *another* Golden Rule which states that no two men shall *ever* engage in conversation whilst pissing, not even father and son. I think the punishment is death.

As we ambled back toward the car—me dragging the tops of my shoes through the tall, damp grass for reasons that were embarrassingly obvious—Dad stopped to look at the night sky. "Where are we?"

"Just a little southeast of Charleston," I said. "I wanted to get some decent directions before we lost internet."

Dad snorted. "I thought the internet was *everywhere* nowadays."

"Hardly," I said. "Even around Lymont, there are whole pockets where you can't get signal, but I guess since you don't use a cellphone, it's something you'd never notice. I know for a *fact* that Briarstaff doesn't have it." I shuddered at the recollection.

"This place really got to you, didn't it?"

My smile was more of a wince. "You could say that."

Silence stretched between us as we stood near the car, reluctant to get back in. After spending much of the day in one vehicle or another, it felt good to stretch our legs, despite the chill in the air.

"You saw her?" asked Dad.

"Hmm?"

"You really *saw* her—like with your own two eyes?"

The look on his face was so hopeful it broke my heart, and I found myself hedging almost by default. "I thought I did, but honestly, Dad, I was pretty messed up. Michael Arthur had injected me with something before the cavalry came, and I was pretty heavily sedated after that."

"You said you saw her in the ambulance."

"Well, yeah, I thought I did, but—"

"But nothing, son. Did you see her or didn't you?" His eyes locked onto mine, desperate for a confirmation I could no longer deny.

I sighed. "Yeah. Yeah, I saw her."

He nodded numbly, wandering toward the rear of the car, presumably to cross over to the passenger side and get in. He paused near the trunk with his back to me, and I watched as his shoulders slowly began to hitch.

Oh, shit. Was he *crying?* No, no, no...

I crossed over to him and laid a hand on his shoulder. "Dad, I didn't mean to—"

He turned around, a smile spreading across his face. "She's alive," he said, and he wasn't crying at all. He was laughing. "Gina's *alive!*"

127

I grinned and nodded, and he grabbed me in a bear hug. We clung to each other, laughing like a couple of idiots until Dad suddenly stiffened, pulling away. The corners of his mouth quirked downward, and as his eyes darted everywhere but to me, I realized he had gotten caught up in the moment, and all was far from forgiven. I swallowed the lump in my throat and took a couple of steps backwards, giving him some space.

"I thought it would be a good idea to catch a little sleep before we move on," I said, changing the subject. "I'm pretty much dead on my feet, and I think we should both be sharp for tomorrow, don't you?"

I was afraid he'd offer to drive, and there was simply no way I'd be able to sleep while worrying about him slipping into another of his fugue states while behind the wheel. I was relieved when he yawned and nodded. Once we were back inside the car, I decided to press my luck before I lost my nerve.

"Dad? Now don't get mad or anything, but don't you think that after what—you know, *happened* back there, maybe I should carry the gun?" I asked, and for a second, I thought he was going to become obstinate and refuse, proclaiming his complete competence. Again, he surprised me with a brief nod before fishing the gun from his pocket and handing it over.

Having managed to satisfactorily assuage my immediate concerns, I nestled into my seat where a deep, dreamless sleep was patiently waiting.

······•••••◉⊖⊙●•••••···

The morning sun served quite nicely as an alarm, gently pulling us both from sleep shortly after seven. I was appalled to see how much gas we had used by simply idling.

"Shi-i-oot," I muttered, remembering Dad's aversion to the 'top tier' swear words and deflecting at the last second. For reasons beyond my comprehension, 'hell' and 'damn' were perfectly fine, but anything above and beyond was crass and entirely unnecessary, and Mom pretty much agreed. They were all just words to me. Thinking about it, I'm not really sure *where* I got my mouth.

"Something wrong?" asked Dad, adjusting his seat back into its upright position.

"Nothing critical," I said. "But I think we better backtrack before we head out and fuel back up. Our options are gonna get a little few and far between if we stick to secondary routes, which feels like the smart thing to do."

"Agreed."

According to the temperature gauge, the car was running a little hotter than before, but I kept that to myself. I hoped it would cool back down once we started moving again, and I didn't want to cause Dad any unnecessary stress. I ground through all the gears on my way to reverse, slowly easing us out of our hidey hole and wincing as the underbody scraped pavement when I pulled back onto the highway.

Dad exhaled loudly. "I see you *still* haven't—"

"Yeah, yeah, yeah," I interrupted. "I know. I still haven't learned how to drive a stick."

His chuckle was a short, sharp bark, and we lapsed into silence that was only slightly more comfortable than before.

"Dad?"

"Yes, son?"

"Are we—" My tongue stuck to the roof of my mouth, and I had to clear my throat. "Are we—you know, are we okay?"

He looked at me sideways as he bit into a cheese Danish I had picked up for him while refueling. He took his time chewing before washing it down with a sip from his coffee. "Why wouldn't we be?"

I stared at the road ahead while wondering the best way to ask for absolution. We had resumed our meandering course toward Briarwood underneath a bright, sunny sky that practically seemed to encourage me to try and clear the air. I honestly *did* feel awful about keeping Gina's secret for all of these months, but in my defense, it was a horrible position to be in, and I wouldn't have wished it upon anybody else. If only it were as easy to discuss these sorts of things with Dad as it was with Mom. I didn't want to anger him all over again, but the guilt was steadily gnawing away at my gut.

"I hope you know that I would never intentionally do something to hurt you and Mom," I said, keeping my eyes on the road.

"I'd like to believe that's true," Dad said evenly, taking another bite of pastry.

"You *can* believe it, Dad. I honestly thought I was doing the right thing."

His nod was so vague, I nearly missed it.

I sighed. I wasn't sure what else I could say without drawing his ire. My decision to keep Gina's fate to myself wasn't one I made lightly, nor was it because I had promised her that I would. It was her reason for swearing me to secrecy that ensured my compliance. How could I make Dad understand that I was only trying to protect him and Mom, Matt and Sheila—their newborn granddaughter, Abbie? Sure, I could tell him that if I had it to do all over again, I would have done things differently, but that would be a lie, and I wasn't about to compound what he considered a lie of omission with the real thing. As much as I hated to admit it, there was no guarantee that we would even *find* Gina, much less safe and sound if we ever even reached the end of this rainbow we were chasing. He was resigned to needing my help, but if this story didn't have a happy ending, the blame would forever lie at my feet, disappointment forever reflected in my father's eyes—provided he should ever deign to look at me again. It was exceedingly difficult to be in such close proximity with something of this magnitude hanging between us but forcing him to discuss it when he wasn't ready was only asking for trouble.

I didn't have the right words anyway, so for the moment, I let it go.

····•••••◦◦••••••····

The next two hours felt like twenty, the rumble of the Monza's exhaust our only source of entertainment. I made a cursory scan of the car's AM radio band—its only option—but talk radio and religious programming reigned supreme, and even awkward silence was preferable to *that*. I started to switch it off before deciding it would be a good idea to at least stick around for the news stories at the top of the hour. I wanted to see if there was any mention of our deceased friend back at the Sleepytime Motel or perhaps a father and son who were on the lam and were currently being sought for questioning in same. It was a story that had yet to break.

More than likely, it was being suppressed.

It was a little after ten, and the sun had risen high enough that I no longer needed to use the visor to keep from being blinded. The car's temperature had stabilized, but it still had a tendency to creep upwards when the engine labored, and as we navigated the footholds of the Allegheny Mountains, it was often enough to notice. We were on the last leg of instructions I had jotted onto the Cheez-Its box, leaving the highway behind and traversing a two-lane ribbon of road that wound through foliage that was only beginning to thin, so it wouldn't be long before we reached our destination. With every mile that passed, I grew a little more uneasy. It was a different perspective approaching from the south, and with every bend in the road, I expected Briarstaff to loom large before us like a predator lying in wait. I could feel perspiration collecting in my armpits and dampening my shoulders, bracing for a jump scare I knew was inevitable.

One more bend, and I gasped, slamming on the brakes and throwing Dad into his seatbelt. Thank goodness it caught him, and thank goodness there was no one behind us; we would have been rear-ended for sure.

To our right, an eleven-foot fence stretched on for miles save for an open gate hanging askew on busted hinges. A squat, cinderblock bunker stood like an abandoned dugout with its own door open wide, its interior dark, its walls almost completely covered in brightly painted graffiti that was as artistic as it was obscene. A narrow ribbon of pavement meandered through the gate and continued through overgrown grounds, and the burnt-out husk of a once-grand three-story building loomed far in the distance. A couple of 'No Trespassing' signs were posted near the gate but based on the number of bullet holes riddling their sheet metal, they weren't much of a deterrent.

"What is it, son?" Dad asked, alarmed by his near miss with the windshield.

"The Academy," I said, my voice flat. I had never been this close to its campus before, but there was no mistaking it from Gina's description. My feet were numb as I eased up on the clutch and pulled the car off the road and onto the wide berm near the bunker, switching the engine off and setting the parking brake. "I need a minute."

I got out of the car and wandered toward the open gate, feeling like I had stepped into a dream. I could almost imagine the facility as Gina had seen it during her brief visit, the ghosts of young recruits engaged in regimented training exercises on the campus grounds while others were brainwashed in classroom settings by misguided individuals like Michael Arthur, all of it contained behind the secured perimeter of a gate monitored by an armed guard. I peered inside the darkened bunker to find a collection of crumpled beer cans, cigarette butts, and other refuse suggesting local teens had found themselves a new place to party on weekends. The interior walls had been subjected to as much inventive vandalism as the exterior.

"Are we going inside?"

Dad was right behind me, and I nearly jumped out of my skin. *"Dad!* You've got to stop *doing* that!"

"Sorry," he said. "I thought you heard me get out of the car. You're shaking. Are you alright?"

I was startled to find that he was correct. My reaction to this place was visceral, and I took a deep breath to calm my racing pulse. "I'm fine."

"So, we're close, then," he said.

I nodded. "Maybe just a few miles more."

He shielded his eyes from the bright sunlight and scanned the grounds. "Aren't you worried this place might still be under some sort of surveillance?"

"No," I said. "The rats who didn't drown have already abandoned this sinking ship."

"Then why are you so afraid? I'm not going to let anything happen to you. We'll just go down there together, maybe shake a few trees to see what falls out—"

"No," I said sharply, and Dad took a step back.

"Well, then, why are we even here?"

"Because it's the only thread I know to chase," I said. "Believe me, I don't want to be here, and it's not like I think we're just going to find Gina somewhere in Briarstaff. This is the *last* place she'd be, I'm sure."

"So, what's the plan? Isn't there some sort of investigative roadmap that you follow when you're trying to locate a missing person?"

I laughed. "'Investigative roadmap?' I work for *Doug Boggs*, Dad. Exactly how intensive do you think my training has been? I'm literally just making this stuff up as I go."

"Okay," said Dad, slowly nodding. "Still, you must have *some* sort of plan."

"The plan is to get in and out of town just as quickly as possible," I said. "I want to see if Delphine Bartlett might be able to offer a little guidance."

"Delphine Bartlett? Isn't she that woman you claimed could see into the future under the guise of Madame Anaphylaxis?"

There was no mistaking the condescension in Dad's voice, and frankly, it irritated me. "Madame *Phalange*. And this is coming from the man who has literally been following his dreams? You might want to cut the lady a little slack, Dad. I know a lot of what she does is for show, but she was pretty darned specific about things she had no way of knowing, and while I may not be one hundred percent sold on her supposed gift, I can't entirely discount it, either. I can't see how talking to her could hurt, provided she's even willing to see us. My face will probably just upset her, reminding her of things she's trying to forget. Like I told you before, her oldest daughter was a victim of everything that went down last July. I'm hoping she'll be empathetic to your position, parent to parent."

"*Pfft*," he said dismissively. "And I'm supposed to what—let her read my palm or something?"

"Yes, if she wants to. She might want to read your cards—I really don't know. Whatever she comes up with, we should just roll with it. She's a little eccentric, but the last thing I would ever want to do is insult her."

"I still don't see how it could hurt to ask around," Dad persisted. "Didn't you just say that all of the bad guys were gone?"

"You just don't get it, Dad," I said, beginning to regret that I had ever mentioned this place. "I mean, yeah, the worst of the worst were rounded up and taken into custody, but some of the town elders had insulated themselves from culpability well enough that they're still out there, thoroughly pissed off that I managed to disrupt the iron-fisted control they've had over this town and its people for *decades*. I'm not a popular guy in these parts, and you better believe our presence will not be even remotely welcome. Lying low is really our only option."

He considered my words before finally nodding. "Fine. We'll do this your way. But if that Phalange woman starts speaking in tongues, I'm going to have one hell of a time holding my own."

CHAPTER ELEVEN

The door opened, and it was difficult to suppress my shock. Delphine Bartlett was a shadow of the woman who had glided across the town square in a rainbow blur of flowing silk and jangling bangles. Her gaunt face was pinched beneath slicked-back hair that was significantly grayer than before, and she looked as though she had dropped at least twenty pounds, none of which she could afford to lose. Gone were the festive colors and the hint of mischief that caused her eyes to sparkle. She wore an oversized, plain t-shirt over faded, ill-fitting jeans. Her shirt was damp in its lower left quadrant from a stain that looked like coffee but reminded me of something else entirely. My mouth ran dry at the memory of Hattie Bartlett stumbling toward me, her pale-yellow top rapidly turning scarlet as confusion clouded her eyes. I pushed the thought away before my throat could close entirely.

"Hi, Del," I finally managed, my smile more of a wince.

"Oh, hi," she said tonelessly. "Come on in. I've been expecting you."

I shot Dad a knowing glance before following Del into her darkened living room. Heavy drapes covered the front windows and none of the table lamps were on, steeping the room in a pervasive gloom that seemed to emanate from its owner's broken spirit. She cleared a couple of piles of unopened mail from the sofa before taking a seat in its matching recliner. Dad and I settled side-by-side on the sofa, waiting for our eyes to adjust.

"Who's this you've brought with you?" asked Del, drawing a smirk from Dad.

"You mean you don't already know?" he asked snidely.

"Dad!" I snapped.

"He's your father?" Del sounded surprised. "I don't see the resemblance."

"The boy takes after his mother," said Dad.

"Hmm. I suppose he must," she said, assessing Dad with a slight frown. "He certainly has more hair, doesn't he?"

Dad's smirk dropped like a stone, and I couldn't help but laugh, a sound that felt foreign within these four walls. On the mantel above the fireplace, a picture of Hattie sitting on her bicycle caught my eye, clotheslining the laughter in my throat.

"You didn't park in front of the house, did you?" asked Del. "It wouldn't be good for either one of us if Emmitt Brown were to catch sight of you."

The memory of the town elder's scowling face came unbidden, and I shook my head. "No. I parked around the corner, and we walked from there."

"Good, good," she said absently, and I wondered if she might be on some sort of antidepressant. I couldn't detect any trace of the vibrance she had nearly radiated when we had met the previous summer. Her expression remained distressingly blank, and I realized it would be up to me to carry the conversation.

"I was actually hoping we might have a word with Madame Phalange," I ventured, and at least that earned the hint of a smile.

"Ah, Madame Phalange," she said wistfully. "I'm sorry, dear, but the spirits have been quiet for some time now. Ever since—" Her voice trailed away, but I could finish the thought on my own.

Ever since Hattie died.

"But you said you were expecting us," I said, curious about her cryptic greeting.

Her gaze swept from me to Dad and back again. "Well—I was expecting you. Not necessarily this one." She swept an arthritic hand dismissively in Dad's general direction. "I still get whispers here and there, but I have such a hard time concentrating. You have unfinished business here. It was inevitable that you would return."

I was less certain. "I only just decided to come back last night. No offense, but Briarstaff is the *last* place I want to be."

"None taken," she said. "It's the last place I want to be, too, but I can't bring myself to leave this house. I swear there are times I can hear her in the next room singing. She was always singing." A kaleidoscope of emotions crossed her face before evaporating in an instant. "I'm afraid I haven't been able to rely on my gift anymore. I haven't done a single reading in all of these months. I don't see how I can help you."

Dad cleared his throat and sat forward, clasping his hands in front of himself. "Miss—um, Phalange—? I want to apologize for my earlier comment. I didn't mean to be rude, but I don't know what to make of—"

"All this psychic mumbo-jumbo," she finished for him, scowling. "Yes, Mr. Morrow. I know your type. If you can't lay hands on it or explain it with logic, it must be some sort of trickery designed to separate you from your hard-earned dollar. I'll admit, there are plenty of charlatans out there making it harder for honest folks like me to share our special gift, and yes, there is a certain amount of showmanship that is expected when doing a reading, but it isn't like I'm over here speaking in tongues or something."

Dad's startled look was priceless. Just like that, Del had managed to put a chink in his disbelief, and it was more than a little vindicating.

"Let me try that again," said Dad, smiling apologetically. "I'm sorry for offending you. That was never my intention, but I'm really out of my element here. As it turns out, we have more than a little in common, and I hoped you might be willing to listen to what I have to say before shutting me down completely. I mean, we both understand what it's like to lose a child, and believe me, I'm so sorry about your Hattie. I didn't have the privilege of meeting her, but Dwayne told me how special she was."

I held my breath, waiting to see how Del would react to Dad's approach, which was sincere but more direct. My foot would have been in my mouth ten times trying to get that out, and I never once would have been able to meet her eye.

"Thank you," she said. "Yes, she was. But I'm a bit confused. You've lost a child, too?"

Ah, shit.

Even though I believed it myself at the time, I had never told any of the locals that Gina was presumed dead. I had pretended to be there to get additional pictures from the Apple Festival to supposedly supplement the article that Gina was writing when she had been in Briarstaff a couple of weeks earlier.

"Um, yeah," I said sheepishly. "I'm really sorry about the confusion, but I sort of misled everybody when I was here before. I didn't have any idea who to trust. He's talking about Gina. I was in town trying to find out what happened to her after her funeral, not to get photos for her story."

She stared at me for a long moment, processing my words. Her expression barely shifted, and it was impossible to tell if she was upset by my deceit. Slowly, she began to nod before turning to Dad.

"I see. So, what did you come here to say, Mr. Morrow?"

"Please—it's Todd," Dad said, looking at her earnestly. "I seem to have a little something wrong with my brain that doctors are having some difficulty quantifying. There's a cloud on my cerebral cortex, but we're still waiting for an actual diagnosis. In the meanwhile, I've been experiencing side effects that are growing more frequent over time, and one of the most persistent is my dreams. I'm not the sort of guy who typically remembers his dreams at all. With very little exception, they dissipate as soon as my alarm clock goes off, but these dreams are different. Not only do I remember them, but they are more vivid than any dreams I've ever had. I can smell what I was smelling, taste what I was tasting—it's such a tactile experience that I'm frequently disappointed when I wake up, if that makes any sense at all."

Del's nod was nearly imperceptible. "You're dreaming about your daughter." It wasn't a question.

"Yes," said Dad. "And in my dreams, she's alive. Look, I know this sounds ridiculous—a parent's last desperate grasp for a highly improbable straw, but I know she's out there. I can *feel* her."

Del remained stoic. "I dream about my Hattie, and I can feel her, too. It doesn't mean she's ever coming back."

"It's more than that," I said, leaning in. "I saw Gina. I spoke to her. She was in the ambulance that took me away from here. I don't know where she is now, but I know she didn't die in the accident that supposedly took her life."

From the expression on Del's face, I may as well have slapped her. She looked at Dad in disbelief. She was finally feeling something, and it only took a second to realize that it was anger. "So, I guess that's one less thing that we have in common, Mr. Morrow. My daughter is dead. Did you come here to *gloat?*"

"*No!*" insisted Dad, tossing me a dirty look. "My entire family has been grieving Gina's loss for nearly a year, and this guy here is the only one who knew the truth. I only just found out last night." He jerked a thumb in my direction, drawing Del's ire toward me.

"You *knew?* You *knew* she was alive, and you let your parents languish in misery?"

All eyes were on me, and I squirmed uncomfortably. "She made me promise not to tell," I said, cringing at the whiny sound of my own voice.

140

"The folks behind The Academy were threatening all of us if she didn't back off, and she thought faking her death was the only way to keep us safe." I turned to Dad. "I didn't even tell Melanie for the longest time, and it almost destroyed us."

Dad inhaled sharply as his indignation grew. "You told *Melanie*, but you didn't tell *us?*"

Of course, *that* would be his only takeaway from what I was trying to convey.

I kept my focus on Dad despite the heat of his glare. I wasn't happy that I had upset Del, but this was the man who taught me right from wrong. I needed him to understand that I had taken those lessons to heart, even if my good intentions frequently got lost in translation.

"Look, I'm not going sit here and litigate this. Good decision? Bad decision? It doesn't really matter at this point, does it? What's done is done, and if we've got any shot at all in finding Gina and bringing her home, we're going to have to work together."

"So, why now?" asked Del, her eyes boring holes through me. "What makes you think it's safe to poke at this monstrous beast that has already taken so much from all of us?"

"Things have changed," I said. "Gina could connect three powerful senators to The Academy, and two of them have died."

Del scoffed. "And that still leaves one behind. In my experience, one person is more than enough to inflict everlasting damage, wouldn't you agree?"

It wasn't something I could dispute. I simply nodded.

"So, exactly what is it you're asking me to do here?" asked Del.

"I was hoping for a reading," I said. "My last contact with Gina was inside an ambulance that was taking me away from here to a hospital. I have absolutely no idea where to start looking, and I hoped you might be able to point me in the right direction."

"I already told you I'm not doing those anymore," she said, staring at her hands.

"Can't you make an exception—just this once?" I asked.

"I don't see the point," she said. "I never could force it, and it feels like my gift has abandoned me."

I sighed. "*Del.* I'm going to be perfectly honest with you. When I met you last July, I thought you were a fake. Fun, but a fake. I thought this whole fortune-telling thing was just a bit you trotted out to make a little extra money during the Apple Festival. The things you told me that night completely set me on my ass. You knew things you couldn't have possibly known. You made a believer out of me that night, and that's why we're here. I don't know where else to go. Won't you at least *try?*"

Her lips moved soundlessly as she mulled over my request. Finally, she pushed herself out of her chair. "*Fine.* Give me a few minutes to get myself set up, but I'm telling you, this is probably just a big waste of time."

We gathered around the small Formica table that was pushed up against the back wall of the avocado green kitchen. It felt even smaller than the last time I'd been here, and I sat in the same space I had occupied while eating the messiest peanut butter and jelly sandwich ever made. My heart clenched again at the memory of Hattie's sweet face, her tongue firmly wedged in the corner of her mouth as she had diligently prepared the monstrosity for me, pleased with her handiwork.

Del sat to my left, shuffling a deck of tarot cards she had already dealt twice. Both times, she had aborted reading them midway through the process, muttering to herself before starting all over again. Her dusty crystal ball stared vacantly at us from the center of the table, devoid of any of the inner luminescence I remembered from my previous reading. It looked every bit as empty and defeated as Del, who hadn't bothered with the whole "Madame Phalange" persona, although she had put a pot of potpourri on the stove to set a mood. It smelled like a mixture of cloves, patchouli oil, sodden earth, and feet, and I wasn't entirely sure what mood she was aiming for.

Dad sat across from me, looking about as uncomfortable as I'd ever seen him, but thankfully, he kept whatever thoughts were going through his head to himself.

Del began placing her cards into five neat stacks, taking a deep breath once she had placed the final one. She grimaced as she began flipping cards, offering none of the narrative that had accompanied my first reading while shielding the cards from us as if they were a poker hand. This wasn't nearly the spectacle I had witnessed before, and I got the distinct feeling she was only humoring us so we would leave her to her misery.

I was so focused on Del's reading that I nearly jumped out of my seat when her tuxedoed housecat landed in my lap, seemingly from out of nowhere. She looked at me and peeped, a rumble already ramping up in her throat. I absently stroked the soft fur between her shoulder blades.

That's Kinsey. She don't bite.

Hattie's voice whispered in my ear, and the vacuum of her loss was like a black hole, swallowing everything inside these four walls. It more than explained Del's current state of despair. I was already itching to get out of there, but she had nowhere else to go. I wasn't entirely surprised when she finally swept the cards to the floor in disgust.

"It's no use," she said, cupping her head in her hands. "The voices are gone. They've abandoned me like everything else."

She began sobbing in earnest while Dad and I looked at each other helplessly. I certainly hadn't meant to cause this sort of distress. Behind me, a door opened and closed in the small mud room off the kitchen, startling me and sending Kinsey off to investigate.

"Mama?"

Del's youngest daughter, Joy Beth, bustled into the room carrying a towheaded toddler in her sinewy arms. She eased him to the floor and leaned down to pull her mother into her arms, gently rocking and shushing her, while her son stared at his grandmother with a finger in his mouth. Only then did Joy Beth seem to realize that we were even there, and she nodded and smiled at me without missing a beat.

"It'll be okay, Mama," she said, cupping her mother's chin with one hand while dabbing at her tears with the other. "Did you take your pills this morning?"

"Pish!" Del groused. "Those pills don't do anything."

"Well, they surely don't if you don't take them, Mama," reasoned Joy Beth. "You have to take them every day for them to level out your ups and downs. Dr. Swanson told you so."

Dr. Swanson. It would seem the town had found itself a new family doctor after Dr. Morris retired.

"Gamby?"

The little boy was apprehensive, approaching his grandmother with big wide eyes that threatened to spill tears, and that seemed to be all the tonic Del needed to pull herself out of her funk. She sat forward, wiping her eyes, the first hint of a smile gracing her face.

"Oh, my little guy," she said, boosting him into her lap and giving him a big hug. "Gamby is just fine now that her little man is home." She sniffed the air and scowled. *"Ooo!* I think someone's had a little accident."

The boy grinned impishly, admitting to nothing as his finger returned to his mouth. Del set him back on his feet while fanning the air beneath her nose exaggeratedly.

"Mama, why don't you take JJ to his room and get him cleaned up?" suggested Joy Beth, shooting me another grin. "I'll get your medicine and have it all ready when you get back."

"Of course!" said Del, reaching for her grandson who promptly squealed and ran into the living room. Del's smile widened as she got to her feet, prepared to give chase. "Now, you come here, you little monster, you!"

Another squeal from the living room and Del was off in hot pursuit, the most lively I'd seen her since we had arrived. Frankly, it was a relief. I stood as Joy Beth turned her focus to me.

"Dwayne Morrow!" she said, hugging me while I squirmed awkwardly. I was happy to see her again, but I was never very good at the touchy-feely stuff. "I never thought I'd see *you* here again!"

I grinned at her. "Honestly? I never thought I'd be back. This is my dad, Todd Morrow. Dad? Joy Beth Perkins. She's Del's other daughter." I winced as the last two words escaped my lips, unnecessarily drawing attention to the ever-present ghost in the room. If Joy Beth noticed, it rolled right off of her.

"Ms. Perkins," Dad said, standing to offer his hand to Joy Beth.

"Oh, please," she said, her cheeks brightening as she took his hand. "It's Joy Beth. Pleasure to meet you, Mr. Morrow."

"The pleasure's all mine, but let's go with Todd, alright? 'Mr. Morrow' just sounds so *old*."

She nodded, first noticing the tarot cards scattered about the kitchen floor and then the darkened crystal ball in the middle of the table. She began picking up the cards from the linoleum floor, and Dad stooped to collect the cards that had landed behind his chair. I would have joined in, but the kitchen was too small, and I would have only been in the way.

Dad handed her a small stack of cards to add to the pile in her hands, and Joy Beth smiled crookedly at me as she squared the deck. "I was going to ask what brought you back, but I guess I see. Huh. Impressive."

"How so?" I asked, as the three of us sat down, Joy Beth taking her mother's empty seat at the table and placing the tarot cards beside the crystal ball.

"Mama hasn't touched any of this stuff since—well, you know," said Joy Beth, the shadow of a cloud flitting across her face. "I can't believe you managed to get her to pull all of this out of her closet. You must have been pretty persuasive with your reasons."

Dad and I exchanged a glance, wondering how much detail I should go into as to why we were sitting at her mother's kitchen table. I stalled for time to contemplate.

"So, you're calling you little boy JJ?" I asked. "That's new."

She shrugged. "'James, Jr.' is such a mouthful, and I really don't want all the other kids calling him 'Little Jimmy' either. It would just be setting him up to get teased. You know how cruel kids can be."

Amen to that. She didn't need to add that removing her abusive ex-husband's name from daily utterance was an understandable blessing.

"So, how have *you* been?" I asked, still filling the air with the sort of inane banter that came far easier than the truth.

Joy Beth brightened. "Good! Really good. Well—*mostly* good." Her eyes flitted toward the living room. "Mama's still having a really rough time, but of course she is. She figured Hattie would always be right here until the day she died, not the other way around. It helps that me and JJ have moved back in. He seems to be the only one who can truly lift her spirits."

"That makes perfect sense," I said, nodding. "He's really adorable."

She beamed. "Thank you. We certainly think so. You wouldn't believe how he's taken to Shane! It's so nice to have a positive male role model for a change." She referred to one of the teens who had tried their darnedest to get me out of that town when everything started to go downhill. They were good kids, all of them.

"That's terrific," I said. "What's Shane been up to?"

Joy Beth glanced at a wall clock that was shaped like an oversized apple. "Right about now, he's heading into Advanced Math." Her feelings about him were transparent; she was practically aglow. "You're never gonna believe this, but he asked me to go to prom with him. Isn't that nuts? I can't go to *prom!* I'm twenty years old!"

"Doesn't the school allow it?" I asked. My own school back in Lymont had some pretty restrictive policies setting its age limit for prom attendees to eighteen while most of the other schools in the area allowed up to twenty-one.

"Oh, sure, but I don't know. I mean, Shane's eighteen now, but I wouldn't want everyone to think I'm some sort of cradle robber or something. Still, I never went to my own. They don't exactly make prom dresses in maternity sizes. I have to admit, I'm a little curious."

"Pfft," Dad interjected with his favorite exclamation. "There's ten years between me and my Jo. Nobody's going to think you're robbing cradles."

"I don't know. We'll see," she said, but it was pretty clear from the look on her face that she wanted to go. "So enough about me. Are you ever going to tell me what you were wanting Mama to help you with? I'm guessing from the mess she left, it didn't go the way you'd hoped."

"No, it didn't," I said, sighing. "Listen, Joy Beth, I have to fess up about something. When I was here last July, it wasn't to get pictures for my sister's story on the Apple Festival."

Her smile faltered as she raised an eyebrow. "It wasn't?"

"No. I was here because my sister had supposedly died in a suspicious automobile accident right after my brother's wedding. I was trying to find out what happened to her."

"Oh, my goodness! I'm so sorry!" she said. "Well, you sure shook things up around here, and I, for one, am glad. Didn't you get your answers before you left?"

"Yes and no," I said, looking at my fidgety hands. "I—uh—I actually found out she wasn't really dead, but *please.* I need you to keep that to yourself."

"But why?" she asked, confused.

"She's gone into hiding," I said. "Gina is the only witness who can connect some powerful senators to everything that was going on at The Academy, and it isn't safe for her whereabouts to be known, not even by us. *Especially* not us."

"Okay, so why are you trying to find her now?" asked Joy Beth.

"Two of those senators have died, and my father's been having visions of his own in his dreams. He's not like your mama. This is a whole new experience for him. For reasons I'd rather not go into again, he didn't know Gina was still alive—"

I tried to ignore the sharp look Dad sent across the table.

"—but his visions have been eerily accurate. It feels like we have a chance to bring her home, if we can just find her," I said. "But Briarstaff is where the trail runs cold. We were hoping Del might be able to help us."

"Oh, I'm sorry," said Joy Beth. "But like I said, Mama hasn't really been able to see things for quite a while now. So, who are these powerful senators you mentioned?"

Dad opened his mouth to answer, but I nudged him gently under the table with my foot, shaking my head.

"I really can't say," I said. "The less you know, the better. Ironically, none of them were from West Virginia."

"Well, it's not like The Academy was exclusive to West Virginia," she said, instantly grabbing my attention.

"What do you mean?" I asked.

"You remember my ex, Jimmy, worked at The Academy as a custodian, right?"

I nodded.

"When he was first hired, he was sent away for six weeks of basic training to some little piddly town over in Pennsylvania—the name's right on the tip of my tongue," she said, her face squirreling up as she pursued the memory. "Anyways, I always thought it was a little odd that he would be required to take basic training just to work as a custodian, but what do I know? I would assume that wherever he went would have to be connected to—ooh! Templar! That's it. Templar, Pennsylvania."

Just then, Del bustled back into the kitchen with little JJ on her hip. Tending to her grandson had restored her composure. "I'm really sorry I couldn't help," she said, shrugging. "The voices are barely a whisper these days, and the only thing even close to a word was 'Nancy.'"

Dad's gasp was barely noticeable over the rapid burst of knocking that erupted at Del's front door.

CHAPTER TWELVE

"Were you expecting company?" I asked, the tiny hairs on my neck prickling as I stiffened in my seat.

"No. Folks around here aren't prone to just drop by," said Del, setting her grandson down only to have him bolt toward the front door. "Hold up there, JJ! Let Gamby answer that." She hurried after the toddler while Dad and I stared at one another, still a little stunned.

Nancy.

It couldn't possibly be coincidence.

"Is everything alright?" asked Joy Beth pensively, and I held up a finger to silence her. Del was already opening the front door, and it felt prudent to listen.

"Lydia."

Del sounded less than pleased, and Joy Beth's nose crinkled like she'd smelled something foul. She leaned in and whispered conspiratorially, "Lydia Pruitt. One of the biggest busybodies in town. I'm sure you remember her brother, Tommy. He was part of that lynch mob you kept from burning down Trevor Anderson's house."

I remembered it all too well. Tommy was also the grandson of Emmitt Brown, Briarstaff's eldest elder, which would make Lydia his granddaughter. I wondered if evil was hereditary.

"Hi, Del," said Lydia, her high-pitched, nasally voice full of false cheer. The acoustics were good, and her voice carried clearly through the house, along with JJ's persistent jabbering. "Pauline thought she saw a couple of strange men on your porch a little while ago. Is everything alright over here?"

Del's heavy sigh was audible even from this distance. "Pauline should be paying more attention to the hair she's styling, not what's going on outside her plate glass window. The fumes must be getting to her. I don't know what you're talking about."

"Oh—I see," said Lydia, momentarily thrown, but it didn't take long for her to regroup. "Well, aren't you going to invite me in?"

Another heavy sigh escaped Del's lips.

"I don't think so, Lydia. I was just about to put JJ down for his nap, so if you'll excuse—"

"At *10:30?* Isn't that a bit early for a nap?"

Lydia's persistence was incredibly grating, and just when I thought Del was really going to let her have it, the unthinkable happened. Just as plain as day, JJ said, "Morrow."

Shit.

The silence was deafening.

Dad looked at me, and I nodded toward the mud room and its rear entrance to the house. I leaned in toward Joy Beth and whispered, "Give us just a minute or so to clear the back yard, and then invite Lydia in. Show her that there's no one else here."

Joy Beth nodded, whispering, "I wish we could have helped."

I smiled, getting out of my seat as Dad tiptoed across the room to join me, avoiding the archway that led to the living room. "Maybe you have," I whispered. "You gave us someplace else to go."

I waved goodbye as we crossed into the mud room, carefully avoiding the clutter that lined its periphery and letting ourselves out through the back door.

···•••••⊖⊙•••••···

If Pauline Dixon had sent Lydia Pruitt over to investigate, it was only a matter of time before she had the entire neighborhood watch on alert. Fortunately, we hadn't encountered any prying eyes as we fled through Del's fenced-in backyard and hustled down the alley toward the side street where I had parked the Monza. We rode in silence as I focused on backtracking through the neighborhood, careful to avoid the town square. Once we managed to work our way down to Route 5, I headed west and out of that godforsaken town.

"She said, 'Nancy,'" Dad muttered absently, pulling me from my thoughts.

"I told you," I said, feeling even more vindication for my belief in the self-proclaimed psychic. It wasn't what we had come to hear, but it was jolting, nonetheless.

"But what did she mean? What in the world could Nancy have to do with any of this? I haven't seen the woman in almost forty years."

"I'm sure it's nothing," I said, sounding more certain than I actually was. "She was probably just picking up on whatever's been going on inside of your head. I don't know how these things work, and I guess it doesn't really matter. It's what Joy Beth said that caught my attention. It's the first real lead I've had on another Academy facility."

"I thought you said you hadn't been pursuing this."

"I wasn't," I said. "But apparently, now we are. Briarstaff was the only place I knew to start, at least until now."

"So, we're headed off to Templar, Pennsylvania?"

I glanced at him sideways. "Do you have any better ideas?"

He shrugged. "Maybe lunch. I'm getting a bit hungry. You?"

"I could eat," I said. "In about thirty miles, there's this little town called Shawnee. They have cell service, and it would give me a chance to plot a course. It would also give me time to touch base with Melanie and Mom, although I'm a little reluctant to call them."

"I thought that was why you bought that burner phone?"

"It is, but that doesn't mean that their phones aren't being monitored. I hadn't really given it much thought, but after what happened at the motel last night, it feels like a frightening possibility. Speaking of which—" I reached down to switch the radio on. "See if you can find the local news. It's probably a good idea to know whether we're fugitives before we put in any public appearances."

The big news was a bad accident involving a school bus and a semi-truck on I-64, but nothing about a man found dead outside a motel, and it only served to reinforce my belief that whoever had sent our assassin was somehow containing the situation. It was more than a little unsettling to realize exactly how much news can be suppressed by those in power. Their resources were seemingly unlimited and completely unpredictable, and it cast a shadow of paranoia over every single move we made. Mercifully, traffic on Route 5 was light, and we didn't seem to have anyone tailing us as we arrived in Shawnee.

I was having a serious case of déjà vu as we pulled into the little strip mall off to our left.

The last time I had been here was with Michael Arthur—I've since learned his real name is Duncan Moore, but that isn't the name I'm accustomed to using. I stared at the ATM mounted into the cinderblock wall near the entrance to Foodland. It had declined my card, and I never once suspected it had been Michael who had sabotaged both its chip and the magnetic strip on its back, giving him the opportunity to loan me cash for the duration of our stay and further ingratiate himself to me. At the far end was Shoe World, but large signs proclaiming, 'GOING OUT OF BUSINESS – 50% OFF EVERYTHING!' covered most of the storefront windows, indicating it wouldn't be anchoring the mall for very much longer. Only a handful of cars were parked in the lot, and I opted for the row farthest from the highway, tucking in between a shiny black heavy-duty Ford truck on obnoxiously oversized wheels and its great-granddaddy, an ancient Ford F-100 whose prevalent color was gleaned from the rust that held it together.

"What are you in the mood for? I've had the brisket from the Barbeque Palace, and it was pretty good," I said, as we got out of the car and eyed our choices.

He frowned, deliberating. "I think I'd rather have Italian. Says they serve Pepsi right there on the door. You okay with that?"

"Sure," I said, and we headed toward Little Italy's Secret Garden, a low-rent Olive Garden knockoff whose interior was obscured by red-and-white checkered curtains strung across its plate glass facade. Dad held the door for me, and I was assaulted by the heady scent of garlic and tomato sauce as soon as I passed through.

An elderly woman was seated behind the hostess stand thumbing through *The National Enquirer*. She placed the tabloid aside, turning it upside down to preserve her place as she got to her feet and greeted us with a weary smile. I was guessing she was the 'mom' of this mom-and-pop establishment. She carried the sort of innate condescension that wouldn't be tolerated from a mere employee. It was borne of ownership and fatigue.

"Just the two?"

"Yes, ma'am," I said, and she reached for a dry-erase marker tucked into the salt-and-pepper bun at the back of her head. She studied a laminated seating chart that only indicated a couple of other occupants, and as she started to place us at a table near the others, I cleared my throat. "Could we have one of the tables near the back, please?"

She didn't actually sigh, but the look she sent me spoke volumes. I simply returned her smile sweetly. "Whatever you say, honey, but the restrooms are back there, too. Hope that won't 'compromise your fine dining experience.'" She didn't even have to fly the air quotes for me to see them just as plain as day. "Follow me."

She grabbed a couple of menus and led us through a sea of mostly empty tables in the center of the restaurant. Booths lined the outer perimeter, and all of the table coverings matched the red-and-white checkered curtains that ensured an ambiance that would never be brighter than dusk. The only source of pallid light trickled down from wall sconces that were mounted between framed paintings of the Italian countryside, or at least I thought it was Italian. I honestly had no idea. Geography was never my thing. They were pretty, anyhow. She motioned to the booth in the center of the back wall, and true to her word, the restrooms were only fifteen feet to our left. Thankfully, the only thing that stank was our hostess's attitude.

"How's this?" she asked, and she didn't really give a shit. She hadn't even bothered to offer her name; she just wanted to get back to *The Enquirer*. She laid a menu down on each side of the table.

"It's fine, thank you," said Dad, sliding into the booth. I pulled the prepaid phone from my pocket before taking the seat across from him. We both slipped our jackets off and laid them in the space beside us.

"Jess will be out shortly to take your orders," she said, and she was already retreating to the front, bellowing, "*Jess!* Couple of big spenders in the back!"

"Wow," I said, picking up the menu and flipping it open. "I'd hate to see her in a *bad* mood."

Dad chuckled, picking up his own menu. "Mmm-hmm."

There were a surprising number of choices, but after waffling for a moment between the lasagna and the chicken parmigiana, I made my decision and set the menu aside, powering on the phone. "Whenever Jess comes, I'll take the chicken parm and a Pepsi. I'm going to start plotting our course and get the phone calls out of the way. I'm still not sure that it's a good idea to call anyone, but maybe if I keep it brief?"

Dad was still busy studying the menu, but he nodded. It wasn't exactly the reassurance I was hoping for. I pulled up Google Maps and searched for Templar, Pennsylvania, discovering its tiny little dot nestled in the north central portion of the state and surrounded on all sides by state parks and forests. It was ideal for any number of illicit enterprises that valued privacy above all else. I groaned. It was almost six hours from where we sat.

Dad looked at me over the top of his menu. "Trouble?"

"Not really. It's just a bit of drive," I said, trying to find a combination of interstates and backroads to get us there without driving straight through Pittsburgh. It was a little too convoluted to commit to memory, and I didn't have anything to write on. Or with. I sighed. "I'll be right back."

Dad nodded as I slid out of the booth and tentatively approached our gracious hostess, a benevolent smile plastered across my face. She had already seated herself behind the lectern and had returned her full attention to whatever scandalous article we had dared to pull her away from. She didn't even look up until I cleared my throat, and even then, she only gave me one eye.

"What now?" she asked.

"I don't suppose you might have a pen and a piece of paper I could borrow?" I asked.

One of her penciled eyebrows leapt to her hairline. "Are you planning to give it back?"

She didn't miss a beat.

"Well—the pen, anyway," I said, my smile turning sheepish.

She made a big show of putting her paper down and pulling herself to her feet, reaching into the bottom of the hostess stand to retrieve her rather sizable handbag. She began rooting through it, finally extracting a sanitary napkin and a crayon, which she offered me with a smirk.

"Best I can do," she said.

This woman *must* be related to Loretta Boggs.

"*Ummm*, thanks," I said, taking them gingerly with my fingertips before retreating to our table.

"I think I've decided on pizza," said Dad, closing his menu. "You sure you wouldn't rather split one with me?"

"Nah, I think I'll stick with the chicken parm," I said, unlocking the phone and preparing to transcribe directions as best as possible with the tools I had.

"You can have your choice of toppings on half."

"No, thanks."

Dad scowled. "I'll never be able to eat a whole pizza by myself."

"Dad."

"Fine, fine, fine. Chicken parm it is. I'm just sayin'. It's an awful lot of food is all."

"*Dad!*"

He held his hands up in surrender as I returned to the task at hand.

"What on earth are you writing on?" he asked, leaning across the table. "Is that what I think it is?"

I buried my face in my hands. "Yes, Dad. It's exactly what you think it is. Believe me, it isn't what I asked for. It makes me a little afraid of what we're going to get once we place our orders. Speaking of which, has Jess made an appearance?"

"Not yet."

"Not even for drinks?"

"No is a very small word, son. I should think you would be used to the sound of it by now." He scanned the room. "I haven't even seen her yet. All the other folks seem to already have their food."

I nearly jumped out of my skin when the prepaid phone rang. The number on the screen wasn't one that I recognized.

"Who is it?" asked Dad.

"I don't know."

"Aren't you going to answer it?"

I frowned. "I don't know."

Dad sighed and reached for the phone. "Here, I'll answer it."

"No!" I said, my voice a little louder than intended. I smiled at the elderly couple whose attention I had drawn. "I'm not even sure we *should* answer it. I mean, who could it be? Nobody has this number."

"Well, you're never going to find out that way," said Dad, snatching the phone right out of my hand and answering it mid-ring. "Hello?"

His face got very serious as he listened.

"Um, yes. He's right here. Hang on." He moved to hand the phone to me, and I recoiled like he was offering up a rattlesnake.

"Who is it?" I whispered.

He just thrust the phone forward, nodding for me to take it.

I put it pensively to my ear. "Hell-oooo?" I sounded a lot like Mrs. Doubtfire.

"Dwayne! I've been trying to call you for hours. I was beginning to get worried!"

"Mel?" I pulled the phone away and looked again at the number on the screen. "Where are you calling from? How did you get this number?"

"It was in my call history from when you called last night, and I thought it might be smart to pick up my own prepaid phone—you know. Just in case."

"Very smart," I said, smiling. Leave it to Melanie to solve my communications dilemma. "It sure is good to hear your voice."

"Likewise, mister. What's with the radio silence? My calls just went straight to a voicemail box that hasn't been set up."

"I've been keeping the prepaid phone turned off out of an abundance of caution."

"Are you alright?"

"I guess that depends on your idea of alright," I said.

I proceeded to give Melanie a condensed version of events since I had spoken to her the previous evening, including our current plans to head to Pennsylvania, which would likely entail another overnight stay somewhere. By the time I was finished, the silence was so complete, I thought the call had dropped.

"Are you still there?" I asked.

"Oh, I'm here, alright," she said. "I don't like this, Dwayne. I don't like this one bit."

"It's not exactly my idea of a good time, either, but what can I do? We've caught someone's attention, and we're just going to have to see it through," I said. "Besides, this might be the chance I've been waiting for to—you know. Resolve things once and for all." I didn't have to tell her I was talking about Gina.

"You've got your gun with you, right?"

I chewed on my bottom lip. *"We-e-e-ll—"*

"Dwayne! I thought we had come to an understanding about that! What good does a gun do you if it's always locked in your nightstand drawer?"

"It wasn't like this started out as a case or something," I said. "I thought I was just taking Dad back home to Lymont. How was I to know that things were going to go completely off the rails?"

"Because they always do," she countered, clearly irritated. She wasn't wrong.

"Well, you can relax," I said. "As it turns out, we are not unarmed. Dad brought his little peashooter with him."

"Oh, my," said Melanie. "I'm not sure *that's* a good idea, what with all of his cognitive issues and all."

"And that's one thing we've actually been able to agree on," I said, eyeing the slight bulge in my jacket pocket where the gun lay. "It's safely in my possession."

"Well, thank God for that," she said.

"Do you think you could call Mom for me?" I asked.

She groaned. "Do I have to? That woman hates me."

"She doesn't hate you," I said. Knowing I'd never change Melanie's mind on that particular issue, I plodded ahead. "Tell her Dad and I decided to go—oh, I don't know—hunting or something."

Melanie and Dad laughed in surround sound at my ludicrous suggestion.

"Okay, fine," I said. "Let's just stick to the truth but stretch it a little. I already told her we had a little fender bender yesterday and had taken Mr. Wheeler's truck to Craig's garage for repair. Just tell her we're out with Craig trying to find parts."

"What do I tell her when she asks why you aren't calling her yourself?" asked Melanie.

"Tell her that the last time we spoke, the call kept dropping. Tell her I asked you to call her rather than put her through all that."

"She's never going to buy it."

I sighed as Jess finally made an appearance. She wandered our way with her pad in hand, and I nodded toward Dad who proceeded to recite both our drink and food preferences. No sense in letting her escape without our full orders. Who knows how long it might be before we saw her again. I took advantage of Dad's distraction to lower my voice and say, "You might just be surprised at what she'll believe. I think she's kind of enjoying having the house to herself, if you know what I mean."

"Fine. Can you at least keep me posted? I don't like not being able to reach you."

I looked at my watch. It was a little past noon. "I'll call you once we settle in for the night. It probably won't be until sometime this evening, though."

"I'll keep my phone on. I don't feel quite the same need for your abundance of caution."

That only caused a new worry to manifest. "I'm not sure it's safe for you and the kids to be staying at the house all by yourselves. I mean, what if someone comes by and—"

"I've got a gun of my own, remember? And I'm a damn good shot, too. I guarantee that mine is always closer to me than yours is to you. If somebody is stupid enough to threaten me or my kids, they won't know what hit 'em. I can hold down the fort. You've seen me in action."

I smiled. "I most certainly have. I love you."

"I love you too. Get yourself home to me just as soon as you possibly can. That's an order."

"Yes, ma'am."

I disconnected the phone and returned to transcribing our directions onto—well, technically, I guess it's still a pad—a dopey grin firmly in place. As I powered down the phone, I realized Dad was staring at me and smiling.

"What?" I asked.

"You two are the real thing," he said, and I felt my ears beginning to burn.

"I'd like to think so," I said as a long shadow fell over the table. I turned, expecting to find Jess with our drinks, but what I saw wiped the grin right off of my face.

Briarstaff's most powerful town elder, Emmitt Brown, stood at our tableside, scowling down at us from beneath his big bushy eyebrows.

"Pardon the intrusion, gentlemen," he said, his voice dripping with false sincerity. He pointed to the space beside me. "Is this seat taken?"

CHAPTER THIRTEEN

Totally blindsided, I could only gape at the elderly gentleman. He loomed over us in his customary two-piece black suit with a matching string tie that hung from his stiff white button-down collar. The smirk on his angular face revealed his delight in catching me unawares. He turned and snagged a chair from an empty table and placed it at the end of ours.

"Never mind," he said. "I'll just sit here."

I could practically hear his old bones creak as he sat, his faux smile still firmly in place.

"I'm sorry," said Dad, clearly perplexed. "Is there something we can help you with?"

"Emmitt Brown," I said, finally finding my voice. "Let me handle this, Dad."

Dad looked at me. "You know this man?"

Emmit's chuckle was a rusty hinge as he turned his attention to my father. "He most certainly does. When Pauline Dixon described the gentlemen she saw approaching the Bartlett residence, I thought one of 'em sounded awfully familiar, but I never dreamed he'd actually have the balls to show his face 'round these parts again. So, you're the father, huh? Must make you real proud, this one. Are you also the one who done taught him how to cheat at cards? Pretty slick if you ask me."

Dad scowled at the implication, and my own smile was tight.

"I wasn't the one who was cheating, and you damn well know it," I said, doing my best to keep my voice low and even. I didn't want to cause a scene but might not have much choice in the matter. I reached to my right and pulled my jacket closer, taking comfort in having Dad's pistol right underneath my hand. "What do you want, Mr. Brown?"

"I might ask you the same thing," he said. "Haven't you ruined enough lives already? You're the reason my grandson is wasting away behind bars."

I chortled. "Tommy is in jail because he was part of a lynch mob that tried to burn a family's house to the ground while some of them were still inside. Seems to me he's exactly where he belongs."

The memories from that night came rushing back, and I could almost taste the acrid smoke that had burned my eyes and lungs as I struggled to free a man from certain death, his wheelchair making the task nearly impossible. His family's only transgression was the color of their skin.

The smile finally disappeared into the wrinkles of his craggy face. "Those folks didn't belong in Briarstaff any more than you did," he said. "We have a way of keeping our streets—clean. I should think you would know that by now, which again begs the question, why exactly *are* you here?"

My smile only widened. "Not that it's any business of yours, but I wanted to introduce my dad to a friend."

"Young man, *everything* that happens in that town is my business," he said. "What business could you possibly have with Delphine Bartlett? That woman hasn't been playing with a full deck in all the years that I've known her—oh! Pardon my pun. She's even worse since you went and got her Hattie killed—"

"Shut your fucking mouth!"

So much for not causing a scene. All eyes were on me as the handful of other patrons tuned in, mouths open and utensils suspended in midair. I took a deep, calming breath and tried again.

"What happened to Hattie wasn't my fault," I said. "It was The Academy. Delphine *knows* that."

Emmitt frowned. "If it makes you sleep easier at night, you go right on believing that. But we all know that if you hadn't been here in the first place, that young woman would still be alive, dumpster diving behind the IGA and riding that ridiculous bicycle all over town, making up words to all those songs she sang so very off-key."

All I could do was grind my teeth. The old bastard was purposefully baiting me, and I could feel heat flooding into my face.

"Besides," he continued. "We don't talk about The Academy anymore. That's a done deal, and it's best to just let it go. I'd hate to think what might happen if someone started poking their nose where it didn't belong. Might I suggest that you and your father take heed while it's still a choice? Get yourselves back to wherever it is in Ohio that you call home before someone gets the wrong idea and makes that choice for you. Consider it a friendly warning."

He folded his bony hands in front of himself, his smile radiating a confidence that was entirely unsettling.

Undeterred, Dad leaned forward, offering an easy smile of his own in return. "Excuse me, Mr.—Brown, is it? I'm starting to get the idea that you're threatening us—well, mostly my boy, and I'm really feeling the need to offer a little warning of my own. If you don't get yourself away from this table in about two seconds flat, I'm going to plant my foot so far up your withered old keister that you're going to be tasting the tips of my toes in the back of your throat, and that's a guarantee. I don't give two shakes who you are or how old you may be—*nobody* threatens my boy. Are we clear?"

Go, Dad, go!

I watched the smile fade from Emmitt's face as he slowly unclasped his hands and got to his feet. He nodded once at Dad before returning the chair to the table behind us and beginning his slow return to the front of the restaurant. Our gracious maître d' was eagerly waiting, and they huddled near the hostess stand to confer, her expression growing stormier by the second.

"Well, *that* can't be good," I said, watching her wrap a meaty arm around the old man's bony shoulders and kiss him on the cheek. He headed toward the door while she made a beeline to our table, hands planted on her ample hips.

"I'm going to need you to leave," she said.

"Beg pardon?" asked Dad. "We haven't gotten our food yet."

"And you won't be getting it anytime soon," she said. "We reserve the right to refuse service to anyone for any reason. Says so right there." She pointed to a sign near the door that reinforced her assertion. "And I'm choosing to exercise that right, right now. Get out."

"I don't understand," I said. "We weren't looking for trouble, but that man came in here threatening us."

Her scowl only deepened. "That 'man' is my father," she said, and everything fell into place. Of *course* he was! "If you don't leave, I'm calling the sheriff, and believe me, you don't want that. He and my dad go *way* back."

"No need for all that," I said. "We're not particularly fond of supporting this family's local economy anyway. Come on, Dad."

I was careful to keep Dad's gun tucked safely in my jacket pocket as I slid it back on, pocketed the sanitary napkin bearing our mapped route, and got to my feet. I offered to return the crayon to our hostess, but she only glared at me. Dad looked particularly pleased with himself as he gathered his things and joined me. The other diners stared openly as we were purposefully shown the door.

That was fine. I had lost my appetite anyway.

"Do you think we're far enough away that we might entertain the thought of food again?" asked Dad from the passenger seat. "I'm starting to get a headache."

I looked at him sharply. "Are you alright?"

He sighed. "Sometimes, a headache is just a headache, son. I need something to eat. That's all."

It had been nearly an hour since we parted ways with Emmitt Brown, and I was quite frankly relieved when his black Lincoln Town Car had turned right out of the strip mall's parking lot when we turned left. His driver was a square-headed behemoth who looked like he could tie me and Dad into a pretzel without ever breaking a sweat, and it wasn't a theory I wanted to test. We were still in West Virginia and passing through Clarksburg on US 50.

"Sure," I said. "It probably wouldn't hurt to top off the gas while we're at it, but we should probably just stick to a drive-thru this time."

"That's fine. Do you want me to drive for a while?"

"No."

"Are you sure? You've been driving for hours. You need a break."

"*No.*" I ground the gears as I downshifted on the WV-20 exit, signaling right and slowing the car.

"Fine, fine, fine," he muttered, staring through the passenger window at the tidy little neighborhood visible through the trees. "Poor transmission probably needs a break, too. Are you *ever* going to learn how to work a clutch?"

I shot him a stormy look but kept my mouth shut. Honestly, I was still a little in awe of how he had handled Emmitt Brown. The look on that old bastard's face was *priceless.*

"There's a Hardee's up ahead," I said. "Will that work?"

"Fine, fine, fine."

We navigated the drive-thru without incident, grabbing a couple of burger combos with only a minimum of grumbling from Dad regarding their failure to carry Pepsi products. He opted for sweet tea, and we parked in the back of the lot to tuck into our food. By then, my stomach was nearly audible.

"Do we have an actual plan yet?" Dad asked in between bites.

"I'm working on that," I said, my mouth still full.

"I mean, other than just showing up in this Templar and asking for directions to this mysterious Academy of yours?"

I shot him a dirty look. "We won't be doing *that*. If Templar is anything like Briarstaff, we won't exactly be welcome there."

"So, what will we be doing?"

I took another bite of my sandwich, stalling. I'd already told him that I was just making this stuff up as we went along. What more did he want from me?

"You don't know, do you?" he asked, scowling.

"Well—*no*, but I will by the time we get there," I admitted.

"Okay," he said, plucking a few fries from their cardboard sleeve. "If you say so."

"I do."

"*Hmmm*," he said, shoving the fries into his mouth.

I sighed. "Do *you* have a plan?"

He washed the fries down with a swig of his sweet tea. "I'm going to find my daughter and bring her home."

I looked at him as he bit into his sandwich. As far as plans went, his wasn't very specific, but based on the set of his jaw and the steely determination in his eyes, I had zero doubt that he would achieve his goal or die trying.

I had trouble envisioning the former, but the latter hardly required any imagination at all.

· · · ● ● ● ◯ ◯ ● ● ● · · ·

We had only just crossed into Maryland when I suspected we had a problem.

Dad had nodded off in the passenger seat shortly after we had gotten onto I-79N, and by the time I took exit 148 to merge onto I-68E, he was sawing logs. Traffic was on the light side, but a late model, white Chevy truck caught my attention in the rearview mirror. Utterly nondescript, there were hundreds of others just like it on the roadways, but this one had a noticeable blemish—the Chevy bowtie in the middle of its black grille was split in two, apparently the victim of a minor traffic mishap that hadn't compromised the actual body of the vehicle. It wasn't exactly dogging us, its driver preferring to keep a vehicle or two between us, but as those drivers either passed to the left or exited for their intended destinations, its presence was a constant shadow. I even modulated my speed to see if its driver might pass when I slowed or gradually fade into the distance when I accelerated, but it was subtly keeping pace, never getting too close nor falling too far behind.

"Umm, Dad?"

He startled awake with a snort. "Are we finally there?"

"Not exactly. Am I being paranoid, or is that truck following us?" I asked, and as he moved to turn in this seat, I nearly shouted, "Not like that! Use your mirror."

He shifted the other direction so he could stare into the passenger side mirror. "The Chevy with the busted grille?"

"Uh-huh."

"I suppose it's possible. What makes you think so?"

"He's been behind us for at least ten miles now. It speeds up when I speed up. It slows when I slow. It's staying just far enough back that I can't even see how many people are in the cab. Can you?"

Dad studied his mirror. "Not really. Why don't we find out?"

I looked at him dubiously. "How would you propose we do that?"

"You've got an exit coming up in a couple of miles. Take it and let's see if this bozo follows us."

"And if he does?"

Dad thought about it for a few seconds. "I don't imagine we can outrun him in this little dune buggy," he said. "You still have my gun, don't you?"

"Oh, yes," I said. Its weight in my jacket pocket served as a constant reminder. "But I'm really hoping to avoid any sort of gunfight in broad daylight."

"I guess you could look for someplace public to pull off. Maybe a gas station or someplace where there are lots of witnesses. If they're following us, I doubt they're looking to make a spectacle of themselves either."

I found it ironic that we were nearing Friendsville, and I waited until the last possible second before veering right onto Exit 4 without signaling my intention. The Chevy followed suit and a lot more smoothly, maintaining its distance while my sense of dread intensified. I only had a quick moment to decide whether to continue straight and merge onto MD-42S or to hang a left on an offshoot that provided access to the opposite direction at a stop sign. Signage indicated an Exxon was located in that direction, so I sped up and cut left, noting a semi hauling a double-wide trailer creeping along from the south. MD-42, also known as Friendsville Road, was only two lanes, and the trailer was like a slow-moving clog working its way through narrow plumbing. It was being escorted by a smaller truck with flashing lights and a big yellow-and-black sign warning of the oversized load.

The Chevy was only a few car lengths behind us and showed every indication that it would be opting for the offshoot as well. If I could time it just right…

"Hang on," I said, calculating my lead time and hoping like hell that I wouldn't stall the engine when I made my move.

I didn't so much comply as roll right through the stop sign, pulling out in front of the double-wide's escort and cutting my wheel sharply to the left. The driver of the pilot vehicle laid on the horn in protest, and I can't even describe the grinding I put those gears through until I finally found second and punched the gas pedal to the floor, chirping my tires and rocketing ahead, the startled little Monza emitting a horrific plume of blue-gray exhaust. I watched the Chevy truck fade into the distance, trapped at the stop sign by an obstacle too big to overcome. The road veered to the left, and I lost sight of it altogether. I took advantage of whatever time I'd bought us to push the Monza even faster, only slowing when the pull off for the Exxon service station appeared on our left. There was a cluster of vehicles at the pumps, while others had parked along both sides of a quaint little country convenience store that was aptly named 'Good To Go.' The facade was sided in natural wood, and its roof was corrugated green tin, propped up by square wooden posts spaced equidistantly across the storefront. I looped around to the far-right side, where I could tuck in behind a panel van that totally obscured us from the road.

Perspiration had sprung up in all of the uncomfortable places, no doubt prompted by my galloping heartbeat. I turned to find Dad grinning at me from the passenger seat.

"That was some pretty good driving, son," he said, and despite our unresolved status, his expression of pride was too rare to go unnoticed. I could feel the tips of my ears burning. "Do you really think they were following us?"

"We'll know in a few minutes," I said, unfastening my seatbelt and opening my door. Dad started to do the same, but I motioned for him to stay put. The biggest advantage of parking beside the panel van was that we couldn't be seen from the road. On the flipside, I couldn't see the road from inside the car, either. My plan was to hover near the front of the van and scope the road from across its hood, hoping its owner didn't return too soon and catch me lurking. I had no idea how I might explain myself, but even worse, our cover would most likely be driven away.

I didn't need to worry for long. The oversized load made its appearance and slowly swept past the gas station, the white Chevy truck directly behind it. I felt foolish ducking down and watching through the windows of the van, but the Chevy didn't even hesitate as it passed, disappearing around the bend as Friendsville Road veered left again.

I fought the urge to giggle hysterically as I got back into the car.

"We're all clear," I said. "They drove past. This is so stupid. I'm making myself crazy! It was probably some local, heading for home, just like back in Chillicothe."

"You can't know that for sure, son," said Dad. "That guy back at the motel was no local."

"True."

"Better safe than sorry," he added. "That old chestnut exists for a reason."

I nodded. "Agreed. Are you ready to get back on the road?"

"I don't suppose we have time for me to run to the restroom, do we? That burger is running right through me."

"Go ahead but hurry," I said. I couldn't help but worry that whoever it was might circle back once they realized they had lost us, but I didn't want to give voice to the paranoia, afraid I might inadvertently manifest it into reality.

"Don't you have to go?" he asked, unfastening his seatbelt.

"I'm fine," I said. "But I could use a Pepsi, if you wouldn't mind."

"You got it," he said, whistling a nameless tune as he exited the car and sauntered around to the front of the building.

I sank down behind the steering wheel and took a few deep, steadying breaths. What in the hell were we even doing? My sister's face flashed through my mind, and I could almost hear her voice.

You will do exactly what I'm telling you to do. You are going to leave it alone.

It was a promise I had only grudgingly made, but nothing was going to stop Dad from pursuing his visions, and it felt more than a little coincidental that the only lead we had was taking us straight into the home state of the last standing senator who was at the center of everything. I needed to learn a little bit more about Senator Amelia Gorham than just her affiliation with The Academy, but until we arrived safely at our destination, I wouldn't have the opportunity.

I closed my eyes and rubbed them, wishing with all my heart that Doug Boggs was a better mentor. At this point, it felt like I had taught him more than he had ever taught me, and that didn't really amount to much.

When I opened my eyes, I was startled by the sensation of moving forward, an optical illusion created by the panel van as it backed out of its parking spot. I grinned at my misperception, but the smile dropped from my face, and I sucked in a deep breath as soon as I realized the white Chevy truck now occupied the spot to the left of the departing van. The cab was empty, suggesting its occupant or occupants were inside—with Dad.

Shit.

I scrambled out of the car and spent a moment waffling, my right hand automatically seeking comfort from the gun in my jacket pocket. I couldn't just charge into the building with a gun drawn. There were too many people around, but by that same reasoning, whoever was stalking us couldn't be too aggressive in apprehending us, either. It was a perverse sort of logic that hinged on our aggressors' sanity, which was anything but guaranteed. If only I had the time to put more distance between us. As I eyed the truck's big, knobby tires, an idea came to mind.

I reached into the car and pulled the keys from the ignition, hurrying around to the Monza's trunk. I popped it open and prayed I'd find what I was looking for.

A-ha! A jack lay in the bottom of the trunk, along with a lug wrench, which was reminiscent of a crowbar. Its head was used to loosen or tighten lug nuts while the other end was beveled to an edge to pry hubcaps away from a tire's rim. I grabbed the lug wrench and made a beeline for the Chevy's passenger rear tire. Fortunately, I was still shielded from view of the customers in the parking lot, because I was fueled by adrenaline and caution had pretty much gone out the window. My first couple of attempts at driving the beveled edge into the tire's sidewall were futile, but the third time was a charm. Air whooshed out in a rush, and the truck listed noticeably as the rim dropped to the pavement.

Now—to rescue Dad.

I stepped around an ice merchandiser near the front of the store and nearly ran into Dad as I turned the corner.

"Whoa!" he said, nearly dropping the bottles of Pepsi he carried. "Why the big rush? I guess you needed the bathroom after all?"

"We've got to go," I said, nodding toward the truck behind me just as a large man exited the store empty handed. Taller than me and built like a tank, he looked completely out of place, despite his redneck attire. His square jaw was clean shaven, and his dark hair was close-cropped and tidy, almost military in style. He stopped to scan the pumps, his eyes hidden behind mirrored sunglasses, but once he spotted us, he turned in our direction. It was like we were trapped in a *Terminator* movie, and Arnold had just locked onto his target.

"Go!" I urged, my feet already moving.

We ran back to the car in what felt like slow motion, and I had the engine running before Dad even dropped into the passenger seat. I popped the clutch, backing out just as the man rounded the corner. Any concerns I had about being paranoid evaporated when he moved to intercept us, but I had already found first gear and was rolling forward, angling around him. He weighed the odds of stepping directly into our path, but the determination on my face must have been enough of a deterrent because he pivoted at the last moment and headed for the driver's door of the Chevy truck.

I suppressed my urge to drive like a maniac out of the parking lot, unwilling to draw any more attention to us than necessary. There wasn't any need. I drove to the edge of the parking lot and paused, allowing a little old lady in a boxy Lincoln to access the service road ahead of me.

"What's the matter with you?!?" asked Dad, craning to look through the Monza's rear window and watching as the big white truck began to back out of its spot. "Let's put some distance between us while we've still got the chance!"

I ignored Dad's urgency and watched the rearview mirror, smirking.

I know something you don't know. Sure, it was childish but supremely satisfying.

Once the truck began to move forward, its hobbled gait was immediately noticeable, even from a distance. I didn't wait for the driver to investigate the cause. I eased my foot off the clutch and followed the Lincoln back out to Friendsville Road. The Lincoln turned left while I went right, heading back toward the interstate and leaving our troubles behind at a downright leisurely pace.

Our Terminator wouldn't be following us any time soon.

CHAPTER FOURTEEN

My sense of triumph was fleeting at best.

As we continued east on I-68, something was niggling at me, and I found myself paying nearly as much attention to the road behind us as what lay ahead. I kept expecting to see that broken Chevy bow tie loom large in the rearview mirror, and it didn't take Dad very long to notice.

"What's the matter, son?"

"I'm sure it's nothing," I said, my eyes continuing to ping-pong back and forth from the windshield to the rearview.

"You're not acting like it's nothing," he said. "Spill it."

"It's just—" I began and then sighed. "We left Briarstaff hours ago, and I only noticed that joker tailing us for maybe the last ten miles or so. Where did he come from?"

"Maybe he was there all along, and you just didn't notice before then," suggested Dad.

"Well, that's a little insulting," I grumbled. As an aspiring private investigator, my powers of observation were my stock in trade, an essential tool in my deductive toolbox. Even if I hadn't noticed the truck immediately, it wouldn't have taken *hours* for me to catch on. I couldn't possibly have been *that* oblivious—could I?

Self-doubt was a quicksand in which I couldn't afford to get trapped. There had to be another explanation.

"Don't get yourself in a twist. I wasn't trying to insult you," said Dad. "I'm just thinking this through. What about that prepaid phone? Are you sure it can't be tracked?"

"I really don't see how," I said. "I paid for it with cash, and loaded it with minutes from a prepaid card, also paid for with cash. There's nothing to connect me to it whatsoever. I've also kept it powered down when I'm not using it."

"You thought you had your other phone turned off, too," he reminded me, but I still wasn't buying it.

"That phone's been connected to me for years," I said. "While I don't understand exactly *how* it was remotely turned on, I've read articles online that acknowledge it's something that can be done. There's just nothing to connect this prepaid phone to me."

As sure as I sounded, it didn't prevent me from picking the burner phone up from the center console to ensure that it was as cool to the touch as I thought it would be.

"You don't think that Phalange woman or her daughter would have told Emmitt Brown's granddaughter where we were headed, do you? I mean, it was the Phalange woman's daughter who put us on our current path," said Dad.

"Never. It has to be something else."

Dad unfastened his seatbelt and cranked his window down. Cool air buffeted around the car's interior, and my eardrums weren't even remotely amused.

"What are you *doing?*" I asked.

"Hang on," said Dad, easing his head and shoulders through the window and craning his neck to stare at the sky above. After a minute, he dropped back into his seat, rolling the window up and buckling himself back in. "I don't see anything above us, either."

"Above us? Like what? A helicopter?"

"More likely a drone," he said. "Isn't that the latest and greatest in tracking technology? I'd really think you would be up to speed on this sort of thing, son. Drones are everywhere these days."

I scowled, ignoring his barb. We could bicker all day long and never find resolution, but my crawling skin suggested that time was of the essence to figure this thing out before we found ourselves in the crosshairs of our next opponent. The Monza pre-dated GPS as standard equipment by about three decades, so it *couldn't* be the car.

Unless…

I jerked the steering wheel hard to the right, nearly hanging Dad with his shoulder belt as we crossed solid white lines and abruptly took Exit 14A at the last conceivable moment.

"It's gotta be the car," I muttered, accelerating along the ramp that led to US 219S and Oakland. Now that I had a theory, the need to validate it was urgent.

Dad looked at me questioningly as he pulled a little slack into his belt. "Son?"

"Hold that thought, Dad," I said, checking our surroundings in the rearview mirror.

For the moment, the coast was clear.

I merged onto the two-lane highway before braking hard and taking the first right, a tar-and-gravel expanse somewhat ominously christened Devils Half Acre Road. The hardscrabble fields that straddled the intersection soon gave way to woodlands only just beginning to show the first signs of spring. The Monza's suspension bumped and shuddered along the rural pavement as I accelerated. Mercifully, there were no eyewitnesses to my lunatic maneuvers, and just as soon as we were out of sight from the highway, I pulled over onto the hard-packed berm and stopped the engine. I hadn't realized how tightly I was gripping the steering wheel until I let go, blood rushing back into my fingers in a tidal wave of pinpricks. For the briefest of moments, the only sound was the *ping-ping-ping* of the engine as it cooled.

Dad's expression hadn't changed one iota. "Son?"

"It's gotta be the car," I repeated, unfastening my belt and stepping out onto the road. Dad followed suit and leaned his arms against the flat sienna paint of the Monza's roof.

"What are we doing, here?" he asked, and I was already lowering myself to the ground.

"We're looking for a bug," I said, examining the rust-dappled undercarriage from the driver's front tire to its rear while Dad worked in the opposite direction along the passenger side.

"Do you even know what a bug looks like?" he asked.

"No," I said. "But I think we'd recognize one if we saw it."

"Where would we have even picked up a bug? The motel?"

"Doubtful," I said, running my fingers along the inside of the front wheel well. "If we got tagged last night, I don't think we would have lived to see the sun come up." I shifted position to inspect the rear tire well. "No—I think we probably picked this up while we were trying to eat Italian back in Shawnee."

Dad chuckled. "I'm having a hard time picturing that old buzzard down here on the ground."

"I suspect the old buzzard was distracting us while his driver did his dirty work," I said. I had run out of places to search, so I scrabbled around to palpate the inside of the rear bumper. "It's the only thing that makes any sense."

"I don't know, son. I'm not finding anything over here. How about you?"

"No," I grumbled. I was getting frustrated. The ground was hard underneath me, and jagged bits of rock were biting into my back. I was just about to extract myself from underneath the trunk when I caught a tiny red flicker out of the corner of my eye. "Wait—what's this?"

"Did you find something?" Dad asked as he got to his feet in front of the car.

"Maybe," I said, waiting for a recurrence of the tiny red light, and it didn't take long. After about five seconds, it blipped again. It seemed to be coming from the innermost right corner of the fuel tank. I ran my fingers along the area, discovering a small rectangular appendage affixed to the tank with an epoxy that wouldn't yield to my tugging. "Pop the trunk and hand me the lug wrench, would you?"

I followed Dad's feet as he crossed to the driver's side of the car and retrieved the keys from the ignition before moving to the rear of the car and releasing the trunk. He stooped to blindly pass me the wrench underneath the car. I used its beveled edge to try and pry the device free, and for just a scary moment, I thought I was going to puncture the fuel tank when the device finally broke loose and fell to the ground. It continued to wink at me as I carefully picked it up by its edges. I had exactly zero desire to get this sucker stuck to the flesh of my fingers. I scooted out from underneath the car and sat up, showing it to Dad.

"Voila!" I said, recoiling as he reached out to take it from my hand. "Don't touch it! It's covered in some kind of mega-adhesive."

"Son of a gun," he said, shaking his head slowly. "This is like straight out of a spy movie or something. What are you going to do with it?"

I got to my feet and carried it over to the tar-and-gravel roadway where I dropped it onto the pavement.

"This," I said, raising the lug wrench over my head and pounding the shit out of the damned thing. It took me several blows before its red eye finally winked out of existence. "There. That should do it."

"Ya think?" Dad asked, smirking at the shards of fractured black plastic lying on the tarmac. "Hard to believe something so tiny could cause this much trouble."

"Yeah, well, now we need to put some distance between us and this thing while we still have the chance. How are you feeling?"

"Invigorated!" he said, throwing a couple of punches into the air in front of himself as he bounced about like a boxer. "Ready for the next round!" His rhythm faltered when he saw the pained look on my face. "Why?"

"Do you think you could drive for a little while? We should probably adjust our route a bit."

It wasn't a question I wanted to ask, but I didn't have much choice. I couldn't drive the car while negotiating a re-route to our destination, and with Mr. Broken Bowtie only a few miles back, resuming our path along I-68 didn't feel very smart.

"Of course!" he said, scowling. "I've been offering to drive for *hours!* I feel just fine. You need to stop treating me like an invalid."

"But Dad—"

"Seriously, Dwayne! I'll tell you what—if I start to feel like I'm spacing out, I'll pull over. I promise."

"Do you usually feel it coming on?"

"Well—no, but it's not like I know how to work that map thing on your phone."

"Fine," I said, crossing to the passenger side. "You've already got the keys. Let's do this before I change my mind."

Dad's satisfaction was evident as he slid behind the wheel, and our reversal of roles was jarring. It was like I was the parent, granting permission against my better judgment, and I just had to hope for the best. Faced with nothing but bad options, having a little faith in my father seemed like the best I could do.

⋯•••••●◦◯◗●••••⋯

"I have to say, this is a fun little car," said Dad, winding his way along National Pike and enjoying a little too much of the view for my comfort. His tendency to drift while gawking was an accepted fact long before he started having issues. "I haven't driven a stick in *years*."

"It shows," I muttered, unable to resist the temptation while studying the map on the burner phone.

"*Pfft*. Didn't Craig say something about the clutch plate slipping? I'm not doing so bad if you take that into account."

My jaw dropped, and I glared at him. "You've *got* to be kidding me. You've been riding me mercilessly about my supposed inability to drive this thing, but the minute I point out that you're not exactly smooth yourself, it's suddenly the *car's* fault?"

He struggled mightily to maintain a straight face, but eventually it proved to be too much, even for him. "Oh, relax. You never could take a joke."

"A *joke?*" Now, I was sputtering. "When were you ever joking? At least I never buried my car in a giant culvert right in front of you and all your bosses at Pepsi."

Okay, so maybe it wasn't exactly fair to drag my brother into this, but I referred to an incident that forever lived in Morrow family infamy. During the summer months between his semesters at the University of Kentucky, Matt worked as an intern at the Pepsi-Cola bottling plant where Dad was the sales manager. On his first day on the job, Matt was zipping along at fifty miles per hour when he suddenly realized he was about to overshoot the entrance to employee parking. Rather than continue on, turn around, and try again like a normal person, he cut the wheel hard, skittering off the road and planting his little VW Dasher wagon at the bottom of a ravine, and just as Dad was escorting a bunch of visiting dignitaries from Pepsi's upper management across the parking lot.

"Well, *that* wasn't funny," said Dad, scowling.

"Depends on who you ask," I said. "I heard you had to call for a second, heavier duty tow truck when the first one couldn't negotiate the incline to retrieve Matt's car. I also heard you refused to acknowledge that he was your son to your co-workers for over a week until your buddies on the slow-pitch team finally outed him as the team's statistician."

Dad sniggered. "See? Now that *was* funny."

"Not to Matt it wasn't," I said. "And that's my whole point. You have no idea how *unfunny* some of those jokes were. You turned Matt into a laughingstock for weeks and made him wish he'd never even applied for that stupid internship."

"First of all, that was *not* a stupid internship. It was an opportunity for a college-age kid to earn better than minimum wage, and I guarantee you that Matt didn't regret *that*," Dad said, turning serious. "Second, Matt brought that on himself. I mean, who drives like that? I just diffused the situation with a little levity. It might have been a whole lot more uncomfortable if I hadn't."

"Still, I've never once heard you criticize his driving, but me? Every single chance you got, and you're *still* doing it. I've never had an accident—"

"Didn't you wreck that Optima you used to have?"

I gawped at the side of his head as he kept his eyes on the road. "I've never had an accident that was *my fault*. I've never rearended a car because I thought I had enough clearance. I've never—"

Dad sighed. "For heaven's sake, Dwayne, *breathe*. Making fun of Matthew's driving would be mean-spirited, a little like beating a dead horse, don't you think? It just isn't one of those things that comes naturally to him. I know you can drive. I mean, you were the one stealing my company car out of the driveway at fourteen, remember?"

"*Borrowed*," I corrected. "And I only took it around the block."

He chuckled. "Try again. You drove t all the way out to Brenner Hollow to joyride with your buddy, Ryan."

"How do you know that?"

"You passed your Aunt Eunice on the way out of the neighborhood, and you'd better believe she made a beeline to rat you out."

I blinked. "You never told me that."

"No, I didn't," he said. "I mean, sure, if you had made a regular habit out of it, we would have had words, but you didn't, so I let it go. Driving was never a thing I worried about with you, even when you weren't technically old enough to be doing it. I was just happy you and the McGregor boy weren't into anything worse than that. At least, not at *that* point."

He cast me a knowing look that was unsettling, and I decided it was best to let it drop, afraid to discover exactly how much of my adolescent exploration had worked its way back to his ears through his seemingly omniscient Lymont grapevine. I returned my attention to the map on the phone, amending our evolving route on a sanitary napkin that was nearly covered in furious orange crayon scrawls at this point.

We traveled the next few miles in awkward silence.

Dad cleared his throat. "You know, that's just how I am. I make people laugh. People like to laugh. I'm never out to hurt anyone's feelings, and I thought you knew that."

I shrugged, keeping my focus on the phone. "Well, I didn't."

We passed another few moments in silence before Dad cleared his throat again.

"You know, you do the very same thing."

I looked at him, surprised. "I do not."

He scoffed. "You most certainly do. I've heard some of those comebacks you lob at Doug Boggs and his mother, and I have to admit, you're pretty darn funny. You're not trying to hurt *their* feelings, are you?"

The corner of my mouth quirked up as I briefly considered his question. "Bad example, Dad."

"Okay, fine, but you know what I'm trying to say."

I slowly nodded. "I do."

As Elton John once immortalized, sorry seems to be the hardest word, but this was close enough for me.

I only meant to rest my eyes for a moment.

I don't know if it was the relative silence that clued me in or the gentle breeze drifting across from the driver's side door that stood wide open, but I awoke with a start, disoriented as hell and completely alone. Dad was nowhere to be found. The car was pulled about twenty feet off the road and into a gravel clearing, shrouded in shadows cast by a sun that had already taken cover behind the densely wooded acreage surrounding us.

Shit.

I scrambled to release my seatbelt and nearly faceplanted in my haste to get out of the car, not fully aware that my legs were still slumbering. I hobbled around in a semi-circle, scanning for any sign of my father's bald head and trying to keep panic from overwhelming me as I came up empty.

A floodgate of concern opened wide as I had zero trouble picturing Dad lost and confused, calling out for his former wife, Nancy, as he wandered deeper and deeper into the dense foliage and away from the car. As if I weren't already going to have enough trouble explaining to Mom our extended sojourn, now I'd gone and *lost* the man.

"Dad?" I called out, listening for any sign of him amongst the sound of birdsongs and the rustle of wind rippling through the lofty treetops. There was no reply. *"Dad?"*

I wandered toward the two-lane highway, looking one way and then the other for any sign of him, but there was nothing to see. The road was completely devoid of traffic in either direction. In fact, I wasn't even sure where we were, or if this was still the same highway we had been traveling before I nodded off. I glanced at my watch and was shocked to see that almost three hours had passed. I hadn't gotten much sleep the night before, but I guess I didn't realize how bone weary I had become while driving.

This wasn't good.

"Todd Richard Morrow!" I bellowed, anxiety spiking as my words echoed through the surrounding hills and back to me. The only response was the taunting caw of a crow hidden somewhere in the crown of new growth sprouting overhead, and I felt like I was going to be sick. I needed to *do* something, but what? I scanned the perimeter more slowly, looking for anything that might indicate which way he had gone, but nothing leapt out and the possibilities were endlessly overwhelming.

"DAD!!!"

I pulled the burner phone from my pocket and powered it on, hoping to at least get a fix on our current location, but this was simply not my day.

SEARCHING FOR SIGNAL…

SEARCHING FOR SIGNAL…

SEARCHING FOR SIGNAL…

Fuck!

I nearly threw the damned thing as far as I could to combat the helplessness that threatened to pull me under, but I forced myself to take a few deep, steadying breaths. I would simply have to go and get some help. That was all there was to it. I could leave a note for Dad tacked to a nearby tree telling him to stay put—I still had part of an orange crayon and some napkins left over from our lunch at Hardee's. I could drive until the phone registered service, and then I could call for help. Maybe local authorities would have some sort of search and rescue team that had a helicopter at their disposal to scan the woods from above.

Was it a good plan? No. As hard as we'd worked to get off the grid, I'd be putting us right back on it. For all I knew, we might already be on the radar for local authorities, wanted for questioning in the death of a man at a seedy Charleston motel, but it would be dark soon, and once the sun set, the temperature would undoubtedly drop. Dad wasn't dressed to spend the night out in the elements, and I had to do *something*.

I felt marginally better for all of twenty seconds. I slid behind the wheel and reached for a set of keys that weren't in the ignition. Dad must have taken them with him. I battered my fists against the steering wheel, laying on the horn repeatedly while issuing my own anguished cry to vent my frustration. I pushed back against the seat and huffed as hot tears came unbidden, stinging the corners of my eyes.

As the reverberation of the horn faded, I caught the faintest hint of mechanical noise in the distance. I scrambled out of the car and hurried back to the road, trying to pinpoint the direction from which it came while the natural acoustics worked against me. The only thing I could tell for certain was someone was coming. I was determined to flag them down, even if I had to prostrate myself across the pavement to make them stop, and that seemed fairly likely. I'm sure I looked like a crazed madman as I pivoted in quarter-turns in the middle of the road, anxious to catch sight of the approaching vehicle whenever it eventually came into view. When it finally did, I froze in place.

It was a white, heavy-duty Chevy truck with a broken bowtie centered in its grille, and it accelerated as soon as its driver spotted me.

Shit!

I ran back into the clearing and was beside the car when I suddenly spotted Dad emerging from the woods in front of me.

He wasn't alone.

A gigantic Sasquatch of a man was right behind him, brandishing a rifle and scowling through a nest of bushy red facial hair.

I watched helplessly as the truck pulled into the clearing behind me, closing us in from behind.

We were suddenly out of options.

CHAPTER FIFTEEN

The driver of the Chevy switched off his engine, and the sudden silence was deafening. He climbed down from his seat, and to say he looked pissed would be a total understatement. The muscles in his square jaw visibly clenched and released as he ground his teeth together, his eyes shielded behind his mirrored sunglasses. I froze in place in the loose gravel beside the passenger door of the Monza.

"Dad? Are you alright?" I called out. It was a ridiculous question, considering its answer was likely temporary.

"Yes," he said, sounding far less concerned than he should be. "Isn't that the guy from before?"

"Why, yes it is," the man said, pulling a gun from where it was holstered in the small of his back. It was so much larger than Dad's tiny pistol, which suddenly felt heavy in my pocket. I had practically forgotten it was there. "I guess you thought that was pretty clever, what you pulled back there, but all you really did was delay the inevitable."

I couldn't take my eyes off his gun as he slowly raised it in my direction.

"Now, listen carefully," he said, his voice low and menacing. "We're gonna do this one of two ways, so don't be thinking you ain't got a choice in the matter. You can either offer yourselves up so I can restrain you, or I'll just put a bullet between your eyes and call it a day. Either way, you're going in the back of this here truck."

My mind was racing, calculating the odds that I could extract Dad's pistol from my pocket and get a shot off before this asshole simply squeezed his trigger. I wasn't good at doing math in my head, but even I could see those odds were abysmal. Nevertheless, I allowed the tips of my fingers to dip into the pocket of my jacket, feeling for the gun's handle without being overly obvious. I flicked the safety off. If I could get just a momentary distraction, I would forego extracting the pistol from my pocket and attempt to shoot the bastard straight through the thin fabric of my windbreaker. Of course, that would only account for one of these goons. For all I knew, the one leading Dad out of the woods already had me in his sights and would cut me down before I even heard the bullet leave his rifle.

"This don't exactly feel right."

I frowned. While it came from the same direction as Dad, it certainly wasn't his voice, and it drew the Mr. Bowtie's attention away from me, as if he had only just noticed the other man's presence. Sensing this was the only chance I might get, I wrapped my hand around the handle of the pistol in my jacket pocket and awkwardly pulled the gun up, jacket and all. I leaned to my right and out of his immediate trajectory, squeezing the trigger and hoping for some of that 'Dead-Eye Dwayne' magic.

The next few seconds passed in a blur.

I could tell my shot went wide almost instantly, and my jacket was smoking from where the bullet had torn through its pocket. My sudden movement pulled our assailant's attention right back into focus, and as he leveled his gun at me, the tension in his trigger finger tightened. I leaned further to my right, bracing for the inevitable when my feet suddenly slipped in the gravel below me, and I could feel myself falling toward the side of the Monza.

The sound of a gunshot was followed by a piercing pain in my head.

Everything went dark.

Was this death?

I certainly hoped not, because it hurt like hell.

Oh, shit.

Was this *hell?*

Probably not. Sure, my head throbbed with each beat of my heart, and my left arm was on fire, but it wasn't the sort of pain and suffering I equated with eternal damnation. I thought my eyes were open, but I must have gone blind because I couldn't see a thing. At least the ground below me was soft and comfortable. My tongue was thick, and my throat was like sandpaper, and when I tried to clear it, it triggered a bout of coughing that exacerbated the pain in my arm. It also brought a flicker of light into the room, as someone approached from the direction of my feet, carrying a candle on a chamberstick.

The ginger Sasquatch towered over me, his scowl even more menacing underlit by the flickering candlelight.

"You still alive?" he asked, his voice low and gravelly.

"Umm…yes?" I croaked, although not entirely sure for how much longer.

His stare was discomfiting. "Just stay put."

"Dad," I said, struggling to sit up. "Where's my dad?"

"You'll be reunited soon enough," he said. "I've got a body to dispose of, and the sooner I start, the sooner I can call it a night."

His words hit me like a punch to the gut.

Dad.

My throat tightened as he walked away, taking the candlelight with him along with most of my hope. How could I even begin to explain this to Mom, Matt—*anyone?* Gina had told me to leave all this alone, warned me of the dire consequences, but did I listen? No. That last image of Dad being

191

led out of the woods by this monster wielding a rifle would be burned into my memory forever, and I would avenge him or die trying.

The door latched, plunging me back into darkness. I cautiously moved my legs, and they didn't seem to be restrained. Neither were my arms, although my left arm was stiff and continued to ache. My jacket was gone, the gun along with it.

Shit.

I gently palpated the area only to discover that my upper arm had been swaddled securely in gauze. I seemed to be on a twin mattress, and after finding the edges with my fingers, I swung my legs over and sat upright, placing my stockinged feet on the uncarpeted flooring. I had no idea where my shoes had gone.

This didn't make any sense. Why would my captors leave me alone and unrestrained? Surely, they knew I would try to escape, even if it was without my shoes. Maybe it was some sort of trap, but for the life of me, I couldn't imagine what kind. They had me dead to rights. Still, I wasn't about to just sit there and wait to be executed. I got to my feet and swept my right arm around, searching for obstacles in my path. I promptly sent something crashing to the floor, and I froze, holding my breath as I waited for that murderous Sasquatch to storm back into the room to end me.

Nobody came rushing in.

After a few seconds that felt like eons, I proceeded with caution, shuffling slowly and adjusting my direction as needed, staying close to the bed as I inched toward where I assumed the door must be. My eyes weren't adjusting to the pervasive gloom, and I wondered if I was maybe being held underground somewhere. After more cautious fumbling, my fingers brushed the hinge of the door, and from there, I was able to find the doorknob. I wrapped my hand around it and slowly turned, expecting it to be locked.

There was a click, and the door opened inward.

I slipped out into a short hallway that was only marginally brighter than the room from which I came, but at least I could finally see again. The walls were rustic, rough-hewn lumber, and the flooring was planked. Across the hall and straight ahead was a closed door with a window to my left. A heavy canvas blind was pulled halfway down, allowing a narrow rectangle of moonlight to spill through, and clearly, I had lost more time.

When did the sun set?

Underneath the window was a handcrafted table where a Bible lay open, held up by a sculpture of alabaster hands. I paused to listen, but there was nothing to hear. No voices, no sounds from a television or radio—nothing. The house was nestled in a silence so complete it was eerie, and it took me a long moment to realize it was the absence of white noise that made it so. The walls were lined with wrought iron wall sconces holding candles, none of them lit, and I realized there weren't any electric outlets to be seen. Were these people Amish? I stepped over to peer outside the window at the dense woods beyond, the full moon high in the sky above.

What *was* this place?

I crossed the hall and gently eased the other door open, peeking inside.

"Dad?" I whispered, still in denial as I scanned the darkened room. If there was any chance at all that he was somewhere in that house, I had to find him before making my escape.

It was empty. A king-sized bed occupied the space between two windows along the far wall, a heavy steamer trunk centered along its footboard. The curtains were opened wide to bathe the room in nocturnal luminescence, and the bed was neatly made up and topped by a patchwork comforter that looked to be handmade. An assortment of antique bottles lined a dressing table to the right of the bed. Some of the bottles were decidedly feminine, suggesting this was likely the bedroom of Sasquatch and whoever he had dragged home to be his mate.

I backed into the hallway, pulling the door closed behind me. As I traversed the short passage, my eye was drawn to an oval mirror mounted to the wall on my left. I paused to examine my reflection, noting an abrasion on my forehead that culminated in an angry, raised knot. Well, that explained my throbbing head. I pressed on.

Another door led into a bathroom on my right before the hallway opened out into a small, living space centered around a stone fireplace whose facade bore sooty evidence of frequent use. Like everything else, it was softly lit by incandescent moonlight streaming in through a handful of windows. A larger picture window to the right of the front entrance looked out into a shadowy yard of indeterminate depth, but the property appeared to be bordered on all sides by woods as thick as the ones I had spied through the window in the hallway.

Centered along the wall across from the fireplace, an enormous, cedar armoire crowded the hodgepodge of mismatched furniture staged around a braided, woolen rug. The seating looked comfortable and cozy, if not particularly color coordinated, but it was more than a little claustrophobic. There wasn't a single piece of consumer electronics to be found. It was like I had traveled back in time. To my left was an open kitchen with a small refrigerator and an ancient stove, both of which must be powered by natural gas or propane as this small cabin showed no signs of electricity whatsoever. A small folding table was in its center, with just a single chair at each end to accommodate the cabin's occupants at mealtimes.

Apparently, Mr. and Mrs. Sasquatch weren't big on entertaining.

I approached the front door and was reaching for the doorknob when I heard the familiar sound of an engine drawing closer. By that point, I would have known that leaky exhaust anywhere. I opened the door a crack and peeked out just as twin headlight beams swept across the yard. It was the Monza, emerging from an overgrown trail at the edge of the property. Leaving the car abandoned at the side of the road would only raise questions, and I had a sinking feeling the grave that was currently being dug was large enough to hold two bodies and a vintage Chevrolet to serve as their casket. I wasn't sticking around to find out. I pulled the door shut and made a hasty retreat through the living room and into the kitchen, prepared to crawl through the window above the sink, if necessary.

Fortunately, it wasn't.

Another door to the left of the stove led to the back yard, and I had my hand on its knob when it abruptly turned in my hand. I stepped back as the door pushed open, the red-headed giant filling the door frame. His bushy eyebrows registered surprise at my unexpected appearance.

"I thought I told you to stay put," he grumbled.

I was already reaching for the cast iron skillet occupying one of the rear burners on the stove to my left. I brought it around and clocked him right in the face, knocking him off his feet and out onto the back porch. He landed on his backside with a grunt, and I wasted no time reversing course to race toward the front door. I kept hold of the skillet in lieu of any better option, hoping the element of surprise might allow me a similar opportunity with his accomplice. I grabbed the doorknob and steeled myself, prepared to greet Sasquatch's accomplice with an iron skillet kiss he wouldn't soon forget. If I could just regain control of the car, I'd be out of there faster than you could say—

Shit!

What about Dad? While the odds were anything but good, I couldn't give up hope until I knew what had happened to him for certain, and that stutter in my resolve was just enough for the bearded ogre to seize my shoulders from behind. A sharp jag of pain erupted in my left arm, and I dropped the skillet as he pulled me back into the room and wrapped me in a tight bear hug. I scrambled, clawed, and kicked, but he simply lifted my feet off the ground as easily as if I were made of rags, squeezing even harder.

"Let me go, you asshole!" I raged with far more authority than I had, my legs pinwheeling in the air and knocking over a table by the entryway.

The front door opened, and my panic intensified, fueling my efforts to break free, but it was an exercise in futility. This guy was unyielding, and despite the endless stream of profanity spilling from my lips, he remained eerily calm. It took a second to realize he was right up against my ear, steadily whispering something.

Was he *shushing* me?

He *was!* He was shushing me like a parent soothing a hysterical child, and it only made me fight harder. I pulled his arm up, leaning down to plant my teeth deep into the flesh of his forearm. A cacophony of noise erupted all around me, including a stream of threatening growls and snarls that only barely preceded the source, an enormous beast who began pummeling me from below, jumping and snapping ferociously.

"Dwayne! Dwayne! *Dwayne!*"

Dad's voice cut through the fury that blinded me, and I lifted my eyes to find him standing in the open doorway, his hands held out with fingers splayed open to stop me. He was accompanied by a lady with short red hair who was every bit as petite as Sasquatch was ogrish, and her mouth formed a perfect 'O.' She finally found her voice, commanding, "Wolfie! Come! Sit!"

The German shepherd immediately complied, abandoning his assault and parking himself beside the woman. Tasting copper, I relaxed my jaw and saw that I had broken Sasquatch's skin.

"Dad?!?" My head was reeling. "You're *alive?"*

"I surely hope so," he said. "What do you think you're doing? Did you just *bite* Burt?"

Burt? Who the fuck was Burt?

"I was trying to escape," I said, all of the fight going out of me. I remained suspended in midair in this beast's vicelike grip, my feet still inches from the ground. "I—I was trying to find you. What's going on here?"

"Oh, for heaven's sake, Dwayne," said Dad, advancing into the room while the lady scowled at me, stooping to right the table I had kicked over. His eyes shifted to Burt. "You can let him down, Burt. I'm so sorry about that."

"Are you sure?" Burt asked dubiously, his breath hot on my neck. "He's a wee bit of a scrapper, this one is. Teeth like an otter."

"Tell him you're sorry, son."

I gawped at him. "Are you *serious?*"

Dad sighed. "Burt saved us. You should be thanking him, not biting him."

I looked over my shoulder to find myself staring into Burt's cavernous nostrils. "I—*uh*, I'm sorry," I said. "You said you had a body to dispose of, and I thought—well, I thought that—" I shook my head. "Never mind what I thought."

A slight smile played across Dad's face, and I knew my unspoken thought had been received, loud and clear.

Light began to chase away shadows as the woman circled the room's perimeter with a box of matches, lighting wall-mounted sconces. Wolfie trailed along beside her, keeping his muscular, black-and-brown body between his owner and the stranger that was me, still unsure if I was friend or foe. Burt's iron grip relaxed, and I dropped to the ground, my arm throbbing underneath its nest of gauze. I turned around to face our savior and was surprised to see a wide smile had broken across his face, instantly erasing any threat his rugged countenance projected by default. He thrust a big hand out toward me.

"Burt Givens," he said, as I accepted his arm-wrenching handshake. "And that purty little lady lighting our way is my one-and-only, Reba."

She nodded at me curtly, still not sure if I should be forgiven. After all, I had only just bitten her man.

"Much as I'd love to stick around and chat, I really *do* have a body to tend to," said Burt as he crossed to the fireplace and scooped a ring of keys off the mantle. "Feels like time's of the essence, if you know what I mean. Forgot to grab the keys to my barn, and I'll need my gardening gloves."

"Are you sure I can't lend a hand?" asked Dad, as I struggled to follow a conversation that made no sense.

"Naw, you're not familiar with the area, and I've got this. Shouldn't take me too long. You'd best spend the time bringing your boy up to speed."

"I hate to put all this on you," said Dad.

"Hey, I'm the one that shot that no-account bastard," he said. "And Burt Givens always cleans up his own messes. Reba, hon? Maybe you could find our new friends something to eat?"

"Of course," she said, pivoting to the kitchen where she lit more candles and fired up the oven. "Since you're headed that way anyhow, would you care to move Todd's car in beside mine? It's probably not a good idea to leave it parked out front where it can be seen."

"On it," Burt said, and Dad tossed him the keys to the Monza. He followed Reba into the kitchen and paused at the back door. "I'll try not to be too long. Come along, Wolfie!" He slapped his leg, and the German shepherd moved to his side, his big tail sweeping the air.

"I'll keep a plate warm, babe."

He bent down and planted a quick peck on the top of his wife's head. "Keep your eyes and ears open. Feels like a storm's a-brewin', and I wouldn't be surprised at all if we had ourselves more visitors tonight."

"Roger that, but I always keep my eyes and ears open. This world is getting darker every day," Reba said absently as she opened the fridge and began rummaging through its shelves for possibilities. "You fellas make yourselves comfortable, and I'll let you know when dinner is on."

I couldn't even begin to hide my perplexity as I looked to Dad for guidance. He simply smiled and indicated the overstuffed sofa across from the fireplace. "After you."

······•••••⊙⊙•••••·····

In no time, the air was redolent with the scent of roasted pork and vegetables warming in a Dutch oven. Reba continued to busy herself in the kitchen while Dad filled me in on everything I'd missed. Apparently, I'd brained myself on the passenger door of the Monza when I'd slipped in the gravel, knocking myself cold. As it turned out, that was a *good* thing. If I hadn't fallen, the bullet that only grazed my arm might have been lethal. Turning his weapon on Dad and Burt had proved to be a fatal mistake for our assassin. Burt didn't take kindly to having his life threatened, especially by someone who hadn't bothered to identify himself or state his purpose for being on his property. Burt used his own rifle to put the gunman down as a matter of self-defense, considering it his constitutional right to protect himself. Whether the courts would see things his way or not was a debate he hoped to avoid. He had temporarily hidden the body in a thicket of foliage where it was unlikely to be seen from the roadway before throwing me over his shoulder like a sack of potatoes and carting me back to his cabin for Reba to tend to, apparently having some sort of field training I still wasn't quite clear on.

Once she had determined that none of my injuries were life-threatening, the unlikely trio sprang into action, dividing and conquering the tasks necessary to cover up what had happened, because no one believed that our gunman was acting on his own. Sooner or later, someone would be following up on their missing comrade. Reba had accompanied Dad back to the Monza to try and determine how we had been located since I had already ditched the bug I found affixed to the car's gas tank. Burt had gone to retrieve the body, his intention to load it into the big Chevy truck and drop it into the depths of a nearby reservoir, rendering the truck's GPS useless for tracking. He had only returned to the house upon the realization that he had forgotten his gloves, and he didn't want to leave fingerprints behind to connect himself to the crime scene, should the truck and its driver ever be recovered. Once back at the house, he had apparently gotten distracted by checking in on me. He hadn't been comfortable leaving me with a head injury and unattended, especially since I had yet to regain consciousness. It was an unexpected act of kindness I would have never suspected from his otherwise intimidating demeanor. He was currently on his way to finish the task at hand before some random passersby made a grisly discovery and phoned the authorities.

"Hold up," I said, massaging the bridge of my nose as important questions came to mind that had yet to be asked, much less answered. "Where *are* we? How far off course have we drifted, and why didn't you wake me up?"

"Relax," Dad said. "We're not off course at all. We're only about thirty miles south of Templar. I let you sleep because you were exhausted. You left your modified directions where I could see them, and I was feeling just fine. Rejuvenated, in fact. That little car handles like a dream."

"So, why did you pull off the road?"

"I had to pee," he said. "Seemed like a perfect place. I had just finished up when I heard someone rustling through the woods. Burt was hunting wild game. I guess I'm lucky he didn't shoot me."

He chuckled at the thought, but it was too soon for me to find it even remotely funny. I lowered my voice so as not to offend the woman who was busily preparing a meal to share with us. "Why in the world would you take Burt's wife back to the Monza with you? That seems needlessly reckless and dangerous. What if someone else had been at that guy's truck checking up on him?"

Dad scoffed. "Don't underestimate Reba, son. She may look petite and demure, but she's ex-military, and her specialty is covert surveillance. She's got this handheld do-dad that can sniff out bugs, and after all the evasive action we took to lose that guy, it only made sense that there must be another one somewhere on the car."

I looked at him dubiously. "Did she find it?"

"I sure did," she called out from the kitchen, and I felt heat flooding into my face with the realization I hadn't been as quiet as I thought I was. "It was lying in the floorboard of your backseat. Your daddy said it was probably the handiwork of some old geezer you ran into earlier today when you were trying to have lunch."

"Emmitt Brown," I said, as much to myself as to anyone else. "Of course. Cagey old bastard had a backup plan."

"Well, it's not transmitting anything now," she said. "But you better believe whoever was monitoring it will find it more than a little coincidental that both your bug and the GPS in that fella's truck stopped working at roughly the same time and in roughly the same location."

Alarmed, I looked at Dad. "We should really go. I think we've already brought enough trouble to these nice folks' door."

"Oh, *pssh*, we're not worried about that," said Reba as she continued about her business in the kitchen, pulling a pan from the counter by the sink and removing the kitchen towel that covered it before putting it into the oven. "Besides, Burt wanted to talk to you both about this Academy of yours."

My alarm transformed into astonishment as I continued to stare at Dad. "You *told* them about The Academy? What were you *thinking?*"

"Well, it's not like we didn't know *something* was going on out there," said Reba, joining us in the living room, as the yeasty smell of dinner rolls intermingled with the mouthwatering aroma of roasted pork. "We just never heard it called that."

I got to my feet, anxiety flooding through me. "We really need to go. Dad? Come on. We can't get these nice folks any more involved than they already are. They aren't equipped to deal with the sort of trouble we're bringing their way."

Reba smiled, casually crossing to the towering armoire and sliding back a heavy bolt that secured its doors. She opened them wide to expose a veritable armory of munitions mounted within. "I'd say we're better equipped than most, wouldn't you?"

CHAPTER SIXTEEN

I stared at the collection of rifles, which appeared to be an eclectic blend of automatic, semi-automatic, and single-shot. Mounted against the inside of the armoire's left door was a wicked assortment of hunting knives and sabers while the right held machetes, axes, nunchucks, and even a medieval-looking mace. Lined across the top shelf was an assortment of ammunition for the guns.

Burt chose this exact moment to burst through the front door with Wolfie bounding in after him, scaring the shit right out of me. Burt scowled as I nearly jumped out of my skin. "Well, I guess there's no turning back. Reba's gone and shown you too much, so now I guess we'll have to kill you."

I backed away so quickly I almost fell over Dad, and it took a moment for everyone's laughter to penetrate through my panic, Dad's being the loudest.

"Oh, very funny," I said, my ears burning as their laughter only intensified.

"Now, Burt," Reba finally managed. "It's not nice to spring your sort of humor on someone so soon. He thinks you're serious."

"Dwayne never *did* know how to take a joke," Dad interjected between chuckles, earning the dirty look I tossed him.

"I'm sorry, man," said Burt, patting me on my right shoulder with a mammoth hand. "I couldn't help myself. I didn't mean nothing by it, I swear."

"Your timing is perfect, honey," said Reba, pulling the heavy drapes over the picture window before pivoting to the kitchen. "I was just getting ready to put dinner on the table. Did you get everything taken care of?"

"Yes, ma'am," he said, just as easily as if he had rolled the trash cans to the curb.

"Grab some folding chairs for our guests and get your hands washed up," she said, opening the oven door and grabbing a pair of potholders. "You may as well put Wolfie out back with his dinner. Otherwise, he'll be making a nuisance of himself begging for ours. I reckon we've got lots to talk about."

Burt crossed to the back door with the dog on his heels while Dad and I stayed out of the way. I gaped at the weaponry that filled the armoire to capacity. Leaning in toward Dad, I kept my voice low. "Who *are* these people?"

"What's the big deal?" he whispered back. "Lots of folks believe in the right to bear arms." He wandered toward the kitchen while I took a last lingering look at the Givens' excessive arsenal.

"Folks like the Unabomber," I muttered to myself before following after him.

···•••••◌◯•••••···

"My Lord, this is good," said Dad, tucking into his pot roast with enthusiasm.

Burt practically beamed from his end of the table. "No one cooks like my Reba."

"Oh, stop it, you two," said Reba, waving the compliment away although she was clearly pleased.

We had congregated around the small table, bowing our heads as Reba said grace before passing the serving dishes in a clockwise rotation, beginning with her husband. She circled behind us, filling our ice-filled glasses with fresh lemonade before taking her own seat at the opposite end from where Burt sat. Between the scent of freshly baked rolls and the succulence of the pot roast and chunky vegetables floating in its broth, I was practically salivating. I hadn't had time to realize how hungry I was. We settled into a surprisingly comfortable silence, considering everything we still had hanging over our heads. It was only after our momentum slowed that Burt wiped his mouth with a cloth napkin and pushed away from the table, snagging a toothpick from a tiny Mason jar on the table and putting it to good work.

"I suppose you've still got some questions," he said, eyeing me in particular. I guess it wasn't all that surprising, considering how many not-so-subtle glances I had stolen at the cabinet in the living room. Its doors were still splayed wide, its fully stocked contents on proud display. "I've got a few of my own, but by all means—you first. Shoot."

The corner of my mouth twitched at his choice of words while I filtered through the queries flooding my mind, sorting them in the order least likely to offend. "Oka-*a-ay*—why are you helping us? I mean—don't get me wrong, we're grateful and completely in your debt, but—*why?*"

Burt set his toothpick aside. "You fellas were in trouble and needed a hand. Felt like the right thing to do."

I smiled, shaking my head at the absurdity of his nonchalance. "When most people talk about the right thing to do, they mean helping someone change a flat tire—or maybe giving you a ride home when your car breaks down. They don't mean shooting a man and disposing of his body along with all the evidence."

"Dwayne!" Dad barked, shooting me a reproachful look, but Burt only returned my smile evenly.

"I'm not most men," he said. "Look, this isn't the first run-in I've had with those folks, and I'm sure it won't be the last."

"Aren't you worried about repercussions?" I asked.

Burt shrugged. "No more worried than usual. We're prepared to defend our position if it should come to that."

His self-confidence was both reassuring and unnerving, but who was I to question it? Having just saved both mine and Dad's bacon, he clearly put his money where his mouth was. I studied the cabin's interior and changed the subject.

"Am I just missing something, or is this place completely without electricity?" I asked.

"We've been off the grid for the better part of twenty-five years now," Reba interjected with more than a little pride. "We own this property free and clear. One hundred and fifty acres of woodland, complete with a natural gas well that supplies most of our basic needs. Most of it is forested, but we've carved back enough to grow our own vegetables and keep a little livestock to supplement, should Burt have a lean year of hunting. Every few months, I do a little bartering with the folks over in Darbydale for sundries in exchange for handcrafted quilts I work on in my spare time."

"Darbydale?"

Reba nodded. "It's the closest town from here, and it's a wee bit bigger than Templar, which would be the next closest."

"Do you have any children?" I asked.

"Do you?" she countered, raising an eyebrow.

I nearly shook my head before hesitating, realizing my ready answer no longer applied.

"I do," I said, a slow grin spreading across my face along with an unexpected surge of pride. "Or at least I will. I'm engaged. My fiancée has a twelve-year-old daughter from her first marriage and custody of her daughter's three-year-old brother from—well, it's a long story."

She nodded appreciatively. "Ours are a bit older than that," she said. "I'm guessing our oldest is about your age with a family of his own, twin boys and a girl. They've been in Wyoming for—what, Burt? Nearly ten years?"

"Pert near," Burt said, nodding.

"He and his lady head up the resistance in the Mountain West," she said. "We're lucky if we see 'em once or twice a year." She gathered her plates and stood, carrying them back to deposit on the counter beside the sink.

Dad and I exchanged a glance before I echoed, "The resistance? Like domestic terrorists?"

"Dwayne!" Dad's eyes nearly bulged out of his head. He kicked me under the table before hissing, "Why would even you say a thing like that?"

Burt chuckled. "Well, we sure ain't Amish, although I reckon some of the locals probably think we are. We're quite a bit north of the Old Order Amish, but folks are quick to assume whatever is easiest to believe. Works for us. We stay out of their way, and they stay out of ours. But *no*. We aren't terrorists, domestic or otherwise. We're survivalists."

"Sort of like doomsday preppers?" I asked, and he shrugged.

"Sort of. Let's just say we've had good reason to lose faith in these self-serving idiots running things in Washington, and you can only push people so far before they start pushing back. Over the years, the American people have lost their way, and I can't see any way back. Greed and special interests continue to eat away at the fundamental principles this country was founded on, and I can only imagine our forefathers are rolling over in their graves. This sort of democracy isn't sustainable. I'm not saying it will happen today, tomorrow, or even in our lifetime, but we're ready when it does, and we're not the only ones. We have our own little underground network all throughout the country."

"Like your son and his family in Wyoming," I said.

"That's right," said Reba, nodding as she returned to gather more plates.

"Does your boy have a name?" I asked.

She paused, fixing me with the slightest of smiles. "They both do."

I looked away, vexed by her deliberate nonanswer.

She continued to stack dishes, prompting Dad to stand. "Let me help you with that."

"Please sit," she said, nodding toward his chair. "You're our guests. I've got this."

"You may as well do as she says," Burt said as Dad grudgingly sat back down. "Doesn't do any good to argue with her, and I surely ought to know. Anything else you'd like to ask before I take a turn?"

I didn't really see the point. They were being purposefully evasive, and it felt like knowing too much about these people could be hazardous to our health. I shook my head.

"Alright, then," said Burt, sitting back in his chair. "Your dad tells me that you're here looking for your sister, and it has something to do with—" He looked at Dad. "What did you call it? The Academy?"

I scowled at Dad across the table. I still couldn't believe that he had spoken so freely to people who were essentially strangers. What part of discretion did he not understand?

Dad raised an eyebrow, getting my message loud and clear. "What did you expect me to say?"

"You could have just said that you had to pee," I said.

"Well, he could already *see* that," said Dad, rolling his eyes before becoming indignant. "Since we were trespassing on the back end of Burt's property, I thought I owed him a little better explanation, especially considering he had a rifle pointed at me. Frankly, I'm glad I did. It sounds like he knows more than a little about the place we're looking for, and we could certainly use the help."

"You should never, *ever* volunteer information," I practically scolded. "For all you knew, he could have been one of them."

Dad folded his arms defiantly across his chest. "Well, he wasn't."

"But he *could* have been," I said. "You had no way of knowing!"

"You know," interrupted Burt. "It's not too late to change my mind and shoot you both."

My double-take must have been comical because Burt's stern countenance dropped away in a fit of contagious laughter that spread to Reba, her melodious giggle floating in from the kitchen.

"Stop it, Burt," she chided, carrying some sort of dessert to the table and placing it in front of her husband along with a knife, a spatula, and a big serving spoon. "Anyone save room for dessert?"

This was the weirdest fucking dinner party I'd ever attended.

Dad eyed the golden-crusted confection longingly. "Oh, my. Is that apple crisp?"

"It is," Reba confirmed, pivoting back toward the kitchen. "Still warm from the oven, and I've got homemade vanilla ice cream to top it."

Dad made a sound in the back of his throat that could just as easily have come from Homer Simpson. "Yes, please."

Reba returned with a stack of bowls and a container of ice cream, passing them off to Burt before taking her seat across from her husband. We fell into anticipatory silence as Burt began meting out healthy portions and distributing the bowls around the table.

"Let's get back to the matter at hand," said Burt, turning his attention back to me. "Why don't you tell me what you know about this Academy?"

I sighed. Discretion was already out the window, so what the hell? I told our story as succinctly as possible, trying not to go too far down into the weeds. A trio of powerful senators—probably more—had spearheaded an initiative to relieve the world of such pesky modern conveniences, most notably an information highway that was toll-free to just about anybody.

The internet's ability to shine a global light onto their dirtiest of deeds was more than just irksome—it was recognized for the threat that it was. Whether you attribute the saying to Francis Bacon, Thomas Jefferson, or Schoolhouse Rocky, knowledge *is* power, and uninformed voters make for very compliant sheep. Whatever agendas these elected officials had beyond dismantling the internet were pretty much unknown, but if operating in a vacuum was a prerequisite, how virtuous could those agendas possibly be? I shudder to think. I struggled through the events surrounding Gina's alleged death, still feeling plenty of guilt for keeping the truth under wraps from Dad, and he didn't make it any easier. He glared at me from across the table while he ate his apple crisp while mine grew cold and soggy.

"So, who were these senators your sister saw in West Virginia?" asked Burt, dragging a spoonful of his dessert through the puddle of melted ice cream in his bowl.

"Parker Ghant was from Ohio, Errol Warren was from Wisconsin—"

"Wait a minute," interrupted Reba, holding up her empty spoon. "You said 'was.' Are they no longer in office?"

I shook my head. "No, they both died earlier this year. Warren was older than dirt and had an aneurysm, but Ghant was murdered. It was all over the news a couple months ago. I don't know how you could have missed it. It was on pretty much every channel—" It took longer than it should have for Reba's expectant look to register. "Oh. No TV. Never mind."

"It sounds like your situation has almost resolved itself," said Burt. "But your sister still can't come home?"

"No," I said. "The third senator is alive and well, and it just so happens that she's from your state. Her name is Amelia Gorham."

Reba's spoon clattered into her bowl as she and Burt exchanged a dark look.

"I'm getting the distinct feeling you've heard of her," I said, eyeing them both as they continued to bristle.

"You could say that," said Burt, standing. "Reba? A word?"

She nodded and stood, solemnly trailing after Burt as he crossed the kitchen and stepped through the door and out onto the back porch. Dad and I were left to gape at one another as the muffled sound of their conversation was blunted by the cabin walls.

"Did I say something wrong?" I asked.

"Probably, but I can't imagine what," said Dad around a mouthful of apple crisp.

I strained to listen as their conversation became animated, but it was useless. Nothing intelligible made its way inside. The minutes passed in slow motion until the door finally opened and Burt came in, Reba right behind him. Their expressions remained somber.

"You know, we've taken too much of your time already," I said, pushing my untouched dessert away. I started to get up. "We should just go ahead and—"

"Sit," said Burt, waving me back to my seat. My wariness must have been apparent, because his expression softened ever-so-slightly, and he added, "Please."

I did as he said, looking up at him expectantly.

"The two of you are going to get yourselves killed if you try and tackle this alone," he said. "We need to come up with a plan."

"We?" I repeated, and his nod was nearly a wince.

"We can't let you take this on by yourselves in good conscience," he said. "I mean, where would you go anyway?"

Dad and I looked at each other vacantly.

"Exactly," said Burt, crossing into the living room. "So, it's settled. It's already getting late, so you'll stay here tonight. It will give us a chance to put our heads together and—"

I inhaled sharply as I looked at my watch, drawing Burt's attention.

"What?" he asked.

"It's just—I didn't realize how late it was," I said. "I told Melanie I'd check in with her once we got settled, and if I don't, I'm afraid she might just try and track us down."

Burt grunted. "I don't see how you're going to do that. It's not like we have a telephone."

"I've got a phone in my jacket pocket," I said. "Although I don't seem to have my jacket anymore."

The corners of Burt's mouth twitched. "Ah, yes, and that cute little toy gun. They're still safe and sound. I believe Reba hung your coat in the closet."

"Mmm-hmm," said Reba, passing her own judgment with the hint of a smirk. "But you won't be able to use your phone here."

"Oh," I said. "No service?"

It made sense. There were less desolate areas in Southern Ohio where my cell phone was utterly useless.

"We don't allow cell phones on our land," she said. "This is our air space, and we control it. We have solar powered signal jammers positioned around the perimeter of our property."

I smiled at her uneasily. "It's a burner. It can't be traced, but okay. I can always drive out to wherever there's service, make my call and come back."

She shook her head. "That isn't a good idea. You and your father may have lost your tail, but he's sure to have reported the make and model of what you were driving to whoever he's working for. It's not safe for you to be out there." She paused, her smirk broadening. "Especially if all you've got is that tiny little gun for protection. Is that your mama's gun?"

I scowled at Dad before nodding toward him. "No, it's his."

"Oh, my," said Reba, her hand fluttering up to cover her smile. "Is all this really necessary? I understand not wanting to worry your girlfriend, but would she really try to track you down?"

I looked at her evenly. "If it was Burt, wouldn't you?"

Her smile faltered. "I suppose I would. Okay, how about this? I'll drive you into Darbydale so you can make your call while Burt digs out some topographic maps of the area to familiarize your dad with the lay of the land."

Dad was eager to agree.

I nodded. "Sounds like a plan."

"Wait a minute—are you telling me you were *shot?*" asked Melanie, her voice rising sharply.

"Just a little bit. I'm fine," I said. "It only grazed me, and the threat has been—neutralized."

Her sigh was loud enough for Reba to hear it from the driver's seat of her vintage VW Beetle. I had assumed we would be stopping at a gas station or some other public place, but it was after nine, and apparently, Darbydale rolled up its sidewalks once the sun set. Staying in any one place for too long would have been conspicuous, so we crawled through the residential neighborhoods of the tiny township at a leisurely pace while Reba pretended not to eavesdrop on our conversation.

"Neutralized? What does *that* mean?" Melanie shot back.

"I'll fill you in later," I said, smiling nervously at Reba. "I promise."

"You're not alone, are you?" she asked.

"No, but it's okay," I said. "We've made a couple of new friends, and I think they might be able to help us find what we're looking for."

After a lengthy silence, Melanie said, "Alright. I get it. I don't *like* it, but I get it. When will you be home?"

"I'm not exactly sure. Hopefully, not too much longer. I really hate to ask, but can you—"

"*No.* Absolutely not."

"Mel," I implored. "I have to get back so we can work out a plan on how to proceed. The sooner I get back, the sooner I get to come home. I don't have time to get stuck on a lengthy call with Mom."

"What am I supposed to tell her? That you're still with Craig looking for parts?"

"Sure," I said. "That should work. Tell her we located the parts but had to drive to Pennsylvania to get them."

"And what am I supposed to tell her when she asks why you didn't call her yourself? That your 'bad reception' is following you across state lines?"

"I don't know," I said. "Just make something up. Tell her my battery died when I was talking to you, but you didn't want her to worry— something like that."

"Sure. Let's give your mom yet another reason to hate me. She *knows* when I'm lying to her," said Melanie skeptically. "I can just feel it."

"Psssh," I said. "She doesn't hate you. Tell her I'll call her tomorrow, and she can speak to Dad herself. You'll be fine."

"Mmm," she noted dubiously before switching gears. "How's your dad been? Any more episodes?"

"No, he's been fine," I said, sounding more confident than I actually felt. I reflected on his last break from reality inside the Sheetz near Charleston. It had been a bad one. Had that only been the previous evening?

"Well, that's good," she said. "Please be careful."

"I will," I said. "I'll call you around this same time tomorrow, okay?"

"You better. I love you."

"Love you, too. Tell Jaz and Jordan I love them, too."

We disconnected, and Reba put the car in gear, reversing course and taking us out of the quiet neighborhoods and back toward the town's main thoroughfare. After a few moments of silence, she cleared her throat.

"I didn't mean to listen in, but it was kind of hard not to," she said. "Is your dad okay?"

"Not really," I said. "But we don't exactly know what's wrong with him. He keeps having these spells where he sort of comes untethered. He doesn't recognize the people around him or know where he's at. He's had every test imaginable, but so far, all we know is he has a small dark spot on his brain. No real diagnosis."

"I'm so sorry," said Reba, her voice sincere. "I'll keep him in my prayers."

"Thank you," I said, staring absently through the passenger window as the township fell behind us. Soon we were traveling underneath a canopy of interlocking branches that nearly obscured the starry night sky.

We fell into a comfortable silence for the next few miles.

"Brock," said Reba, startling me out of my reverie.

"I'm sorry?"

She glanced at me, smiling. "Our oldest son," she said. "His name is Brock. His wife is Jenny, and our grandbabies are Jackson, Jacob, and Jessica."

I returned her smile. "Nice."

She nodded, but her smile slowly faded. "And then there's Boyd."

"Boyd?"

"Our other son. He's almost five years younger than Brock," she said. "We don't see him anymore."

I waited for her to expound, but we fell back into a silence that suddenly felt heavy.

Finally, I asked, "What happened?"

"That bitch, Amelia Gorham—that's what happened," she said, her voice tight. "She took our boy away from us, and now he's one of *them*."

215

CHAPTER SEVENTEEN

I knew something was wrong as soon as the cabin came into view. Burt was pacing the covered porch, his big dog underfoot and nearly tripping him. The front door stood open behind them, and Dad was nowhere to be seen. Reba bypassed the rutted path to our left leading back to the barn and drove right through the front yard, pulling up to the porch. I was out of the car before she had it completely stopped.

"What's wrong?" I asked, my eyes darting around frantically. "Where's Dad?"

Burt met me at the bottom of the porch stairs. "Inside," he said. "On the couch. I wish I could say he's fine, but frankly, I'm not all that sure. At least he's not agitated anymore."

"Oh, no," I said. "Was he looking for Nancy again?"

Burt blinked. "Yes! How did you—"

"I should've said something before we left," I said, stepping past him and into the darkened living room. Burt had extinguished the candles nearest the couch, and the sight of Dad huddled beneath a multi-colored afghan made my heart clench. His eyes were closed, his pale skin frighteningly corpselike. "Dad?"

I exhaled pure relief as he turned his head to face me, his eyes fluttering open. "Hi, son," he said, offering a weak smile. "I guess I did it again."

I perched beside him on the couch while Burt and Reba hovered near the door, their concern evident. "I guess you did. Are you feeling okay now?"

The corners of his mouth dipped and trembled as he slowly shook his head, struggling with a frustration so strong it nearly brought me to tears. My dad was utterly old school, and showing fear was a weakness he wouldn't indulge, even when it was completely outside of his control.

"I'm just so tired," he admitted. "My head's been splitting ever since I— uh, came back, or whatever you want to call it."

"I should get you to a hospital." I started to stand, but his hand snaked out from underneath the afghan with surprising speed and grabbed my wrist.

"*No*," he said. "We are too close to finding her, and we're not turning back now. I just need to get some sleep, that's all."

I stared at him for a long moment, but he only held my gaze, his chin jutting out defiantly. I sighed and turned to our hosts. "I don't suppose you have anything for a headache, do you?"

Reba nodded, pivoting toward the kitchen. "I do. Burt? Would you mind moving my car into the barn while I get these fellas situated for the night?"

Burt went back outside while Reba lit a candle mounted onto a chamberstick and leaned in toward Dad. "Are you able to walk?"

He glared at her before tossing the afghan aside. "Of course, I can walk," he grumbled. "I'm tired, not incompetent."

"Of course," she said, backing up to give him a little room.

I stood so he could swing his feet to the floor, and as he sat upright, he massaged the bridge of his nose, trying not to wince and almost succeeding. I reached out to offer a hand and received the scowl of a lifetime. I let my arm drop to my side and cleared a path.

We followed Reba back to the room where I had awakened, and now I could see that there were two twin beds inside, one of which was still neatly made. Reba guided Dad toward it, setting the candleholder on its nightstand.

"Make yourselves comfortable. The bathroom's right next door, and there's a box of matches in both nightstands if you need to relight the candle. I'll get you something for your head, Todd," she said, backtracking toward the hall.

Dad sat on the bed with a sigh, his expression strained.

"Are you sure you're alright?" I asked, hovering near the other bed.

"I'm fine," he groused. "Or at least I will be after I get a little shuteye."

The flickering candlelight offered an opportunity to more fully survey a room I had previously navigated only by touch, trial, and the occasional error. The red, white, and blue sheets on the other bed were reminiscent of bedding my brother and I had as children in the room that we shared. Most of the handmade furniture was stained dark walnut, making the room feel even smaller than it was. The far wall housed built-in shelving that held an eclectic collection of reading materials on its left-hand side, with titles ranging from *The Hardy Boys* to *The Hobbit* with a little Stephen King thrown in for good measure. Model airplanes and sports memorabilia lined the shelves on the righthand side, the line of demarcation precisely centered at the wall's midpoint. It didn't take a private investigator to realize this must have been the room that Brock and Boyd shared at some point in time.

There was a tap on the door before Reba entered with a glass of water and a couple of analgesic tablets, which she handed to Dad. He tossed the pills into his mouth followed by half the water, pausing to swallow before drinking the rest.

"Thank you," he said, handing the glass back to Reba.

"Now, if you fellas need anything at all, we'll be just across the way. We can pick this back up in the morning," she said, pausing at the door. Her eyes locked on mine, and almost imperceptibly, she nodded toward the living room. "Dwayne? I should probably change the dressing on your arm before you call it a night. Wouldn't want it to get infected."

"Oh, okay," I said absently, trying to match the subtlety of her cue. I had only shared the basics of Dad's condition, not how frightening it could be when it manifested. She and Burt undoubtedly had questions. "I'll be right there."

She nodded and stepped into the hall, shutting the door behind her.

Dad pulled the bedcovers back and slipped his feet under the patriotic sheets that mirrored the linens on the other bed. He was still awfully pale, and the skin around his eyes had taken on a purplish hue. He looked as frail as I'd ever seen, and I had to look away.

"I'm going to go take care of this," I said, holding up my bandaged arm. "I'll be right back. Do you need anything else before I go?"

"I'm fine," he said before rolling over and burrowing into the covers like he was freezing.

I took the candle from his nightstand and used it to guide myself out of the room and back into the kitchen where Burt waited anxiously at the table. Reba busied herself at the counter, putting away the dishes she had washed before we had taken our little jaunt into town. Burt stood when he saw me coming down the hall.

"Is he alright?" he asked, keeping his voice low.

"I think so," I said, sounding less than confident. "He says he just needs rest." I could only shrug.

"I shared what I knew, not that it was all that much," Reba added quietly from where she stood at the sink, filling a pan with warm, sudsy water. "I hope you don't mind."

"That's fine," I said, pulling out a chair and taking seat at the table. It felt like I'd been awake for days.

Burt sat back down as Reba carried the pan of water, a couple of damp rags, and a box of first-aid supplies in to set them on the table. She pulled one of the mismatched chairs over and sat to my left so she could get to work on my arm.

"Is Nancy your mom?" asked Burt.

"No," I said, surprised at how bitter one tiny word could sound. "She was my dad's first wife, a fact I only recently learned. I'm not really sure why he's fixating on her during these—spells. You'd have to ask him, although he claims not to know either."

"How long has he been having these episodes?" asked Burt.

I did some quick math in my head as Reba gently unwound the gauze from my arm. "I found out back in February, but I suspect it's been a little longer than that. It's hard to be certain. My family kinda excels at keeping its secrets. If I hadn't run into my mom and aunt in the ER, I probably *still* wouldn't know."

"Are they frequent?"

"Frequent enough," I said, wincing as the soapy water hit the abrasion on my arm. "What happened?"

"We were going over a county map," said Burt. "I'm pretty sure the place you're looking for is the New Horizons Boys Ranch. It's about ten miles southwest of Templar, and you'd never be able to find it on your own. Its campus is set way back in the woods for privacy reasons, though I suspect privacy runs both ways, if you catch my drift. I've seen federal prisons with less security. I was showing Todd some vantage points through the woods to get a better view of the place when he suddenly grabbed his head and just sort of staggered off. I thought he was having a stroke."

"I'm sorry," I said. "We should have said something."

He waved my apology away. "It's not like you exactly had time. We've been at a dead run since I stumbled over him pissing in my yard. But the look in his eyes—the way he called out for this Nancy woman—" He shuddered at a recollection I had no problem envisioning. "The gun cabinet was still open, and he was giving it a serious once over. For a scary minute, I thought I was going to have to take him down."

"Oh, God," I said, dropping my face into my free hand. I had no problem envisioning how that might have played out, either. I inhaled sharply as Reba applied something that felt like liquid fire to my wound.

"Hold still," she said. "I'm almost done."

"So, what's the deal with this Boys Ranch?" I asked through gritted teeth.

"It's a fancy name for what we used to call reform school back when I was a lad," said Burt. "It's a last chance stop for boys before they can be charged as adults for the mischief they can't seem to stay out of."

"Like Boyd?" I asked.

Reba's hand slipped, pulling the fresh gauze a little too tight. She gave me an apologetic look as she adjusted the bandage. Burt's cheeks flushed a deep crimson as he looked away.

"Yes," she said. "Like Boyd."

"So, what's the story?" I asked, wading into the inevitable, despite the obvious discomfort it was causing Burt and Reba. I'd already shared our secrets, so it only seemed fair.

Reba put the final touches on my bandage and sighed, leaning back in her chair. "Do you have any brothers, Dwayne?"

I nodded. "One. Matthew. He's almost three years older than me."

"Are you close?"

I shrugged. "Yeah, I suppose so. I mean, we pretty much got along after he went away to college. Not so much when we had to share a room. I can't count the number of times we tried to kill each other during *those* years."

Her smile was wistful before it dropped away entirely. "You're joking. Boyd never joked. The hatred he felt for his older brother was almost biblical, a modern-day Cain and Abel."

"He actually—?"

"Just the once," she said. "He also chased me around the kitchen table with a butcher knife, but that's neither here nor there. I can take care of myself, but I would have never forgiven myself if something had happened to Brock. Boyd's temper was always completely off the chart. There was no such thing as 'too far,' and there wasn't a threat in the world that fazed him. Thank the Lord, Brock was always bigger and stronger—he's almost five years older than Boyd. I swear, I'm still not sure where we went wrong—"

"Now, stop it, darlin'," Burt interjected gently. "This wasn't our doing. I mean, Brock turned out fine. *More* than fine. It wasn't like we played favorites. Their personalities were just *so* *different*. As much as I hate to say it, I think some folks are just born bad."

"Burt!" Reba glared at her husband, and he clammed up. Apparently, this was one sore subject on which they agreed to disagree. When she looked back at me, her expression practically begged for absolution. "He just needs some professional help, that's all."

Burt snorted, and she leveled another glare in his direction.

"You said that Senator Gorham took him away," I said, attempting to stick to facts versus prickly speculation. The last thing I wanted was for the Givens to break out into a full-fledged argument over something that even experts disagreed over, especially with an arsenal of guns looming in the background. "How does she fit into the picture?"

"She's been very instrumental in securing the funding needed to keep New Horizons running," said Reba. "The institution is privately held, and she's on the board of directors. Every campaign cycle, her ads lean on her reputation as the last-chance savior for wayward boys. I doubt she has much to do with the day-to-day operations of the place, but she sure keeps tabs on its delinquent population. Isn't that like most politicians? Do none of the work but take all of the credit."

"So, how did she get her hooks into Boyd?" I asked.

"Boyd was out with some of his buddies raising hell for his seventeenth birthday. Before the night was over, they burned a family's house down in Darbydale. They thought the family was on vacation," said Burt, his face clouding over. "They were wrong."

Reba pushed away from the table, grabbing the pan of tepid water and sloshing some on the table before heading into the kitchen to empty it into the sink. She stood there with her back to us as tension rippled through her shoulders, her discomfort evident, but Burt wasn't quite finished yet.

"Eddie and Joyce Holland woke up to a roomful of flames closing in on their baby girl who still shared a room with them and thank God for that. They got her outside to safety before Eddie went back in for his seventy-three-year-old grandmother who, ironically, had just moved in with them because she kept forgetting to turn the burners off on her gas stove. Eddie ended up with third-degree burns on over half his body, and Dorothy nearly died of smoke inhalation but after weeks in the hospital, she managed to pull through. Otherwise, those boys would have been looking at murder charges instead of arson and reckless endangerment, which was bad enough." Burt paused as the memories threatened to overwhelm him. "Teddy Bickle and Frankie Osborne took the brunt of it. They were eighteen and were tried as adults. Boyd was driving the car and claimed he didn't know what the other two boys were up to, though I find that hard to believe. In any event, he caught what we thought was a break. Instead of going to jail, he was remanded to the care of New Horizons."

"How long ago was this?" I asked.

"Eleven years ago," said Reba, finally turning around to rejoin in the conversation. "He could have been sent to prison on his eighteenth birthday, but the courts allowed him to remain at New Horizons until he was twenty-one. He was supposedly doing well in their programs and seemed to settle down under their care. I don't know. We were never allowed to see him."

I blinked. "Never? Is that even legal? Wouldn't they have to have some sort of visitation policy for parents?"

"They do," said Burt. "But Boyd refused to see us."

"Surely, he's not still there," I said.

"No," said Reba. "Now he works for Senator Gorham. He's part of her security detail and has been for years. New Horizons turned him into a mindless robot—a foot soldier for that bitch and all of her crazy agendas. That place is a cult, I tell you. It's taking these troubled boys and turning them into a militia."

I pondered that for a second, and it made a certain sort of sense. The Academy in Briarstaff was geared toward developing cyber soldiers to fight technology with even smarter technology. New Horizons sounded more like basic training, a place for readying troops for—what? Ground warfare? Against whom? A shudder rippled through me at the thought of an invading force that was already fully entrenched on American soil.

"So, what are you and your dad hoping to accomplish here?" asked Burt, snapping me out of my reverie. "Surely, you're not thinking of trying to get onto the New Horizons grounds. It would only be a matter of moments before you were rounded up, and if what happened earlier is any indication, ejecting you from the grounds is only wishful thinking. I'm guessing you'd never be seen again—at least, not alive."

"You know, I've gotta be honest," I said. "I don't really know what we're doing here. We're kind of just winging it. Dad's been having these dreams about Gina, and that's what convinced him she was still alive. I've tried to dissuade him, but he was pursuing it whether I came along or not. I thought it would be better to be with him than to let him go it alone, especially considering these spells he's been having."

"But you *knew* she was alive," said Reba, taking her seat again at the table. "Why wouldn't you share that with your parents? That seems horribly cruel."

"I'm not exactly *proud* of it," I said, bristling. "The last time I saw Gina, she made me promise to keep it under wraps. She said the safety of our entire family was at stake. What would you have done?"

"I don't know," she admitted. "It's not like we've done much for our own boy."

Burt snorted. "There's not a whole lot we *can* do, hon. Boyd is twenty-eight. He made his choices a long time ago."

"But we *know* people, Burt," she said. "Kirby and Wilson have loads of experience in deprogramming. If we could just get Boyd away from these people, we could—"

"Enough, Reba," said Burt irritably. "We've been over this."

Her mouth snapped shut, but the look she gave him spoke volumes. I wanted nothing more than to slink away back to my room, but Burt shifted his attention back to me.

"Okay, so you need to have some sort of plan, here," said Burt. "'Winging it' isn't going to cut it. You're only going to get yourselves killed."

"You're right," I acknowledged, tugging at my bottom lip as I mulled it over. "Gina had pictures of the three senators placing them at The Academy's grounds in Briarstaff, and although it wasn't an association they wanted to be made public, that alone wouldn't have been much of a threat. It was the combination of the pictures and what she overheard when she found a way into the facility that set them after her."

Burt leaned forward on his elbows, clasping his hands together. "New Horizons isn't some sort of brain trust. They're training these men for combat, but it's not like they're conducting these training exercises right out in the open where anyone could sneak some pictures and leak them to the press."

I rubbed my tired eyes and sighed. "I have no idea how to get us out of this mess, but there's no turning back. So far, they've sent two assassins after us, and I don't think they're going to give up that easily."

"Two?" asked Burt, surprised.

I nodded. "Last night, they sent a guy to the motel we were staying at. We managed to take care of that one ourselves—well, Dad did. I just stood there like an idiot and watched while he pitched the guy over a second-story handrail to the parking lot below. He didn't—land well."

I didn't think Burt's eyebrows could raise any higher. "Your dad managed to neutralize a professional hit man?"

"He's tougher than he looks," I said. "You can't really judge him based on what just happened here."

Burt sighed. "But you can't discount it, either."

"What are you saying?"

"Whatever you decide to do, you have to understand that your dad is a liability," he said. "You never know when he might have another one of his episodes."

I stared at him. "Well, I can't just take him back home. There's no way he would stay put, especially now that he knows that Gina is out there somewhere. I can't let him do this by himself."

We fell into awkward silence as inspiration failed us all, and while I didn't have any ideas, one thing seemed perfectly clear—we had already taken more than enough advantage of the Givens' hospitality.

"If you're still alright with us staying tonight, we'll clear out in the morning," I said, pushing away from the table. "I appreciate everything you've done, but we can't pull you any further into this."

"Oh, now, settle down," said Burt, waving away my concerns. "We're not putting you out. We just need some time to think about what we're going to do."

I stood behind my chair and eyed him dubiously. "I don't get it. Why are you helping us?"

"I could say it's just the right thing to do, but I'm not fond of lying," he said. "Truth of the matter is, we've been looking for a way to bring that

Gorham bitch down for years. Helping you helps us. What we all really need is a good night's rest, so we can tackle this again with fresh eyes. Sound good?"

"If you're sure," I said warily.

"I am."

I nodded. "Thank you."

Reba's cheeks remained flushed, and it was clear she was peeved at Burt for cutting her off earlier. She definitely had some thoughts on the matter, but this wasn't the time nor the place. I retreated down the hallway and quietly let myself back into the bedroom.

I stared at the darkened ceiling, worry spiraling.

As I lay there, trying to manifest a tangible path forward, I began to grow anxious when I couldn't hear Dad breathing across the room, no matter how hard I listened. He was utterly still, an indistinct shape submerged in a lumpy sea of bedding. Normally, he would be peeling the paint off the roof with his obnoxious snoring, and the vacuum of silence had my imagination running amok. I was just about to feel my way across the pitch-black void separating us to do a well-check when he abruptly snorted, rolled over and hit his usual stride.

I nearly giggled with relief, but that relief was short lived.

Burt and Reba must have continued their discussion after I left the room. It was beginning to leak through the walls, and it wasn't getting any more amicable with time. If anything, it was getting worse. While I couldn't make out any of the specifics, the tone was argumentative, with Reba's agitation growing the longer they went at it. Eventually, heavy footfalls sounded in the hallway, followed by the thunderous slam of their bedroom door. It was a wonder it didn't wake Dad, but now that he had found his normal rhythm, nothing else was penetrating his slumber.

I lay awake for hours, wondering what in the hell we had gotten ourselves into.

Just when I thought sleep would never come, it finally pulled me under.

CHAPTER EIGHTEEN

M y eyes opened wide as a hand clamped over my mouth.
      "Shhh."

It was Reba, and I struggled to get my bearings. Vestiges of daylight crept around the heavy blinds, just enough to see that Dad was no longer in the bed to my right. The covers were strewn halfway across the floor, as if tossed aside in haste. I shook my head ferociously to displace her hand. "What have you done with my dad?"

She reasserted her hand, clamping down even harder, her eyes projecting urgency. *"Shhh!* Your dad's fine, but we have to move quickly. We're not alone."

Wolfie's incessant barking finally registered through the cabin walls, and I thought I could vaguely make out Burt's voice in animated conversation. I shut my mouth and nodded, ready to follow Reba's lead. She stood and motioned me out of the bed before moving toward the door. She held up a finger as I approached, turning the doorknob carefully and slowly easing the door open. She peered out into the hallway, and once she determined the coast was clear, she waved me forward, pointing to the open door across the hall. It led to hers and Burt's bedroom. I scuttled along in my stockinged feet, and she followed me in, quietly closing the door behind us. The blinds were pulled in here as well, but visibility remained slightly higher as there was a greater number of windows leaking tendrils of sunshine around their covered panes.

"What is going on?" I whispered, but she waved my words away, pointing toward the foot of their king-sized bed. I did a double take. The steamer trunk that had previously been centered along the footboard was lying on its face at an odd angle, exposing a rectangular cutout in the planked flooring. She nudged me toward it.

As I got nearer, I could see a set of narrow steps leading down into utter darkness, and I hesitated, looking back toward Reba with uncertainty. She sighed, impatiently shooing me down, and what's a guy to do? The voices were getting louder from the living room, and I had exactly zero idea what was happening. I eased my way down into the darkness, narrowly avoiding braining myself on the narrow opening as I ducked beneath the floor and fumbled blindly into the void.

I had only just reached the earthen floor at the bottom when the trunk sprung back into place on hidden hinges with a definitive click, effectively sealing me within a dark, soundless, subterranean tomb.

I'll be the first to admit that I've got issues—thank goodness claustrophobia isn't one of them.

I couldn't see my hand in front of my face, but I had the distinct impression that I wasn't alone. "Dad?" I ventured, keeping my voice low.

"*Dwayne!*" His response seemed impossibly loud, coming from somewhere ahead and to my right.

"*Shhh!*" I scolded automatically, afraid he'd be heard by whoever or whatever we were hiding from.

"I don't think we have to worry about noise, son," he said, although he took his voice down a notch. "I think this space is a veritable bomb shelter. You'll have to watch your step. Everything happened so fast, I didn't have a chance to grab a candle on the way down, but there's plenty to fall over.

I learned that the hard way. I did find a place to sit that's fairly comfortable, if you want to follow the sound of my voice."

"Umm, okay," I said, flailing about blindly with my hands in front of me, shuffling forward in halting half-steps for fear of faceplanting. I was having a serious case of déjà vu from the previous evening and wasn't nearly as convinced that we wouldn't be heard if I sent something crashing to the ground.

"Marco," Dad said in a flat monotone.

It was so ludicrous, I couldn't help but giggle. "Polo."

We traded prompts until I finally located him in the far corner of the dungeon-like space, and I managed to cover the distance without significant incident. While I had no real sense of the size of the space, it felt like it was bigger than the cabin above. Dad guided me down to the seat beside him.

"How are you feeling?" I aimed my question in his general direction, blinking into the darkness.

Huge sigh.

"I'm *fine*." I didn't need to see his face to picture his sour expression. "Like I told you last night, I just needed to get some rest. That's all. Everyone needs to stop treating me like—"

"An invalid," I interjected, massaging the bridge of my nose. "Yeah, yeah—alright. So, what happened up there?"

"Woke up around dawn like normal," his disembodied voice said. "You were still sawing logs—also like normal. You know, son, you really need to see someone about that snore of yours. It could be sleep apnea."

My turn to sigh. "I don't have sleep apnea."

"How would you know?" he asked. "You're *asleep*. You have no way of knowing that for yourself. It's like saying you don't snore at all, and Lord knows *that* isn't true. You need to do one of those sleep studies to find out—"

"I'm *fine*, Dad," I snapped, wondering how he had managed to effectively swap out my concerns for his health for his concerns about mine. As a conversationalist, he was a master at this sort of diversion.

"I just don't want you to die in your sleep, son," he added, unable to resist taking one last, well-placed jab.

"I'm not going to die in my sleep, Dad. I promise."

"Well, I'm not going to either, so can we just give all this a rest?"

"Fine," I said.

"Fine," he agreed.

We lapsed into silence until I finally prompted, "So—?"

"Hmm?"

"So, what *happened* up there?" Heaven help me, I tried to keep the exasperation out of my voice, but it was impossible. "What are we doing down here? Is this a hostage situation? I'm not accustomed to being lurched out of sleep only to be thrown into an underground pit."

"Pfft. It's hardly a pit. This has the feel of decent furniture, not that I can see it—"

"Da-a-d! What *happened?"*

"The dog," he said. "That's what happened. I was just getting ready to have a nice cup of coffee with Burt and Reba in the kitchen. We were trying to decide what to have for breakfast when their dog started barking his fool head off outside. Burt went to see what all the ruckus was about, and next thing I knew, Reba was hustling me down here, telling me to stay put and be quiet while she went to get you. And now you're pretty much up to speed."

I tugged at my bottom lip. "I don't like this. Do you think somebody found that guy's body in the reservoir?"

"Maybe."

"Do you think someone saw Burt dumping the truck and the body, and they're taking him in for questioning?" My imagination was beginning to run wild with a decidedly dark slant. "What if they hold Burt and Reba for questioning. I mean, they can do that for what—a couple of days at most, right?"

"I would think you would know that better than I would, son," said Dad, remaining cool and collected while I began to eye my internal panic button.

"If they get charged, we could be locked down here for *days*," I realized. "We could starve to death—or run out of oxygen. How long do you think the air in here will last? I mean, nobody knows we're here!" My throat began to constrict, and suddenly claustrophobia was right back on the table.

I jumped as Dad placed his hands firmly on my shoulders.

"Relax," he said, his voice warm and soothing. "We're not going to run out of air *or* food. Like I said earlier, this is some sort of fallout shelter or something. It was specifically designed for survival. And I'm sure that Burt or Reba will be back soon. Just *breathe.*"

I nodded, taking his sage advice and feeling my racing heartbeat slow with each breath, but there was only so much worry I could dispel.

"Dad?"

"Yes, son?"

"If we get out of here—"

"When we get out of here," he corrected.

"Okay—*when* we get out of here," I said. "I think we should leave just as soon as possible."

"I agree we shouldn't overstay our welcome, but it seems that the Givens know a little bit more about this Gorham woman than we do," said Dad. "Shouldn't we at least stay to find out what that might be?"

"I don't know," I said, reflecting on the events of the previous evening. "There's something about all this they don't agree on. I heard them arguing after we went to bed last night, and it got a little heated. I'm not sure I want to be in the middle of all that."

We sat in silence as Dad considered my words. "Okay," he finally said. "Your reservations have been noted. I say we proceed with caution, and if we don't like the direction things are headed, we hit the road. Sound like a plan?"

I nodded as if he could see me. Sure, t sounded like a plan—a somewhat shitty plan. But it was better than any plan I currently had.

Side by side, we sat in the inky darkness, listening to each other breathe while time dragged its sluggish feet toward whatever fate our futures may hold.

The sound of the latches releasing was like unexpected gunfire, causing both of us to jump. We stared as a small rectangle of light was cast down from above at the far end of the room, illuminating the narrow stairs and the shelves of canned goods that were directly across from it.

"Knock, knock!" Reba's flat voice sounded from above. "You fellas can come up now. Coast is clear."

I followed Dad back to the stairs, noting box after box of what I could only guess were doomsday supplies lining the walls. Off to the side and stacked on pallets was quite an assortment of bottled beverages and spring water. It would seem that this whole survivalist thing was more than just a passing hobby. As we climbed the stairs single file, I was never so happy to see my father's blue-jeaned backside appear before me in the scant daylight.

We followed Reba back to the kitchen table where Burt was already waiting, a serious expression on his face. All the curtains remained drawn, but a few candles had been lit to push back the gloom. Wolfie was apparently still outside, standing guard. At least all was quiet now.

"I'm guessing that wasn't the Avon lady," said Dad, taking a seat at the table.

"No, it was not," said Burt, nursing a cup of coffee. "It was a couple of fellas looking for their missing comrade. It was honestly a little sooner than expected, but I'm not entirely surprised."

"What did you tell them?" I asked, taking my seat from the night before. Reba went to the fridge and retrieved a carton of brown eggs, carrying it to the kitchen counter. Apparently, breakfast was underway.

"Not a goddamn thing. I said this was private property, and it's posted all over the goddamn place. I told them they had best get their asses off my land before I got my gun," he said.

I blinked. As far as reactions go, Burt's felt a little extreme. "Is that how you—*normally* answer the door?"

The corner of Burt's mouth quirked up. "Matter of fact, it is. Reba and I enjoy our privacy, and we make no bones about it. We keep company by invitation only. It would have been a hell of a lot more suspicious had I invited them in for coffee. Besides, they didn't know anything. They were just on a big ol' fishing expedition."

"How can you be so sure?" I asked.

"Well," said Burt, pausing to take a sip of his coffee before ticking his points off on his fingers. "They didn't come in any official capacity, they just claimed to be looking for a friend who didn't come home after a day of hunting. They didn't ask about the two of you at all. They didn't push it when I told them to skedaddle. For now, they'll just move on to our nearest neighbors and see if their luck gets any better."

I raised an eyebrow. "For now?"

"Oh, they'll be back," he said. "Or at least somebody will. Probably several someones. With badges, guns, and a warrant. Smartest thing would be for the two of you to be gone by then."

"Oh," I said, unable to hide my disappointment. Less than twelve hours ago, Burt had said they wouldn't turn their backs on us, but I guess his morning visitors had been reason enough to reconsider. I exchanged a glance with Dad. "Come on, Dad. We should go."

"Not so fast," said Burt. "I told you we weren't putting you out, and I meant it. But I also feel obligated to point out that the smartest path forward is for the two of you to hightail it back home and let this whole thing go. Somehow, I'm pretty sure that's not gonna happen."

"Not while my daughter is still out there," said Dad, the muscles in his jaw flexing defiantly. "Not a chance."

Burt slowly nodded as Reba beat the hell out of a bowlful of eggs. It may have just been my imagination, but she still seemed mighty out of sorts.

"Alright, then," said Burt, leaning in. "Let's discuss strategy."

Reba made the rounds distributing coffee mugs before circling again with a carafe to fill them. "There's sugar and creamer on the table. Help yourselves," she mumbled before returning to pour the frothy bowl of eggs into a cast iron skillet on the stove. She immediately began whisking with a vengeance.

Burt's eyes followed her, his expression unreadable while the tension in the room was anything but. Their differences from the previous evening were still hanging heavy in the air, and I snuck a glance at Dad to see if he was picking up on it, but his attention was laser-focused on measuring just the proper amount of sugar to sweeten his coffee.

"The objective is to bring your daughter safely home," Burt said, restating the obvious to Dad. "And to do that, you need to eliminate any obstacles that are standing in your way, namely Senator Amelia Gorham. Sound about right?"

Dad looked to me for confirmation, and I nodded.

"So, were you thinking about trying to do this yourself, or are you looking to hire someone? I mean, this isn't the sort of thing that we do, but I might have a few folks I could reach out to. This won't be cheap, though."

Burt warned, and I have to admit, I was a little slow on the uptake. But once I caught his meaning, my eyes widened.

"We're not planning to *assassinate* the senator," I said. "I need to find a way to discredit her—make people see her for who she really is and what she's up to at this New Horizons facility."

Burt shook his head doubtfully. "Well, good luck with that. It's not like she's been hiding her affiliation with the place. It's a point of pride."

"An operation that's been around as long as New Horizons is bound to have had its fair share of scandals over the years," I said, my brain finally responding to the coffee. "I mean, you and Reba can't be the only two parents with complaints. I need to do a little digging to see what I can uncover."

Reba made the rounds again, this time distributing plates of scrambled eggs and toast. "Good luck," she said, echoing her husband's sentiment but with even less conviction. She didn't join us at the table but instead bustled out of the kitchen and back toward the bedrooms, leaving an awkward silence in her wake.

"Is she alright?" Dad asked around a mouthful of eggs. I rolled my eyes and wondered how he and Mom had ever managed to stay together for nearly four decades.

Burt's smile was more of a grimace. "It's a touchy subject for her."

"I think these should fit you pretty well," said Reba as she handed me a folded pair of jeans, a ribbed A-shirt, and a navy plaid flannel shirt. "You look like you're about Brock's size. Can't help you with the underwear, though."

That was just fine with me. Borrowing someone else's underwear was never really a goal of mine, but after breakfast, we had all come to the rather blunt conclusion that we were getting a little whiffy. I smiled at her as I took the stack of clothes. "Thanks, I'll figure it out."

"Towels and washcloths are in the bathroom closet," she said. "I make my own soap and shampoo, and you'll find both in the stall. They may not smell as pretty as what you'd find down at the Walmart's, but they get the job done. I can't help you with shaving supplies. Burt hasn't shaved in years, and we're just coming out of winter, so I haven't either. Just give me a holler when you're ready, and we'll get this show on the road."

"Thank you."

She excused herself while I got to the task at hand. Dad was queued up after me, although we'd decided to go our separate ways after that. I was about to undertake my least favorite part of the whole 'detective' thing—research. Typically, it involved hours and hours of going down endless rabbit holes to nowhere, hoping to stumble across something useful, if only by accident. Since the Givens didn't have a computer, much less electricity, it would require me to avail myself of someone else's resources, and in this case, Reba had offered to drive me back into Darbydale where there was a small public library that made the internet available to its patrons via shared computers. It wasn't ideal, but it was better than nothing. The very idea of spending that much time in a library was repugnant to Dad, and when Burt suggested that they discuss alternate strategies, he was all over it. I suspected Burt was trying to keep Dad busy and out of the line of fire—whatever that may be—and I was perfectly fine with that. With each of Dad's subsequent episodes, my confidence in him was shaken a little more, and as much as I didn't want to admit it, Burt was absolutely right.

In his current state, Dad was a liability

Convincing him of that would be next to impossible, however. Distraction seemed like the best option at this point, but that would only work for so long.

I pulled the cloth shower curtain back to find a corrugated metal stall with a concrete basin. A wire caddy was looped around the neck of the shower head, containing the aforementioned clump of soap and a bottle of cloudy liquid that smelled of eucalyptus. I stripped off my grimy clothes and turned the water on, disappointed by the lack of pressure. I stepped under the tepid water, careful to keep my bandaged left arm out of the lazy spray.

How was it only Wednesday?

It felt like I hadn't seen Melanie or the kids in weeks, and it was beginning to feel like I'd never see them again. Even if I was able to find something to use against Senator Gorham, it was going to take time, and I was pretty much out of excuses to tell Mom as to why I wasn't bringing Dad home. I couldn't tell her about Gina—at least not yet, but I couldn't be sure that Dad wouldn't let it slip.

Gina.

Did she know what was happening? Was she monitoring from afar or completely oblivious to what was going on? Would she even know if we managed to clear the path for her to come home? It had been nine long months since I had last seen her face hovering over mine in that ambulance, a recollection that was hazy at best. Any number of things could have happened in all that time, and my imagination tended to dip toward darkness.

Was she even still alive or had they found her first, finishing a job that was contracted the previous July?

For a moment, I could barely breathe, overwhelmed by the certainty we were already too late. Hot tears came unbidden, and all I could do was let them mingle with the water spiraling down the drain.

Dammit! I needed to pull myself together. There was no sense in worrying about all the things that were beyond my control. We had decided on a course of action, and I needed to focus on my part. I didn't need to have all of the answers now, and the realization served to release the pressure that was currently threatening to suffocate me.

I worked the viscous minty shampoo into my hair before picking up the clump of handmade soap to try and coax it into a lather. It was waxy and gritty, and eventually I just dragged it along my torso with a washcloth. True to Reba's word, it smelled like nothing, but after letting the water sluice through my hair and down my body, I felt undeniably better. The water was just beginning to turn cold when I finally rinsed the last of the grainy soap off of me.

I had no more turned the water off and stepped out onto the thick braided rug lying outside the shower basin when a short, sharp knock sounded at the door.

"Let's pick up the pace, son," said Dad from the hallway. "What did you do, fall in? Other folks need to shower too, you know."

"I'll be out in a sec," I said, coaxing the moisture out of my hair with a surprisingly absorbent bath towel. "Umm, but you might want to wait ten minutes or so."

Dad's sigh was plain as day through the door. "Did you plug the toilet?"

"No!" I barked irritably. "I just—uh, I—"

"You used all the hot water, didn't you?"

I dropped my head. "Yes."

Another heavy sigh. "For pity's sake, Dwayne! I don't know what's wrong with you kids these days. When I was in basic training, we had exactly thirty seconds to get washed up and rinsed off—period. None of this lollygagging like it was some kind of luxury spa. Jeez. Good thing they don't have electricity, or I'd probably be waiting for you to blow dry your hair, too."

I couldn't help but smile as he grumply padded back down the hall. He certainly sounded like himself, and for just a moment, I could almost make myself believe it was true.

CHAPTER NINETEEN

"Can I ask you a question?" I couldn't take another second of the awkward silence that consumed the VW's cramped interior.

Reba kept her eyes on the winding road as her knuckles tightened on the steering wheel. "Sure."

"Are you okay?" I asked, watching her from the corner of my eye.

"I'm fine," she said, her voice flat and unconvincing.

I paused, choosing my next words carefully. "Thing is, you don't *sound* fine. You sound pissed. Did we do something to upset you?"

She shook her head almost imperceptibly. "Not at all." Her words said one thing while her whitening knuckles said something altogether different.

I stared at the sun dappled pavement as it disappeared under the blunt snout of the Beetle. Traffic was practically nonexistent, and for the most part, we had the road to ourselves. I plucked at the undershirt that Reba had lent me, uncomfortably aware of how it clung to my frame like a second skin. Brock was either a lot thinner than me or had a penchant for exhibitionism that was never my thing. I toyed with the buttons of the navy plaid shirt I had worn over top of it and wished I would have fastened it at least partway up.

"I seriously don't mean to put my nose where it doesn't belong," I said, unable to just let it go. "But I heard you and Burt last night—after I went to bed."

That caught her attention. She looked at me sharply. "Oh."

"I wasn't eavesdropping," I quickly said. "And I really didn't hear anything specific. I could just tell you were arguing, that's all. I'd hate to think that we were the cause of that."

She chuckled humorlessly, showing the first hint of a resigned smile. "I promise you, that wasn't your doing. For the most part, Burt and I are completely sympatico. There are just some things…"

Her voice trailed off as she focused on the road, a logging truck trying to suck us into its vortex as it roared past in the opposite direction.

"It's Boyd, isn't it?" I ventured.

She sighed before scowling at me. "It is."

We lapsed back into silence. The woods that bordered the tarmac were beginning to thin with a handful of unremarkable one-story dwellings popping up at irregular intervals along both sides of the street. Just when I thought I was going to have to find another way to get her to open up, she took a deep breath and cleared her throat.

"Let me ask *you* a question," she said, her eyes still locked onto the road ahead.

"Okay."

"You've got a couple of kids of your own, right?"

"Well, technically, they aren't mine, they're my fiancée's, but yeah," I said, nodding. "I do."

"I know you said they were young, but can you imagine a scenario where one of them did something so awful that you would completely turn your back on them?" She glanced at me, carefully gauging my reaction.

"Well—no, I don't suppose I can," I said after a moment of reflection. "Is that what's going on here? Didn't Burt say that he wanted Senator Gorham to pay for what she's done to your family?"

Reba scoffed. "Oh, sure. He wants payback for what she's done. He's all about the payback and stopping her from victimizing anybody else, but he doesn't want anything more to do with our own boy, and I just simply can't understand that. I mean, I know Boyd's troubled. He's *always* been troubled. But with the proper care, he might be able to control himself—actually function like everybody else."

"Is he bipolar?" I asked.

"How should *I* know?" she responded, her agitation growing. "Burt is so goddamned anti-establishment that he would never let me take our son to a psychiatrist to be evaluated. He thinks psychiatry is just an expensive way for people to get professional absolution for their bad behavior. He says it's just another way for big pharma to turn us all into mindless cattle."

"I'm sorry," I said sincerely. I honestly couldn't imagine what it might take to turn my back on Jasmine or Jordan. Of course, I couldn't imagine them doing the sorts of things they'd said Boyd had done, so it wasn't exactly an apples-to-apples comparison. Still, it wasn't a nightmare I'd wish on anyone.

"Yeah, well, it's been a point of contention for a lot longer than you and your dad have been around, so you can let yourselves off the hook. We agree on far more than we don't. We'll find a way to work through it. Eventually."

Reba slowed the car to twenty-five as we approached Darbydale, the city limits delineated by a faded sign celebrating the town's bicentennial back in 2003 and proudly proclaiming the province "A Real American Original!" The city itself was a lot less celebratory, a cluster of squat brick buildings laid out in tidy squares. The geography was flat as a pancake, with buildings maxing out at three stories, although most of them had fewer. Daylight revealed nothing breathtaking about the architecture or landscaping that was noteworthy, the town's aesthetic strictly utilitarian. Residents were taking full advantage of the good weather, strolling the wide sidewalks both leisurely and with purpose, and I couldn't help but notice several heads pivoting to watch as we drove by.

243

"I hope we weren't supposed to be flying under the radar," I said, trying hard not to return the growing number of stares that followed us. "Do you always get this sort of reaction?"

Reba shrugged. "I've gotten used to it. People don't really know what to make of us, so I'm sure we've inspired some pretty tall tales. While they may not be the warmest folks you'll ever meet, at least they keep their distance."

"Aren't you worried about being seen with me?" I asked, trying to make myself smaller in the passenger seat.

"Not really," she said. "If anyone asks, I'll just tell 'em you're Brock. It's been years since anyone's seen him, and even when he lived here, he didn't exactly hang out in town. You're close enough to his physical type to pass."

She used her signal and turned right into a mostly empty parking lot that was clearly marked, "For Library Patrons ONLY! – Violators will be TOWED at the Owner's EXPENSE!"

"Friendly," I noted, nodding at the sign.

"Full of shit is more like it," she snorted. "The closest tow service is Bob Gentry's, and he's two counties over. Take a look around. Parking isn't even an issue in Darbydale."

Nevertheless, she pulled toward the back of the lot and nosed the VW into a slot behind a maroon Buick, largely obscuring us from the inquisitive eyes of passersby. She turned the engine off and swiveled in her seat to reach into the back and grab her purse. She extracted a small wallet and flipped through it to produce a small white card, which she handed to me. "Here. You might need this."

I looked it over. "Brock's library card?'

She nodded. "I seem to recall that you need to have one to access the library's computers. Since you're trying to stay off the radar, I wouldn't advise using your ID to get your own."

"Thanks," I said.

244

"So, I'll leave you to it," she said. "I have a few errands of my own to run that will keep me busy for quite a while. When would you like me to come back and pick you up?"

I glanced at my watch, noting it was just after nine. "I'm sure it's going to take a while. Maybe three?"

"Three o'clock it is," she confirmed. "Did you grab your cellphone and charger? This will be your only chance to top it off, and you should probably make any calls you need to make before we head back."

I patted my pocket, feeling the outline of the burner phone. I had its charger wound around my wrist, and I held it up. "Got 'em."

"There's a decent café just down the block where you can grab some lunch when you get hungry. Do you have enough money to get through the day?"

I grinned, amused by the maternal instincts suddenly kicking in. Reba sounded a lot like my own mother seeing me off in the morning on a school day.

"I'm good—*Mom*," I teased. I had made a pit-stop to the bowling bag in the backseat of the Monza before we had gotten into Reba's Beetle, loaning myself a hundred dollars from Dad's stash. He knew I was good for it.

Reba's cheeks brightened, before she treated me with her first real smile of the day. "That's my boy. Now, get in there and try to blend in. Most importantly, turn up some dirt on that lousy, skeezy bitch. Do your mama proud!"

The automatic doors whooshed open to provide hands-free access, and I paused just inside the second set of double doors to give my eyes a chance to adjust to the relative gloom after coming in from the bright sunlight. I was one of only three people in the small building, and as my eyes came into focus, I realized the other two were staring at me with unbridled curiosity.

So much for blending in.

Turning my head left, I nodded to the elderly gentleman scowling at me from where he was seated on a pleather sofa in the periodicals section and proceeded to the circulation desk in the center of the room. A short, heavyset woman with tight, steel-gray curls lifted her own chin in acknowledgement as I approached, the corners of her mouth dipping down ever so slightly, as if she were smelling something foul. She had a short stack of books in front of her that she was scanning back into the system at a languid pace while her eyes never looked away from me.

I eyed the spines, spotting Patricia Cornwell, Lisa Regan, and Charly Cox. I gestured toward the books with a knuckle.

"I see someone really likes strong female protagonists," I said, grinning crookedly.

I was hoping to break the ice, but she looked at me like I had just broken wind. She ignored my observation and scooted the stack aside, clearing her throat. "May I help you with something?"

"Um, yeah," I said, unconsciously tugging the front panels of my plaid overshirt together to cover my midsection. "I understand that you have computers for public use?"

"For library patrons," she said, somehow managing to look down her nose at me while also angling up to meet my gaze.

"Sure," I said, fumbling Brock's library card out of my pocket and casually handing it to her. I examined my surroundings, trying to play it cool, but the intensity with which she studied the card had my pits gently weeping down my ribcage. It wasn't a picture ID. What could be the issue? "Is something wrong?"

She slapped the card down on the counter and slid it back to me. "It's expired," she said flatly. "Nearly ten years ago. You'll need to register for a new one." She reached below the counter and pulled out a clipboard with an application attached and a pen tethered to the board. "Fill this out and bring it back. I'll need to see an ID with proof of address."

My smile faltered.

"Oh," I said, struggling to hide my disappointment. "I didn't think these things ever expired."

"Well, they do," she said evenly, thrusting the clipboard toward me with one hand while feeding Brock's expired card into a shredder with the other.

Shit.

I hoped Reba wasn't expecting that back. I took a seat at one of the open tables to the left of the circulation desk and stared at the form in front of me, wondering how I might get around that whole "ID requirement." It felt a lot more likely that I'd be spending the next six hours waiting for Reba to return. What a colossal waste of time!

Oh, stop it, said a little voice inside my head. *Just fill out the form and worry about the ID later. And look! It might not be so bad. Only the fields marked with an asterisk are required.*

I sighed and picked up the pen.

NAME (Last name first, First name last)*

That was easy enough. I printed GIVENS, BROCK in precise block letters.

DATE OF BIRTH*

I had no idea! But then again, they couldn't really verify much of anything, so I just had to make it seem reasonable. Reba had said that Brock was approximately the same age as me, so I jotted down my own birthdate.

ADDRESS*

Well, of *course*, they would require an address! I hadn't quite gotten around to swapping contact information with the Givens so we could exchange Christmas cards during the holidays. The only signage I had seen anywhere near the Givens' property was of the "No Trespassing" variety, not street signs. I didn't know if they even had a mailbox. It was like they lived in the middle of Sherwood Forest.

Hmm.

I poised the pen over the form, hesitating only a second before jotting down 4345 SHERWOOD LANE, DARBYDALE, PA. I figured what the hell? In for a penny, in for a pound. I applied the same logic with the mandatory phone number field, using the ubiquitous 555 area code that was prevalent in movies and television, followed by the only slightly less well-known 867-5309, banking on odds that Lucretia the Librarian had never even heard of Tommy Tutone or his beloved Jenny.

The rest of the form was comprised of optional information—demographics, hobbies, and interests. The only required field left was for my signature, and I'll be damned if I didn't almost scrawl 'Dwayne Morrow' and ruin the whole thing. I caught myself at the last second and signed 'Brock Givens' instead.

Now what?

What possible excuse could I have for not having an ID that might persuade the old battle-axe to give me access to the internet? I could tell her I forgot it, but I didn't feel that lack of preparedness would earn me any latitude. It only took a single look at her stern countenance to realize this lady was strictly by-the-books. I smiled at my own pun, but it was short-lived as she suddenly leveled a knowing look in my direction. It was like she read my mind.

Spooky.

I was distracted by an annoying squeak from somewhere within the rows of shelving behind me. With each iteration, it grew louder, and I turned just in time to see a young woman emerge from between two rows pushing a shelving cart laden with books. A crown of loose brown curls framed her oval face, and she was dressed for summer in a lightweight one-piece floral print dress that showed a whole lot of tanned leg. White plastic dongles trailed from each ear, explaining the rhythmic bob of her head to music only she could hear.

"Miss Whitney?" called the librarian from behind the circulation desk.

The young woman rounded the corner without even looking up, and I could hear the older woman's sigh from where I sat. She bustled out from behind the desk and approached Miss Whitney in a huff, pecking her on the shoulder and scaring the living shit out of her.

"Ms. Appleby! Oh, my *Lord*, you startled me!" she exclaimed, clutching her chest.

"What have I told you about wearing those earbuds?" Ms. Appleby asked irritably.

"I'm sorry, ma'am," said the younger woman, but the twinkle in her eye suggested she wasn't all *that* sorry. "I just figured it wouldn't matter since we don't get busy 'til closer to noon."

"It isn't up to you to decide what is permissible and what is not. This is the last time we're going to have this conversation. I would suggest leaving those things at home before they end up costing you your job."

"Yes, ma'am."

"I need you to cover the front desk for me, please," she said. "I need to make use of the facilities."

"Yes, ma'am," said Miss Whitney, plucking the buds from her ears and noticing me for the first time. She grinned and pulled a face as Ms. Appleby waddled toward the back of the building, winking at me before she headed over to the circulation desk.

This might just be the opportunity I was hoping for.

I picked the clipboard up and headed for the circulation desk, hoping my smile was warm versus creepy and desperate. I was startled to realize she wasn't looking at my face, and thank goodness for that, because my ears felt ready to burst into flames. Her eyes roamed my torso from top to bottom and back again, and it was pretty clear she liked what she saw. I laid the clipboard on the desk in front of her and opened my mouth to speak, but the only thing that came out was a high-pitched peep. I cleared my throat and tried again.

"Hi," I said. "I guess my library card was expired, and I was hoping to get a new one."

She flipped the clipboard around and pulled it toward herself, running her finger down the form as she read its contents.

"Let's see what we've got here—Brock," she said, the corner of her mouth quirking up as her gaze lingered. "This all looks good to me. Can I see your driver's license, please?"

"Well, umm, I've got a little problem with that," I said, squirming uncomfortably.

"DUI?" she asked, her grin widening.

"*No!*" I said, feeling my cheeks flush. I hoped my two-day stubble provided adequate cover. "I just didn't think to bring it with me. I've had my library card forever, but I guess it had expired. That other lady shredded it before I even knew what was happening. I'd go get my license, but—uh, my car's in the shop, and my mom dropped me off on her way out of town. I don't want to borrow any library materials. I'd just like to use the internet for a bit. Do you think you can help me, Miss—it's Whitney, isn't it?"

"Laurel," she said, batting her thick lashes at me. "I don't know. I'm already on Ms. Appleby's shit list. She'd have a stroke if she knew I bypassed another stupid rule."

Apparently, the thought was appealing, because the next thing I knew, she had stepped over to the keyboard and began pecking away, entering the information from my application. I scanned the back of the building for Appleby's imminent return, a sudden wave of guilt washing over me.

"Are you sure about this?" I asked, shifting nervously on my feet. "I wouldn't want to get you into any trouble."

"Don't worry about it," she said, clicking the submit button with satisfaction. A printer came to life under the counter, spitting out a couple of labels with matching barcodes. She peeled one off and attached it to my application and applied the other to a generic Darbydale Public Library plastic card and slid it across the counter to me. "There you go, Mr. Givens. You have your choice of computers as no one else is using them at the moment. Each workstation has a hand scanner attached. Scan your card, and it will start a one-hour clock running. If you're not finished when your time is up, and there's no one waiting, you can scan your card again and just keep right on going."

I picked the card up and smiled at her. "Thanks. I really owe you one. I was afraid I was about to waste a whole afternoon."

"No worries," she said. "Can I ask what you're researching?"

Whoop! Curveball. It hadn't occurred to me that anyone might give two shits about why I needed the internet. I stared at her while formulating what I hoped would be a reasonable response.

"The Indigenous tribes of eastern Pennsylvania—?"

It came out as much a question as a reply, and I looked away, certain she knew I was lying.

"Indigenous tribes, huh?" she repeated, the hint of a smirk playing at her lips. "I'd say it sounds intriguing, but I never really was a very good liar. Aren't you a little past your college days?"

I tried not to look offended. "You're never too old to learn. How old do you think I am, anyway?"

She shrugged. "I dunno. Forty?"

My face dropped. *"Forty?"*

I was nothing short of incredulous, and her laughter did little to lessen the sting.

"Hey—you asked," she said. "But I've never been good at those sorts of guessing games, anyway. Besides, I didn't mean anything bad by it. I find older men intriguing, although I have to say, I would have never pegged you as an academic. You look more like the hands-on type."

My mouth went dry, and words failed me entirely. I mean, how do you respond to a comment like that?

"I'm thirty-five," I finally muttered, my wounded pride preventing me from letting the obscene fallacy stand. *Forty.* For fuck's sake!

She giggled before affecting a pout and leaning across the counter. "I really *am* sorry. I didn't mean to offend.'

I shrugged it off, mentally making a note never to ask *that* particular question again. "It's fine."

A door closed somewhere in the back of the building followed by heavy footfalls coming our way. Laurel straightened and plucked my application off of the clipboard, feeding it into the shredder.

"Go grab a computer," she advised. 'It wouldn't do for Frau Appleby to catch you fraternizing with the help."

I goggled and pointed at the rapidly shrinking application being consumed by the shredder. "Isn't that, like, destroying evidence or something?"

"Um, *no*," she said, favoring me with another grin. "It's what we always do after entering applications into the system and verifying identification." She winked and turned away just as Ms. Appleby came into view.

I took my newfound library card and headed for the computer furthest away from the circulation desk and Appleby's prying eyes.

CHAPTER TWENTY

Research may not be my favorite investigative activity, but I have to admit, once I resign myself to it, I pretty much lose myself in the task. After I located an available electrical outlet to charge my prepaid phone, I logged into the computer and got down to business. I started by checking the tri-state news to ensure that Dad and I had yet to land on the FBI's Most Wanted List. So far, so good. Then I wasted a bit of time googling Senator Gorham directly, but it soon became abundantly clear that I wouldn't find anything horribly shocking in the public arena. Hers was a carefully cultivated image that harbored no serious scandals over the course of her forty-plus years in politics, just a series of strategically placed photo ops to advance whatever agenda the senator was currently pursuing. All of the images had been carefully staged with happy people surrounding their smiling representative. She had aged gracefully, her auburn hair silvering only slightly as fine lines appeared on her face to mark the passage of time. Her expression was nearly identical in every single picture, offering a ready-made smile that never quite reached her eyes. Her affiliation with New Horizons was anything but secret. Several of the articles I found lauded her commitment to the disenfranchised young men of Pennsylvania, lost souls whose adolescent transgressions had set them on the wrong path due to circumstances mostly beyond their control. Her goal was behavioral reform, to alter their trajectory so they might realize their own potential and return to a path of meaningful contribution to society. No one seemed to question why the beneficent senator's goodwill didn't extend to her own gender as well.

I shifted gears and began searching for anything I could find about the facility itself. New Horizons wasn't always a private reformatory. In fact, it began its existence as a state-run coed orphanage under the name, The Holloway House. The main dormitory was constructed in the 1950s and housed nearly a hundred children at the height of its operation in 1964. Over the next decade, Pennsylvania phased out institutionalized housing in favor of smaller group homes and foster care as they were deemed more conducive to individual growth and development. The building stood empty for nearly five years before it was bought by a private group of investors who expanded the campus and turned it into the juvenile detention facility that it was today. The place was only sporadically referenced in articles throughout the years, and in most cases, it was from Senator Gorham's own campaign materials, citing various impressive statistics to validate her ongoing commitment to the rehabilitation of Pennsylvania's underage male miscreants. The only blight on the facility's sterling history happened over nine years ago, when a fire broke out in one of the dormitories housing the youngest of New Horizons' residents. Several boys were hospitalized due to smoke inhalation while two of the less fortunate had succumbed to injuries sustained in the blaze. A photo of firefighters battling the blaze accompanied the article, and it was a sobering sight.

"*Hmm.*"

I jumped at the sound of Laurel's voice, which was surprisingly close to my ear.

"Well, that's a first," she said, grinning crookedly. "I've never really thought of our local home for wayward boys as a habitat for Indigenous tribes, but okay."

I closed the browser, feeling like I'd just been busted looking at porn. "I, uh—I was just taking a little break," I said, heat flooding into my cheeks. "I didn't hear you sneaking up on me."

She raised an eyebrow and leaned a hip against the computer desk. "I wasn't exactly sneaking, but sorry, I didn't mean to scare you. You *were* pretty focused, so I guess that's my bad."

"No problem," I said, smiling up at her. "Did you need something?"

"I just wanted to alert you to the fact that you're going to need to take at least an hour's break in about twenty minutes," she said. "The other workstations have all filled up, and Edna Lafferty comes in like clockwork every day at noon to catch up on her emails and the latest Hollywood gossip from TMZ. She won't use any more than an hour, but she won't use any less, either."

I looked around, surprised to see that the library had filled up considerably since I had started my quest.

"Oh, okay. Thanks for the heads up," I said.

I turned my attention back to the screen and reopened the browser, only to realize Laurel was still hovering just behind me.

"Was there something else?" I asked.

"As a matter of fact, there is," she said, turning coy. "Earlier, you said you owed me one."

My eyes narrowed. "I did. What did you have in mind?"

"*We-ell*—I get my break about the same time you'll need to surrender the workstation," she said. "How about taking me to lunch?"

"Oh, um—sure," I said warily, not really seeing any other option.

She laughed. "You don't have to sound so thrilled about it. I promise I won't bite."

I chuckled, despite the heated flush I felt engulfing me once again. "I'm sorry. As you saw, I was just really focused on what I was doing. Of course, I'll have lunch with you. It would be my privilege."

"That's better," she said with a wink. "I'll meet you out front in twenty."

· · · · ● ● ● ◉ ⊖ ● ● ● · · · ·

We crossed the street and headed for the café that Reba had told me about, although it was Laurel's idea, not mine. Working in such close proximity, she was a regular, a fact confirmed as soon as we entered the glass-fronted establishment.

"Hey, Laurel! I see you've got company today," called an olive-skinned, dark-haired man, grinning from behind the register as he made change for a departing customer.

"I do, but hands off, Tony," she said, waggling a warning finger in her friend's direction. "This one's mine."

I wondered exactly how much embarrassment it might take to actually kill a man, because I was surely reaching my quota. I nodded sheepishly and looked at my feet.

Tony just laughed. "See how you are. Fine. Grab yourselves a seat and take a minute to look at the menu. Today's special is salmon, teriyaki or grilled. I'll be over in a sec to get your orders." He cast one last lingering look in my direction. "Pity."

The floorplan was open and airy, and over half of the tables were already occupied. I followed Laurel to an empty table along the far wall and near the back of the restaurant. She took a seat facing the room, and that was perfectly fine with me. It felt like everyone in the room was watching us, and depending on how things played out, the fewer people who could identify me, the better. I sat down and pulled a couple of laminated menus from where they leaned against the wall and handed one to her.

"Um, Laurel," I said, looking at her over the top of my menu. "I should probably tell you—I'm not—you know, single."

257

She continued to peruse her menu without looking up. "And who said I was?"

Oh, good Lord.

My face dropped, and she couldn't keep a straight face. "Oh, my goodness, you're *fun!* You should just *see* your face. I'm only toyin' with you. Relax."

Yeah, right.

Tony appeared beside the table looking inquisitive. "Did I give you long enough, or should I come back?"

"I'll just have the chicken caprese salad and a glass of water with lemon," said Laurel, setting her menu back in its place. "Thanks, Tony."

He pivoted toward me. "How 'bout you, handsome?"

"Um—how's the Reuben?" I ventured.

"Everything here is worth tasting," he replied cheekily.

"Okay. Sounds good."

"You got it," he said, writing absolutely nothing down. They say that's the sign of a good server, but in a world just chock-full of worry, it feels like an unnecessary bit of grandstanding. "It comes with fries, but you can swap those out for house-made kettle chips. And what to drink?"

"Fries are fine—and Pepsi?" I asked hopefully.

His lips formed a perfect moue. "So sorry—unlike the rest of the Keystone State, you're deep in the heart of Coca-Cola country here, my friend."

I couldn't help but grimace. "Fine. As they say, when in Rome…"

Tony looked me over again before turning to Laurel and smiling. "I wouldn't say he's yours quite yet, girl." He winked at me and headed back to the kitchen with a spring in his step.

Laurel giggled, leaning forward on her elbows. "I think somebody likes you," she teased in a sing-song cadence.

"Stop it," I grumbled, flustered and unable to meet her impish gaze.

Laurel's sigh was exaggerated as she slumped back into her chair. "Okay, fine. So, tell me, Brock Givens, how long will you be in town?"

"Probably just another day or so," I said. "I'm not entirely sure yet."

"Well, normally, I'd offer to show you what little there is to see around this backwater hole in the ground, but seeing as how you're a local and I'm not, I reckon there's not much I could show you that you haven't already seen."

"Probably not," I agreed. "How long have you lived here?"

"Almost ten years," she said before blanching at the thought. "Oh my *God!* Has it been that long? Wow, time sure does fly! I'm originally from upstate New York. Moved here straight out of high school with He Who Shall Not Be Named."

I blinked. "You moved here with Lord Voldemort?"

That got a genuine laugh, her eyes crinkling at the corners. "No, silly. Just some loser I met on the internet—Marcus Bellamy. Everyone tried to tell me I was nuts, but what can I say? I always have to learn my lessons the very hardest way possible."

She shrugged as Tony returned with our drinks, setting them on the table unobtrusively before backing away.

"Do you have any kids?" I asked.

"Thank the sweet Lord above, *no,*" she said, squeezing the wedge of lemon into her water and stirring with her straw. "The very thought of being tied throughout all eternity to that abusive, alcoholic son of a bitch makes me shudder. Let's just say I was very diligent about taking my birth control every single day."

"I'm sorry you went through all that," I said sincerely. "Were you married long?"

"Not even a year," she said with a tight smile.

"What happened?" It was absolutely none of my business, but curiosity has a way of overriding good manners.

"He died," she said as casually as if she were discussing the outcome of a local sporting event. "Enough about him. Why don't you tell me a little bit about yourself."

I took a sip of my Coke and stalled. I didn't have a backstory prepared as I hadn't anticipated much in the way of prolonged social interaction, and my knowledge about the Givens family was fairly limited. "What do you want to know?"

"Tell me about your significant other," she said. "Have you been together long?"

"I can't say I remember a time before we were together," I said.

"What's her name?"

My mouth opened, but my mind drew a complete blank. Angie? Debbie? Janet?

"Jenny!" popped out of my mouth just a little too enthusiastically as the mental fog lifted. "Her name is Jenny."

"Any kids?" she asked, and I nodded. "How many?"

"Three?"

She arched one perfectly sculpted eyebrow. "Are you asking *me?*"

My chuckle was a little high. "No, of course not. Three. It's three."

"Yikes, that must be a handful," she observed, taking a sip of her water. "Boys or girls?"

"Yes."

She lifted both eyebrows at that one. "*Huh?*"

Mercifully, Tony chose that moment to return with our food, sparing me the indignity of not knowing my own children's names, and make no mistake—they weren't anywhere near the tip of my tongue.

"Everything look tasty?" asked Tony, standing back and eyeing his culinary masterpieces with satisfaction.

"Looks delicious," I said, smiling and tucking right in. I figured it would be hard to get my foot into my mouth if it were already filled with Reuben.

Laurel nodded appreciatively. "Perfect, Tony—as always. Thanks."

"I'll be back to check on you in a bit. Enjoy," he said, before pivoting and gliding away.

Laurel stared at me across the table, the hint of a smile playing at her lips as I struggled to chew the oversized bite I had shoved into my maw.

"Mmm-*mmm*—very good," I somehow managed without spitting food across the table.

She stared at me for a moment longer without touching her salad. She leaned forward, keeping her voice low. "So, exactly how long do you plan on keeping this up?"

I nearly choked, my cheeks extended like a squirrel preparing for winter. I took a moment to focus on swallowing before leveling the most innocent look I could muster. "Keeping what up?"

She sighed. "You're not Brock Givens."

I could feel my face falling before I could even begin to catch it. "I'm not?"

"Huh-unh. I went out with Brock a couple of times just after Marcus died. While my parents would undoubtedly disagree, I tend to remember the men I've slept with."

"Oh."

"'A' for effort, though," she said, finally sampling her salad. "And clearly, you're acquainted with the Givens. I recognized Reba's car when she dropped you off this morning."

Shit. The jig was up. I eyed the door and contemplated making a run for it.

"So, who are you?" asked Laurel. *"Really?"*

"Richard," I said, and technically, I wasn't lying. Richard Dwayne Morrow was the name given to me at birth.

"Hi, Richard. Can I call you Ricky? You look more like a Ricky."

"Sure," I said.

261

"You got a last name, Ricky?"

"Um, yeah," I said. "But I'd rather not say, if it's all the same with you."

"*Ah.* A man of mystery. Okay, I can let it slide." The corner of her mouth curled up. "For now."

I nudged my plate forward, my appetite entirely gone. In fact, I felt more than a little queasy. "I should go."

She reached across the table and placed her hand over mine. "Please don't. This is the most interesting thing that's happened to me in, like, *forever*, and seriously—who am I going to tell? I just helped you obtain a fraudulent library card. It's not like I love the job, but I can't really afford to lose it. Please tell me you're not here to do something stupid, like blow up that reform school or something."

I couldn't tell if she was serious. "*No!* Of course not," I objected before lowering my voice. "Do I look like some sort of domestic terrorist?"

"Well, no," she admitted. "But then again, I've never been the best judge of character when it comes to cute guys. Case in point—Marcus Bellamy, but again, I digress. Where do you fit in with the Givens? Are you family or just part of that whack-a-doodle doomsday cult they belong to?"

Whack-a-doodle doomsday cult. That brought a bemused smile to my face.

"Neither," I said. "In fact, I only just met them yesterday."

"Well, that's unusual," she said, taking another bite of her salad. "The Givens aren't particularly known for their hospitality to strangers. Quite the opposite, in fact. What makes you so special, Ricky?"

I shrugged. "I couldn't say. I had a little car trouble yesterday, and they were kind enough to lend a hand."

"Mmm-hmm—well, *that* tracks," she said, successfully keeping the sarcasm from her voice but her eyes twinkled with mischief. "Especially the part where Reba brings you to the local library. I would have guessed you would be looking for a qualified mechanic, but maybe you're the do-it-yourself type—is that it? Were you searching for a Google tutorial but got sidetracked with all that New Horizons nonsense?"

"Maybe."

"Did you find what you were looking for?" she asked, her wide eyes playfully inquisitive as she coaxed another sip of water through her straw.

Her effortlessly cool demeanor had me sweating bullets, and the room felt like it was closing in on me. I reached for the wad of twenties I had stuffed into my pocket and extracted three, placing them on the table. "I really should go."

"Oh, stop." She nudged my plate back toward me. "You're letting a perfectly good sandwich go to waste, Ricky. Eat up! Your secret is completely safe with me, I promise. Surely, you don't think I'm lying?"

I couldn't contain the short burst of laughter that erupted. "I don't even *know* you, Laurel."

"This is true," she agreed. "But let me tell you what I've come to suspect about you—correct me if I'm wrong or don't—that's entirely up to you. You have exactly zero interest in the Indigenous population of anywhere but are focused instead on that damned institution. I'm guessing you're some sort of investigative reporter, looking for a human-interest piece to catapult you from the little leagues and into the big time—but *no!* Don't tell me."

I just stared at her and waited for her to continue.

"Folks in Darbydale like to turn a blind eye to the place because it keeps a lot of tax dollars flowing into the local economy, but that doesn't keep 'em from talking behind closed doors. In the time that I've lived here, rumors have swirled about alternative methods of reform that they are allegedly testing behind closed gates, but no one's ever gotten close enough to corroborate. Lots of folks think the place is haunted. Did you read about the fire several years back?"

I nodded.

"A couple of boys died in that fire, and their angry spirits are supposedly tethered to the scene—if you believe in that sort of thing. Do you believe in that sort of thing, Ricky?"

"Not really."

She smiled. "Yeah, me neither. But something weird is going on out there for sure, and I, for one, would love to know what that something is."

I eyed my sandwich and talked myself into picking it back up. Admittedly, it didn't take much encouragement. The first bite had left me nostalgic and longing for more. "What exactly are you saying?"

"I'm saying we should eat our lunch and then head back to the library," she said. "We've both got work to do, although yours sounds a lot more interesting than mine. I'll try and stay out of your way if you promise to give me a heads-up when the shit's about to hit the fan."

I narrowed my eyes. "Sounds to me like you've got a whole lot more than a passing interest in New Horizons."

She shrugged, dabbing the corner of her mouth delicately with her napkin. "Maybe."

I stared at her expectantly until she finally grinned.

"Fine. My job at the library keeps me off the streets—*literally*, but the thought of slowly transforming into Lacy Grendel haunts my nights," she said. "I'm going into investigative journalism myself, and you have to admit, I sure can smell a story."

Oh, good Lord—she was the female Brady Garrett.

It made a certain sort of retroactive sense, and oddly, I suddenly felt a whole lot better. She saw in me a potential quid pro quo and was smart enough to realize that I wasn't the biggest story here. I took another bite of my most excellent Reuben, feeling capable of chewing and swallowing without endangering my life.

"So, do we have a deal?" asked Laurel, her confidence on full display.

I sighed before leaning in and lowering my voice. "Look—I can't tell you anything now. It could—jeopardize things, and the last thing I want to do is endanger anybody else."

Her hazel eyes gleamed with anticipation. "But—?"

I allowed myself the hint of a smile. "But—*if* anything comes of what I'm doing, you'll be the very first to know." I could almost hear Brady calling me a traitor—as well as several other colorful obscenities, but he'd just have to scratch and get glad. A guy's gotta work with what he's given.

"Oh, thank you—*thank you!*" she enthused, clapping her hands lightly. I hoped I wasn't getting her hopes up for a big bunch of nothing, but it felt necessary to keep my own investigation on track. "One thing you should probably know."

"What's that?" I asked.

"You really need to be careful around the Givens," she said.

I looked up from my lunch. "How so?"

"If you've spent any time with them at all, you know that they're anti-establishment, but it runs a whole lot deeper than that. Brock's little brother got himself into a whole heap of trouble and ended up inside that place," she said. "He's never been the same."

I nodded. "Yeah, so I've heard."

"Boyd always had this thing for fire. It's what landed him there in the first place, and a lot of folks believe he's the one that started the fire that killed those two young boys."

"Oh, geez," I said, sitting back in my chair.

"But that's just one theory," she said. "The other says it was Reba Givens. She was caught on premises that night trying to break her son out. She assaulted three guards and was in the general vicinity of the dorm when they took her down, but the fire had already been started."

"Took her down?"

Laurel nodded. "Everyone says you shouldn't get between a mama bear and her cubs. It took three bullets to stop her."

CHAPTER TWENTY-ONE

"N^{o.}" I sighed into the prepaid phone as I paced the sidewalk that lined the library parking lot. "But *Mel*—"

"Absolutely not. You are just going to have to call your mother yourself, and I'd advise that you have your dad with you when you do it since you already had me tell her he'd be on the next call. She's convinced that something horrible has happened to him, and you're still punishing her for not spilling what she knew about your dad's first wife."

"That's ridiculous."

"Yeah, *you* tell her that. She's done listening to me," said Melanie. "She literally accused me of sleeping with the enemy, and just in case there's any doubt, *you* are the enemy, so technically, she isn't wrong."

"Fine, fine," I said. "But it will have to be later. I don't have him with me at the moment. I'm doing a little research at the local library here in Darbydale, Pennsylvania. That's where the trail of breadcrumbs has led us."

I proceeded to bring her up to speed with everything that had happened since the last time I was able to speak freely and was once again surprised by how much had happened in the last forty-eight hours. I concluded with what I'd just learned in my lunch with Laurel, then added, "I've got a couple more hours of research ahead of me before Reba is due to pick me up. With any luck, I might find something that will get us a little closer to coming home, although I honestly don't have a clue what I'm looking for."

"You might want to do a little digging on these Givens folks while you're at it," she said. "There's no way that Reba's siege on the facility would have missed the local news. She didn't mention any of this to you?"

"Not a word, but then again, the Givens aren't real big on volunteering information."

"Three bullets?"

"That's what Laurel said," I said. "It would seem that Reba's got a little bit of Sarah Connor in her."

"Please be careful," she said. "These people sound dangerous, and you don't know what their real motivation might be. They may not be as friendly as you think."

"I will," I promised. "How are the kids?"

"Missing you," she said, warming my heart. "Oh, and somebody else has been missing you, too."

"Yeah?" I asked, my grin widening.

"I'm not talking about *me*, you goon," she said, popping my balloon before it was fully inflated. "I'm talking about Brady. He called me a little while ago looking for you. He says your phone goes straight to voicemail and you aren't returning his calls. I tried to tell him that you were spending a little time with your dad, but your total lack of communication has him convinced there's more to it, and you know how he is once he smells a story."

"Dammit!" I groused. "Don't you *ever* tell him I said this, but why does he have to be so darned good at his job? You didn't give him this number, did you?"

"Of course not," Melanie said indignantly. "I just told him I'd pass along that he was trying to get hold of you next time we spoke. I'm pretty darned good at *my* job too, you know."

"The best. I'll call him tonight."

"You do that," she said. "And once you've soothed the jangling nerves of your mother and your best friend, you damn well better circle back around and soothe mine again, too. Are we clear, mister?"

"Yes, ma'am."

I smiled as we disconnected. Somebody else was missing me too, whether she wanted to admit it or not.

······•••●●○○●●●••·····

Two of the library's workstations had opened up while Laurel and I were at lunch. I claimed one of the seats for myself, using my fraudulent library card to secure another hour's worth of computer time. Laurel was nowhere to be seen, and as I ignored Ms. Appleby's blatantly hostile glare, I wondered if she had been relegated to some menial task as punishment for going to lunch with me. Even if Appleby hadn't seen us crossing the street together, word had likely already gotten back to her. In towns like Darbydale, news traveled fast.

I picked up where I left off, opening the article I had been reading about the fire when Laurel had interrupted me. It was attributed to *The Tri-County Tribune*, which appeared to be the area's primary source of local news. I re-read it with fresh perspective, now that Laurel had added details that I didn't recall from my first pass. There wasn't much in the way of detail as the story was still breaking, and while there was no mention of Reba by name, the article did mention a person of interest who had been detained at the scene.

I searched *The Tribune*'s news archive for other articles related to the fire, and over the next few days, a slow trickle of supplemental information was added, including the names and pictures of the two young men who had perished in the fire, William Martin and Eddie Brickey. Martin had been a resident of New Horizons for a little over a year, but young Mr. Brickey had only arrived a few weeks prior. Their adolescent faces stared back at me from the computer screen, projecting both apathy and attitude, and I briefly wondered what each had done to be assigned to the facility. As both boys were minors, those details were likely sealed by the courts, and who the hell cared, anyway? Neither deserved the horrific fate they met.

I almost missed Reba's name when it finally made an appearance in the Tri-County Beat section, a roll call of all the arrests that had been made in the areas the paper serviced. She was a line item wedged between a guy charged with drunk and disorderly conduct and a woman who had beat the living daylights out of her husband. Reba's own charges included trespassing and criminal mischief, and if Laurel hadn't told me she was at the scene of the fire, I would never have connected those dots from the scant bit of information before me.

Her name made its second appearance several months later in the paper's For the Record section, a daily roundup of all the criminal proceedings and the sentencing handed down in each case. Reba had been found guilty on both counts and had been sentenced to five years in the State Correction Institution in Muncy.

Well, that was disconcerting.

I mean, *sure*, it wasn't the sort of thing you lead with when you're meeting someone new, so I could understand why it hadn't come up over dinner the previous night, but it also made me wonder what other skeletons were lurking in the Givens' collective closet. I was just about to turn my search in that direction when another result caught my eye. It was a human-interest story broadcast on the local news on the one-year anniversary of the fire. The segment was entitled, "Clearing the Air—Restoring Faith in New Horizons." It was a real puff piece hosted by a somewhat local CBS morning correspondent, Tiana Tikani, and likely sponsored by its featured guest, Senator Amelia Gorham. I had barely started playing the clip when

Ms. Appleby swooped in, her penciled-in eyebrows dipping low, nearly meeting just above the bridge of her nose.

"Just what do you think you're doing?" she asked, her volume low but full of condescension.

"I was interested in watching this interview," I said, pointing to the screen. "Is that against the rules?"

She sighed. "Of course not, but you'll need to use headphones or earbuds if you plan to listen to the audio. You're disturbing the other patrons."

I glanced around the room. No one was even paying attention to me, but okay. "I'm sorry. I didn't realize. Do you have a pair I could borrow?"

She looked at me like I'd asked to use her toothbrush. "Certainly *not!* I *do* have inexpensive earbuds that may be purchased at the circulation desk if you're interested."

"Well—sure," I said. "How much?"

"Twenty dollars."

My own eyebrows shot to the heavens. She thought *that* was inexpensive? Many airlines offered earbuds as a complimentary courtesy, but then again, it was something they could afford considering the exorbitant cost of air fare.

"Alright," I agreed, reaching into my pocket to pull a twenty from my rapidly dwindling stash of cash. I started to hand it to her, but she turned on her heel and clomped toward the desk, pausing midway to turn and stare at me expectantly. I guess delivery wasn't included in the purchase price. I followed her to the desk and exchanged one crisp twenty-dollar bill for a pair of cheap, corded, plastic earbuds that undoubtedly cost about three at Dollar Tree. I thanked her and returned to my seat.

Plugging the earbuds into the front of the PC, I inserted the hard plastic nubs into my ear canals and resumed my video.

"Taking time out of her busy schedule to join us this morning is our very own Senator Amelia Gorham," Tiana sa d, every single one of her brilliant white teeth on display. "Thank you for being here, Senator."

The senator offered her own carefully cultivated smile, nodding appreciatively toward the camera. She wore a pastel pantsuit strategically chosen to soften her naturally sharp edges while projecting warmth and confidence. "It's always my pleasure, Tiana—and good morning to all your lovely viewers!"

Tiana's expression downshifted as she turned to the camera, affecting a serious disposition. "Senator Amelia Gorham is known for her numerous accomplishments for the people of Pennsylvania, and today we are here to reflect on a passion project that is near and dear to her heart. Sadly, it also marks the one-year anniversary of a tragedy that claimed two young lives at that very facility."

The senator nodded, her face exceedingly contemplative.

"Of course, we're talking about New Horizons, a residential treatment center for troubled male adolescents." She turned to the senator, her nearly irrepressible smile just itching to make another appearance. "Tell us, Senator Gorham, why is New Horizons so important to you?"

"Thank you, Tiana," said the senator before shifting toward her intended audience who were viewing from home. "Perhaps my biggest disappointment in life is that my late husband, Arliss, and I were unable to have children of our own. We both came from big families, and we looked forward to continuing that tradition. Sadly, it wasn't the hand we were dealt. It simply breaks my heart that there are so many unwanted children brought into this world every single day. Neglected. Mistreated. *Abused*."

She paused to dab at eyes that looked suspiciously dry while Tiana nodded empathetically.

"Very early on, my late husband and I decided to open up our home, adopting three children whose parents couldn't provide for themselves much less their children."

The camera cut to a picture of three pitiful urchins, three boys, none of them older than six. Their family resemblance was never more apparent than from their identically haunted eyes staring mournfully into the camera. Their faces were nearly as filthy as their raggedy clothes, and they were clearly malnourished.

The camera cut back to Tiana just as she gasped. "Oh, my goodness, look at those precious faces."

The next images displayed showed the children as they flourished throughout the years while in the care of the Gorhams, ending with a picture of the three of them as middle-aged adults, surrounding their mother and beaming proudly just outside the gates of New Horizons. The camera pulled back to focus on the senator admiring the collage displayed on a large screen centered between the two women on the wall behind them.

"Jonathan, Davis, and Nelson," said Senator Gorham, beaming. "The lights of my life, and members of the New Horizons Board of Directors."

"So, New Horizons is a family affair," noted Tiana with a knowing smile.

Gorham's chuckle was right on cue. "Literally. Over the years, we fostered dozens of other children above and beyond the three we adopted, providing the sort of stability that every child deserves. But even with our considerable means, there was only so much we could do. I wanted to do more—no, I *needed* to do more. New Horizons was the realization of a dream. It was an opportunity to provide stability, rehabilitation, and healing to young men who had lost their way, victims of a system that had failed them."

"But it was a dream that was nearly cut short," said Tiana, the screen showing the same picture I had seen of firemen battling the horrific blaze.

"Last year, a fire broke out in one of the dormitories, claiming the lives of two young boys."

The senator's face turned grim. "Yes. William Martin and Edward Brickey. Such a tragic loss."

The boys' faces graced the screen next, although these were different pictures than what had accompanied the article I had read. In them, the boys looked impossibly younger, more lost than ever and yet completely unaware their final chapter had already been written.

"It was a very traumatic night," prompted Tiana.

"It was," said Senator Gorham. "It was the same night that a deranged mother of one of our other residents used her Jeep to breach our security perimeter, making a bad situation even worse. At first, we thought the two events were related, but a thorough investigation into the incident confirmed the fire was a result of an overloaded circuit, prompting a campus-wide upgrade to the facilities' electrical wiring."

The camera shifted its focus to Tiana's lovely face. "While these repairs were certified by the state, they couldn't restore the sense of security that had been stolen from these young men who had already suffered so much in their short little lives, but you once again refused to abandon them in their hour of need."

"That's right, Tiana," said Senator Gorham, offering another calculated smile. "The board unanimously voted to create a staff position for an individual suited to dealing with both troubled youth and grief counseling, and we were extraordinarily fortunate that our top candidate was able to come aboard almost immediately."

Tiana turned toward the camera. "Up next, we'll meet New Horizons' resident counselor, Dr. Jillian Whittier, and she'll share the incredible progress she's made in such a short time. That's right after the break."

My fingers gripped the mouse so tightly it nearly squeaked. As the clip abruptly ended, I scrambled to back it up and replay that last little bit over again, certain my ears must have deceived me.

Dr. Jillian Whittier.

It suddenly got very hard to breathe. This couldn't be a coincidence. Dr. Whittier was the couples' counselor Melanie had dragged me to when we were having issues she didn't think we could resolve on our own. I had never cared for the woman, but Melanie had always attributed my animosity to my indisputable disdain for therapy. It's not that I think psychotherapy is the hippy-dippy scam my father does; it's just for other folks—not me.

Of course, Melanie hadn't seen the way Dr. Whittier watched us from her second-story window as we left our sessions and returned to our cars. Her interest extended beyond the professional, and as our troubles all revolved around the secret I had kept from Melanie for far too long regarding my sister's actual status, I had convinced myself the good doctor was a plant working on behalf of the three senators who had ordered my sister's execution, tasked with discovering if we knew anything that might further endanger their future plans.

This was the connection I could never make.

During my last big case—and maybe even because of it, Melanie and I had worked through our differences on our own, and I had finally asked her to marry me. When she agreed, I could hardly wait to tell Dr. Whittier that we were no longer in need of her services, but when we had gone to our next appointment, I was denied the vindication I craved. Dr. Whittier had disappeared without a trace, her office stripped of all her belongings, any trace that she had ever occupied a suite in the medical plaza removed. All that remained was a cantankerous custodian working diligently to remove a sizeable yet stubborn stain from the otherwise immaculate beige Berber carpeting.

After listening to Tiana Tikani utter the name no less than five times, I allowed the clip to continue, holding my breath as I waited for the doctor to make her appearance once the internet ads that had replaced the original commercials could be skipped. I thought I must have clicked something wrong when the video resumed with a fire-eating magician named Lucy Darling, dressed to the nines in a blue satin gown and wearing a helmet of crimson hair, playfully riffing on her captivated audience.

I stopped the video and tried again. There was nothing more to see. Apparently, the second half of the interview had either been truncated or had never been uploaded. I felt robbed all over again, unable to confirm beyond a shadow of a doubt that this Jilian Whittier was the same woman who had casually inserted herself into our lives.

Frustrated, I tried searching for the doctor by name and found absolutely nothing. She wasn't even tagged in the metadata for the original video, which I watched again. My hour was quickly running out, and I didn't have much to show for it. I decided to switch gears and look into Burt and Reba Givens in *The Tri-County Tribune*'s archives.

I almost wished I hadn't.

Both had extensive public records, and both could easily be linked to various protests throughout the past fifteen years. At a glance, their causes were admirable—protecting national resources, reducing pollution, and curtailing government oversight, but several of these demonstrations had turned violent, with local police using force to disperse protestors, occasionally getting themselves hurt in the process. Both Burt and Reba had spent various amounts of time behind bars for their involvement in these and other things, and I had a hard time reconciling the occasional angry images of them that accompanied these articles with the middle-aged couple who had quite literally saved our lives. Twice. I briefly considered printing out all that I had found, but if a set of cheap plastic earbuds had cost me twenty dollars, I didn't think I could afford the cost. Besides, I wasn't sure how Reba would feel about me compiling a dossier on her and her husband after all they had done and continued to do for us. I made a mental note to ask Melanie to use some of Boggs' resources to dig deeper into the Givens' history. It would probably be good to know exactly who we were dealing with.

The screen of my workstation suddenly flashed a warning that I was down to my last three minutes of borrowed time. Checking my watch, I saw that I had almost another hour before Reba was due to pick me up. I fished the library card back out of my pocket, preparing to scan it again once the countdown clock struck zero, and a shadow fell over me.

I turned to find Ms. Appleby standing directly behind me, her hands on her hips and her scowl dipping deeper into her jowls than ever before.

"I'm sorry," I said, smiling up at her. "Is there someone waiting to use the workstation?" I sincerely doubted it. Two of the other workstations had freed up since the last time I looked.

"I'll need you to come with me," she said, turning and taking a few steps toward the back of the building before stopping to see if I was following.

I just sat there, smiling stupidly and wondering what the hell was going on. "Excuse me?"

She sighed. "Ms. Tieman, our director, would like to have a word with you in her office."

Oh, shit.

I glanced at my ill-gotten library card and figured I was busted. I scanned the room for Laurel, but she was still nowhere to be seen, and my heart sank as I wondered if she might have been fired for facilitating the fraudulent identification for me. I certainly hadn't meant to cost the young lady her job.

Another sobering thought landed.

Was falsifying a library card illegal? It took exactly three seconds for me to decide that it most probably was. Were the police already on their way to handcuff me and take me into custody? The library didn't appear to have any security officers in the building, and I eyed the door, wondering if I should just make a run for it. Of course, Reba wouldn't even be looking for me for another hour, and—

"Are you coming?"

When is a question not a question? When it's said in the tone Ms. Appleby used, and I cleared my throat and looked at my feet, nodding.

"Bring your belongings with you, please."

I didn't have much to collect, just an overpriced pair of earbuds, the prepaid phone I'd charged on the library's dime, and a stack of napkins I had swiped from the café should I need a makeshift notepad. I hadn't written a single thing down, so I stuffed it all into my pocket and trudged along behind Ms. Appleby as she led me toward the back of the building like a delinquent student being shepherded to the principal's office. We stepped into a short tile hallway that led to an industrial emergency exit. On the left were public restrooms and a water fountain, and further along was a swinging metal door marked, 'Employees Only.' Through its lone porthole, I could see stacks of books lined up neatly on tables in the room beyond, waiting to be sorted and reshelved. Along the right wall, an alcove opened into a small anteroom, and that's where Ms. Appleby turned. An empty reception desk occupied the back wall, and a pair of matching upholstered chairs stood sentry to the only other door in the room. It was closed. Mounted at eye level on its solid maple surface was an engraved placard that read, 'Lee Tieman, Director.'

Ms. Appleby stopped short of the door and turned toward me, holding up a forefinger. "Wait right there, please." She rapped a knuckle on the door, and after receiving a muffled response from the other side, opened the door and leaned in. "He's here."

"Please ask him to step inside," a disembodied female voice said from somewhere within.

Ms. Appleby opened the door wider and looked at me expectantly. I smiled meekly, keeping my eyes down as I stepped into the room. As she backed away and pulled the door shut behind her, the latch was impossibly loud. I looked up to find a petite woman with a platinum blonde pixie cut seated behind a desk, her rapt attention on the document before her. She followed its text with the shiny tip of a Cross pen and didn't even bother to look up or acknowledge my presence.

"Won't you have a seat?" she finally said, absently pointing toward a pair of chairs that faced her desk; they matched the ones in the lobby.

"*Umm*—sure," I said, opting for the one farthest away, if only by a couple of feet. There were no windows to admit natural light, and the effect was nothing short of claustrophobic.

We sat in heavy silence as she finished reviewing the document, finally applying her signature to the bottom with a flourish. When she was finished, she slid the paper to her right and set her pen aside, finally lifting her bespectacled gaze to meet mine.

"Would you *please* tell me what in the literal hell you are doing here, Dwayne?"

I blinked, startled by the sound of my own name and the voice that said it. The audio didn't match the video, and my world tilted uneasily on its axis as I leaned in for a closer look.

"*Gina?*"

CHAPTER TWENTY-TWO

I just sat there with my mouth hanging open as my world slowly came back into focus.

The hair was all wrong, as were the glasses perched on the end of her nose, but I knew every inch of the face that was currently scowling at me.

"Dammit, Dwayne, you *promised*," she said, her fists clenched on the desktop.

"Gina?" I repeated, a slow smile spreading across my face. "Is that really you?"

"Of course, it's me," she said, irritably, removing her glasses and setting them aside. "Are you trying to ruin everything? You're not supposed to be here!"

By then, I'd gotten a case of the giggles. "Oh, for shit's sake, you can yell at me later. For now, how 'bout you give your little bro a hug?" I stood and leaned across the desk, my arms opened wide.

She just sat there, and my smile began to falter.

"Oh, come *on!*" I urged, waving her in, but she didn't budge. Her face was completely unreadable.

That's when I noticed the narrowness of her chair's armrests, the thin, oversized wheels along each side, and the shiny, chrome hand rims that were inset, glistening beneath the overhead lighting. I could feel the blood draining from my face as I gestured toward the chair, terrified of what it signified.

"Wha—what *happened?*" I finally managed.

"Don't change the subject!" she snapped, still furious. "You're not supposed to *be* here!"

"Pl-please tell me this is—," I stammered, my mind racing while my heart sank. "—I don't know. Part of your disguise? Part of your new identity? Part of—"

"Part of my new life," she said, using the hand rims to back up and propel herself around the desk. My throat clenched as I sat down hard, the wheelchair coming to a stop beside me. "There was—an incident."

Now I was gaping, trying to make sense of what I was seeing. At a glance, Gina could have been seated anywhere. She wore cream-colored slacks and a mint-green blouse, her feet shod in stylish black flats and resting on the chair's footplates. The most startling difference by far was the close-cropped icy white crown of hair that covered her head like fine down. I couldn't ever recall seeing my sister with hair shorter than shoulder length, and its color had always been midnight black like our mother's.

"An incident?" I croaked, my throat like sandpaper.

She sighed, avoiding my probing gaze. "About a month after I left you in that ambulance, I was settling into the new identity that had been established for me through Homeland Security in a small town in central Illinois—Shelbyville. I was Madeline Ensley, work-at-home data analyst for a Fortune 500 company with so many global employees my credentials would never be questioned. I was to lay low and mind my own business while Joe Greene and his team continued to collect information about the network of sister facilities to the one I had stumbled across in Briarstaff. One night, he dropped by to see how I was getting by, but there must have been a leak somewhere in his team. One minute he was reinforcing the dos and don'ts of being in WITSEC, and the next thing I knew, my living room was being riddled with machine gun fire. We were both hit."

Her eyes glossed over at the recollection, and she looked toward the ceiling to keep herself in check, taking a shaky inhalation.

"I guess I was the lucky one," she said, smiling feebly as a single tear rolled down her cheek. "Joe threw himself over top of me, shielding me from the brunt of the attack. I was shot twice. Joe—" She inhaled sharply. "Joe never stood a chance."

"Oh, my God," I said, slumping in my chair. "Is this—is this permanent?"

"My spinal cord was pretty severely damaged in the lumbar region, so barring some innovative new medical procedure that has yet to be invented, I'll be sitting the next few out," she said, smiling weakly, and I just lost it. I knelt before her, taking her hands into my own while I sobbed like a baby, my mind desperate to find a rewind button that could undo all of the terrible things that had happened to us in the past year.

"This isn't *fair!*" I wailed. "It's not how things were supposed to go. We were going to bring you home, give you back your life—"

Gina pulled her hands away from mine and looked at me sharply. *"We?'* What do you mean, *'we?'* You're not supposed to be looking for me at all! Who else have you involved?"

My blubbering subsided as I scrambled to reframe my words. "No one! Well—I mean, almost no one. I told Melanie—"

Gina groaned, dropping her head into her hands.

"—but I *had* to. She knew I was keeping secrets from her, and even after I told her, she left me!"

"Well, that's just *tremendous!"* Gina said, throwing her hands into the air. *"Goddamn* it, Dwayne! So, now she's your ex and she's pissed. Do you *really* think she's going to keep quiet? *Fuck!* What in the hell is *wrong* with you?"

I sat back, completely stunned. "N-no—it's not like that. You don't understand. I was about to lose the best thing I ever had—"

Gina's eyes blazed. "You wanna talk about *loss?* I lost a kidney, and the ability to use my own two legs! I'll never walk or use the bathroom like a normal person again!"

A fresh wave of anguish washed over me as her words hit home. "I— I'm *sorry!* I couldn't *be* any sorrier, but you can trust Melanie, I promise you that."

Gina's laugh was derisive. "You *promise* me? You *promised* me that you wouldn't come looking for me, but here you are! Oh, my *God*, Dwayne! I'll have to start all *over* again. I can't—I just *can't*—"

There was a sharp knock on the door, followed by Ms. Appleby's concerned voice. "Is everything all right in there, Ms. Tieman? Do you need me to call the police? I've got the phone right here in my hand."

"*No!*" said Gina, a little too sharply. She took a deep, steadying breath before trying again. "We're fine, Karen. Mr. *uh*—Givens and I are just having a little difference of opinion. It's nothing to worry about, I assure you."

A few uneasy seconds passed before Ms. Appleby asked, "Are you sure?"

"Absolutely certain, and I'd appreciate it if you could return to the circulation desk. Laurel is due to leave any minute now, and someone needs to mind the shop."

"Of course, Ms. Tieman. I'll keep the phone with me—just in case," she said, and we waited until we heard her heavy footballs receding.

"'Karen,' huh?" I asked. "I always wondered who inspired all those memes, and now I know."

Gina laughed in spite of herself, pinching the bridge of her nose as the worst of the storm between us passed, and soon we were both giggling uneasily. "Yeah, she's a bit uptight."

"A *bit* uptight? She makes Loretta Boggs look downright friendly." I rolled my eyes, and we laughed a moment longer, more of the tension between us dissipating. Once it felt safe, I waded back in. "What you asked of me wasn't fair, and if I had to do it all over again, I would have told Melanie sooner. I knew I could trust her, but I held back because of your damned promise, and it almost cost me my relationship. She didn't say a word about you when we were apart, but we eventually managed to work things out. We're getting married. She's *not* going to tell anyone."

A slight smile flickered across my sister's face. "Married? Wow—I never imagined both of my little brothers would tie the knot before I did. *Especially* Matty." We both had a laugh at our brother's expense. For a few seconds, it almost felt like old times. "Of course, there's *lots* I never imagined."

She didn't have to spell it out as her gaze flitted over her lower extremities. Her meaning was loud and clear.

"Other than that one little tiny transgression, I have kept your damned promise, despite seeing what it's done to Mom and Dad and the rest of our family," I said. "I understood the risks as you outlined them, and I'd never do anything to jeopardize the people we love. Believe it or not, me being here was *not* my idea."

Her eyes narrowed. "Then whose?"

"Dad's," I said.

She regarded me doubtfully. *"Dad's?* I'm not following."

"He's—he's not well," I said, reluctant to acknowledge an illness I couldn't quantify, but fat chance of that. Gina sat up straight, the alarm evident on her face.

"What do you mean, he's not well?" she asked.

With a sigh, I got up from my knees and returned to the guest chair to relay a story that had begun—was it only a couple of months ago? After all of Dad's inconclusive tests, it felt like so much longer. I hadn't made it very far along when Gina held up a hand, interrupting me.

"*Whoa, whoa, whoa*—hold up. Did you say Dad's *first* wife?" she asked, incredulously.

"I did," I said. "Her name is Nancy. I'm guessing this is news to you, too? Matt didn't know anything, either, and Mom refused to discuss it. I didn't get any real details until Dad and I hit the road—"

"You and Dad hit the road? He's here?" she asked, alarmed.

"Not with me, but yes. I'll get to that in a minute. Shall I continue?"

She waved me on, but she was clearly reeling from the revelation. It's a hard pill to swallow when you discover that one of the people you trust the most has been holding back on something so very significant. Once I finally reached the events of this week, she was beyond dismayed, her concern for our father overriding any of the anger and anxiety that she had directed toward me.

"And there's *still* no prognosis?" she asked, as if I might have a better answer if she repeated the question enough times.

I shook my head. "It's maddening. And in the meanwhile, these 'episodes' he's having seem to be increasing in frequency. I probably shouldn't have left him alone with the Givenses. He's already had one incident and practically scared the daylights out of Burt."

She sat back in her chair, chewing on her bottom lip. "So, this little road trip was Dad's idea? That's so hard to picture. He doesn't like sleeping away from home. And he's never, *ever* believed in clairvoyance, precognition, or anything like that. Do you remember when I went through my paranormal phase back in high school? He used to laugh at me when I told him Lainie and I had actually communicated with a spirit from the 'Great Beyond' while using a Ouija board."

"Did you?"

"Probably not," she admitted. "I mean, *I* didn't push the planchette, but I can sure see Lainie doing it, if only to get me riled up, and that's exactly what Dad insisted had happened. I don't know."

Lainie Kramer had been Gina's best e since second grade, and the one most likely to get her into trouble. She was to Gina what Ryan McGregor was to me, and our parents had always paid a little more attention when we were running around with them. Almost twenty years later, Ryan was dead and Lainie undoubtedly believed Gina was. Everyone else did. If only that fucking Ouija board could have warned us all of what was to come.

"But you're telling me that you've basically been using his dreams as a sort of—guide?" she asked.

I nodded. "He's been so damned close to the truth of what I know—at times, it's been downright spooky, and you know how he is once he gets an idea into his head. He's out to rescue you, and nothing I could have said or done was going to stop him. I thought it was better if I tagged along rather than let him blunder through and make a lot of noise, especially if anyone out there is paying attention."

"And based on what you've told me, clearly they are," she said.

"Well—yes. We've managed to evade two attempts on our lives," I said. "I doubt they'll be the last."

"*Dammit!*" she said, her frustration resurfacing with a vengeance. She looked cornered, her eyes darting around the room and desperately searching for a way out. "Everyone thought I was dead! You were all *safe!* I didn't need any help navigating this! Two of the senators have died, and I was working on neutralizing the third, but now everything's been compromised, including yours and Dad's safety. I don't know how to fix this! I'll have to start all over again, and I'm not even sure how to do that anymore, now that Joe's gone—"

I leaned in, gently taking hold of her arms, careful not to hurt her. I expected her to be fragile and was surprised by the sinewy musculature of her limbs. "Hey, hey, *hey*—just take a minute and breathe, okay? We will figure this thing out, and we'll do it together, do you understand me?"

"But—"

"*Shhh,*" I more or less commanded, and she fell silent, her tear-filled hazel eyes staring up at me. "There's no need to panic just yet. If your cover were blown, they would have already been here, don't you think?"

"I-I-I suppose," she agreed, visibly relaxing. "I've been here since late November, so that's what—five months? I had only been in Shelbyville for a couple of weeks before they found me."

"You said there must have been a leak in Joe's team. What makes this identity any more secure than the last one?" I asked.

"Barb Whittington," she said. "She arranged everything."

"I'm sorry—*who?*"

"I was rescued by Joe's partner, Barb Whittington. She was riding with Joe but had stayed behind in the car to catch up on some paperwork while he checked in on me. They were parked along the curb across the street. She didn't give it much thought when an old Ford Crown Vic coasted down the street toward her, slowing down in front of my house so the driver could unleash a quick burst of hellfire into the front of my house before getting the hell out of there. It all happened so fast. Barb didn't even have a chance to get a look at the driver, much less get a license plate. She pretty much oversaw everything from there, calling for backup and an ambulance."

"And you're sure that Barb wasn't the leak?" I asked.

"Positive," said Gina. "I mean, if she were the leak, why would she have gone to all this trouble? She would have just finished the job once she saw that I was still alive. No—Barb's good people. Unfortunately, I can't exactly reach out to her now."

"Why not?"

"Barb's the one who suspected a leak, so she personally oversaw everything that happened after I made it through surgery, starting with the fact that I died on the table."

"Wait—*what?*"

"More specifically, my 'Madeline Ensley' persona died on the table, and anyone who knew that I was Madeline would assume the assassination attempt had been successful."

I scowled. "What about the doctors who worked on you?"

"I was admitted under another name and discharged under yet another. Barb was the only one who knew for certain what was going on, and when it was time to leave the hospital, she picked me up herself. She hadn't been able to identify the leak, so she worked a sort of double blind—it's hard to explain."

I took her hands in mine and smiled at her reassuringly. "Try."

"Essentially it was like a computerized lottery. I was assigned a random number which was fed into a system. It generated a new identity for me, but I was the only one privy to those details. It was the only way to ensure that no one else could find me—including Barb."

I stared at her, more than a little outraged on her behalf. "They just *abandoned* you?"

She squeezed my hands. "Not at all. Barb discussed several options with me at length, and we both decided it was my safest choice. She and her team would continue trying to identify other facilities related to Briarstaff, and I was free to do whatever I wanted. I mean, she could probably find me if she really applied herself. It's a little harder to just blend in when you come with all this hardware, but she's the only one who knew about my condition, and after all that she's done, I'm sure I can trust her."

I looked at her skeptically. "And you just happened to get placed within a few miles of the only surviving senator's pet project? Sounds more than a little convenient."

"It wasn't like that," she said. "I received one-way ticket to Seattle, and that was where I was supposed to stay, but I wasn't quite ready to give up my own investigation. I wanted my real life back, and the only way to get that was to neutralize the remaining threats. I looked into all three senators—using a VPN out of abundance of caution—but I couldn't find anything on Errol Warren or Parker Ghant that might indicate the presence of a facility in either Wisconsin or Ohio. But I found plenty of articles on Amelia Gorham and her precious New Horizons, and I knew I had to be onto something. Part of the relocation process included occupational aptitude testing—you know, sort of like Mrs. Rucker administered during our senior year at Midland, remember?"

"Sure," I said. "According to that stupid standardized test, I believe I was equally suited to civil service, warehouse work, or lawncare."

She laughed. "I guess that explains your general disdain for college, but clearly, they've never seen you work a lawnmower. Dad had to threaten you every single time."

I rankled at her implication. "Hey, I have an aversion to extreme heat. When it comes to perspiration, I'm an overachiever. I don't recall you being pushed toward library science."

"No, I tested equally well across the board. I pretty much had my pick of careers. But the process has evolved since we were subjected to it in high school. It produced a range of likely professions and a variety of documentation supporting my new identity's qualifications in those areas. It was designed to get me into any number of doors that weren't entry-level, but it was never gonna qualify me as a surgeon. It was up to me to prove myself, and of course, entry-level was always an option if nothing else panned out. I started looking for work in the area and was lucky enough to secure this position as Director of the Tri-County Library System. My main office is at the branch in Norton, but I also have satellite offices here in Darbydale and Hammel."

"So, what have you learned?" I asked.

She sighed. "Not nearly enough. In her lengthy career, Senator Gorham has never been involved in anything controversial, and she's very popular with her conservative constituents. Her holdings are private, including her personal property, but that's not all that unusual for elected officials. It's a matter of security."

"Yeah, that's pretty much what I found," I said. "I was trying to find more information on the fire that broke out in one of the dormitories, killing those two young boys."

"It's funny you say that—well, not *funny*, but—"

"What do you mean?"

"I was following a similar line of thinking," she said. "The tri-county area has an alarmingly high mortality rate for young male adolescents."

I sat up in the chair, my Spidey sense activated. This felt important. "Was there a connection to New Horizons?"

"With some but not all. I was still trying to figure it out. Aggregated statistical information is a lot easier to come by than the details, especially since we're talking about minors. Of course, someone could have actively been working to suppress those details, and if so, they did a damned good job."

"This sounds promising," I said. "We should work on this together."

"*No*," she said.

"Why not? I'm uniquely qualified to be of assistance. Have you forgotten that I'm a private investigator?"

She scoffed. "*In training*. No." She grabbed her hand rims and backed away, putting the desk between us.

I was more than a little offended. "I was good enough to help bring The Academy down in Briarstaff, and I've been good enough to solve three more cases since then, including the murder of Senator Parker Ghant. Are you serious?"

After she repositioned herself behind her desk, she leveled a glare at me. "Completely." She sighed. "Look, I'm not trying to cast aspersions on your capabilities, little brother, I promise. But you've got one objective here, and that's to get Dad to go home and stay put—focus on getting himself well."

It was my turn to scoff. "Fat chance! Have you *met* our father?"

"I hate to suggest this, but can't you lean on his medical condition to convince him that his dreams are nothing more than delusions?"

"Don't you think I've tried that?" I asked. "He's not buying it. And besides, what makes you think it's even safe for me to take him home? At this point, he's made too much noise. He's never going to believe that these attempts on our lives aren't connected to you. What else could they be?"

"I don't know!" she said, her agitation mounting again. "Maybe you could convince him and Mom to move in with you for a while. I mean, aren't his specialists in Columbus, anyway? That way, you could keep an eye on him while I—"

"While you *what?*" I asked. "Tackle an investigation you're completely unqualified for? You *need* me. Stop pushing me away."

I stared her down, refusing to blink as she considered my words. She looked like she was about to explode. Finally, she said, "Fine! I'll share with you what I've got, and you can do with it what you will."

She rummaged around in the desk drawer to her right and extracted a flash drive, pulling another from the purse she had stowed somewhere behind her desk. She shook her mouse to wake up her computer screen and plugged the two drives in. She started copying files from one drive to the other.

"But you will leave here and never, *ever* come back," said Gina, her expression brooking no denial. "We both understand the objective, but we *cannot* be in contact with one another. It's too dangerous. Hopefully, we can find something we can use against Senator Gorham sooner rather than later. I don't care how you do it, but you've got to convince Dad to back off."

"That's a lot easier said than done," I said, looking away. "I don't think he's going to back off without a concrete reason for doing so."

"I didn't think it would be easy, but—oh, no," she said, realization dawning. "You told him, didn't you?"

Shit.

I was hoping it wouldn't come to this. I looked at her apologetically and shrugged. "I really tried not to, but his dreams started getting spooky, you know? They lined up almost perfectly with what happened, and I thought that maybe it was a sign."

"Oh, my *God!*" she said, lifting her head toward the ceiling and laughing hollowly. "You are *unbelievable!*"

"So, sue me," I said, sounding like the petulant bratty brother she knew best. "I just want you home—where you belong."

After a moment, she slowly began to nod. She reached behind her neck with both hands and unfastened the necklace that was draped around her throat. It was a golden unicorn on a slender chain, a gift our father had given her when she was still in school. I hadn't even noticed it. She reached across the desk and handed it to me.

"Here," she said. "Tell him this is my idea, and I need him to do what I say. I'll be in touch just as soon as I possibly can." As the necklace dropped into my open palm, she cupped my hand into both of hers and squeezed. "It really *is* good to see you again, Dwayne."

I smiled as my throat tightened. I was in danger of blubbering again. "You have no idea," I managed. Another thought suddenly occurred to me. "So, how did you know that I was here? I kinda usurped the identity of one Brock Givens."

Gina pivoted her computer screen toward me and reached for her mouse. "Closed circuit surveillance," she said, clicking an icon on her desktop. "I nearly shit myself when I saw you seated out there using one of our—oh, no."

"What?" I said, leaning in at the alarm in her voice.

The monitoring system had filled her screen, the lower left quadrant focused on the circulation desk. Ms. Appleby was currently in deep discussion with two uniformed police officers, and she was clearly pointing toward the rear of the building and the very office in which we sat.

CHAPTER TWENTY-THREE

Gina plucked the flash drives from the front of her computer and handed one of them to me.

"Go," she said, waving me away with one hand while the other returned to her mouse. "Use the emergency exit at the end of the hall. I'm disabling the alarm."

I stood, pocketing the flash drive and her necklace while remaining rooted to the spot. "What about you?"

"They aren't here for me," said Gina, her focus on her monitor. "This is all about you. They're here to make sure that I'm alright. That goddamn Appleby bitch is overstepping her authority, yet again. She didn't take me at my word when I said I was okay. *Damnit!* She's still pissed that the board passed her over for my position. She's been a thorn in my side since Day One."

"Are you sure?"

"Completely," she said. "Those are local boys, but Len Whisman has been on the force long enough to realize that you aren't Brock Givens. You need to get out of here before he sees you."

"But—"

"*Now!*"

I nodded, nearly knocking over my chair in my haste to reach the door. I opened it carefully and peered out into the reception area. The coast was clear.

"*Dwayne!*" Gina hissed.

I looked back over my shoulder.

"Be careful," she said, grinning lopsidedly. "I love you, baby bro."

I returned her grin. "Love you too."

"Now, *hurry!* They're heading this way!"

I took a deep breath and plunged forward, not quite running but almost. Ms. Appleby's voice was getting closer, and I didn't dare look back once I stepped into the tiled hallway and turned right. I hurried to the end of the hall and held my breath as I pushed the crash bar, halfway expecting the emergency alarm to sound even though Gina had assured me she had disabled it. The door swung out silently and with little resistance; I had to scurry ahead to keep it from slamming into the back of the building, a noise that would have undoubtedly brought the officers running. I eased the door shut and paused to catch my breath and get my bearings. My heart was jackhammering in my chest, and I fully expected someone to burst through the door at any moment.

I had to get out of there.

I shielded my eyes against the afternoon sunlight to check my watch. It was only a little after two-thirty, and Reba wouldn't return to pick me up for nearly half an hour. I couldn't just stand there waiting. The portion of the parking lot in which I found myself was virtually empty, save for a trio of vehicles that probably belonged to library employees. There was no place to hide. Even the dumpster across the way was freestanding and accessible from all sides.

I was seriously contemplating diving into whatever lurked within its covered interior when one of the three cars, an older white Chevy Impala sedan, suddenly lurched forward and cut in front of me, blocking my path. The passenger window lowered with a hum. I leaned down to peer inside.

"Get in!" said Laurel, gesturing urgently from behind the wheel.

She didn't have to tell me twice.

I opened the passenger door, and dropped into the bucket seat, fumbling for the seatbelt.

"Are you fucking *kidding* me?" she said, swatting the belt out of my hands. "Get down."

I looked at her questioningly as she rolled the passenger window back up.

"Just do it!" she insisted.

I located the control that adjusted the incline of the seat and laid it back as far as it would go. It wasn't perfect, but it kept me from being seen through the passenger side window. I folded my hands over my stomach and stared at the ceiling as the car began to inch forward.

"Just—stay—down," she mumbled, carefully navigating a lot I couldn't see. I nodded, almost afraid to breathe. "We're almost free."

Our forward momentum abruptly stopped, and a jarring image sprung to mind of Darbydale's finest surrounding the car with their weapons drawn. Before the idea had a chance to really take hold, Laurel turned the wheel to the right and eased into traffic, gently accelerating. I watched as overhead power lines appeared to be pacing us through the passenger window.

After a few moments and some serious study of her rearview mirror, Laurel finally said, "We're all clear. You can sit up now."

I fumbled for the button to raise my seatback and reached for my seatbelt again. Some habits die hard, and I felt naked without it.

"Thanks," I said, craning to look behind us to verify that no one was in hot pursuit. I was suddenly aware of the sheen of perspiration that glued my muscle shirt to my midriff. I subconsciously pulled my outer shirt together. "I guess I owe you another one."

"I guess you do," she said, her smile widening. "So, *Ricky*—where to?"

Laurel pulled off the road across from the overgrown trail leading back through the woods and to the Givens' cabin. She put her car in park and left the engine idling.

"This is as far as I go," she said as she shifted in her seat to face me.

We had spent most of the ride in awkward silence, but I could tell she was just itching to riddle me with questions. So far, I had staved them off with monosyllabic replies as I kept my eyes on the foliage whipping past the passenger window.

"Oh—okay," I said, unfastening my seatbelt. I didn't know where else to have her take me, but I could understand her reticence about driving down a lane that was clearly marked as 'No Trespassing.' I didn't have any way of reaching Reba to warn her away from the library, but I figured the police car parked in the parking lot would be a sufficient deterrent. She'd make her way home eventually. I opened the door to get out of the car, but Laurel held my arm.

"Listen," she said. "I'm serious—you really need to be careful around these folks. They play by their own set of rules."

I smiled at her. "I hear you."

"Do you?" She didn't return my smile. In fact, she looked troubled. "I mentioned earlier that Marcus, that douchebag I moved here with had died. What I didn't say was that I think that Brock Givens may have killed him."

My smile fell away. "Excuse me?"

She shrugged and stared at her hands. "I may have started seeing Brock just a wee bit before Marcus died. I didn't want it to sound like I was 'that' kind of girl, but I was really unhappy, and Brock was just so sweet." Her eyes locked onto mine. "He was also very protective."

I settled back into my seat and pulled the door shut. "So—do you *think* he killed Marcus, or do you *know* he did?"

I was cautious with my phrasing. I didn't ask if Brock had done it at her behest, but I'd be lying if I didn't admit the thought crossed my mind.

Her smile was tight. "I don't *know* anything. But the timing was awfully coincidental."

"How so?"

She sighed, visibly disturbed by the memory. "Marcus's idea of fun Friday night included drinking until he was blackout drunk—but beating the shit out of me before he got to that point. It wasn't only on Fridays, but it was *every* Friday. He wasn't much of a day-drinker. He worked down at the mill, and even *he* wasn't stupid enough to try and use a table saw while drunk. Towards the end, I had his routine pretty much down. I could tell when he was having a shitty day because he'd light up my phone, getting nastier and more demeaning with each call. I learned to wait him out, find someplace else to be until at least ten. By then, he'd be passed out inside our trailer in his underpants, dead to the world until morning. By then, he'd forgotten what he was even angry about. He'd shower, get dressed, and go about his day, acting like nothing ever happened."

"Until the next time," I said.

She nodded. "There was always a 'next time.' It was a miserable way to live."

"So, why did you stay?"

She scoffed. "Why does *anyone* stay? I was young. I was stupid. I was *proud*. It felt like I'd burned all the bridges with my family, and I'd rather take a smack to the mouth than admit they were right about Marcus. Looking back, I honestly don't know. I certainly wouldn't put up with that sort of bullshit now. I spent most of my Friday nights down at the Legion, just waiting until it was late enough to feel halfway safe going home. I wasn't twenty-one, but their dances were open to anyone eighteen and above. That's where I met Brock, and ain't that some shit? If I'd met him first, I would probably currently be Mrs. Brock Givens, happily married and mother to some fine-lookin' children." She chuckled. "He was one handsome man."

"Did he know about Marcus?" I asked.

"He knew I was married," she said. "He knew I was unhappy—but no. I never told him everything I was dealing with. What we had was too new, and I was afraid of scaring him off."

"But he found out anyway."

She bit her bottom lip, reflecting on a past that clearly still haunted her. "It was on one of those Friday nights," she finally said. "Brock and I had just had the most wonderful evening. He dropped me off at the entrance to the trailer park, and I damn near floated home, finally seeing a way out of this bottomless pit I had fallen into. It was the first time he told me he loved me. He wanted to *be* with me."

Her face clouded over.

"Marcus was waiting up for me," she said, her eyes filling with tears. "Sitting in the pitch-dark in our broken-down La-Z-Boy. I never saw him coming." She turned to me and smiled, running a forefinger over her teeth. "Wanna guess how many of these are real?"

"Oh, God," I said, appalled. "I'm so sorry."

"When Brock saw what he'd done, he went wild," she said. "I don't think I've ever seen anyone so angry—not even Marcus on a bad day. He swore that Marcus would pay for what he'd done, and I honestly relished the thought of Brock teaching that bastard a lesson he'd never forget. But things didn't exactly play out the way I expected. Marcus just— disappeared."

"Disappeared?"

She nodded. "He went to work the next morning, but when he clocked out for lunch, he never came back. It was like he vanished into thin air. You'd think I would have been relieved, but I wasn't. I just kept waiting for him to turn back up, and it was making me crazy. After the third day, I was pretty much taking Brock around the bend with me. Nothing he said could calm me down, but he kept insisting that it was over. Marcus would never hurt me again, and the very next day, he was proven correct. Marcus's body was fished out of the reservoir, and he'd apparently suffered some sort of blunt force trauma to the back of his skull. Next thing I know, I'm being hauled in for questioning in the murder of my husband. I really thought I was going to jail, and Lord knows I couldn't afford a decent attorney. Fortunately for me, once they figured out the time of death, pretty much all of my time was accounted for. I was either at work or at the Legion, and there were plenty of witnesses to confirm my whereabouts."

"How about Brock?" I asked. "He was with you a lot of the time, right?"

"He was," she said. "But not the afternoon when Marcus first disappeared. He claimed to be out hunting with a couple of his buddies, and they all backed each other up, but—" Her voice trailed away as she shook her head. "It never rang true with me. These guys were part of that doomsday cult or whatever it is that Brock's parents belong to. I have zero doubt that they'd lie for one another if push came to shove."

"Did you ask him?"

Her smile was tight. "I couldn't bring myself to do it. It was easier to cling to innocence if I didn't have my suspicions confirmed. Otherwise, I would have felt like an accomplice. Marcus was *my* problem, not Brock's. I would have *never* asked him to do something like that, no matter how bad things had gotten. You have to believe me."

And I did. After seeing how Burt and Reba had handled the goon who was sent to kill me and Dad, I didn't question Laurel's intuition. She was undoubtedly right.

"After a couple of weeks, Brock asked me to leave town with him. He had some new opportunity out west and thought the timing was perfect for us to make a clean break. I wasn't quite ready to join that crowd. As much as I liked Brock, his entire family had a scary reputation around town, and frankly, I was a little scared of them, too. I told him it would look too suspicious if we both left town together, and he didn't argue the point. He said he'd send for me once he got settled."

"But you're still here."

"I am," she said. "I never had any intention of following Brock out to Wyoming. I'd already spent too much of my life feeling uprooted and out of place, and I didn't want to lose the handful of friends I'd made since I'd landed here in Darbydale. I spent the next couple of months dreading Brock's return and what I'd say to him to break things off, but wouldn't you know? Seems he wasn't all that different from any other man out there. All it took was another fine piece of ass for Brock to forget all about me. When he came back, it was to tell me that he'd gotten married. I had to pretend I was angry, but I was *relieved*. I couldn't begin to imagine looking at his face every single day until the end of time."

"You're certain he did it," I said. It wasn't a question.

"Wouldn't you be? Point is, you need to watch yourself around these people. They aren't afraid of the local authorities, and 'thou shalt not kill' doesn't seem to apply. There's really no limit to what they might do."

I nodded, receiving her warning loud and clear. "I will. Thanks."

I opened the car door and started to get out when she grabbed my arm again.

"Give me your hand," she said, and I looked at her, puzzled.

"My hand?"

"*Mmm-hmm*," she said, pulling a pen from the center console. She splayed the fingers of my left hand open and began writing on my palm. It tickled. "It's my number. Call me if you need anything else. After everything

I've shared with you, maybe someday you'll be ready to share with me what you're *really* doing here—*Ricky*."

I got out of the car and stepped off the road, giving her plenty of space to execute a three-point turn before heading back into town. I waved as her taillights receded in the distance.

I looked at the poorly demarcated entrance that would lead me back to the Givens' isolated cabin and whatever lay beyond.

It didn't feel all that promising.

Wolfie announced my arrival long before I saw the cottage, barking ferociously and reminding me that I wasn't exactly a known commodity. I could only hope he wasn't about to tear me to pieces. By the time I reached the clearing, Burt was already standing in the front yard with a shotgun in one hand, Wolfie's collar in the other, ready to release his straining hound depending on who was trespassing on his land. It seemed to take a lifetime for him to recognize me, but once he finally did, he muttered a command that immediately tamed his ferocious beast.

"Hey, there," called Burt. "Where's Reba? Y'all left together. I kinda figured you'd come back together, too."

"Yeah, so did I," I said, crossing to where he stood. I started to offer a hand to Wolfie so he could catch my scent, but he bared his teeth, a low growl issuing from his throat. I pulled my hand to safety, reconsidering the thought. "I ran into a little trouble at the library."

"What kind of trouble?" called Dad from somewhere to my left. I followed the sound of his voice to find him approaching from the weathered barn, and I burst out laughing. "What's so funny?"

He wore a pair of borrowed jeans two sizes too large for him and cinched at the waist by a length of rope. His shirt was a black, sleeveless

Red Hot Chili Peppers tee that put his respectable guns on full display. The entire look was completed by a bright red knit cap covering his bald head. He looked like the world's oldest gang member, and it was everything I could do just to catch my breath.

"Have you taken a good look at yourself, son? I believe you're a little long in the tooth for that outfit, too," he said, reaching down to scratch Wolfie behind the ears. The dog only stared at him adoringly, his tongue lolling from his grinning maw. I have a healthy respect for dogs, but there's a reason I'm a cat person. "What kind of trouble?" he repeated.

"Just a busybody librarian," I said. "She pretty much had it out for me from the minute I walked into the place. She called the local cops over something stupid, and I got out of there before they saw me." I looked up at Dad and held his eyes, hoping he would pick up on what I was putting down. "It was no big deal. We can talk about it later."

"I reckon that was smart," said Burt. "Reba wouldn't have stopped once she saw cops. Too much history. She'll be along sooner or later."

I let that one go. I knew so much more about the Givens than I did that morning, and I wasn't sure how they'd feel about that. It felt safest to feign ignorance while I processed all that I'd learned.

"What have you been up to today?" I asked Dad, looking to change the subject. "Still feeling alright?"

"Right as rain," said Dad, puffing his chest out a bit. "Worked up a bit of a sweat out in the barn. Burt had some camouflage netting we strung over top of the Monza that makes it hard to see if you don't know what you're looking for. It felt proactive. I imagine he's right. Eventually someone else will be out here poking around. Did your 'research' yield anything useful?" His disdain for due diligence was apparent by the air quotes he flew.

"Possibly," I said. "I'm still sort of processing it."

I was spared from having to elaborate by the sound of Reba's VW Beetle, nosing its way into the clearing. Wolfie leapt around the yard, unable to contain his excitement at her return. She pulled alongside us and rolled down the window.

"I sure am glad to find you here," she said, smiling at me. "I was a little worried when I saw police. You okay?"

"Yeah, I'm sorry about that," I said. "It didn't feel like a good idea to stick around. I didn't mean to put you out."

"No worries," she said. "As long as everyone's safe and sound. Did you find what you were looking for?"

"It's given me some things to consider," I said, and I wasn't lying. "Say, how would you feel about me and Dad borrowing your car for a little bit? We need to check in with the folks at home before we call it a day, and Mom isn't going to be satisfied unless she talks to Dad herself."

Reba cut the engine and set the parking brake. "Sure. Do you think you'll be long? I was just about to get dinner started. How do you fellas feel about venison burgers?"

I fought to keep from pulling a face while Dad looked absolutely thrilled. I can't help it. I still eat with my eyes. Eating Bambi was never on my bucket list.

"Sounds delicious!" said Dad, rubbing his hands together. "Count me in!"

Reba left the keys in the ignition and the car door open as we traded places. I motioned for Dad to get in, trying not to appear too eager. We had some things that were better discussed privately, and this felt like the perfect opportunity to make ourselves scarce.

• • • • • • ● ⊖ ⊖ ● • • • • •

I wasn't planning to drive all the way back into town, just close enough to get cell reception.

I used the time to bring Dad up to speed on the shady shenanigans I had learned about the Givens, and he grew more somber with each allegation. I halfway expected him to write everything off as the paranoid ravings of a woman scorned, but he seemed to appreciate the gravity of the situation as well as our currently precarious position. We owed the Givens a debt of gratitude, for sure, but there was only so much we could realistically offer in return. It was a potential source of contention I wasn't looking forward to exploring.

I pulled into the parking lot of a small Sunoco gas station just outside Darbydale's corporation limit, nosing the car into a slot at the side of the cinderblock building. I hadn't found the courage to discuss Gina yet and was more than happy to procrastinate for long enough to get our calls out of the way.

"You first," I said, turning on the phone and handing it to him. "You can tell Mom we should be back by the weekend."

His eyebrows nudged his knit cap up. "We should?"

"Fingers crossed," I said, although I truly meant it. I was hoping I could convince him of the logic in Gina's plan. "At least it buys us a little more time to figure things out."

"Thanks," he said dryly, entering his home phone number and pressing 'Talk.' Mom answered the phone on the second ring, her agitation apparent even from a distance.

"Hi, hon. It's me," said Dad, already halfway out of the car to continue his conversation in the relative privacy of the parking lot. He was never very fond of getting dressed down publicly, and from the pained look on his face, Mom was reading him the riot act.

I used the time to process all the disjointed facts I'd managed to collect over the course of the day. An idea was beginning to take shape, but it wasn't without its own set of risks, and I wasn't quite sure I was willing to take them.

I wasn't sure I had much choice.

I continued to deliberate until Dad returned, looking somewhat defeated. He handed me the phone and scowled at my smirk. "Don't look so happy, son. She's mad at you, too."

My smile fell away. "Mad at *me?* What did *I* do?"

"Humoring the ravings of your lunatic father, I believe she said. You'll find out soon enough. Now, call your lovely lady and let's get back to the Givenses. I'm starving."

I got out of the car and punched in the number to Melanie's prepaid phone. We didn't talk for long. She had the kids in the car, and she passed the phone off to Jasmine so she could concentrate on driving. Her car wasn't Bluetooth enabled, and in Ohio, it's illegal to talk on your phone while driving unless it's hands-free. Frankly, Melanie wasn't the best driver to begin with, so I was glad she wasn't attempting it. It gave me a chance to banter with Jaz and Jordan for a few. After Jordan told me a somewhat circular version of his day including an imaginary dinosaur that had wreaked havoc upon his room, Jasmine took the phone back.

"So, when are you coming home?" she asked.

"Hoping for this weekend, kiddo," I said. "If everything goes as planned."

She paused. "Are you okay?"

My laugh was a little high pitched. "I'm just fine. I'm with my dad. What could possibly be wrong?"

"Well—okay," she said dubiously, and I marveled at her ability to read a room. "Mom wants to know if you'll call her back tonight?"

"Not tonight," I said. "Tomorrow. I won't have another chance until then. Tell her I love her."

"Ugh," she groaned. "Fine."

"I love you and that goofy brother of yours, too."

"Yeah, me too. Bye."

As she disconnected the call, I smiled, more than a little homesick. Taking a deep breath, I tapped out another number into the screen.

It was time to phone a friend.

CHAPTER TWENTY-FOUR

"Everything alright?" asked Dad as I got back into the car. "You were on the phone for quite a while there."

"Yeah," I said, starting the car and backing out of the parking spot. It was a little past four-thirty, but it felt so much later. I dreaded the conversation we were about to have, and I was having trouble figuring out where to begin. "I had more than one call to make."

"Oh? Anything to do with the phone number that's smearing in your palm?"

I glanced at my hand and laughed. "No," I said. I had already forgotten it was there. "That's just Laurel's number."

"Isn't she the girl from the library who gave you all that gossip about the Givenses?"

Gossip.

It would seem that my earlier expectation of how he might react to Laurel's information was merely premature, and he had landed firmly on the side of our current benefactors.

"One and the same," I said. "She told me to call her if I needed anything else."

We lapsed into silence for several miles while I continued to try and find a delicate way to update him on Gina. I took a deep breath, just about to dive in when Dad decided he wasn't quite finished with the subject at hand.

"Are you *planning* on calling her?" he asked, looking at me sideways.

"Laurel?" I asked, surprised. "No. I mean, I can't imagine why I would. But it's nice to have her number just in case, isn't it?"

He made a sound in the back of his throat that reminded me of Dexter processing a hairball.

I chuckled. "Apparently not. If you've got something to say, why don't you just come out and say it?"

"A woman doesn't write her digits on a man's palm unless she's got her eye on him," said Dad. "Don't be stupid, son. We surely didn't raise you this way."

My bewilderment gave way to irritation. "What, exactly, are you implying, Dad?"

"I'm not implying anything. I'm just stating facts. You've got a remarkable young lady waiting for you to come home and start a life with her and those two precious children. Don't blow it."

"What would make you think I'd ever do a thing like that?" I asked, feeling more than a little attacked.

"Hey, I was young once, too, you know," he said. "I remember how tempting a smile, a wink—a little flash of skin can be. But your days of carousing ended the minute you asked Melanie to marry you, do you understand me?"

I gaped at him, my entire face burning. *"Carousing?* Have you even *met* me? Where is all of this coming from?"

He shifted in his seat, looking away. "I just don't want you to ruin a good thing, that's all. I mean—you aren't getting any younger."

"If I somehow manage to screw things up, I *guarantee* you it won't be because I'm cheating," I said. "You *do* realize that you're accusing me of something that would never even cross my mind, right? What do you want from me?"

He stared at me pointedly. "I want you to wash your hands, son. That should just about do it."

It was everything I could do to keep my mouth shut, pithy retorts piling up like a trainwreck behind clenched teeth. This wasn't how I envisioned us utilizing this time. Before we found ourselves back in the close quarters of the cabin, I needed to present our options so Dad might have the evening to really consider our next move before committing to a definitive plan of action. I didn't want to confirm Gina's proximity in front of folks who were little more than strangers, regardless of what they'd done for us, but the longer I held my tongue, the angrier he was going to be once I finally spilled the beans. I suspected keeping Dad from doing something rash was going to be a challenge.

We were rapidly approaching the cabin and running out of time. I wasn't any closer to figuring out how to broach the subject when Dad gave me as good an opening as I was likely to get.

"You told me to tell your mother we'd home by this weekend," he said. "That only gives us a few days. I'm guessing you have some sort of plan. Would you care to let me in on it?" He already sounded skeptical, so I couldn't imagine this was going to go well.

I pulled into the same spot where Laurel had earlier dropped me off and put the shifter in neutral, applying the parking brake. I took a deep breath while Dad bored holes through me with his eyes.

"I'm going to tell you something, and I need you to remain calm," I said, realizing as I returned his stare that I was asking the impossible. "Can you do that?"

"Of course!" he snapped. "When am I *ever* not calm?"

I sighed, resigned to the unpleasantness I could no longer avoid. "I saw her."

For a moment, he was perplexed. His face squirreled up underneath that ridiculous red hat, but I saw the very second that realization dawned, his expression heartbreakingly hopeful.

"G-Gina?" he croaked.

I nodded as a tsunami of emotion washed over him. He turned away from me and stared through the passenger window, unwilling to let me see the tears that were spilling from his eyes, completely unaware that I could see them reflected in the glass. His hands clenched repeatedly as he struggled to contain the feelings that were threatening to undo him. I gave him all the time he needed to compose himself, nearly certain that his next words would be an angry outburst aimed at me.

Instead, he cleared his throat and simply asked, "Where?"

"In the library," I said. "As a matter of fact, she's the director of the entire Tri-County Library System. They know her as Lee Tieman."

He nodded slowly, subtly wiping the moisture from his face. "Okay," he said, his voice eerily calm. "Let's go."

I blinked. "Go?"

"To the library. I want you to turn this fucking car around and take me to see my daughter."

Ah, *shit*. There it was. Dad rarely dropped an F-bomb, but when he did, it was best recognized as an early warning of the storm about to break. The anger bubbling just underneath the surface, the muscles in his jaw flexing as his steely look dared me to defy him. Here was where I ran the risk of getting smacked in the mouth, and reasoning with him was going to be next to impossible, but I had to try.

"We can't," I said, watching his face race through a spectrum of deepening red until it was fully purple.

"We *can't?!?*" he roared, and I flinched at the sheer volume of his response. "After all that we've been through—all that you've *knowingly* put us through, you're going to tell me we fucking *can't?!?*"

Two F-bombs. I was toast.

I withered under the heat of his angry glare. "Dad, I—"

"You can either put this *goddamn* car in gear right this second, young man, or I'm going to drag you out from behind the wheel and—"

"She doesn't want to see you!" I yelled, cutting him off. I watched my words land like physical blows as his face crumpled, but I had to stop this thing in its tracks. "She doesn't want to see *any* of us, at least not yet. Not until it's safe. It took everything I had to convince her that nobody was following me. She was ready to pull up stakes and go back into hiding again, and she was *pissed*. Do you want to chase her away?"

Dad's frustration was apparent from the furrows in his forehead. "No," he finally said. "Did she realize I was with you?"

"Yes."

"And she *still* didn't want to see me?"

"I'm sorry, Dad. No."

It was heartbreaking to crush his tiniest glimmer of hope, but it had to be done. I wasn't exactly lying when I said that Gina would bolt. I couldn't bring myself to tell him about her current condition. It was something I had only barely begun to process myself, and just thinking about it nearly made me sick to my stomach. I wasn't relishing my role as harbinger of doom, and that particular bit of news wasn't going to be coming from me. I was afraid it would only make him that much more determined to seek her out.

"What does she expect us to do?" he asked.

"She wants us to go home," I said.

"No."

"She wants us to wait for her to find a way to discredit Senator Gorham so she can come home safely."

"I will *not* come *this* close to seeing my daughter only to turn around now," he said with steely determination. "There's *got* to be another way. We can help her!"

"I suspected that's how you would feel," I said, and when he opened his mouth to argue, I held up a hand to ward off his next argument. "I agree with you."

He blinked. "You do?"

"I do," I said. "In fact, I'm trying to figure out the best way to help right now, I've just got a little more digging to do. I think that Amelia Gorham's Achilles' heel is also the thing she's most proud of—New Horizons."

"How do you figure?"

"I'm still trying to sort that out. In Briarstaff, everyone knew about the Academy, but nobody really talked about it. Gorham's approach to New Horizons is just the opposite. It isn't open to the public, and if Joy Beth Perkins' ex-husband got his 'basic training' there, it's clearly being used as more than just a reformatory for troubled young men. Still, Gorham uses it at every opportunity to illustrate the kind of person she is, or at least the kind she wants us to believe she is. She wants to appear completely above reproach, and her record bears her out, but there's just something about her. Of course, we know about her involvement with Gina and this whole mess at the Academy, so maybe I'm jaded, but—"

"I know what you mean," Dad said. "I've seen her on CNN. Everything she does feels scripted. She thinks she's the smartest person in the room, no matter who else is in the room with her."

"Exactly. And I swear, I think she's taking some sort of perverse pleasure in hiding the true purpose of New Horizons right in plain sight. The place has had a handful of scandals over the years, and that's what I was trying to dig into at the library, but most of them were glossed over in the news as if they were insignificant. My gut tells me there's a lot more to the story, and Gina agrees." I used a forefinger to fish the flash drive that Gina had given me out of my pocket and held it up for Dad to see. "Apparently, this area has been plagued with an unusually high incidence of mortality amongst its male juvenile population. Gina's been trying to connect the dots but hasn't been able to do it so far. I managed to convince her to share copies of what she'd found with me."

Dad took the flash drive from my hand and turned it over in his hands, looking at it with nothing short of wonder. "Gina gave you this?" The question was pensive, his voice unsteady.

I smiled, nodding. "She did."

His eyes locked onto mine, guardedly hopeful. "I swear to you, son, if you're just messing with me, I'll—"

"I'm not," I said, hooking my finger back into my pocket. I pulled out the slender gold chain, holding it up so the afternoon sunlight glinted off the unicorn dangling from it. "She really hates that she can't be here to tell you herself, but it's best that these assholes continue to believe she's dead. Whatever we do, we can't lead them straight to her door."

He traded the flash drive for the necklace, tears once again threatening to overwhelm him. He gently pulled the length of chain through his fingers, carefully inspecting it like he wasn't sure it was real. His bottom lip betrayed his emotional state with the tiniest of quivers as he closed his fingers around the necklace and turned away, unwilling to share his vulnerability. It wasn't how his generation was raised, and some things would never change.

I yelped as a series of rapid knocks sounded against the driver's side window, directly behind my head. Dad hurriedly composed himself as I turned to find Burt staring in at me from the side of the road. I reached for the hand crank and rolled the window down while placing my other hand over my racing heart.

"*Jesus*, Burt! You scared the shit out of me!" I said, forcing a smile I didn't feel.

"Umm, sorry about that. Y'all okay in there? I could've sworn I heard shouting." Burt asked, squinting first at me before shifting his attention toward Dad.

Wolfie paced circles around his ankles, observing anxiously from below and looking confused by the strangers who occupied a vehicle normally driven by his mother. He abruptly raised on his haunches, resting his front paws in the open window frame and blasting me in the face with his hot, fetid breath so he could take a closer look inside the VW's cabin.

"We're fine," I said, trying to avoid the dog's wet, probing snout without looking as repulsed as I felt. It smelled like he'd been recently feasting on feces.

Dad nodded, already looking remarkably calmer and more collected. "Just a little difference of opinion, but you've got a couple of boys of your own. You know how that goes."

"Yep, that I do," confirmed Burt, slapping his thigh and coaxing Wolfie away. "This fella got himself all excited when he heard Reba's car, and I started to get a little worried when y'all didn't pull in. You sure you're alright?"

My enthusiastic "Absolutely!" collided with Dad's "Right as rain!"

Burt's smile was nearly as convincing. "Well, all right, then. Dinner's just about ready. Let's head back before it gets cold."

I nodded, putting the car in gear. We pulled across the two-lane road and onto the overgrown trail that led to the cabin. Wolfie bounded after us, and Burt trudged along behind.

Even from a distance, there was no mistaking the scowl that had settled onto his face.

"Smells wonderful!" Dad exclaimed as we entered the cabin, and I was reluctant to admit that he wasn't mistaken. Admittedly, I was still equating our dinner with a beloved Disney woodland creature, and it was hard to feign enthusiasm. It almost felt like cannibalism.

"Thank you," said Reba as she bustled around the kitchen, bringing an assortment of homemade condiments to the table where she had already staged freshly sliced tomatoes, onions, and whole leaves of romaine lettuce. "By the time you fellas get your hands washed up, everything should be ready."

Dad looked pointedly at me. "After you, son." His eyes drifted to where Laurel's number was written on my left hand.

My smile was tight as I struggled to keep from rolling my eyes. I headed for the bathroom while the others engaged in polite banalities. Once inside, I closed the door and figured I may as well make use of the facilities while I was there. After I flushed the toilet, I turned the water on and stared at the smudgy numerals while I waited for the water to get warm. A small wicker basket rested on the tank of the toilet, containing the sorts of things you might find in a junk drawer. A handful of batteries, a box of matches, some loose change—but my eyes landed on a pencil buried amongst the paraphernalia. I extracted one of the wadded-up napkins I had stuffed into my pants pocket and plucked the pencil out of the basket, using it to transcribe the number that was in my palm to the paper.

I had no intention of ever calling Laurel, but it felt foolish not to preserve the option.

· · • • • • ● ⊖ ⊖ ● • • • • • · ·

I eyed the burger as I was surrounded by the sounds of voracious mastication. Dad was showering Reba with enough praise for both of us while I picked at the macaroni salad on my plate and wondered how I might slip my murdered deer carcass to the salivating canine stretched out below the table without being busted. It wasn't looking likely.

"Aren't you even going to try it?" asked Reba, calling me out.

I looked up to find everyone staring at me expectantly.

"I—uh—" I stammered, trying to manufacture an excuse that wouldn't be offensive. Dad looked thoroughly embarrassed while Burt continued to chow down like he hadn't eaten in days.

A giggle erupted from Reba's throat. "It's okay," she said. "I saw how you reacted earlier when I mentioned venison. Yours is just plain ol' hamburger. You can dig right in."

I could feel my face brightening. "Really?"

"Really," she said. "You may have borrowed Brock's identity earlier, but you sure do remind me a whole lot more of Boyd." She looked across the table at her husband. "Don't you agree, honey?"

Burt barely grunted, his focus confined to his own plate.

My stomach growled as I picked up the burger, eyeing it with renewed purpose. It was thick, juicy, and now it was practically calling my name.

I know, I know—it's completely ridiculous. Why the preferential treatment for deer over cattle? The short answer? Before I ever learned about the horrific and sobering reality of the food chain, I believed ground beef came from the grocery store. I stubbornly held tight to that belief, and even after thirty-five years on this planet, I wasn't about to give it up now.

I took a bite and groaned audibly. It was heaven on a homemade bun.

"Did you have a productive day?" asked Reba, picking up her own sandwich.

"I think so," I said, not bothering to swallow before answering and earning a reproachful glare from Dad. I took a moment to finish chewing and cleared my palate with a swig of iced sweet tea. "I found a few things to follow up on, but I'm hoping we'll be out of your hair in the next day or two—provided that's alright with you and Burt, of course."

"No hurry," said Reba, pausing to corral a bite of macaroni salad onto her fork. She paused with her fork halfway to her mouth. "What sort of things did you find?"

"There seem to be an awful lot of young men dying around here," I said. "A handful can be traced back to New Horizons, but I think I can probably link even more. Senator Gorham's ability to control media coverage about that place is pretty remarkable. If it hadn't been for someone pointing me in the right direction, I probably wouldn t have found it."

"And who would that be?" asked Reba, eyeing me over the rim of her glass.

My pause was nearly imperceptible. I couldn't admit that it was Gina— I had already shared that information with too many people. I decided to keep it generic.

"Just someone who works at the library."

"Didn't you say her name was Laurel something or the other?" Dad volunteered, and Reba's fork fell with a clatter onto her plate.

"Laurel Whitney?" she asked sharply, and I froze with my burger halfway to my mouth, wondering if discretion was even a possibility with Dad. He just sat there looking pleased with himself.

"I think that's what she said," I said through gritted teeth.

"Well, that explains the police, then," said Reba, pushing her plate away. "She would've known you weren't Brock the moment you flashed that library card. I had no idea that Laurel was working at the library these days. That girl has been nothing but trouble since the first moment I laid eyes on her." She said Laurel's name like it was bitter on her tongue.

"That's not what happened at all," I said, wishing Dad had just kept his big mouth shut. Reba's agitation was only growing. "She was actually pretty helpful. Brock's library card had expired, and I wouldn't have gotten anywhere if she hadn't helped me renew it without any identification."

"And why would she do a thing like that?" asked Reba. "She knew damn well you weren't my son."

"I honestly couldn't say. It was the head librarian, Ms. Appleby, who called the police. Maybe she caught on that I wasn't who I said I was? I really don't know. What's the story with this Laurel, anyhow?" I asked, deciding that feigning ignorance was my best option.

Reba opened her mouth to respond, but Burt issued a low warning. *"Reba."*

She took a deep breath while glaring at her husband. "Only that you can't trust a single word that girl says, that's all." She jabbed at the macaroni salad on her plate, pushing it around with her fork while the muscles of her jaw flexed beneath her skin.

We lapsed into an awkward silence, everyone's appetite seemingly obliterated with the exception of Dad's. He continued to shovel food into his mouth with wild abandon. I picked at my own food so as not to seem rude. Finally, Reba broke the silence by asking me, "So, how's your burger?"

"Delicious," I said, taking another big bite to illustrate my point.

"It's venison," she said, and I nearly choked. "Amazing how much better it tastes when you don't know what it is. It was the only way I could get Boyd to try it, too."

Apparently, Laurel wasn't the only one who couldn't be trusted.

To say that sleep was elusive is an understatement.

I tossed and turned while all the bells I couldn't unring kept jangling away inside my head, reminding me of all the holes riddling a plan I had already set in motion. The probability of all the stars aligning was so low I had a better chance of hitting the Mega Millions.

Eventually, I fumbled my way through the dark and out into the hall, staggering to the bathroom like a zombie—a zombie who really needed to pee. I stepped back out into the hall after washing up only to be startled by a disembodied voice floating in from the darkened living room.

"Dwayne? Is that you?"

I squinted into the gloom, easing my way toward the sound. "Reba?"

As I exited the hallway, I found her sitting alone on the couch, her outline barely visible. Wolfie's eyes glistened in the dark from where he lounged at her feet. "Will you sit with me for a minute?"

"*Umm*, sure."

"Here, let me light a candle so you can see where you're going," she said, just as a match flared and seemingly levitated through the air. She pressed it to the wick of a candle resting on the end table and blew out the flame as amber luminescence pushed back the gloom. "That's better."

I chose one of the chairs across from her, perched on its edge, and wished with everything I had that Dad would join us. Something about her forlorn expression in the flickering candlelight was deeply unnerving, and I couldn't imagine why she had called me in.

"I won't keep you but a minute," she said, smiling listlessly. "I just wanted to apologize for earlier."

I exhaled in a whoosh, as relief washed over me. "I'll get over it," I said, grinning crookedly. "I mean, it wasn't all that bad when I didn't know what it was, but you really shouldn't fool someone like that."

She stared at me vacantly for a second before throwing her head back and laughing throatily. "I wasn't talking about the venison. You're a grown-ass man. You shouldn't be eating with your eyes."

I was grateful for the limited lighting. I could feel my embarrassment burning to the tips of my ears. "I don't understand."

"I'm talking about Laurel," she said, and saying the name still seemed difficult. "You need to be careful of that girl. She's trouble with a capital 'T,' and believe me, I know what I'm talking about."

"Okay," I said. "Anything you'd care to share?"

"She's the reason Brock lives so far away, and I'll never forgive her for that."

"I thought Brock moved away to head up another branch of your survivalists, or whatever you call yourselves. I'm sorry—I'm not trying to offend."

Reba smiled. "No offense taken. Sure, that's what Brock is doing now, but that's not why he went. He moved to get away from that black widow before she could do any more damage. She had no sooner moved to Darbydale with her deadbeat husband when she started eyeing my boy. She had Brock wrapped around her finger so fast I didn't even see it coming. Next thing I know, the husband's dead, and she's doing everything she can to pin it on Brock."

I kept my expression neutral as I listened to a decidedly different version of a story I had already heard from Laurel, wondering who was telling the truth and realizing I had no way of knowing for certain.

So much for sleep.

CHAPTER TWENTY-FIVE

Getting away from the cabin proved easier than I had anticipated, although I was really dragging ass. I had gotten maybe an hour-and-a-half of sleep at best, and my swollen, bloodshot eyes were the undeniable proof. At least there were no more unexpected visitors in the wee hours of morning requiring us to take shelter in the claustrophobic space below the floorboards. World's worst alarm clock, I promise you. I had managed to scrounge an oversized navy t-shirt from the back of Brock's dresser, and while I was beyond scruffy, at least I was a lot less self-conscious.

When I asked Reba if she could take me back into town, she tossed me her keys and begged off, citing a towering pile of laundry that she'd been putting off. I figured Dad would be harder to dissuade, but when I told him I had another day of research ahead of me, he decided helping Burt with some menial tasks around the cabin was a better use of his time.

I hurried out of there before he could change his mind.

As the Darbydale corporation limit came into view, I powered up the burner phone and held my breath, waiting for it to connect to its cellular network. A few seconds later, the telltale sound of a text sounded, and I thumbed the messaging app open to find a single new message waiting.

I'm a little early, but I'm here. Parked in back, like you said.

I closed the app and powered the phone down, setting it aside. Much like the morning before, traffic was light, and pedestrians stared, undoubtedly wondering why Reba Givens wasn't driving her own car, but I kept my eyes on the road, hoping to avoid another run-in with the local authorities I had only barely managed to evade the previous afternoon. I doubted I'd be so lucky again.

The café was even busier this morning, its small lot almost completely full. That was fine with me. I wasn't there for breakfast. I drove past its glass storefront, signaling left a block further down. I parked the VW along the curb and got out, checking my pockets to make sure I had everything I needed before locking the door and continuing up the block and away from the main drag. The day was overcast and cool, but it wasn't the weather that raised the flesh on my arms. I was afraid I'd have to share the truth about Gina with the last person on Earth I ever thought I might, but it honestly felt like my only option, and I could only pray that I was doing the right thing.

I crossed the street midway down the block, ducking into an empty alley that ran behind the businesses along the main thoroughfare. A used car lot, a two-story office building, and finally, the café. Tony, our server from the previous day, stood just outside the rear exit, smoking a cigarette and texting away, his thumb practically a blur. I waited in the shadows of the neighboring office building until he finally ground his cigarette out beneath his shoe and picked up the butt, carrying it with him as he reentered the building.

Backed into a spot just beside the dumpster was my cherry-red objective, and I never thought I'd be so happy to see it. I hurried onto the lot and circled around its rear, pecking on the passenger window. The door unlocked, and I opened it, sliding into its black leather interior.

"Shoes! Shoes! Shoes!"

I pulled the door shut and sighed. "For fuck's sake, Brady, if and when we get through this thing, I'll pay to have your car detailed, alright? Can we just get out of here? *Please?*"

Brady grinned, his dimples on full display. "You got it, mi amigo. But it's gonna cost ya. I don't trust this baby to just anyone."

He lovingly stroked the dashboard of his Dodge Charger before shifting into gear and pulling away.

Brady had already gotten a room in a small hotel on the edge of town. Once upon a time, it had been a Red Roof Inn, but these days the roof was more orange than red, faded after decades in the hot Pennsylvania sun. A hand-stenciled sign in the office window proclaimed, "Beds by the Hour!" and I felt the immediate need for a tumbler of penicillin.

"Is this the best you can do?" I asked and he smirked.

"I needed a base of operations, not a weekend retreat," he said. "This'll do just fine. Now, come on. We've got a lot of ground to cover."

"Did you stop by the house?"

"I called ahead. Melanie had a bag packed and waiting for me."

"Did you remember—"

He laughed. "Would you stop it, man? I remembered, I remembered."

He got out of the car and popped the trunk with his key fob, extracting a couple of laptop bags, one of which was familiar. He handed it to me.

When I called, I had tempted him with the story of a lifetime, a political scandal that involved Senator Gorham and a rash of deaths that appeared to be connected to her New Horizons initiative. Convincing him to come had been easy, especially once I explained that I wanted him to conduct a live interview with the senator, during which he could level my accusations at her however he best saw fit. The senator's schedule was a closely guarded secret, but her love for publicity was a well-known commodity. Brady Garrett had just enough clout to request an audience with Her Majesty while I wouldn't dare try. I couldn't risk her making the connection between Gina and me.

"I have to admit, I'm surprised you called," said Brady, using his key card to let us into a room whose only notable attribute was its stagnant warmth. "We might have to crack a window. The AC is on the fritz."

"Why didn't you ask for a different room?"

"They said they were full up," he said, rolling his eyes. "But since they're the only game in town, what's a guy to do?"

He laid his laptop bag on the double bed and unfastened it, extracting his computer.

"You have no idea how many things I had to rearrange to accommodate this," he said, setting his laptop on the room's small desk and plugging it in. "I've already managed to schedule a sit-down with Senator Gorham tomorrow morning at ten. I'm gonna need a lot more than what you've told me so far, or else I'm conducting an interview better suited to *Good Morning, America* than *The Associated Press*, and that's not exactly how I see myself, you get me?"

"*Tomorrow?*" I was startled. "That was fast."

"What can I say? You were right," he said, running his hands through his dark mop of curly hair as he dropped into the only task chair in the room. "The senator was more than eager to talk about New Horizons and all the good it's done. So, show me what you've got."

I eyed his computer. "You're not using the motel's public wi-fi, are you?"

He sighed. "I'm using my mobile hotspot and running it through a VPN. I'm an investigative journalist, Morrow. Discretion is my middle name."

"Manuel is your middle name," I said. "And an abundance of caution is more than warranted here. Believe me."

"Are you ever going to tell me the whole story?" he asked.

"I don't know what you mean," I said, avoiding his probing stare. I extracted my own laptop from the bag that Melanie had sent and laid it on the bed, powering it up.

"You know *exactly* what I mean," he said. "You've been keeping something from me for months. I had hoped when you called that you were finally ready to let me in, but you're still just feeding me as little as you can get by with and only on a need-to-know basis. It's bullshit, man. I dropped everything because I thought you needed my help."

"I do," I said. "But don't act like you haven't got a horse in this race. If there wasn't something in it for you, you wouldn't be here."

He scowled. "You don't know that. We're *friends*, you asshole. You seem to keep forgetting that."

"You're right. I'm sorry," I said sincerely. "I really do appreciate your help."

Brady grinned. "I mean, I probably wouldn't have come as *fast* if there wasn't something in it for me, but I would've shown. Eventually."

I laughed, happier than I'd ever admit that he was here. "There's the Brady Garrett I know and loathe," I said. "All good things in time, my friend. Let's start with this."

I pulled the flash drive from my pocket, suddenly certain that I had overestimated its value. I hadn't had a chance to review the contents myself, and I was relying on a smoking gun that Brady needed in less than twenty-four hours. I felt a little lightheaded as anxiety threatened my resolve. With Brady staring at me expectantly, all I could do was hand him the drive and hover as he inserted it into his laptop, pulling up its contents in File Explorer. There were thirty-one folders, each bearing a man's name followed by a date from sometime over the past fifteen years. Brady opened a few of them randomly, and it was soon apparent that each folder had a variable number of files within. Some had as few as two while others had a dozen or more.

This was going to take a while.

"Copy half of the files to your laptop while I get myself set up," I said, "This will go a lot faster if we divide and conquer. I'm gonna need your wi-fi password."

I sounded so much more confident than I felt. What we really needed was a miracle.

Brady closed his last document and sighed, massaging the bridge of his nose. *"Fuck."*

I was wading through the last of my half of the files and couldn't really disagree with his assessment. A couple of hours had passed, and we didn't have a single thing to show for it. Lots of unfortunate deaths, but only a handful of the young men could clearly be traced back to New Horizons—and by handful, I meant exactly three. Two of which were the boys we already knew had died in the fire at the freshmen dormitory.

"Please tell me you've found something useful," he said, sounding about as hopeful as I felt.

"Well—no, but let's not give up so easily," I said. "Think of it as a starting point—a nice, focused list. We just need to dig a little deeper, that's all."

His response was a derisive snort. He pushed back from the desk and stood, unleashing a ripple of audible pops as he flexed his back. "These are juveniles. Their records are sealed."

"You're the investigative journalist. Don't you have ways around that?" I asked, rubbing my tired eyes and yawning.

He glared at me. "You're the private investigator. Don't *you?*"

"Touché," I grudgingly acknowledged. "But unfortunately, no, I don't. We've got a couple of programs for doing deeper dives back at the office, but nothing I can access from here."

"Are you fucking kidding me?" asked Brady. "You're an IT guy! Can't you just remote in?"

It was my turn to laugh. "Doug Boggs is both cheap and paranoid, and I don't know which is worse. I recommended we install the software on a shared computer that we could all access as needed, but I was barely able to convince him to internet-enable the office, much less allow remote access. He's only willing to pay for one license for any of the software, and he insists that it be installed on Loretta's laptop. We're supposed to run any and all queries through her since she supposedly works at both Boggs locations. It's less than efficient."

"She won't help you with this?"

"I can't trust her with this," I said. "It's too important, and the timing is too tight."

"But you haven't exactly trusted me with it either, have you?"

"Of course, I trust you," I said. "You're here, aren't you?"

"But to what end?" he asked, pacing the floor. "I can't just go into that interview tomorrow leveling accusations against a prominent senator of the United States without a single shred of proof. It would be career suicide, and I'll be damned if I'm going to give her airtime for a piece that's nothing more than self-serving campaign fodder. I should just call this whole thing off before it's too late."

"*No.*" I said, my tone grabbing his attention. "You're giving up too easily."

"And you're putting me in an impossible situation! There isn't a story here that warrants this sort of investment of my time and resources. I mean, even if we can find something that links these deaths in some way back to

New Horizons or Senator Gorham, what's the almighty rush? We should take all of this back home and do our due diligence before—"

"*No.*" My tone was even sharper as Brady seemed ready to surrender. "I can't let this go on any longer."

"*Why?*" he demanded. "Give me one good reason why."

And here we were—a stalemate over a moment of truth I'd been avoiding for nearly nine months.

"It's my dad," I said.

His thick brows knitted in confusion. "Your *dad?* What does he have to do with any of this?"

"Actually, he's the one who started this whole thing—or at least this leg of it," I said. "He's here. He's been with me the whole while, although I guess it's more accurate to say that I'm with him."

"Okay," he said, waiting for something, *anything*, to start making sense. "Does this have something to do with whatever is going on with his—" He circled his hands around his noggin, and I nodded.

"He's gotten it into his head that Gina is still out there somewhere," I said, carefully gauging his reaction.

"Your sister? Oh—*oh*," he said, comprehension dawning, incomplete though it was. "That's just awful. For *all* of you. I'm so sorry, man. I've heard about cases like this with dementia patients—"

"He doesn't have dementia," I interrupted defensively. I didn't know what afflicted Dad, but surely it wasn't *that*. At least I hoped it wasn't.

"Oh, sure, but you know what I mean. Having to be told time after time about loved ones who have—you know, passed. It's got to be heartbreaking for the whole family. Where is he now?"

"He's staying with some folks across town who've taken pity on us, but we can't really stay much longer. He's been having dreams that he thinks are premonitions. He's convinced himself that he can find Gina and bring her home."

"Have you talked to his doctors? As much as I hate to say it, it sounds like your dad's condition is deteriorating. He should be under observation, not on some ill-advised road trip with you. Aren't you worried that you're making things worse by humoring his delusion?"

I stared at my hands, unable to meet Brady's steady gaze. I'll give him this—it didn't take very long for him to piece the rest together.

"Oh, my God," he said, his hand fluttering to his mouth. "It's *true*, isn't it?"

I slowly nodded, and Brady sat down hard in the task chair, his mouth hanging open. "All this time—*all this time*," he said, clearly stunned. "I knew something was up. I just *knew* it. But what does this have to do with Senator Gorham? *Oh!* It's not just *her*, is it? Of course not! It's Parker Ghant, too! I knew there had to be more going on than the Pendleton case for you to treat him the way you did at Anyssa's and my party. You're not exactly known for your manners, but that was extreme even for you."

"You know what? Fuck you, Brady," I said, perching on the end of the bed across from where he sat and locking my fingers together in front of me. "You got me. Now, do you want to hear what happened, or would you rather just keep guessing?"

He settled back in the task chair, crossing one leg over the other. "By all means, continue."

"Alright, but you cannot repeat a single word of this without my express permission, do you understand me? My sister's life depends on it."

"You have my word," he said, ticking a phantom lock in front of his lips with his thumb and forefinger before discarding the imaginary key over his shoulder.

I scowled at him, wishing I had a little more assurance than that, but we were past the point of no return. I took deep breath before taking us back to the previous July, when a man calling himself Michael Arthur knocked on my front door and changed my life forever.

"Holy shit, Dwayne," said Brady, gaping at me as I finally reached the current bookmark in our ongoing saga. My mouth was dry as sand, and I crossed to the small bathroom to get a drink of water. "I suspected you were involved in something, but never in my wildest dreams would I have come up with anything like this."

"So, maybe now you understand my sense of urgency," I said. After months of playing things close to the vest, I hadn't held anything back—well, not much of anything. I still wasn't ready to discuss the shock of finding my sister in a wheelchair. It almost felt like if I ignored it, it couldn't possibly be true. "Dad's behavior is erratic at best, and he's not going home, especially now that he knows I've seen her here. I'm not at all sure that I can count on his discretion."

Brady nodded. "Well, you can count on mine," he said. "Unfortunately, my discretion isn't what we need. We need to be able to link more of these young men's deaths to Senator Gorham and her facility. As it stands, I've got nothing to work with. The senator's got her information locked down tight. It would be great if we could find an eyewitness or two." He glanced at the clock in the lower right-hand corner of his laptop's taskbar. "Good Lord. It's nearly two o'clock. I'm starving. How about you?"

I nodded, stifling another yawn. I'd been too anxious to eat breakfast, but now that I had unloaded my story onto Brady, I was keenly aware of how empty my stomach was. I pulled up Google and searched for restaurants near us. "Maybe we can have a pizza delivered or something so we can just keep working."

"Sounds like a plan," he said, turning back to his own computer. "Too bad we can't have the answers we need delivered."

My fingers froze above the keyboard. "Maybe we can," I muttered.

Brady looked up at me. "Did you say something?"

I was already digging through my pockets, pulling out one crumpled napkin after another before finally finding the one I was looking for. My penmanship was barely legible at this point, but I could fairly easily decipher the digits.

"What are you doing?" asked Brady.

I pulled the prepaid phone from my pocket and powered it up. "I'm phoning another friend."

There was a pensive knock on the door, and I peered through the peephole to make sure our visitor was the one we were expecting. Tammy's Pizza had already delivered a couple of 20-ounce Pepsis and an extra-large pepperoni pie, much of which had already been devoured. Belatedly, it occurred to me that I should have extended an invitation to lunch, but I was too tired to think clearly. What I would have given for a nap, but there simply wasn't time.

"Hi," I said, opening the door and smiling at Laurel. "Thanks for stopping by."

"I almost didn't," she said, staying put on the stoop with her hands tucked behind her back. "When I gave you my number, I thought you might ask me out, but inviting me to your motel? It's certainly more forward than I expected. Exactly what kind of girl do you think I am?"

My smile collapsed, and instantly, I was a sputtering mess. "Umm, *no*— I wasn't suggesting that you and I—*uh*, what I'm trying to say is that we—"

"*'We?'*" she interjected, peering into the room around me. Currently, there was no one else to see. Brady had taken a potty break. "Who's this *'we'* you speak of, Ricky? I warn you, I'm palming pepper spray, and I'm not afraid to use it. You may be kinda cute, but I'm not up for anything kinky or weird."

I blinked, surprised at how quickly the conversation was going sideways. I laughed and held up my hands in surrender. "No, no—nothing like that, I promise. It's just that you were such a big help before. I thought you might be able to help us with some new information I've come across but can't really make head nor tail of. I've got a buddy of mine helping me, but neither of us are from around here."

"Are we still talking about New Horizons?" she asked, cautiously edging past me into the room.

"I don't know. I was hoping maybe you could tell me," I said, just as the bathroom door opened and Brady stepped out, drying his hands on a towel. He smiled crookedly at Laurel, his eyes twinkling and his dimples dimpling.

"How do, ma'am?" he asked with a nod, and I could practically feel myself slipping into insignificance from the way Laurel openly gaped at him. "I'm—"

"Manny," I interjected, warning him with my eyes. I had already braced him for the fact that Laurel thought my name was Ricky, but we had yet to create a nom de plume for him. I was hopeful she hadn't seen him on television. Most of his televised reporting was restricted to Central Ohio, but he'd also managed to snag some national airtime once or twice, and it would be just our luck for her to recognize him.

"Well, hel-*lo*, Manny," she said with an appreciative smile, and a once over that took him in from the top of his curly, dark hair to the bottom of his well-worn Adidas sneakers. She held out a hand, and Brady scooped it up to plant a delicate kiss on its back. I had to look away before my lunch made an involuntary return appearance. She tittered, her voice suddenly throaty. "I'm Laurel."

"Beautiful name for a beautiful woman," said Brady, dazzling her with a smile that kept his inbox overflowing with messages from adoring fans of

333

literally all persuasions. I wasn't jealous—just incredibly disenfranchised. Until that very moment, I had never known what swooning actually looked like, but I had zero doubt it was what Laurel was currently doing. A nervous giggle issued from her lips as roses blossomed in her cheeks, and if I had left the room, it would have likely gone entirely unnoticed.

Instead, I cleared my throat. Loudly. We still had a lot of work to do.

"I'm sorry," said Laurel, reluctantly directing her attention back to me. "You were saying?"

I inserted the flash drive into Brady's laptop, and with a couple of taps and swipes, I pulled up the directory that showed all the folders bearing the names of thirty-one men.

"Would you mind taking a look at this?" I asked, pulling out the task chair for her to have a seat at the desk.

"Okay," she said, sitting down and letting her eyes roam the screen. "Is there something specific I'm looking for here?"

"Do any of these names mean anything to you?" I asked.

"Especially in relation to New Horizons," Brady added, leaning in close enough for her to catch his musky scent.

She examined the screen more closely. "Well—sure. There's a folder for Eddie Brickey—and here's one for William Martin." She glided the pointer over the two files. "Those were the two boys who died in the fire."

"What about the others?" I asked, trying not to get my hopes up.

"Terrance Tomlin," she said, abandoning the touchpad and using her finger. "Oh, and Jerry Crawford. Felix Pelfrey, and—" She turned to look at us as Brady and I struggled to contain our excitement. "What is all this?"

"Are all of these names connected to New Horizons?" I asked, trying not to sound too hopeful and failing miserably.

"I couldn't say all of them," she said. "At least not at a glance, but several of them are, for sure."

"Define several," said Brady, directing her attention back to the screen.

"Well, *again*, I've only just scanned the screen, but at least six—maybe eight. Probably more."

Brady and I exchanged a smile as she continued to peruse, and it was all I could do to suppress nervous laughter.

Finally. We had something to work with.

CHAPTER TWENTY-SIX

By the time I headed back to the cabin, the sun had already begun to excuse itself behind the western hills. I was beyond exhausted but riding a euphoria that was impossible to contain. Laurel had recognized fourteen of the names on the flash drive including the two young men we already knew about. Considering that some of the dates were before her time in Darbydale, she had still managed to connect nearly half of them to New Horizons, and as far as statistics go, that one was staggering. Apparently, the information highway can be redirected or suppressed entirely when the price is right, and yet the backyard grapevine cannot be bought, and memories run long in a small town. Eventually, the truth will out.

Many of the boys came from broken homes or were wards of the state, and all of them were prone to trouble, eventually earning themselves a stay at New Horizons of indeterminate length. What Laurel *didn't* know was that any of these other boys had died. One was shot in a hunting accident. Another passed away in his sleep due to a carbon monoxide leak. Several had committed suicide. Any single incident was plausible, but what were the odds that this many former residents of New Horizons had met such tragic and untimely fates? It was my contention that for whatever reason, they hadn't met the expectations of Senator Gorham and her cronies, and their experience at New Horizons posed more of a threat than could be tolerated.

After thanking Laurel profusely and sending her on her way, Brady had given me a quick tutorial on a professional grade Sony camcorder he had stowed in his trunk. I would be accompanying him to the interview in the guise of his regular cameraman, Tony Banci, and while I didn't know a thing about operating the damned thing, he assured me that a steady hand was all I'd really need—the camera would do the rest. He provided me with an impressive set of WBNS credentials with my smiling face plastered over Tony's picture, just in case Senator Gorham's security detail required proof of identity. It was a detail I would've overlooked, and I was duly impressed. Once I was reasonably comfortable, he promptly showed me the door, whining about the interview he had yet to script, and I was more than happy to give him his space. If I had any hope of returning by eight the next morning, I'd need to get a good night's rest.

For the first time since Dad had drafted me into service, it felt like our end goal was actually possible.

As I pulled the VW onto the Givens property, Wolfie came bounding into the yard, followed by Burt, Reba, and Dad. I rolled the window down and put the car in neutral, waiting for everyone to catch up with the exuberant canine.

"Is everything alright, son?" asked Dad. "You were gone a lot longer than I thought you'd be. We were starting to worry that something else had happened to you."

"Nope! In fact, it was a very productive day," I said, smiling wearily. "I think we should be able to go home tomorrow."

Dad stepped forward, his face nearly aglow with hope. *"Really?"*

"Well—if everything goes according to plan. Give me a minute to put the car in the barn, and I'll tell you all about it."

"Don't bother with all that," said Reba. "Just get yourself inside! I've been keeping a plate warm for you, although it might be a little dried out after all this time."

I looked at her dubiously, and she laughed, offering a Girl Scout salute.

"It's just chicken! Swear to God."

I rolled the window up and switched the car off, getting out as Reba and Dad headed toward the cabin. Burt hung back, waiting for Wolfie to finish fertilizing the lawn. His face was hidden in shadow, but he didn't look nearly as happy as I'd thought he'd be to see us leave.

Lord knew *I'd* be happy to be gone.

"You actually have an appointment to see her," said Reba, her eyes dancing.

"Well, my friend does," I said through a mouthful of chicken. It was juicy, savory, and not even remotely dried out. Everyone else was partaking in dessert, which they'd held off on in anticipation of my eventual arrival. It was some sort of rhubarb pastry, and I was keeping an eye on the last remaining slice. It was *mine*. "Brady Garrett. He's a fairly well-known reporter back home and has even managed to get his face on the national news a couple of times. Maybe you've seen him?"

She stared at me until I realized my faux pas.

"Ah—that's right. No TV. Sorry."

"But this is a face-to-face interview, not something over the telephone or one of those video conference doohickeys, right?"

"That's my understanding," I said. "In fact, I'm going undercover as Brady's cameraman."

"Where?" asked Reba, and her eagerness didn't escape her husband's notice.

"*Reba*," he warned, his tone low.

She barely took the time to shoot him a dismissive glare. "I'm guessing it's at her estate out on Cobblestone Creek. It's rumored to have an underground level that's twice as big as what's sittin' on the lawn. I sincerely doubt that she'd allow you onto the New Horizons campus—or would she?"

"*Reba!*" Burt's tone was sharper, and so was the look she leveled at him.

"I'm just asking about the plan," she said. "That's all."

He scowled at her before turning his attention back to his plate.

"I honestly don't know," I said. "Brady didn't tell me where we were going. I'm just supposed to meet him back at his hotel by eight."

"Alright," she said. "I've got some errands to run tomorrow, but I suppose they can wait until after I drop you off."

"You don't have to do that," I said, wiping my mouth and reaching for that last piece of dessert. I didn't care for the way Dad was eyeing it. "I figured we could just take the Monza. After the interview, I'm hoping we'll be able to go home."

"Oh," she said, a single syllable steeped in disappointment, but she was quick to recover. "Well, I hope everything goes as planned. I have to admit, it's sure been nice having someone to talk to for a change."

If Burt took offense, it didn't show. He just kept his head down and his mouth full.

I surprised myself by waking early, feeling completely refreshed and ready to get this whole thing over with. I even beat Dad to the shower, breezing through and changing into another set of Brock's old clothes. This time, it was painter's jeans and a Pittsburgh Steelers jersey. The graze on my left arm was markedly better, so I was able to lose the gauze wrap in favor of a smaller, less noticeable bandage. This was a good thing as the Steelers jersey was short-sleeved. Mom would have surely had something to say about it, and it wouldn't have been anything nice. She was a tried-and-true Bengals gal, and I was essentially committing sacrilege.

Dad was left to rummage through more of Boyd's castoffs and emerged wearing a Nine Inch Nails t-shirt, threadbare jeans, and a black knit cap in place of the bright red one. He looked like an extra in a Cheech and Chong movie. We had toast and coffee before thanking Burt and Reba for their hospitality and heading over to the barn to get this show on the road.

It wasn't even a quarter after seven.

My first sign that the day wasn't going to go as planned came once we'd wrangled the camouflage netting off of the Monza. I got behind the wheel and turned the key to no avail. Well—almost to no avail. There was a rapid, urgent clicking that sounded from underneath the hood.

Dad looked at me from the passenger seat. "What's wrong, son?"

"It won't start," I said, trying again. More clicking, but it was a lot less rapid. "I think the battery may be dead."

"Well, pop the hood, and let's take a look," said Dad, unfastening his seatbelt and getting out of the car. I did as he instructed and joined him to stare at the filthy engine and wonder exactly what the fuck was wrong. Neither of us were particularly mechanically inclined, but that didn't stop us from pulling on this and tugging on that to try and find a culprit to our current woes. The dismal lighting inside the barn didn't make it any easier, and after several fruitless minutes of exploratory surgery, I heard footsteps approaching.

"Everything okay?" It was Reba, hands tucked into the back pockets of her jeans. "Y'all have been out here for a while."

"Damned car won't start," I groused, getting frustrated by both our lack of diagnostic ability and how grimy our hands were getting. I'd have to scrub down if we ever got to Brady's motel. I was pretty sure a cameraman shouldn't be covered in grease.

"Maybe it's just the battery," she suggested. "Let me pull my car in, and we'll see if I can give you a jump. Hang on."

By the time she returned, Burt was hovering near the entrance, watching as his wife pulled her VW across the front of the Monza, bringing the passenger door nearly even with the Chevy's hood before stopping and applying the parking brake, leaving the engine running. I was beginning to wonder if she'd ever jumped a car before when she came around the front and opened the passenger door, folding the front seat down. She had a lengthy coil of jumper cables in her hand.

"Battery's underneath the backseat," she called over her shoulder as she leaned in.

Hmm. Who knew?

She tugged forward on the seat and lifted it up, attaching one of the cables to her own battery's terminals before affixing the other end to the battery in our car. She bustled back to the driver's seat and revved her engine.

"Try her now!" she yelled.

I turned the key. Nothing. Not even a click this time. I was steady spouting a stream of colorful obscenities as I got out of the car and pounded on its Brougham roof, our carefully laid plans going right out the window. Our early start was now lost, and we'd be lucky to get to the motel on time.

"Oh, would you *relax?*" Reba laughed as she untethered the cars from each other. "I can drop the two of you off."

"Thought you had errands," said Burt from across the way. It was the first thing he'd said all morning, and it almost came out like an accusation.

Reba glared at him. "I do. But I can drop these fellas off on the way."

341

He shook his head and sighed before turning back toward the house, Wolfie bounding along after him.

Reba scowled for a second longer before snapping the backseat into place and turning toward us. "Who's ready to go?"

· · · • • • • ◦ ◦ • • • • • · ·

I really should have seen the next trouble coming. Dad had been too easy, too compliant as of late. He was more than a little overdue for a display of good old fashioned patriarchal dominance. In his eyes, it didn't matter how old I was. He would always be my father, and therefore, the boss of me.

"I am *not* staying behind," he said, folding his arms across his chest and blocking the exit from Brady's motel room. "This is my *daughter* we're talking about here."

I sighed. "No, it's *not*, Dad. The *last* thing that we'll be talking about is Gina. As far as Senator Gorham and her people know, Gina isn't even alive."

"*Umm*, Dwayne," said Brady from just over my shoulder. "We really need to get going." He pointed to a watch he wasn't wearing before nodding to the parking lot that lay just beyond Dad's stubborn form.

"Okay, look," said Dad, trying another tactic. "You guys have your roles to play, so why can't I have mine? I could be Mr. Hotshot Reporter's security."

I gasped as he pulled his snub-nosed pistol from his belt line to illustrate his point.

"Where did you get that?" I demanded.

From the look he tossed me, it was the most idiotic question he had ever heard. "It's mine. I wasn't about to leave it behind at the cabin. Burt and Reba have enough weapons of their own."

342

"Give it to me," I said, holding my hand out expectantly. "We've already discussed this. Until we know what's going on inside your head, it's not safe for you to carry it around, remember? And Mr. Hotshot Reporter doesn't *need* security. It's typically everyone else who needs security from him."

"Hey!" said Brady. "I'm standing right here, you know?"

I ignored him. "Besides, we'll never get past the senator's security detail if we're armed. This stays here."

He mulled the probability for longer than he should have before finally surrendering his firearm. "Fine," he said, sounding every bit as juvenile as he looked. "But I'm still going."

"Dad!"

"Dwayne!"

Brady impatiently tapped his foot as Dad and I stared each other down, wasting precious minutes we simply didn't have.

· · · • • • ◌◦◦ • • • · · ·

"I'm very concerned about this," said Brady as he slowly crept up the long tongue of asphalt that wound through the senator's vast estate. It had an ornately gated entrance, and we were buzzed in after Brady flashed his press credentials to a surveillance camera mounted on a post that was conveniently the right height. "I'm not sure how I'm going to explain your dad. I've got identification for you, but I wasn't expecting him to tag along. What am I supposed to say?"

"Hey, I'm not happy about this either," I said, scowling at Dad through the passenger side mirror. He wasn't paying a bit of attention. He was focused entirely on the resplendent landscaping that we were rolling through, undoubtedly wondering how long it would take to mow a lawn of that size. "I've seen you doing live reports before. Don't you usually have one guy for cameras and another for sound?"

"Totally depends on what I'm doing, but yes, normally I would. But considering I didn't have a clue what was going on, and you pretty much swore me to secrecy about what little I *did* know, I didn't think bringing anyone else along was an option." He used the rearview to catch his own glimpse of Dad. "What can he do?"

"Other than be a total pain in the——"

"Watch it, son," Dad warned, cutting me off. "Those next words might just be your last."

I rolled my eyes and stared out the window.

"Just so you know, Mr. Garrett," said Dad. "I'm not just some useless old man. I was a decorated soldier in my younger days and the best damn sales manager that the Pepsi-Cola Bottling Company ever had. I'm a quick study and good with my hands. You tell me what you want me to do, and I'll do it. You want me to keep my mouth shut? Done. The only thing I ask is that you let me see this woman with my own two eyes—this horrible woman who has conspired to cause my family so much harm. I need to see her face as you destroy her reputation the way she's destroyed the last nine months of my life. I don't just need it. I *deserve* it."

What could we say? He wasn't wrong.

· · · • • • ◯◯ • • • · · ·

We were asked to remain in the car as a square-jawed, security automaton collected our information and carried Brady's and my picture IDs away, already communicating with someone inside the house through his Bluetooth earpiece. Dad had done a credible job of pretending he'd forgotten his wallet, and Brady stepped in to vouch for him, offering some dude's name—Seth Baker. I'd never heard of him, but he obviously worked on the WBNS crew.

As the minutes ticked by, I grew certain that Dad's obstinance was going to be our undoing. What if they ran a check on this Seth What's-His-Name and his picture came back belonging to a twenty-year-old African American? I'd certainly like to see Dad talk his way out of *that* one. Scratch that—it was the *last* thing I wanted to happen.

Mr. Roboto suddenly reappeared at Brady's window, rapping it sharply with a knuckle. Brady eased the window down and looked up, shielding his eyes against the sun.

"You can leave your car here," the guard said, his face devoid of any and all emotion. "Follow me."

"*Ummm*, okay," said Brady, barely containing his surprise. "Seth? Why don't you and Tony grab our things from the trunk?" He pressed the release, and it opened with a *thunk*.

"Sure thing, boss," said Dad, affecting an accent that sounded suspiciously like Joe Pesci from *Home Alone*. I was so busy smirking that I almost missed my cue; I was the Tony to whom Brady referred. I unfastened my seatbelt and got out of the car, pushing the seat forward so Dad could climb out of the rear.

I grabbed a ring light and one of the video camera bags, handing Dad the other, along with a collapsable tripod. Brady reached in and grabbed his bloated laptop case, looping it over his shoulder. He closed the trunk, and we followed the guard toward the sprawling ranch house's front entrance where another guard stood waiting. He was essentially identical to the first man, save for the strawberry blond, close-cropped stubble covering his head. He wore a matching Bluetooth earpiece which apparently kept all of Gorham's security personnel connected, and he held a security wand in his hand, ready to scan us before admitting us into the senator's inner sanctum.

"Leave your bags with me and please proceed to Mr. Givens, single file," our guide directed, and my ears perked up. *Mr. Givens.* I do believe we were in the process of meeting Boyd, and it didn't take more than a second glance to see Reba's features reflected in her son's solemn face.

By then, my armpits were beginning to feel a tad dewy.

Dad went first, holding his arms out on each side and his legs splayed. Boyd ran the wand systematically around every square inch, giving him a curt nod when he was done. He directed Dad to wait just inside the door before turning his attention to me and eventually Brady. By the time he had scanned us, the first guard had finished rifling through our bags and handed them back to us.

"This way," said Boyd, turning and walking through a large formal living room that looked like a photo spread straight out of *Better Homes & Gardens*—warm and inviting on the surface but unlikely to have ever been utilized, not even for guests. We stepped into a hallway through an archway at the rear of the room. Straight ahead was a spacious kitchen that was nearly as large as the first floor of my house. Stainless steel commercial grade appliances looked like they had never been touched by human hands, gleaming in the bright sunlight as it poured through an enormous skylight recessed into the center of the ceiling.

We turned right and proceeded down the carpeted hall, passing a series of closed doors along both sides until we came to another archway on our left that opened into an expansive living area at the rear of the house. There was a pool table on one end, and a cozy seating area on the other. Everything was white or off-white, including the brick of the fireplace that was the centerpiece of the room. Mounted to the wall above it was the largest flat screen television I had ever seen. The back wall of the room was almost entirely glass, looking out onto a sprawling, emerald lawn with nary a weed in sight. Senator Gorham was apparently fond of natural light; a trio of recessed skylights were mounted into the ceiling here as well, admitting almost enough sunlight to require sunblock.

"The senator will be seated in the Queen Anne chair by the fireplace, and she prefers to be photographed from her left," instructed Boyd. "Feel free to rearrange the furniture as needed and get yourselves set up. Senator Gorham will be in shortly."

He turned to leave, but Brady held up a hand. "Excuse me, Jeeves," he said, his eyes drifting back to the phone he held in his hand. "I don't seem to have any signal in here for my hotspot."

Boyd's smirk was a little condescending. "No, you wouldn't have signal while on the grounds. The senator is very protective of her privacy and doesn't allow it."

"Oh," said Brady, blinking back his surprise. "Well then, can I get a guest password for wi-fi or something? I'll need to get my cameras online before we start the interview."

"Why would you need that?"

Brady's laugh was a little incredulous. "Well—it's very difficult to conduct a live interview if I can't get connected to the internet."

"Oh, no," said Boyd. "This won't be a live interview. The senator doesn't do them."

Brady sputtered. *"Excuse me?* My station has scheduled time to air this interview during today's noontime broadcast. I'm pretty sure I was clear about that when I made my request."

Boyd scowled. "That wasn't my understanding. But it's really irrelevant, Mr. Garrett. If you're interested in interviewing Senator Gorham, you'll have to record the interview first and submit it for her approval before you can air it. Those are her conditions."

"That's *outrageous!"* said Brady, his anger reflected in his eyes.

Boyd shrugged. "In that case, this interview is over. I'll take you gentlemen back to your car."

Dad and I exchanged a worried glance as we sensed that everything was falling apart right in front of us. I leveled a glare at Brady, willing him to salvage things before it was too late.

"Okay, hang on," said Brady, pinching the bridge of his nose. "I'm sure I can make this work, but I'm going to need access to a working phone. I can't just leave my people hanging. They're expecting a live feed in about half an hour. They'll need some time to fill the spot."

"Certainly, Mr. Garrett," said Boyd. He crossed to a tall, blond armoire that rested against the wall behind Gorham's overstuffed sofa, opening its doors to reveal a compact office desk, complete with a computer monitor and landline telephone. "Press '9' for an outside line, but please be aware that all communications are monitored."

Brady stared after him incredulously as he went back out into the hall, presumably to retrieve the senator. "Son of a *bitch*," he spat, heading toward the phone.

Dad was perplexed. "So, what does that—"

Brady held up a finger to stop him, pointing to his own ears. Dad's eyebrows knitted together, and he started to say something else before I grabbed his arm and shook my head. It was apparent that Brady was worried we were being watched, and we needed to keep any questions to ourselves. From the deepening consternation on my father's face, I could only hope to never be teamed up with him in a game of charades. He opened his mouth to say something else, but I cut him off before he could speak.

"You want us to go ahead and unpack the bags, boss?"

"Yes, please," said Brady as he entered a series of numbers on the telephone's keypad. "Give me a few moments, and I'll show where to set up the stationary camera. It's so bright in here, we shouldn't need the ring light."

I nodded and started unpacking the equipment while Dad hovered over me. He was a last-minute addition to a plan that was half-baked at best, and his part was entirely unscripted. We only had the benefit of half of Brady's conversation, but it was readily apparent that he was getting reamed for this last-minute change of plans. After a terse exchange, Brady disconnected and joined us, showing us how and where to position things. His expression was glum.

"Everything okay?" I finally ventured, deciding the question was appropriate even if Big Brother was listening.

"Not really," said Brady with a tight smile. "I'm sure I'll get my ass chewed once we get back to Columbus, but it's really out of my hands. I can only hope the interview turns out as well as I imagined. It might soften the blow with management. I *doubt* it, but—"

His words fell away in frustration, and I sincerely hoped I hadn't just cost him his newfound job. While I certainly didn't anticipate this turn of events, I wasn't entirely surprised. Gorham's ability to spoon-feed the media only the things she felt her constituents were entitled to hear was uncanny.

As if on cue, Senator Amelia Gorham breezed into the room wearing the very same manufactured smile I had seen throughout her online interview. Boyd trailed along behind her, never farther than a few feet away.

"Mr. Garrett, is it?" she asked, her voice bright and every bit as phony as her smile. She only had eyes for Brady, our presence in the room not even registering. She offered him a dainty hard, and he took it.

"Yes, ma'am," he said, using a crooked, dimpled grin that never failed to charm. "But you can call me Brady."

"Very well, then," she said, taking a seat in the Queen Anne chair that looked more like a throne and daintily crossing her legs. "And you can call me Senator Gorham. Shall we begin?"

Brady's smile momentarily faltered a the realization the senator was immune to his usual wiles. "Let's."

CHAPTER TWENTY-SEVEN

The interview started innocuously enough. Brady opened with a brief summary of Senator Gorham's lengthy career in politics before shifting gears toward New Horizons. I followed the back-and-forth between Brady and the senator through the camcorder's viewfinder, always careful to only capture the senator from her left. From my peripheral vision, I could see Dad standing stock-still behind the stationary camera, his arms folded across his chest as the muscles in his jaw tensed and relaxed. He was telegraphing daggers with his eyes but fortunately, the senator wasn't paying any attention to us. We were only Brady's hired help; we may as well have been furniture.

Soon, I was having the strangest sense of déjà vu. While Brady's questions covered the same territory as the previous interview I had seen from almost ten years earlier, his phrasing was all his own. The senator, on the other hand, recited the same answers almost verbatim, sticking to a script that hadn't failed her in all these years. Once they had finished covering the tragedy that I'm sure she wouldn't be discussing at all if it weren't a matter of public record, things began to get interesting.

"So, Senator Gorham, tell me—what is graduation like at New Horizons?" asked Brady.

Gorham's smile dimmed by degrees. "Excuse me?"

Brady's chuckle was made-for-TV. "I'm sorry, I'm probably not calling it the right thing," he said. "But once your wards reach the age of majority, eighteen, they age out of your system—one way or another, correct?"

"Well—yes, but it depends on the individual and the reason for his detention at New Horizons that determines what happens at that point," she said. "While some of our worst offenders are transferred to a state or federal facility to serve out the remainder of their sentence, some are invited to remain with us until they reach their twenty-first birthday. Most of our young men are fully rehabilitated by the end of their terms."

"Meaning—?"

"They are ready to begin their new lives. It's another point of pride for New Horizons. We are truly invested in each and every young man's future. Not only do we provide rehabilitation for the behavioral issues that first brought them into our care, we also provide vocational training and career counseling to help them enter the workforce as productive members of society once they are released. We don't simply abandon them once they turn eighteen."

"What sort of employment are they suited for?" asked Brady.

"Any number of positions," said Gorham. She motioned toward Boyd, who stood sentry just outside the camera's reach. "For example, my Chief Security Officer spent several years at New Horizons, himself."

I panned the camera over to capture Boyd who stood at rapt attention with his arms crossed behind his back. His face was the perfect picture of stoicism. It was like he hadn't even heard the senator's words.

"Do you make a regular habit of hiring former wards?" asked Brady.

"I wouldn't call it a *regular* habit, but yes, it's happened more than once," said Gorham, her confidence returning. "These are good men, and they deserve a second chance. What sort of message would I be sending if I weren't willing to give them an opportunity myself? I think it's more important to note that we have a very high success rate for helping these young men land solidly on their feet—much higher than that of other facilities like New Horizons."

"Very admirable," said Brady, nodding. "But as with anything else, I'm sure New Horizons has its share of regrettable outcomes, too."

"I'm not sure what you mean."

Brady shifted in his seat and leaned forward, his focus intensifying. "I don't know of any rehabilitation program that is one hundred percent successful," he said. "Surely some of these men return to their old ways."

"I really couldn't say," said the senator, her camera-ready smile once again faltering.

"How long does New Horizons typically continue to engage with former residents?" asked Brady.

"Again, it varies depending upon the individual," she said.

"Varies like how? One month? Three?"

"There's no set limit," Senator Gorham said. "We continue to be a resource just as long as we're needed. As I've previously said, we don't just sever ties once our charges become adults."

"Terrance Tomlin. Jerry Crawford. Felix Pelfrey. Do these names mean anything to you?"

The senator's smile dropped away completely. "Where, exactly, are you going with this, Mr. Garrett?"

"You recognize them," said Brady. He wasn't asking.

"I can't say that I do."

"You should. They all spent time at New Horizons," said Brady.

The senator sighed. "I won't discuss specifics about any of our past or present residents. Their records were sealed by the courts, and they're entitled to their privacy."

"You certainly didn't hesitate to share your Chief Security Officer's past affiliation with New Horizons."

"That's different. Boyd is a trusted associate—he's practically my son. He's a shining example of what New Horizons can accomplish, and he's proud of how far he's come." She turned to her stone-faced security officer. "Is that a fair assessment?"

"Yes, ma'am," he said, barely moving a muscle.

I did my best to follow the conversation with the camera, trying to capture the escalating tension in the room. Dad continued to stare from where he stood, his complexion nearly scarlet. I could practically see the angry heat rising from the top of his head.

"Would it surprise you to learn that Terrance Tomlin, Jerry Crawford, and Felix Pelfrey have something else in common other than their time spent at New Horizons?" asked Brady, laser-focused on the senator's face.

She simply stared at him. It looked like she was trying to will his head to explode.

"All three of these young men died shortly after leaving your fine facility," Brady continued. "And that's just the tip of the iceberg. Martin Ramsey, Buddy Thompson, Bernard Shephard—"

"*Enough*," said Senator Gorham, shaking her head. She nodded toward Boyd, and he tapped his Bluetooth earpiece, muttering something unintelligible from where I stood. "This interview is over."

"But Senator Gorham," said Brady, offering the most beautifully perplexed smile. "I've only just begun."

The senator looked at him venomously as she stood. "On the contrary, Mr. Garrett. We're finished here."

"How about Dr. Jillian Whittier?" he persisted, standing and blocking the senator's path. Boyd moved to intercept him, reaching for the sidearm he had holstered at his side. The security officer who had handed us off to Boyd strode through the door, his weapon already drawn, but Brady just kept right on going. "Here's one—Michael Arthur. What can you tell me about him?"

The senator ignored his question and addressed our latest arrival. "Please escort Mr. Garrett off of my premises, Gil."

"Yes, ma'am," said the officer, reaching out to take Brady's arm.

"Are you getting all this?" Brady asked me as I kept the camera rolling to capture the interview as it continued to fall apart. This wasn't the smoking gun I had hoped for. Senator Gorham had shut things down more quickly than I had anticipated, and I wasn't sure we had enough to blow the lid on this whole thing.

"It doesn't matter what your men have recorded," said Senator Gorham, her tone condescending. "We'll be confiscating your equipment—"

"You can't do that!" Brady shouted as the security officer shepherded him toward the exit. "That equipment belongs to WBNS! This interview is protected by the First Amendment of the Constitution of—"

"Oh, settle down, Mr. Garrett," said the senator. "I'll return your equipment—once we've deleted its content, of course."

Dad and I just stood there, unsure of what to do. Eventually, I motioned him toward me as I moved to follow Brady out into the hallway where he was loudly objecting to being manhandled by the guard. I was surprised when Boyd stepped sideways and blocked our path.

"Please," said Senator Gorham, smiling like the Cheshire cat as she took her seat once more. "I'd like a word with the infamous Dwayne Morrow and his father."

Shit.

We froze where we stood, Dad's complexion continuing to mottle. "You know who we are?" I asked. The question was redundant, but she caught me completely off guard, and I didn't know what else to say.

"Of course, I know," she said. "What I *can't* understand is why in the world you people won't leave me alone. I mean what's it going to take? This unusual obsession you have in finding fault with me and my associates is irksome, to say the least."

"You and your associates put a hit out on my daughter, you psychotic cunt," Dad snapped, and I'd never heard such language fall from his lips. I could only gape and watch him go. "So far, karma has already served justice to two of your traitorous compatriots, bitch. Now, it's your turn."

Her smirk was ugly. "Ms. Morrow's death was ruled an unfortunate accident," she said. "You can't prove otherwise."

"She was silenced after witnessing something in Briarstaff involving The Academy," Dad persisted, and I wasn't sure if he was helping our situation or hurting it. "Something that linked you, Parker Ghant, and Errol Warren to an initiative that your constituents might be very interested in hearing about."

The senator laughed from the back of her throat. "Oh, my goodness, you've missed your calling! All those years wasted forcing that sickly sweet, carbonated beverage on unsuspecting folks when you could have been writing bestselling thrillers with that sort of imagination!"

It didn't pass me by that Senator Gorham already knew Dad's background. Her flippant comment confirmed that she'd been studying us for a while. She continued, unabated.

"I *do* recall hearing about some unfortunate business in the Briarstaff area regarding this—Academy, or whatever you called it. Quite a scandalous affair, as I remember. But attempting to connect me or my late colleagues to those events is a rather ambitious undertaking, not to mention a complete and utter waste of time."

"Is it?" I asked, finally finding my voice. "Is that why you sent someone—actually, make that *two* someones to try and stop us?"

"I don't have any idea what you're talking about," she said, the corners of her mouth quirking upward, indicating otherwise. A flicker of surprise crossed Boyd's face, and he looked like he wanted to say something, but he held his tongue.

I only wished that Dad would do the same. "We'll never stop digging," he said. "We won't stop until you are held accountable for every despicable thing that you've done, and we're not alone in this. You've just ejected a respected and well-known journalist from an interview that wasn't going your way. Do you think Brady Garrett is going to give up that easily? Do you—"

"Enough!" roared the senator, slapping her palms down on the arms of her chair. Her calm facade had fallen away, revealing a seething hatred that pulsed just beneath the surface. "Do you want to know what's going to happen? Let me enlighten you. Mr. Garrett is about to have his own unfortunate accident on his return trip to Central Ohio. His cameras are right here, so there's no evidence he'll have on his person when his body is found—"

"No," I said, horrorstruck.

"Oh, yes," she said, nodding confidently. "And this is all your doing. If you and your father hadn't pulled him into this—if you'd just had the good sense to leave things alone, none of this would be happening. And then, of course, there's the other little matter of what to do with the two of you." She turned toward Boyd. "Do you think we could make them disappear as completely as Vance Cooper seems to have done?"

"Vance Cooper?" I repeated. The name meant nothing to me.

"He's one of my men," she said. "Built like a tank and drives a big white Chevy truck. Oh, come now, Mr. Morrow. You may as well tell us what you've done with him. We're going to get that information out of you or your father one way or the other. As I told you, I don't simply abandon my protégés. You may as well make it easy on yourselves and fess up."

Boyd's expression abruptly changed as the piece in his ear delivered some distressing news. *"Umm,* Senator? Gil's reporting a problem out front with—"

A sudden burst of gunfire erupted at the front of the house, and we all jumped, startled by the sound. I had visions of Brady being mowed down in a foolish attempt to circumvent his escort, but when a second round erupted, it was even closer. Boyd didn't hesitate to draw his own weapon and position himself between the senator and the open archway leading out into the hall.

"What's going on?" Senator Gorham demanded, her command of the situation finally shaken.

"I don't know," said Boyd. "Just stay behind me while—"

An enormous clatter sounded behind us, and I turned just in time to see broken pieces of the stationary camera scatter across the carpet from where Dad had stumbled into the tripod and knocked it to the floor. His eyes were glassy and wide, and twin rivulets of blood poured from his nostrils.

"Nancy?" he said, his voice thick as he stared at Senator Gorham. "Why won't you just leave us *alone?* My little girl doesn't need—"

Dad gasped and grabbed the sides of his head, smearing blood across his blotchy complexion before falling face first onto what remained of the camera.

"Dad!" I called, the rest of the world dropping away as I fell to my knees on the floor beside him. He began to convulse, his eyes bulging while his mouth was frozen in a silent scream. I was pretty sure he was having a stroke, and I was watching him die. "I need some help here! *Please!*" It was ludicrous to expect assistance from folks who only planned to kill us later, but panic had robbed me of the ability to think clearly, and I just needed someone—*anyone* to save my dad.

That's when Reba Givens and three of her own associates burst into the room. They were dressed head-to-toe in camouflage and had assault rifles drawn and ready.

"Mom?" Boyd only had time for one small, astonished syllable before one of the men accompanying Reba injected something into his neck, dropping him like a stone.

Senator Gorham practically danced in a circle trying to shrink away from everything that was happening. Finally, she looked at Reba with unadulterated loathing. *"You!"* she hissed. "Five years in a federal prison wasn't *enough* for you? Boyd doesn't *belong* to you anymore! He belongs to me! I've turned his life around, and he's mine! He's—"

"Why don't you just shut the fuck up?" said Reba, lifting a pistol and shooting the senator dead center in the forehead, blood and brains spattering the pristine white brick mantel of the fireplace directly behind her. She dropped back into her chair, a look of stupefied astonishment locked on her face for all eternity.

A pervasive silence fell upon the room, save for a small gulping hiccup that I belatedly realized was coming from me. Tears streamed down my face as I struggled to process what had just happened. Dad's seizure had passed, and his eyes were now closed. He was still breathing, but it seemed shallow and thready at best.

"Was your Dad shot?" asked Reba, looking down on us from above.

"N-n-no," I stammered. "He had another one of his—oh *God!* I need an ambulance. I need to call an ambulance!"

"I'll take care of that," she said. "Just hang tight. I'd appreciate the courtesy of a head start if you'd be so kind."

The men that had accompanied Reba were already carting Boyd's prone body out of the room, careful to avoid the area around the senator.

She smiled. "Burt said it can't be done, but I won't give up that easily. My boy can be deprogrammed. I'm sure of it."

"You—you followed us," I said, suddenly realizing that our automotive issues with the Monza had been anything but incidental.

"Sorry about that. But it was the only way I could get close enough to put an end to this."

"Brady," I said, looking out into the empty hall.

"He's fine," she said. "We gave him just a touch of the same sedative we gave to Boyd to keep him out from underfoot, but it shouldn't last for long."

"And the other guard?"

Reba shrugged. "We tried to convince him to stand down. He won't be bothering you now. Now, just stay put. I'll send help just as soon as we're clear."

"But what do I say?"

She smiled. "Play dumb. There's nothing connecting you and your dad to me. And please know, I'll be praying for him."

I nodded numbly as she hurried after her men out into the hall, leaving us under the steady but unseeing gaze of a senator who was finally finished ruining lives. While I don't wish death upon anyone, I'd be lying if I denied that this one felt justified.

Maybe even good.

After a handful of minutes that felt like an eternity, sirens sounded in the distance.

······•••••○○•••••·····

Dad was taken by ambulance to Darbydale's local medical clinic, a bare-bones facility that could do little more than stabilize him before arranging a life flight to Riverside in Columbus where a team of specialists would be waiting. My brother, Matt, was en route to Lymont to collect Mom and bring her back to the hospital, where I hoped to catch up with them all just as soon as I could extricate myself from the intense round of questioning that Brady and I were subjected to. Fortunately for us, video of the siege on the senator's compound was captured by various security cameras positioned around the property. While it wasn't accompanied by audio, there was never any doubt as to who was responsible, and Reba Givens pretty much leapt to the top of the FBI's Most Wanted List.

Brady walked away with a better story than he ever anticipated, covering Senator Gorham's assassination from inside the scene. Not only was the footage on his cameras still intact, but I had managed to capture most of Gorham's self-incrimination on an old analog microcassette recorder I had insisted Brady bring with him, smuggling it into the senator's home in the spare battery case of one of his camcorders. I had slipped it into my pocket and activated it when we were setting up the cameras. In my lengthening experience with these people, I had already seen them scramble digital surveillance using high-tech wizardry beyond my understanding, so it seemed prudent to have a backup plan to ensure we'd get what we needed from the interview. The only limitation was the thirty minute recording time on each side of the microcassette. Subtly flipping the tape over in the middle of the interview would have been tricky, to say the least. The time restriction actually worked to my benefit. The tape ran out before capturing the conversation I had with Reba just before she left, preserving the illusion that we had never met.

Eventually, we were on our way back to Columbus in Brady's Charger, pushing the speed limit on the nearly six-hour drive and counting on Google Maps to warn us of any speed traps along the way. I would have to figure out how to reclaim Craig's Monza at a later date. I wasn't about to go anywhere near the Givens' property anytime soon.

I called Melanie to bring her up to speed and to let her know I was finally coming home. My sister-in-law, Sheila, had offered to watch the kids, freeing Melanie up to head into the hospital where she could keep me apprised as any news about Dad's condition became available.

After subjecting myself to about ten minutes of terror from Brady's aggressive driving, I closed my eyes. With nothing left to do but worry, sleep was the most attractive option.

· · • • • • • ◯◯ • • • • • · ·

Melanie met me at the door as I entered Dad's room, wrapping her arms around me and holding tight. It was nearly eleven o'clock.

"Finally," she said, rising on her tiptoes to plant her lips on mine. "I've been worried sick."

Mom was right behind her, already nudging Melanie aside. "I'm never letting *any* of you out of my sight *ever* again, do you hear me?"

"I do," I said, kissing Mom on the cheek and nodding to Matt who stood vigil over Dad's bedside. His concern was evident, and it was easy to see why. Dad looked impossibly small and fragile tucked into the hospital bed. His head was wrapped in bandages, and his eyes were closed. If it hadn't been for all of the blipping and whirring of the various monitors stationed around his bedside, I wouldn't have known that he was still breathing.

"They only brought him back to the room about twenty minutes ago," said Melanie, snaking an arm around my waist.

"What happened?" I asked.

"It was that damned spot on his brain,' said Mom, whispering the swear word as if she was afraid her own mother might hear her from her lofty perch in Heaven. "It was an aneurysm that ruptured, but Dr. Gupta feels confident he was able to cordon off the weak spot and bypass the area so blood will flow around it. He doesn't detect any cancer, thank the Lord. As crazy as that man can make me, I can't even imagine life without him."

"Did they say how long he would be out?" I asked, moving in for a closer look. He was just so damned *pale.*

"Hopefully, it shouldn't be too much longer," said a nurse, bustling into the room to check the multitude of monitors attached to him. "I'm Clarice, and I'll be taking care of Mr. Morrow tonight. I'm guessing you all are family?"

Mom nodded. "I'm Todd's wife, Jo, and these are our boys, Matthew and Dwayne." Melanie cleared her throat as a subtle reminder that she was still in the room. "Oh, and this is my future daughter-in-law, Melanie."

"Hi," said Melanie, offering her hand to the nurse.

"Very nice to meet you all," said Clarice. "And while I know you are eager to speak with Mr. Morrow, his recovery is going to depend on lots of rest. You might want to plan your visits in shifts so as not to overwhelm him once he wakes up. Is anyone planning on staying overnight?"

"I am," said Mom.

"I'll bring you an extra pillow and blanket," she said, patting Mom's hand. "The recliner over in the corner is surprisingly comfortable for getting some sleep."

"Thank you," said Mom.

"You're most certainly welcome. You let me know if there's anything else you need while you're here," she said, heading for the door. She stopped just short, and said, "Oh! Excuse me, miss. I didn't see you there."

"It's alright," came the reply. "I saw you coming."

We all turned to find a petite young woman with an icy-blonde pixie cut wheeling herself into the room.

"I'm sorry, ma'am," said Mom. "I think you've got the wrong room."

"I don't believe I do—Mom."

Mom blinked, her hand fluttering to her mouth. *"Gina?!?"*

Gina smiled, her eyes overflowing with tears, and Matt was barely able to keep Mom from hitting the floor when she abruptly passed out.

CHAPTER TWENTY-EIGHT

What followed was an exhaustive round of interrogation punctuated by tears, laughter, anger, and heartfelt apologies. Emotions were running high, and we were asked to keep it down by hospital staff—twice. What can I say? Resurrection is rare, and this was a gift we would be celebrating for quite some time. Our shattered family circle was once again whole, although not in quite the same pristine condition as before. Mom, in particular, was having a great deal of trouble with Gina's lower limb paralysis, fussing over her as only a mother can do. I could tell Matt was pissed I hadn't taken him into my confidence, but he wasn't going to sully the moment by ripping into me in front of everyone else. It would wait for another day, and I was resigned to take my lumps whenever he was ready to serve them up. Honestly, I would have been pissed too, if I were in his shoes.

After about a half-hour into our reunion, Melanie tapped on my elbow and pulled me aside.

"If it's alright with you, I think I'll go get the kids and take them home before it gets any later," she said. "It's getting a little tight in here, and I'm only in the way."

"You are *never* in the way," I said, pulling her into my arms and hugging her. "But that's probably a good idea. I was planning to stick around until

Dad wakes up. I need to see the look on his face when he finally lays eyes on Gina."

"Of course!" she said. "Stay as long as you need to. We won't wait up. But if Gina hasn't already made other arrangements, invite her to stay with us. I'd love to get a chance to know her better. We didn't really get the opportunity last time she was in town."

I smiled. "Thank you for being so understanding. Have I ever told you how much I love you?"

"Just keep right on telling me, mister. But my understanding *does* have its limits. Tomorrow night? You and me. One on one."

My grin widened. "Yeah? Where?"

"Our room."

"What should I wear?"

"As little as possible," she said, sealing the deal with a lingering kiss that left me more than a little weak in the knees. She winked before gently extricating herself from my arms and disappearing down the corridor.

"Nancy?"

Dad's voice was little more than a weak croak, and my heart sank.

Mom, Matt, and I hurried to his bedside and leaned in so he could see us. Gina wheeled in as close as she could, but the bedrail obstructed her view.

"Where am I?" he asked, his eyes searching the room.

"You're in the hospital, sweetheart," said Mom, taking his hand into hers as best as she could with all the wires and such tethering him to the bed. Her dismay at hearing the name of his former wife was evident, but she was doing her best to keep it together.

"Are you my nurse?" Dad asked. "Can you bring me some water?"

"I'm not, but I can page her," Mom said, her voice trembling. She fumbled for the call button at Dad's side and pressed it repeatedly.

Dad glared at me and Matt, his voice lowering to a whisper. "Who are those ugly young men, and why are they staring at me?"

Mom turned to Matt, dabbing at her eyes. "Get his nurse, Matthew. Hurry."

Matt moved like he was on fire, racing out of the room as he called for help.

"Dad?" I said, leaning in.

He scowled and pulled away. "Good Lord—your breath is revolting. Stop bothering me, boy! I have enough kids of my own at home."

My eyes narrowed as I held his gaze, words from my childhood coming back to taunt me. The very corners of his mouth quirked up as mischief danced in his eyes.

"You are the *meanest man on Earth*," I practically roared, drawing a reproachful look from Mom. I wanted to smack him but was barely able to restrain myself despite the overwhelming temptation.

"*Dwayne!* Don't you dare talk to your father that way when he's clearly out of his mind!" said Mom, landing a good one without even trying. She leaned in, still unclear on what was going on. "Todd? Look at me, Todd. Concentrate. Do you know who I am?"

He smiled. "Of course I do. You're my Jo-Jo. Sweetest little hood ornament that's ever perched her pretty little backside on the front of my car."

Mom had held herself together as long as she possibly could. She erupted in tears, showering him from above as she gingerly touched his face, blubbering a load of mushy nonsense that no one needs to hear their parents say. I turned toward Gina, giving them a modicum of privacy while fighting a lump in my throat the size of a football.

Matt burst into the room with Dad's nurse, Clarice, scrambling to keep up. "*We're here! We're here!* Coming through!"

He pushed me aside to give the nurse access before stopping to catch his breath. He was too winded to notice Gina's and my bemused smiles.

"Hi, there," said the nurse, smiling benevolently at Dad. "My name is Clarice. Can you tell me who you are?"

"And no monkey business this time, mister," said Mom, scowling from the other side of the bed.

"Todd Morrow," he said, his voice sounding vaguely stronger.

"And how are we feeling?" asked Clarice, multitasking with her tablet as she recorded her observations.

"I don't know about you, but my head is killing me," he said, and the room erupted in nervous laughter.

"Well, I just might be able to help with that," Clarice said. "Give me just a few, and I'll be back with your meds and something to drink." She shifted her attention to us, adopting a no-nonsense stance. "Other than Ms. Jo, I'm gonna need the rest of you to say your goodnights and clear out. Mr. Morrow needs plenty of rest, and you can all touch base again tomorrow."

"Yes, ma'am," I said, nodding.

As she bustled out of the room, Dad cleared his throat. "Dwayne?"

I stepped closer to the bed. "Hmm?"

"Did we do it?" he asked. "Did we take that horrible woman down?"

I examined the bed and found the button to elevate its head. I gently eased him up a few inches, just enough so he could see Gina sitting in her chair at the foot of his bed. "What do you think?"

"Hi, Daddy," she said, fighting back another round of tears.

Oh, who am I kidding? There wasn't a dry eye in the room.

"This is a very cool ride," I said, examining the controls I could see from the passenger seat.

Gina drove a late model Dodge Grand Caravan that had been modified to be accessible to people in wheelchairs, its floor pedals replaced by hand controls that served the same functions. It had a motorized, folding ramp installed behind the passenger seat, providing access for Gina's chair to roll into the space normally occupied by a driver's seat. Once she had secured her wheels and buckled up, we were on our way.

After confirming she hadn't reserved a room anywhere, I extended Melanie's offer to put her up for the night, belatedly realizing that our guest room was up a flight of stairs she couldn't possibly negotiate. She laughed it off, saying the couch would be just fine but I couldn't help feeling guilty. It was just another jolting reminder that things were never going to be the way they were before.

It was nearly one in the morning, and traffic was light. We took SR-315 south to I-670, following it west until it merged with I-70, continuing on to the outerbelt.

"How long are you planning to stay?" I asked.

"I'm still figuring that out," she said. "I'm thinking it might be nice to move back in with Mom and Dad for a little while. Mom's gonna need some help with Dad. In case you hadn't noticed, he can be a real handful."

"Oh," I said, a little surprised. Lymont was the *last* place I figured she would land. "What about your job with the library?"

"I'll give them as much notice as I can, but I was only there to try and nail Senator Gorham to the wall. I can hardly believe she's really gone," she said. "It's been all over the news. *You've* been all over the news. Again."

An image of the senator's face in startled, final repose flashed through my mind, and I suspected it would be haunting my nightmares for quite some time. "I can hardly believe you're really here," I said, smiling.

She glanced at me sideways. "I owe it all to you. I hope you can forgive me."

"Forgive you? For what?"

"For pushing you away. For not trusting that you could actually help me. I put you in an awful position, and I wouldn't blame you if you hated me. I was just so scared that something horrible would happen to someone I loved, and I couldn't live with that. You know how ruthless these people can be."

"You can let yourself off the hook. I couldn't possibly hate you. Now, the hair? *That* I hate. What in the hell were you thinking?"

She laughed. "I was thinking it was about as different as I could get. I don't know. I think it's cute."

"You look like Billy Idol's granddaughter," I said, rolling my eyes.

"Maybe I should just shave my head and start all over again."

"Not just anyone can pull of the Sinéad look," I warned her.

"I would totally *rock* it."

I smiled. "Yeah, I think you would. You'll want to take the Georgesville exit." I indicated the upcoming ramp on our right.

She activated her signal, taking the exit and driving past the bright lights of the Auto Mall on our right. We fell into comfortable silence for the next several miles as we left the lights of the densely populated neighborhoods in the rearview mirror. We finally reached the entrance to Orin Way, and she turned right onto the narrow gravel road.

"What in the world possessed you to buy a house all the way out here? You might as well live in Lymont yourself," Gina said, staring at the moonlit flatland that stretched on for miles along both sides of the lane. Houses were few and far between, and I truly hoped it would stay that way, but with the rate of expansion in the Columbus metropolitan area, I knew it was only a matter of time before someone got the bright idea to develop it.

"Not true," I said. "I chose this location because it's the best of both worlds. I have my privacy, but when I need something, I don't have to drive fifty miles to get it. Opportunities for employment are better, and people are a lot more open-minded. It's also close enough to Mom and Dad that I can check in on them from time to time. For me, it's perfection."

"I suppose so," she said, shielding her eyes as bright headlights suddenly moved in behind us, blinding her in the rearview. "What the hell? Where did *they* come from?"

I turned in my seat just as red and blue bubble lights flared to life, followed by the unmistakable wail of a police siren.

"I wasn't speeding, was I?" asked Gina. "I didn't see a limit posted, but I couldn't have been going any faster than thirty-five."

"At this time of night, it's probably just a sobriety check. The Grove City PD must be desperate for dollars. You better pull over."

She put her hazards on and pulled to the side of the road, the police car tucking in behind her. "Don't forget—I'm Lee Tieman. It's what's on my ID and registration. We certainly don't want to confuse this poor chucklehead with a slip of the lip."

"Got it," I said.

Time passed as we waited for the officer to approach, keeping our hands in plain sight so he could see we posed no threat. Eventually, a flashlight flared behind us, and the darkened shape of a man about my size cautiously approached the driver's side of the van. He motioned with his light for Gina to roll her window down, and she complied.

"License and registration." The husky directive floated in out of the darkness, and Gina carefully reached for the wallet inside the oversized bag resting between her wheelchair and the passenger seat.

"I'm sorry," she said, handing her information through the open window and squinting into the light shining directly into her face. "Was I speeding, officer?"

Her question went unanswered as the flashlight shifted its focus to me, examining me head to toe. After a lengthy, uncomfortable silence, the officer said, "I'm going to need you both to step out of the vehicle. One at a time, and slowly."

Gina smiled into the darkness. "Umm, easier said than done, officer. As you might have noticed, I'm in a wheelchair."

"Out of the vehicle, ma'am. Don't make me ask again."

She sighed, releasing the locks on her wheels. "If you insist, but I'll have to exit on the passenger side. That's where my ramp is."

"That's fine."

As the automated mechanism began extending the ramp out onto the berm of the road, I started to unfasten my seatbelt and found myself staring into the full intensity of the flashlight's beam.

"Please stay exactly where you are, sir. Once Ms.—*Tieman* is out of the vehicle, it will be your turn."

Something about this wasn't right. All the hairs on the back of my neck were standing on end.

Gina was beginning her descent backwards down the ramp, and the officer used the opportunity to cross around the back of the van to meet her on the other side. As her wheels crunched onto the gravel, a strange sound gained volume. It took me a minute to realize it was coming from the officer. It was the most unsettling laughter I had ever heard.

"Now you—*Dwayne*," he said, his voice vaguely familiar, but I was more concerned with the gun that he held in the hand that wasn't brandishing the flashlight. It was rock-steady and pointed at my sister.

No. This couldn't be happening. We hadn't come all this way just for things to end like this. For the first time since moving here, I wished the area weren't quite so remote.

I ground my teeth as my mind raced, remembering that I had left Dad's handgun in Brady's hotel room back in Darbydale. I was completely unarmed. I kept my hands raised and visible as I unfastened my seatbelt and exited the vehicle.

The maniacal laughter intensified.

"I honestly can't believe my luck," the officer finally said, and suddenly, I knew who it was. It was confirmed once he moved the flashlight beneath his chin to illuminate his face from below.

"Michael Arthur," I said. "Or would you prefer Duncan Moore?"

"I couldn't give a shit what you call me," he said. "It's not like anyone will ever hear you."

He looked like he'd aged a decade since the last time I had seen him. His dark, curly hair, once neatly trimmed and reminiscent of Brady's, had grown scraggly and unkempt. He sported a full beard and mustache and had dropped ten pounds more than he had to spare. His clothes were filthy, and he smelled like he hadn't showered in weeks. Upon closer examination, I realized his car was an old Crown Victoria outfitted with aftermarket bubble lights that gave it the illusion of law enforcement.

I gasped as another realization dawned.

"It was *you*," I said. *"You're* the one who did this to my sister." I pointed toward her damned chair as white-hot anger surged through me.

"Well, I'm just going to call that a happy accident," he said, keeping his gun trained on me. Gina had gone still, watching in horror as past became present once more. "I had really hoped to kill her, but in a way, this is *so— much—better!* I've ruined her life just like you ruined mine."

Gina laughed. "I could never be as ruined as you are, you sick fuck."

His arm lashed out like lightning, pistol-whipping her across the face with enough force to jolt her chair and elicit a sickening yelp.

"Don't you touch her!" I roared, taking an ineffectual step in Michael's direction but getting nowhere near close enough before the gun was targeting my face once more.

"No one believed me," Michael continued. *"No one!* I told them she was still alive. I saw her at her own damn funeral! You did, too. I just needed a little more time to find her, but after the havoc you wreaked in Briarstaff, they started cleaning house—tying up loose ends. They tried to kill me too, you know. Isn't it ironic that after a lifetime of dedicated service, they were more concerned with silencing me than the bitch who could bring The Academy and everything associated with it to its knees? Stupid morons really believed she was dead. Their lack of loyalty to me was truly disappointing."

Gina spat out a mouthful of bloody saliva, her bottom lip split and already swollen to twice its normal size. "Let me grab my violin, asshole," she said.

He drew back to strike her again, and I held up my hands. "Stop! *Please!* If you're going to hit someone, hit me! She's defenseless in that chair!"

"If you insist," he said just before my world exploded in a sea of stars, the grip of the pistol connecting solidly with my temple. I dropped to one knee as a wave of nausea washed over me. "I'd stay down if I were you. Any sudden moves, and—" He turned the pistol on Gina, his implication crystal clear.

"You said, *'they,'*" said Gina, drawing Michael's attention back to herself. "Who are *'they?'*"

Michael leered at her. "You'll never know. We are *everywhere.* There isn't anything we can't infiltrate if we set our minds to it. We're your neighbors, your co-workers, your physicians, your counselors—"

"I get it already," said Gina, surprisingly defiant. "You are Legion. *Whatever.* You're nothing but a bunch of filthy cockroaches, scurrying into the darkness whenever anyone dares to shine a light on the dirty deeds you do. The trouble with cockroaches is that they turn on one another. You said it yourself; look how they turned on you! And yet here you are, continuing to protect the very people who cast you out. I don't understand."

"I wouldn't expect you to. While I may have lost favor with the powers that be, I'm not *entirely* without connections." He leaned in, mere inches from Gina's face. "I was able to find *you*, wasn't I?"

She turned away as he inhaled deeply, taking in her scent. I felt like vomiting.

"What do you want?" I asked, frantically looking for anything I could use against him but finding nothing.

"Vengeance," he said, standing over me and placing the barrel of the gun against the top of my head. "After everything the two of you have done to me, I really think I've earned it, don't you? Make no mistake about it, you're both about to die. It's just a matter of who goes first. Do I have any suggestions?"

"I suggest you shoot yourself, you worthless piece of shit," said Gina, smiling crookedly.

"I've had just about enough of your smart mouth, little lady," he said. "Okay, fine. You wanna leave it up to me? Sure, we can play it that way." He pivoted toward me and pulled the trigger. The bullet slammed into the side of the van right beside my head before the sound of the gunshot even registered. I couldn't suppress the flinch that shook my entire body.

"*Stop it!*" Gina shrieked. "It's me you want. Leave Dwayne out of it."

"I think we're a little past the point of no return here," said Michael. "Although I will admit, I'd love to hear you beg for his life. That would be a real turn on."

"Huh. I seem to recall shooting your tiny little dick off last time we met," I said, unable to contain myself any longer. If I was going to die anyway, I may as well get a couple of shots in of my own. "I didn't think *anything* could turn you on anymore."

Another explosion of stars as he executed a perfect roundhouse kick to the side of my head. I slammed into the van before falling sideways, tasting gravel as I clung to consciousness.

"Smart mouths are a thing we Morrows have in common," said Gina, weirdly calm—almost resigned. "Let's just get this over with. You've already taken my livelihood, my mobility. Put me out of my misery. The only thing I ask is that you be man enough to look me in the eye while you do it."

"*No*," I sputtered, struggling to sit upright.

"Be quiet, Dwayne," she said. "I know what I'm doing. This will all be over soon."

Michael studied us both, deliberating. "I have to admit, as much as I'd love to make you watch me put a bullet in your little brother's head, I think I'd get a lot more satisfaction out of watching his face when I kill you. After everything he's done to bring you home—it just feels like the right thing to do, you know?"

"For God's sake, just shut up and do it," said Gina.

"Well, alrighty, then. If you insist," he said, standing in front of her and taking aim. He looked back at me, an ugly smile playing on his lips. "Pay close attention, Dwayne. This is all for you."

I squeezed my eyes shut. I didn't give a shit what he wanted. He couldn't force me to watch him execute my sister. I just prayed it would be quick. The gunshot was louder than before, echoing in my ears. Hot tears streamed down my face as a strangled cry escaped my throat. As much as I hated giving that bastard the satisfaction of seeing me break, I couldn't hold it together anymore. It was just too much to bear. I could only imagine what this would do to Mom and Dad. It just might kill them, too. I thought about Melanie burying yet another partner and the kids that had almost been mine. I hoped Jasmine would remember to feed Dexter.

"Dwayne."

The voice was muffled, and not at all the one I expected to hear.

I opened my eyes and turned to find Michael Arthur sprawled over top of my sister.

"Can you get this asshole off of me, please?" she asked, and I was on my feet in an instant, pulling him away and letting him fall to the ground. He was completely limp. I gaped at my sister with my mouth hanging open, struggling to understand what had just happened. It took me a moment to register the gun resting in Gina's lap.

It was much bigger than the one Michael still clutched in his hand.

Gina smiled wearily. "It's over."

"But—I don't—where did that thing come from?" I stammered, pointing at her weapon.

"After everything that's happened, I don't go anywhere without it. I don't have a lot of good things to say about being in this chair, but you'd be amazed at how many great hiding places there are in this contraption. I rolled right through security at Riverside, and no one suspected a thing when the metal detectors went off. Surrounded by all this hardware, who would?"

I stared into Michael's unseeing eyes. "He certainly didn't."

EPILOGUE

The weeks that followed were utterly surreal.

The siege on Senator Gorham's private residence and her subsequent assassination sent shockwaves throughout the country. Brady Garrett was well on his way to becoming a household name as his exclusive coverage of the event dominated the national news. His interview footage with the senator was enough to spark an official investigation into New Horizons, and it wasn't long before the governor suspended operations, transferring its wards to other facilities in the state. Staff were subpoenaed and injunctions filed, but not before wagons had circled and years' worth of records were lost or destroyed, making it difficult to hold much of anyone accountable for anything.

Perhaps the biggest surprise came from Brady himself. I was prepared for him to hound us for invasive interviews regarding what had happened with Gina, but he took great care to shield my family as much as he possibly could. When I cornered him, suspicious of his motives, he reminded me that he had lost family members too, and he would have given anything for a second chance with them. He knew we weren't ready to talk and would respect our privacy. Of course, he also made me promise that should that day ever come, those interviews were his and his alone to conduct. As far as bargains go, it seemed more than fair.

Reba Givens eluded authorities for nearly two weeks. Her ten-year-old mugshot made the rounds on every newscast, making her as infamous as a modern-day Bonnie Parker, although she didn't suffer quite the same fate. She was alone when she was finally captured, and I thought it was very telling that all reports referred to Burt as her estranged husband. It was the story she told, and he wasn't coming forward to dispute it. I had a feeling their estrangement began the moment she decided to stage a rescue mission to recover their son, Boyd, with the tenuous hope she could get him the deprogramming she believed he desperately needed. By the time authorities arrived at the Givens' property, the cabin and barn were fully ablaze, and it took the fire departments from several of the surrounding townships to keep the fire from spreading into the woods. There were no reports of bodies nor firearms found, just a smoldering husk of an old Chevy Monza buried deep in the wreckage of the barn. I discreetly urged Craig to play dumb and report the vehicle as stolen. Once the VIN number was recovered, it would trace back to him, and he didn't want any part of this. I'm not entirely sure where Burt went, but if I had to guess, he was most likely enjoying a new life playing with his grandchildren and watching them grow, somewhere in Wyoming. I'm not really sure what happened to Boyd. He wasn't with Reba when she was captured, so I can only assume he's either having his brain wiped or he's still out there somewhere. Same with Dr. Jillian Whittier. I'd sleep a little easier if I knew for sure, but what is life without a little uncertainty?

Dad's recovery has been slow but steady. Since his surgery, he has yet to experience any more of the startling episodes that sent him tumbling into his own past—knock on wood. He seems just as sharp and ornery as ever, and his doctors expect him to make a full recovery. He and Mom were more than delighted to learn that Gina wanted to move back home for a while, and modifications to the Morrow homestead were already underway. A ramp had been built to provide access to the front entrance, and a renovation of the first-floor bathroom was currently in progress to make it fully accessible for Gina's needs. She refused to be coddled for her condition, helping Mom around the house with cooking, cleaning, and carting her wherever she needed to go until Dad was cleared to drive again.

Initially rankled by my unanticipated absence, Doug Boggs had a sudden change of heart after the telephones at Boggs Investigations began lighting up. While Brady had been fairly successful in shielding my family from scrutiny, there was no way to keep my name out of it. I was present when everything went down. I spent countless hours being interviewed by police, and Brady had actually given me credit for conducting the investigation that had led him to Senator Gorham's door. I suddenly found myself in very high demand, which wasn't bad considering I still wasn't officially licensed yet. Business is booming, and Doug is considering adding another associate to our ranks to serve as an apprentice in the Lymont office. I probably shouldn't have been surprised when Gina threw her hat into the ring. I hate to admit it, but with Melanie already on board, Boggs Investigations is beginning to feel like a family business—dysfunctional at times, but then again, aren't all families? I can only hope that Doug and Loretta have the good sense to recognize my sister's worth.

Otherwise, there will be words. Okay, *fine*. With those two, there will *always* be words.

Oh!

I haven't told you the best part. For that, we'll have to return to that first night after Michael Arthur ceased to be a threat to anyone ever again. As you may recall, I had a date with my lady…

I rolled over onto my back, every single inch of me tingling in the best way possible. Melanie tucked herself underneath my arm, laying her head

379

on my chest as our labored breathing found its way back into a normal rhythm.

"My *God*, I've missed you," I said, kissing the top of her tousled head. "If this is how you plan to welcome me home, I need to go away a lot more often."

"You better not," she warned, nudging me playfully before running the tip of her fingernail from my sternum to my naval, leaving a trail of gooseflesh in her wake. "I may never let you out of this bed."

I snorted. "Clearly, you've already forgotten my morning breath."

She poked me again. "Can't you just give me a few moments of ignorant bliss before ruining it with your lethal halitosis?"

I snuggled closer to her. "Whatever you say, my sweet. I didn't think we'd ever get the kids to bed."

"Well, what did you expect? You brought them presents," she said. "You yell at your brother for spoiling them, and yet you do the very same thing."

"Not true!" I said, pulling away in mock outrage. "I do it *much* better."

"You're like one of those claw cranes at Walmart, but you always produce a winner. Jordan may only be three, but he's no fool."

"Oh, come *on*," I said. "The boy is growing attached to me independent of my generosity. Have you noticed how he always begs for *me* to tell him a story before bedtime? Not you—*me*."

"Which reminds me," she said, propping herself up on an elbow to scowl at me. "What's all this about little Prince Jordie and Gloretta, the Troll Queen of Tackytown? It was all that little monkey wanted to hear about, and I could hardly get him to sleep these last few nights. Apparently, you left off on a cliffhanger, and I was completely in the dark. I had to ask Jasmine to help me wind him down, but thank goodness, she had some familiarity with the child-eating swamp hag herself."

A slow smile crept across my face, but I couldn't meet her gaze. "Oh, they're just some silly stories I made up for the kids. That's all."

"You're dead meat if Loretta ever catches wind of this—you know this, right?"

"Loretta Boggs couldn't even catch her own breath," I said. "I'll take my chances, especially since it brings such joy into that little boy's life."

"Yeah, well, like I said, he's no fool. It also takes you twice as long to tell a simple bedtime story as anyone else on Earth. You extend his curfew by almost a half hour every night!"

I grinned, staring at the ceiling. *"Meh.* He's only this age once."

She scowled at me. "And in the morning, I get the grumpy version who hasn't had nearly enough sleep. Thanks."

I laughed, rolling onto my side and sliding down until Melanie and I were practically nose-to-nose. "You're welcome."

I kissed her gently, and she responded by pressing her body even closer to mine. "I'm starting to think you like those kids more than you do me," she said, pouting.

"Not even close," I said, my hands beginning to wander.

"Every time I turn around, all I hear is *DUH-wayne* this and *DUH-wayne* that."

"I have to admit, it melts my heart every time I hear him maul my name."

Melanie inhaled sharply as my fingertips found their target. "It's such a mouthful," she said, and her physical response was contagious. I was ready to stop talking. "How would you feel about 'Daddy?'"

She may as well have doused me in cold water. I lay back and stared at the ceiling. "Oh, Mel—I don't know about that. I mean, you know how much I love those kids. It might be the biggest cliché ever, but I'd die before I ever let anything happen to either one of them. You know that, right?"

She nodded. "Well, sure but—"

"No," I said. "No buts. They're Ryan s kids, and I would never expect either one of them to call me something I'm not. That doesn't mean I won't do my very damnedest to be the best father figure that they could ever have, although I'm guessing there will be some days that will be harder than others. Now, if some day they decide they would like to call me that without any prompting from us, it would be the greatest privilege of my life, but—"

She put a finger over my mouth.

"Would you just *shhh?*" She turned my face toward her own. "I wasn't talking about them."

My brows furrowed in utter confusion. *"You* want to call me 'Daddy?' Umm—I'm all for a little sexy-time fun, but that's just—"

Understanding dropped like an anvil, stopping my flow of incessant stupidity, and she didn't have to say another word. She practically glowed in anticipation.

"Are you sure?" I finally managed.

She nodded. "Jordan wasn't the only one who had a doctor's appointment the other day. It would seem we did a lot more than just make up at Sarah's that night. I know this wasn't what we planned. Are you upset?"

My mouth worked, but for the longest time, nothing came out. Melanie's face registered neither disappointment nor surprise when what finally emerged was utterly redundant.

"Are you sure?"

She simply nodded again.

I cupped her face in both my hands, my lips finding hers once again. There's no adequate way I could ever describe the feeling that washed over me in that moment—equal parts elation and terror, tempered by a profound sense of wonder unlike anything I had ever dared to imagine.

I was going to be a daddy.

THE END

Darin Miller

UP NEXT

The Jasmine Chronicles

Volume One

COMING 2026

INTERCEPTION

Dwayne Morrow Mystery #9

ACKNOWLEDGEMENTS

In 2003, I began writing a story that would eventually become *Diversion, Dwayne Morrow Mystery #4*. I wanted to honor the memory of my sister, Gina Lee Miller, who was born with spina bifida and a host of other medical complications. All of this is fully documented elsewhere, most specifically in a post I keep pinned to my Facebook author page.

We lost Gina in 1987, after she endured yet another invasive but necessary surgery. It was quite a wake-up call—my first real taste of death, and I can't say that I cared for it very much at all. Even after almost thirty-eight years, I can still hear the sound of her sweet voice.

With *Diversion*, I wanted to give Gina an adventure like the ones she always loved to read about but could never have experienced firsthand. Although it took me nearly twenty years to finish that story, I know in my heart that she would have truly loved it.

What I couldn't have known when I started writing that story was that in a few short years, our father would also be gone, the victim of early onset Alzheimer's. Its aggressive progression was both horrific and merciful; to linger in such a state was stealing Dad's dignity, and there were brief moments when he was acutely aware—and utterly terrified.

I've often said, a conceit of being a writer is the ability to provide happier endings when there were none, and with this latest entry in what I've come to think of as the Morrowverse, I've looped the loop, bringing this recurring piece of Miller family history to a far more satisfying, if perhaps bittersweet, conclusion. I really hope you liked it. I'm fairly confident *they* would have—

well, except for all the swearing. Much like Dwayne, I really don't know where I got my potty mouth…

Enough of all that maudlin stuff. Let's get on with the gratitude:

Back for an unbelievable eighth time, my editing team is once again rising to the challenge of making me look oh-so-much better than I really am. Eternal appreciation to Teri Lott, Lynne Hobstetter, and Traci Steele for finding all of the things that I didn't, but make no mistake, any errors that remain are strictly my responsibility.

I owe a huge debt of gratitude to Katie Mettner, kickass Harlequin Intrigue author and reigning Queen of Representation for Folks with Disabilities— a title I may have invented but she completely embodies—for her seasoned advice and guidance, which is helping Dwayne find a bigger audience every single day. When Katie talks, Darin listens. And when I'm feeling down, Charly Cox, author of the pulse-pounding Detective Alyssa Wyatt bestsellers, has the most incredible knack for dropping by just to prop me up. Her kind words and encouragement continue to bolster my faith in myself, making me believe I really *can* do this. And, of course, big, big love to Lisa Regan, who has invited me (and Dwayne) to participate in not just one, but *two* of her Detective Josie Quinn release day celebration extravaganzas on Facebook. Authors helping other authors is such a beautiful thing!

To my growing legion of Dwayniacs—I can't thank you enough for your support, and in the case of Super Dwayniacs Jen Miller (no relation) and Nancy Brady—endless needling. You ladies are experts at keeping me on my toes, and I appreciate it! I remain thoroughly gobsmacked that *anyone* is interested in reading my little books of lies, but it's such a gratifying feeling. I got a little happy with the name-dropping in this one…you just never know who might turn up next.

Coming next is the first entry in *The Jasmine Chronicles*, a YA offshoot from the *Dwayne Morrow Mysteries* that features Melanie's daughter, Jasmine. She's a feisty little thing, isn't she? One can only imagine the shenanigans she gets into when the adults are busy adulting.

But don't worry—Dwayne Morrow *will* be back in 2026, and Nancy and Jen, you'll be the first to know—I promise!

Until next time,
Darin Miller
Grove City, Ohio – July 2025

ALSO AVAILABLE

REUNION
Dwayne Morrow Mystery #1

CIRCUMVENTION
Dwayne Morrow Mystery #2

RETRIBUTION
Dwayne Morrow Mystery #3

DIVERSION
Dwayne Morrow Mystery #4

ISOLATION
Dwayne Morrow Mystery #5

ABDUCTION
Dwayne Morrow Mystery #6

DECEPTION
Dwayne Morrow Mystery #7

OVER CONSUMPTION
*A Dwayne Morrow and Jane Bond
Novella
(Co-written with V.R. Tapscott)*

OTHER WORK

BROKEN BITS AND BOBS
*A Collection of What Ifs, What Was,
and What Never Should Be*

HOUSE OF SECRETS
*Every Room Holds a Story
(Contributor, "Redemption")*

EQUILIBRIUM

THE LIBRARY CENTENNIAL ANTHOLOGY
*Celebrating the Lives and People of the
SPL Community
(Contributor, "Meredith's Bad Day")*

DID YOU LIKE ME?

☐ **Yes!** ☐ **No** ☐ **Maybe?**

May I ask a favor?

If you enjoyed reading this book as much as I enjoyed writing it, won't you please consider leaving a rating and/or review on Amazon, Goodreads, Barnes & Noble, BookBub, or anywhere else you might see fit? It only takes a moment to leave a rating and a maybe a couple more for a short review—even a simple 'I would recommend this book!' will do nicely.

Word of mouth is the single most powerful tool in an Indie author's toolkit, and ratings and reviews help more than you may realize in growing our audience. Think of it as a gratuity you might leave a server after an evening of fine dining, but this gratuity doesn't cost a thing—only a few moments of your time.

Thank you for your kind consideration.

Amazon

Goodreads

Barnes & Noble

BookBub

ABOUT THE AUTHOR

Darin Miller was born in Portsmouth but currently resides in Grove City, both of which are located in Ohio. While he has worked in Information Technology for three decades, he has *not* solved a single, solitary crime to date. He is the BookFest award-winning author of the Ohio-based *Dwayne Morrow Mystery* series, as well as an unrelated short story collection, *Broken Bits and Bobs*, and a standalone psychological horror thriller, *Equilibrium*. With equal parts action, humor, suspense and mystery, the *Dwayne Morrow* series features characters you're sure to love—and in some cases, loathe.

Stay current with updates, short stories, and other special promotions at www.darin-miller.com.